KAYOS
The Bad & The Worse

Tracy A. Ball

BLACK ROSE writing™

The final approval for this literary material is granted by the author.

First printing

This is a work of fiction. Names, characters, businesses, places, events and incidents are either the products of the author's imagination or used in a fictitious manner. Any resemblance to actual persons, living or dead, or actual events is purely coincidental.

ISBN: 978-1-61296-805-6
PUBLISHED BY BLACK ROSE WRITING
www.blackrosewriting.com

Printed in the United States of America
Suggested retail price $19.95

Kayos is printed in Gentium Book Basic

For Malakai

You have changed the world. Now, every day has a bright spot—your smile. Every problem has a solution—your giggles. Every plan has a purpose—your snuggles. And, every action has a reward—your happiness. You truly are, the Little King.

Matthew- My life before you was an apology for all of my flaws. But you see, kiss, and call them gold. You are my haven as I dare to dream. You hold me up while I collect stardust and feed dragons. You anchor me while I ride butterflies and search for sunken treasure. When I reach the end of my imagination, you tuck me in and sing me to sleep.

Kelly- Thank you for seeing potential when other people see problems. Thank you for your keen, analytical mind and your love of psychology. Thank you for your sense of adventure and justice. Thank you for your laser-precision wit and your quirky sense of humor. Thank you for giving me a story worth telling. And, most of all, thank you for being you.

Ramses - The dictionary definition of a hero is: A person noted for courageous acts or nobility of character. In other words, you. To be a loving husband and father is hero work. You do it every day, and you make it look easy.

Daryle- I am awed and inspired by your strength of character. In a world gone mad, you carry truth like a torch and defy any who would attempt to extinguish it. Because of you, I am a better me.

Special Thanks

To Mommie- For telling me stories, giving me books and allowing me to have an imagination.

To my fellow BR and LK authors – In the face of crazy, you remain encouraging and supportive. Despite our different styles/views/beliefs/etc., you go above and beyond to make our communities the place to be.

To the Gutter Flowers – those who have been punished for daring to be themselves.

KAYOS
The Bad & The Worse

April 17, 2058

Chapter 1

Orion didn't need a clock, he knew the time. It was around two a.m., no later than ten after. He'd been waking up at two-ish for as long as he remembered. He lay in his bed, listening for sounds in the dormitory room he shared with five other students. One floor below, the night-shift staff huddled around the television in the common room. Two guards made hourly rounds, their footfalls heavy on the polished wood floors. The building used to be a prestigious Catholic school years before he'd been born.

He shivered. The pajamas they gave him were too short. Miss Elliot said he was going through a growth spurt. Maybe they kept it cold on the third floor. He didn't know, didn't care. Orion welcomed the chill. Tonight, he wanted to be uncomfortable. He wanted to remember this place.

Hillcrest School of Excellence—The Place Where Brilliance Is Revealed. His new school's motto didn't tell the whole truth. The more accurate description would be, Hillcrest School of Excellence—A prison in disguise.

Orion recognized it as a prison as soon as he arrived. The electric outer fence purposed to keep the rebels out. Guards posted at measured intervals inside a second fence; the absolute lack of freedom in class and out. The constant droning about duty to country and cause. They were signs, clues to his new reality. A reality he'd been warned about just hours before his life changed. Not merely changed, destroyed.

Miss Elliot tried to tell him, a hundred different ways probably. But it was the last thing she said to him, although he hadn't realized it at the time. She pulled him aside, reprimanding him with her tone, but not her words. Never her words. Miss Lareina Elliot was always careful with her words.

"Congratulations. You're going to an amazing school. You won't believe it." She smoothed his blond cowlick and walked away. Hasty, stiff steps. Her last mutterings barely reaching his ears. "I'm sorry to see you go."

He felt let down, but had no chance to discuss it with her. No opportunity to ask for an explanation. He thought she would have clarified why she put his essay aside. Why she hadn't included him. She told him, his insights were among the best she'd reviewed. She called him a genius in the making. You don't call someone a genius in the making if you're not preparing to help them advance. You don't accidentally leave their work out of the judging. Hillcrest School of Excellence only accepts the best. He'd been working to be the best for nine months. You don't take that away without justification.

He didn't need justification now. He understood her reasoning; her unguarded moment of horror when he disrupted the panel, waving his paper. The essay she left in her office. It might have been the mistake she excused herself with, but he knew better. He knew better then but regarded her actions with disdain. He knew better now. Miss Elliot didn't want him to attend the Hillcrest School of Excellence, the place where brilliance is revealed, because she knew it was a prison.

Orion had been in the Excellence Scholarship Program for nine months. Not once, to his knowledge, had he let Miss Elliot down. He didn't intend to start now. It was after two a.m. He had to go.

****

R U ignoring me?

Kaiden sent the text. Lareina wouldn't go this long without responding. If he didn't hear from her by the time he closed shop, he'd drive to Michigan, tonight. They had a rendezvous scheduled, but it hadn't been finalized. How were they supposed to finalize anything if Lareina didn't respond? It wasn't her. If it was uncharacteristic for Lareina, it meant trouble. Lareina never did anything out of character.

Kaiden checked the time. He ran a hand across his dark, close-cropped hair, scratching behind his ear. He'd close shop now, but he would miss a thirty-k drop. He wanted his thirty-k, no he needed his thirty-k. If he were going to drive nineteen hours—sixteen, if he avoided stupid drivers—from Red River, Louisiana to Presque Isle, Michigan, he would need his money. He twisted his diamond stud earring a minute or two, realized it, and made himself stop.

Derrick came into the office, knocking once on the already open door. The rest of Kaiden's garage looked like a garage, but not his office. Thick carpet, redwood desk set, eight-seat conference table. High powered deals happened in this room; no tools, equipment, or dirt crossed his threshold. Ever. "Yo, Boss-man," Derrick said, "Ramin's here. He's got four easy-riders with him. Asked to see you."

"Does he have my money?"

"He asked to see you."

"Go find out if he's got my money, or he won't be seeing shit and you're going to be seeing my left foot planted in your ass."

Derrick heaved an aggravated sigh. He left Kaiden's office, passing Fisher, on his way in.

"I got it," Fisher said. "Give Ramin the keys to the Dodge."

"What Dodge?"

"The Meris, you dumbass." Fisher put his considerable bulk behind the shove he gave Derrick. The lanky eighteen-year-old stumbled forward but kept his balance. He didn't retaliate. Nobody retaliated against Fisher's two-hundred and ten pounds of muscle. Fisher tossed a brown package on Kaiden's desk. The torn corner revealed two tightly bundled stacks of one-hundred-dollar bills.

Kaiden nodded his thanks to his right hand. "You got any plans?"

"Nothing I can't change."

"I'm going to Michigan."

"I'd never miss an opportunity to see 'Reina. When are we leaving?"

"As soon as we lockup."

"There's trouble?"

"Something's not right." He tugged his earring.

"Make Derrick lockup. I'm going to pack." Fisher strode from the room.

"I'm packed already." Kaiden picked up his money.

****

"Let me get that for you, son." The UPS man, coming out of the upmarket condominium, held the door open for the teenager to enter.

"Thank you," Alec said. The box he carried wasn't overly heavy. Still, he used it to his advantage. He held it up, blocking his face and kept his obsidian eyes focused upon his footing.

"You're welcome." The UPS man went about his day.

Alec could have taken the elevator, but he preferred the steps. In the past week, he found them to be quicker and considerably less traveled. Even with the box, he could run all four flights before the elevator got to the second floor.

Apartment 428. He unlocked the door and disarmed the security system with the ease of someone doing it for years as opposed to days. He left the box on the spotless kitchen tile and walked through the condo as if he were home. Alec was home.

Bookshelves. She had a million books. Not stupid ones like in the school's library, but good ones. He didn't like reading, but listening to her read was the best, especially when she rubbed his head. He loved that. Here and there, on a shelf, on the corner of her desk, on the end table, the bathrooms too, she kept the oddest knickknacks. Mostly, a collection of silver serpents. Not the kind of thing people would expect from her. He would expect it, but not the majority of people. Alec gave her four of the figurines himself. She kept one in the kitchen, two in the living room, and the big one—he couldn't remember what she called it—watched from the center of her dresser, its black glittery eyes saw everything. Lareina was fond of snakes. So was he. Not fond of them in a creepy, Medusa way. They respected the power. If you threaten a snake, you will remember it. Could be the last thing you ever get to remember. Cats were her other passion. His too. Big cats; lions, panthers, an assortment of pictures, stuffed animals, and miniatures all over the place. Tigers were dominant. She loved tigers.

First things first. He checked her monitor and her hidden security system. Then he checked his own booby-traps. Next, he got his snickers. He left it on the dresser this morning and had been fiending for it all day. Candy bars were rare, but Lareina managed to keep him stocked. Even though he hit the jackpot when he found her stash on the top shelf of her closet, he kept himself on her schedule. Lareina gave him one a day; he only ate one a day...mostly.

Alec tore the wrapper open and moved back toward the kitchen. He munched silently as he thumbed through files, looking for certain items according to the color-coding. Hide anything with a green label. Destroy everything with a yellow sticker. Leave the manila folders in her office and scatter the brown envelopes where they can be found, but not too easily.

He already took care of her office here. He organized everything precisely as she instructed him. He got the files from her office at school the same day the DoP showed up. The *Department of Protection* was trouble. The things they did had nothing to do with protection. He hated them before they snatched Lareina.

This last stack of files, left at the Board of Education, was the hardest to procure. She hadn't meant for him to get them, but he did. Lareina frequently called them arrogant bastards. Alec agreed. Now, all he had to do was wait.

She would expect him to eat dinner; he made a tuna sandwich. She'd expect him to take a shower; he used a lot of the foamy soap. He thought about getting into her bed and watching a movie, but the idea made him lonely. He went into his own room—he knew it was his the moment he saw it. A jungle theme; a palace in the jungle. The cheetah, his personal favorite, in the painting above his bed, had deadly obsidian eyes. He used to wonder if his earliest ancestors came from someplace with cheetahs—a jungle in India before they went extinct, maybe. Those thoughts came before he adopted Lareina. Her ancestors most likely came from Africa which had all the jungle he needed. Yep, he would rather be in his own room. In his bedroom, it would be as if he fell asleep waiting for her to come home.

She was coming home.

Chapter 2

Silas drove his jeep, a Genuine, to the side gate. He had his ID extended before the checkpoint guard approached. Due to his status—Special Ops CT—the guard waved him on, no questions. There were less than one hundred of them in the world. The instant recognition and immediate response would have given most people a jolt of pride. Not Silas. The covert tactician expected star treatment for being himself.

Rather than drive directly to his destination, Corporal McKade toured the area, making mental notes of heights and distances, things that would be relevant to a sharpshooter. He parked in the furthest lot possible and blew fifteen minutes wandering through buildings that had nothing to do with his purpose.

The weather sucks.

The message was a no-brainer for him to translate. If anybody on the planet thought Lareina Elliot sent him a text about the actual weather, they, no doubt, worked for the DoP. Silas smiled at his thoughts. This month, *he* worked for the DoP. His job was to travel around the country on military assignment, legally killing things so the DoP could continue sporting the theory they were peaceful. As if it weren't common knowledge the Dopes—his name for them—were made of slime. They didn't start that way. Originally the Department of Justice, they took over local law enforcement under the ideal of cleaning up corruption. They became a national entity known as the Department of Protection & Peace. Now, all they do is enforce government rule.

They picked the wrong one this time. Corporal Silas McKade did two things without fail. He killed people and he protected Lareina Elliot.

'The weather sucks' meant trouble. Inside of a week, he would have her back and murder whoever fucked with her. If someone injured her, or worse, he'd put an end to the war by removing a few states from the map.

He may remove a few anyway, on principle.

Presque Isle Academy was a cluster of buildings housing classrooms, dormitories, labs, and administrative offices surrounded by trees and overgrowth. He made his way to the cafeteria across from her building. He'd collect intel there. Her office could be found on the back side, facing the woods. She had chosen it for a very specific purpose. To give Silas a clear shot from his favorite tree, a hundred yards out.

Higher ups were about. Agents tried and failed at being inconspicuous. He suspected the activity had something to do with his business.

The lunch bell rang. Good. Nothing like a bunch of noisy kids to tell him everything he needed to know.

****

Orion adjusted the radio. He liked everything about the Acura-Exhibit. It was nice. Burgundy. Mr. Thomas Murer kept it clean. Orion wouldn't have bothered with it if it had been trashed. He switched the station. Country. He hadn't heard this song before. He sailed through the intersection and finished his burger, wiping his hand on his pant leg. It wouldn't be right to mess up Mr. Murer's nice clean car. Especially since Mr. Thomas Murer left his wallet in the glove box, thereby authorizing Orion to take the money and stop for food on his way out of town.

Escaping Hillcrest had been a simple but intense procedure. To the roof and down the drainpipe. They overestimated their control by a ridiculously high margin. Maybe they underestimate new arrivals. Orion snorted. Someone who's interested in parkour and scores 196.8 out of a possible 200 on a test where the top performers average 170 to 180 should never be underestimated. It doesn't matter how many fences you put up.

The GPS informed him of his upcoming turn. It was difficult obeying the speed limit, but he had to. Attention was not what a fifteen-year-old runaway in a stolen car needed most. What he needed most was to get back to Presque Isle and Miss Elliot.

****

Fatigues garnered little notice; many of the older students were in the military training program. Others wore blue and gold school uniforms, depending on their age and curriculum. Some students chose street clothes as daily activity dictated.

Over the past five years, the country's greatest thinkers ate lunch in this cafeteria while waiting to be approved for the next level of the federal government's special education program. Even in this elite environment of over-achievers, more than seventy-five percent of them had already reached their full potential. The academy's purpose was to shuck the oysters and find the pearls.

The din was unbelievable. Forty minutes of food and freedom meant everything to a student. Opposite of the world around them, Silas talked quietly, forcing the girls across the table to lean forward, lest they miss some entertaining tidbit and forfeit an opportunity to flirt. Their sixteen-year-old attempts to be alluring were transparent and humorous at best. Girls always angled for his attention. He expected it. Buzz-cut brown hair, secretive grey eyes, he could bench press two-sixty, and he ran five miles in full gear every morning; at twenty-one, his physique was his best weapon. He wielded it often with ease and with pleasure.

"When did you get in?" asked one of the girls—Tasha/Sasha...whatever she said her name was.

"Just now. They told me to go to lunch and then go see somebody, umm, Miss Elliot, I think."

"I hate her," said the other one. Beth.

He watched her mouth then let his eyes dip lower. *That's a ton of metal to be chewing around. Commendable rack, though.*

"If you don't follow her directions, she will go out of her way to make your life hell."

"I like her," the Tasha/Sasha chick said. Her half-moon earrings were almost as big as her hands. She talked with her hands. "She always helps me whenever I have a problem."

I bet you have a lot of problems. Oily skin, broken flip-flops and whatnot.

Beth shook her head. "I still hate her. I'm glad she's gone." She snapped her fingers. "Miss Elliot's not here—"

No kidding.

"—You'll have to see somebody else. Probably Mr. Deverell. I heard he's the new guidance counselor for Sector A."

"No, he's not." Tasha/Sasha's earrings rattled with her denial. "He's just there temporally."

"Uh-uh," Beth tried to cut her off.

Tasha/Sasha talked over her. "Miss Elliot is my counselor, you'll most likely be in my group. I've been directed to see Mr. Deverell, temp-po-ral-ly." She faced Beth as she punctuated the syllables. "Miss Elliot got sick; food poisoning, he said. Really bad case. She'll be back in a few weeks. And those are the facts." She grinned, clearly declaring herself the victor in the tug-of-war for Silas' attention.

You told me something useful. One point for each of you. Silas nodded, seemingly more interested in Tasha/Sasha's eyes than her conversation; which suited Tasha/Sasha but made Beth frown.

An Asian girl with long legs and short, spiky, red hair balanced a tray of half eaten food in one hand and her book bag over her shoulder as she paused beside their table, waiting for the boy in front of her move. "Tasha, if someone told you pigeon shit was orange, you'd believe it. The real fact is you don't know what you're talking about. You never do."

"Oh, mind your business, Yukiyo," Tasha snapped. It didn't matter. Yukiyo had already walked off.

Beth caught Silas' eye and gave a slight nod of agreement.

Tasha. Silas made a mental note. *And Yukiyo.* She had been sitting at the next table, alone, with her nose in a book when he chose to talk to these flirtatious idiots. Obviously, she'd been listening. She knew something, or at least, she thought so. *Congratulations Yukiyo. You've made my list.*

****

Cute, Yukiyo thought as she emptied her tray and left the cafeteria. He was either up to something or today's brain-dead champ (which was saying something). Those were the only choices she had for the G.I. Joe throwback. While spacing during science, she happened to notice him coming out of building number three about a half hour before lunch. Building three housed storage and maintenance, a research department, a few offices, and a lot of empty classrooms. Guys like him didn't wander anywhere near building three unless they wanted something specific or they were lost. In her opinion, lost equalled stupid.

Beth and Tasha aren't the type of girls new kids cuddle up to, unless he marked them as easy targets, which they were. However, day one is definitely too early for hormones. Conclusion: he was up to something, or brain-dead. He could be both. Fortunately, she didn't have to care.

She did have to think about Miss Elliot though. Yukiyo was not gullible. No one could convince her school hadn't suddenly become ten shades weirder. She didn't know Miss Elliot's whereabouts, but someone better find her fast. Yukiyo had an appointment with her in fifteen minutes. Sorry, but no, a substitute would not do.

****

"Hey, Kaiden. Wake up man." Fisher reached behind him and pushed Kaiden's leg.

Kaiden woke and sat up in the same moment. Part of him remained at the ready. "Where we at?"

"Getting close." Fisher stretched his neck. He'd been driving for the last four hours. "Do you want to go to the school first?"

"No. We'll see what's up at her house first. Then if needs be, we'll blow up the school in the morning." Kaiden tugged his earring. "Pull over. I'll drive, but I need to take a piss."

"Yeah, me too." Fisher put on his blinker. A minute later, the Oneida made a fast turn into a Taco Casa parking lot.

Chapter 3

"May I help you, dear?" the receptionist, Mrs. Biley, spoke without rising from her chair.

Yukiyo sat her book bag down on the paperstone counter separating the office personnel and equipment from students and other undesirables. "I have a one o'clock with Miss Elliot."

Mrs. Biley reached for a spiral notebook labeled APPOINTMENTS. "Your name?"

"Mio. Dia. Yukiyo." Yukiyo rolled her eyes. They played this dumb game every time she came into the office. The stupid witch recognized her, but the school was so tight-assed, their own children had to identify themselves.

"Oh, yes. Here you are." She looked up from her book, apparently happy with her game. "Mr. Deverell is expecting you."

"No, he's not. I don't have an appointment with Mr. Deverell."

Mrs. Biley was a little less happy when she said, "Mr. Deverell has taken over Miss Elliot's duties for the time being."

"Sounds like a personal problem which has nothing to do with me."

Someone came in and sat in a hard plastic chair directly behind Yukiyo.

"I'll be with you in a second, young man." Mrs. Biley leaned to the right so she could peer around Yukiyo without getting up.

The teenager glanced over her shoulder and back as if she hadn't seen anyone. "I'm here to see Miss Elliot. That's my appointment. That's my schedule. That's why I'm here."

The receptionist got up from her desk. She clutched her appointment book. In that office, it was the bible.

"Are you in Sector A?"

"Are we in building 2, room 106, guidance office for Sector A? Did you read my name in your little 'Sector A' appointment book?" Yukiyo pointed to the book.

Mrs. Biley pursed her lips. "The students in Sector A, under Miss Elliot's guidance have been informed she is away. Mr. Deverell will be seeing to her duties until her return. Now, Miss Mio~"

"The receptionist in this office has been informed of my name on several occasions. Yet, every week she has to be told again. What's your point?"

Mrs. Biley glared at Yukiyo a half a minute. "Wait right there, young lady." As stiff as a corpse, she turned her attention to an inner office.

No sooner had she stepped out of sight, did Silas step up to the counter. He glanced at the various papers lined, stacked, or scattered across it. Sign-in sheets, sign-up sheets, information packets, lunch menus. Next, he moved to the far end, interested in the pictures and awards decorating the bland, beige wall.

A door opened. Mrs. Biley strode forward. Mr. Deverell followed her. His blond ponytail was at odds with his dark grey suit. The gold hoop earring dangling from his left ear gave the impression he'd rather be surfing. He'd rather be anywhere less restrictive. His stature could have been considered average, yet, he wasn't average. He flashed an easy smile, full of nonchalance and poison.

"Miss Mio Dia Yukiyo," Mr. Deverell inflated a sigh. "What am I to do with you?"

Yukiyo raised her eyebrows at his tone. She did like him in spite of the situation. Not that it mattered. "You're not going to do anything with me. I'm here to see Miss Elliot."

"Why?" *Why her? Why are you causing trouble? Why won't you cooperate? Why are you insistent on having your way?* A lot of questions, but Mr. Deverell didn't waste words.

Mrs. Biley looked down her somewhat hooked nose as if Mr. Deverell had properly put Yukiyo in her place.

Yukiyo liked that too. She thought Mrs. Biley was an idiot. She found it a pleasure to be proven right. Again. She tilted her head, pretending to ponder the question.

Silas stepped around the counter.

"Whyyyy what?"

Mrs. Biley scowled.

Mr. Deverell didn't change his expression. "Games, Miss Mio? That's out of character for you."

Yukiyo made a mental note to scratch her earlier opinion of him. She didn't like him in this situation, therefore, she didn't like him. Period. "Why what?"

Silas disappeared.

"Young lady, are you aware that people have been dropped from this program for less trouble than you have thus far caused?"

Seeing as the question came from Mrs. Biley, Yukiyo did not acknowledge it.

Neither did Mr. Deverell. "Why do you continue to show up for appointments you have no intention of keeping? I find the ritual fascinating."

Okay, fine. Call him charming. She still didn't like him. "To keep my record clean, why else? I'm not going to miss my assigned appointments because you guys screwed up. Unfortunately, the same can't be said for Miss Elliot."

"Not her fault," Mr. Deverell said. "You haven't kept an appointment since I've been here. What's your issue with me?"

"I haven't missed anything. I'm supposed to be here for half an hour. I'm here. Your name isn't Miss Elliot. You are not my assigned counselor. We have no established relationship. You don't get a half hour of my time just because you happen to be sitting at Miss Elliot's desk."

"Don't I?" Christian Deverell arched his eyebrows. "Out here or in there," he pointed behind him, "we're spending time together."

"You're spending time with her." Yukiyo nodded her head at Mrs. Biley. "She called you out here. I'd be standing here regardless of who's in front of me."

"Why is that?"

"I'm not one of your clients. Analyze somebody who gives a shit."

"Manners, young lady!" Mrs. Biley pointed her finger at Yukiyo.

"You say that a lot." Yukiyo stared at Mr. Deverell but spoke to Mrs. Biley. "Young lady this, young lady that," she mimicked. "It's like you think you're superior to someone. Perhaps *you* should see a counselor. Mr. Deverell has free time."

Mr. Deverell chuckled.

The phone rang. Mrs. Biley turned her back on the rude girl, using her most courteous voice, she greeted the caller.

Silas stepped around the counter. He studied the pictures and awards decorating the bland, beige wall.

"Yukiyo, may I make a suggestion?" Mr. Deverell said. He was serious; no banter, no condescension. "Why don't you schedule an appointment with me? Something different than your regular sessions, but no less important. You can pick up with Miss Elliot when she returns. I would hate to see you fall behind. Especially when you go through so much...trouble to keep your appointments. Besides, I would love the opportunity to become better acquainted with you. I'd consider it a rare challenge."

Yukiyo walked a full circle around the reception area, pondering his proposal. She came back, crossing paths with Silas as he made his way back to his seat. "You owe me," she whispered as he stepped aside to let her pass.

Christian Deverell followed her movements with his eyes. Nothing else on him moved.

When she got to the counter, Yukiyo picked up her book bag. She verified the contents. "Oh, look at the time. One twenty-eight. Have a nice day." Her black mini-skirt swished as she marched out of the office.

Christian watched her go. He stood a moment longer, watching the hallway, assuring himself she would not be returning. Behind him, he heard Mrs. Biley working at her desk. His eyes settled on Silas, the only other person in the waiting area. "In my office." He turned, confident the younger man would be following.

Lareina's office did not resemble her apartment. Here, the walls were decorated with beachy oil paintings; sunrise over the ocean and sandy shores. A handful of seashells and a ceramic dolphin added color to the bookshelf. She had a bulletin board covered with notes and drawings; the adoration of her students. A large picture window, with its ivory drapes drawn back, flooded the room with light. A storage closet held her supplies and two pairs of shoes—emergency footwear.

"Close the door." Christian went to Lareina's desk. His desk. Christian had already made it his own.

"You're in a pissy mood." Silas did as he was bidden. "It can't be over a mouthy sixteen-year-old."

"She's seventeen. She's a pain in my ass. I don't know what Lareina would have wanted with her."

"What makes you think Lareina wanted her?"

"She's uncooperative, which means she knows too much of something." Christian opened a drawer. Nimbly shuffling through folders, he withdrew the one he wanted.

"Do you want me to kill her?"

"Yes." Having found the correct file, he passed it to Silas.

"Umm hmm." Silas thumbed through its contents.

"I mean it." Christian went to a second drawer, a second folder.

"If you do, you're a sicker s.o.b. than I thought, Eugene."

"I don't believe I've given you permission to be informal with me, Corporal. You don't get to call me Eugene." Christian retrieved some forms and filled in the necessary information as he talked.

"I didn't ask your permission. If you're expecting me to kill two people for you, one of them a sixteen-year-old kid, then I'll call you whatever I want. Eugene."

"Don't piss me off. I can do my own dirty work. She's seventeen."

"Where is Lareina?"

Christian pointed to the folder. "At the moment, she's tucked away, sedated. She made a big mistake, which interestingly enough, is the reason she's still alive."

"Mistake. Hmm. Lucky you."

"Lucky me. I'm going to see her in a little while. After I find out what I need to know I'll call you and you can...do what you do best. Where can I reach you?"

Silas made himself comfortable. He propped his feet up on Christian's desk. Lareina's desk. "Nope, I don't think you can."

"Pardon?"

"You can't do your own dirty work. Not where Lareina Elliot is concerned, anyway. You may not care about offing a sixteen-year-old, but," he plucked the folder, "you've got some history here. You don't want to be a part of her destruction."

"Seventeen-year-old. Lareina's destruction is Lareina's business." He handed Silas the forms.

"Lareina used to be your business." Silas gave a cursory glance to the death warrants. Lareina Nicole Elliot. Mio Dia Yukiyo.

"Lareina is still my business. At least, until I get what I'm after.

Lareina's destruction is not my business. Everything you need to know is in the folder. Whatever device you planted in here won't be active much longer. Where can I reach you?"

Silas dipped into his pocket, retrieving a handful of peppermints. "She keeps them in the cupboard." He popped one into his mouth.

"Where can I reach you?"

Having heard a dismissal in Christian's tone, Silas got up. "You can reach me on Yukiyo's phone." Folder and forms in one hand, he used the other to close the door behind himself.

****

Orion circled the compound, debating the best way to enter. A runaway student couldn't exactly drive a stolen car through the front gate and not expect to be noticed. It was a temporary problem. He'd figure something out in a minute. He just needed to think a bit.

****

"This ain't right." Kaiden hit the light switch, illuminating the hallway in Lareina's condo.

Fisher stood in the doorway, behind him. "What's up?"

Kaiden took a cautious step forward. "Don't feel right."

Fisher dropped his duffle bag and withdrew his pistol. That he was still alive, on more than one occasion, had been because of his trust in Kaiden's feelings.

Kaiden didn't pull out his own gun. It wasn't that type of feeling, yet. Besides, Fisher had his back. He wasn't the one in danger. Gradually, they made their way through the place, one room at a time, clicking on lights and searching his sister's apartment. Living room, bathrooms, all three bedrooms, under the beds, in the closets; nothing seemed out of place— not that either of them would know if it were. Kaiden knew the code but had never been to Lareina's secret place. She had school assigned living quarters, however, this condo wasn't the school's business. Regardless, somebody was here. Or, at least, somebody had been here, recently. Kaiden felt certain of it.

Everything was turned off and undisturbed. That was the problem.

Where was the dust? The trash didn't smell. The food in the refrigerator wasn't bad. It didn't feel empty or abandoned and that didn't feel right.

Kaiden sat down in a cream colored, wingback armchair, trying to reason out his impressions. Fisher plopped across the matching sofa, grabbed a pillow for his head and laid back; feet up, gun across his stomach. Waiting.

"Who the hell is in here?" Kaiden called out; his voice bouncing off the ceiling.

Nothing. No sound. No movement. Nothing.

"I said," Kaiden raised his voice an octave, "Who is in here!"

"Do you think somebody will answer?" Fisher shifted to get more comfortable. "We did search the place."

"Who were you expecting?" Alec leaned against the wall, munching on a Twix bar. Where he had been hiding remained a secret. "Why don't you quit yelling." He retrieved his cell phone from his front pocket and punched some numbers. The television clicked on and a few unnecessary lights clicked off. "Get your shoes off the sofa, you moron." As he berated Fisher, Alec joined them in the living room. He sat in his favorite recliner, changed the channel and said, "It's about time you showed up. Kaiden, right?"

Kaiden nodded. "Who are you?"

Fisher sat up. "Give me a piece of candy."

Alec shoved the last bite into his mouth. "Wha' 'andy?"

Chapter 4

Silas stepped into the sun and was humored. *Not hard to keep up with her at all, is it?* Yukiyo waited in the parking lot, leaning against his Genuine. With an easy stride, he made his way over.

She watched his approach with feigned disinterest. "Well?"

Silas hunched his shoulders. *I can play your game better than you, girl.*

"Why were you sneaking into Miss Elliot's office and what did you find out?"

"Are we friends?"

"Buttwipe, I kept his attention and stalled him so you wouldn't get caught."

"Gee, thanks." He unlocked his doors.

"You're a dick, but I'm going to be the biggest pain in your ass until I find out what's going on. They do have cameras in that office if I need to prove my story." She nudged by him and slid into the driver's seat.

Should I? No, I shouldn't. She's funny. I'll make an exception. Silas leaned in close. Too close. He whispered, "I jammed the signal. No film today." While she digested that piece of information, he went on to say, "You've got less than twelve minutes. Go to your dorm, pack your shit—one bag. Walk out of the back gate. Don't talk to anybody. I'll be waiting." Silas straightened up and surveyed his surroundings.

Yukiyo's heart raced. Buttwipe had something going on. She stood up, using both hands to push him back a step. "Bubble space." She gave her skirt a perfunctory tug, to keep it in place. "There's a guard at the back gate. Are you going to knock him out or something?"

"Or something. Hurry up. You're wasting my time."

Silas left by the front gate and drove as close as he dared to the rear entrance. The elderly guard never saw him coming. Silas rendered him unconscious—he would be that way for at least an hour—and he still had to piss away six minutes of his life waiting for Yukiyo.

Precisely twelve minutes from the time he said 'go' Yukiyo marched through the gate. He had to give her credit. She didn't pause at the security booth, being nosey. She looked natural as if she strolled through the back gate every day around this time.

A burgundy Acura made its way down the road. Silas remembered seeing it pass the front of the school earlier. He made a mental note of the out-of-state license. All was cool until the driver hit the brakes and a clear male voice called Yukiyo's name.

Yukiyo stared at the driver in surprise. A delighted smile lifted the corner of her mouth. She went to the vehicle. They talked for a full minute. Yukiyo waved him over.

Silas obliged her. When he got to the car, he saw another kid. He wasn't sure, but he thought he might know him or something about him.

"Orion, this is..." Yukiyo looked at Silas, looked at the spot on his fatigues where his name should have been. "He's not important. The thing is you have something in common."

"What do we have in common?" Orion arched his brows. Other than being white and hanging out back, he couldn't spot the similarities.

"Miss Elliot. He knows something about her and you know something about her. None of us should be here."

"You got that much right, at least," Silas said, "I thought you were smarter than this. We have to go."

"He's coming with us."

Her statement was news to Orion. "I'm not going anywhere."

"Yeah you are," she retorted. "Not like you have a choice. Keep driving around in circles. Eventually, someone is going to spot you. Good luck explaining why you're not wherever it is you're supposed to be. Not to mention, the car." Yukiyo half turned, giving Silas a sideways look of exasperation. "You were snooping around Ms. Elliot's office, probably looking for clues, or leads, or whatever. This guy," she hooked her thumb at Orion, "was just shipped off to the smart people school. Smart people equal answers. He's coming with us."

Silas was collecting intel, of course, he wanted to talk. His beeper went off. "Damn it." Reaching into his shirt pocket, he pulled out a small bottle of pills. Shaking two of them into his palm, he offered them to the bemused teenagers.

"Right." Orion rolled his eyes.

"Are you brain-dead?" Yukiyo put a hand on her hip.

Reflex-quick, Silas reached into his waistband and released a small pistol. He tapped the muzzle to Orion's head. "No, I'm not. I don't have time for this shit. Take the pills."

Eying Silas, his gun and Orion, Yukiyo snatched a pill. She put it in her mouth and swallowed. "If you're going to poison us. May I ask why?"

Silas didn't say anything until Orion took his pill. "Swallow. Both of you."

"I did."

"Don't fuck with me, Yukiyo. Swallow the damn pill." He cocked the pistol.

They didn't know how he knew neither of them had swallowed the pills until they swallowed them in earnest. First Yukiyo and then Orion made a gagging noise. The pill was tasteless until it hit your esophagus. Then it made you want to throw up.

"I have a gun, a death warrant, and not a shits worth of concern for you. I don't need to waste my poison. Get in this car and drive to The Leisure World Condominiums. Whichever building has apartment 428, go to that parking lot and stay there until I tell you to move. Do not go in the building. If you do, the next time I put a gun to your head, I pull the trigger." Silas put his gun away.

"Man, who the hell are you?" Orion demanded.

"What the hell is the pill about?" Yukiyo walked to the passenger side of Orion's car. "Are we supposed to just die there in that parking lot?"

"It's possible." Silas looked left and right. "The pill is a tracking device. For the next seventy-two hours, I'm your daddy. Don't make me hunt you down." With that, he left them. Hopping into his jeep, he sped off.

****

One street over, three blocks behind, Silas wouldn't risk following any closer. His target was lethal and as such, should not be underestimated. Silas wasn't worried his tracking device would be discovered. America wasn't aware his technology had been invented. Regardless, he didn't want anyone's senses tingling, no danger pre-warnings.

"Alpena Regional." Silas watched the car he tracked pull into the hospital's parking lot. "Is this a joke? She better not be there out of necessity." A few quick taps on the screen minimized the GPS and started the search engine that would hack into the hospital's database. Silas owned a Chronos, the most advanced hand-held in the Universe. It was an electronic brain specifically designed and assigned to certain Special Ops CT's and no one else.

Within a minute, his screen lit up.

```
Name: Lareina Elliot
D.O.B 02/04/33 Sex: Female S.S. 148-62-2121
Location: Internal Medicine
Room: 204
Ailment: Food poisoning
Condition: Stable
Medication: Bismuth subsalicylate 4 hr.


*
Name: Lareina Elliot:
ID # 246824
D.O.B 02/04/33 Sex: Female S.S. 148-62-2121

No Records found
Location: Unknown
Room: Unknown
Aliment: Unknown
Condition: Unknown
Medication: Unknown


*
Name: Unlisted
ID# 246824- 4
D.O.B. Unlisted Sex: Unlisted S.S. Unlisted

Location: C.C.U. Isolation
Room: 416
Ailment: Unlisted
Condition: Unlisted
```

Medications: Mephobarbital/Barbiturate/twelve-hour
drip.

"Something for everybody; the well-wishers, the researchers, and me." Silas cross-referenced the lists. The first and easiest to procure was general information. An experienced hacker could uncover the second. The last, most informative list came from a priority clearance or Chronos. "What would she do without me?" Deft fingers made the information disappear. Silas continued driving. Knowing Lareina's location was all he needed.

****

"I'm guessing you're the little shit who's supposed to come with me?" Kaiden asked.

"Nope." Alec flipped through channels too fast for anyone to identify the programs. "Lareina wasn't sending me nowhere."

"How do you know who I am?"

"I said she wasn't sending me nowhere. That doesn't mean she didn't tell me nothing. I know everything."

"Everything?" Fisher repeated. "Who the hell are you, kid?"

Alec stopped surfing long enough to glare at Fisher. "I got your 'kid' right here." He cupped his groin.

Fisher lifted his gun. "You might not be knowing shit in a minute."

Alec made a condescending noise.

"Knowing everything could get you hurt." Kaiden brought the attention back to himself. "If Lareina told you something about me you'll need to prove it. What's your name?"

He considered his options for a full minute before he relaxed. "Name's Alec. I've been waiting for you."

"Why?"

"Why do you think? Do you see your sister anywhere around here?"

"We didn't see you," Fisher said, "and here you are."

"'Cause you're a dumbass," Alec threw a glance in Fisher's direction. "But, you'll improve. I have faith."

Fisher tried hard to hold his frown. The kid was going to be a total pain in his ass. At least, he wouldn't be bored.

"Can we be done with the chitchat? What's up with my sister and why

28

are you in her house? Also," Kaiden tugged his earring. "You can fuck with Fisher all you want, but if you can't tell us something useful, he will blow your scrawny little ass away."

For emphasis, Fisher removed the safety.

Alec pursed his lips. "Ppfff. You are not that stupid. You might be," he half-turned toward Fisher and swung around again. "But, you can't be. Not if you're related to my mother. You touch me and she will kick your ass."

Kaiden and Fisher eyeballed one another. *Mother?*

****

"Where are you going?" Orion had just cut the engine when Yukiyo opened the door.

"To see who lives at 428 Leisure World Drive."

"No."

The authority in Orion's voice made Yukiyo pause. "Don't you want to know why we're here?"

"I know why we're here. Because some asshole, whose name you didn't bother to get, put a gun to my head and poisoned us. The only shot we got is to do what he says, so sit down."

Yukiyo complied. "Don't you want to know why we're here?"

"I bet we'll find out eventually."

"We may not. As you pointed out, G.I. Joe Wish-he-was hasn't even given up his name."

Orion dismissed her. "Go get yourself killed. I'll be right here."

Yukiyo huffed, but she stayed.

It wasn't five minutes before Orion's patience zeroed out. "Alright, let's go see."

They got out of the car, slamming the doors.

Inside the building they didn't speak. Sharing the elevator with an elderly couple, they gave no indication they were together. Yukiyo kept an impassive face when Orion disembarked one floor below their destination. *She wasn't getting out.* She waited a few steps away from door #428 until he rejoined her by way of the stairs.

"Now what?" Yukiyo broke the silence. "Should we knock?"

Orion studied the hall. He counted the doors on the one side and gauged the distance from one end to the other. He seemed satisfied with what he surmised. "You should, but not until I text you."

"Text me from where?"

"I'm going to climb up to their balcony, see what I can see."

"These kinds of places don't usually have back steps or outside fire escapes."

"I don't need them." Orion went back the way he came.

Yukiyo followed him to the stairwell. No sense in waiting out in the open while he pretended to be a monkey. "Hurry up."

****

"I should shoot him and be done with it." Silas stopped his jeep behind the Leisure World complex. Scanning the tops of buildings was a natural habit, he noticed Orion immediately. He retrieved a duffle bag from the back seat. Inside was his favorite—his TS13; a semi-automatic with a triclip chamber and combination muzzle. The lightweight barrel allowed a twenty-five-hundred-meter range. If he didn't have to compete with windage, Silas could hit a target at twenty-seven. He slipped the suppressor on—*no need to wake the baby.* Leaning into the cheekrest, he centered his scope on Orion, leading his target.

Once Orion stood securely on the second-story balcony, hand on the railing, ready to make his next climb, Silas counted, "...two, one," and squeezed the trigger. *Mmm. I love how that feels.* He watched as Orion snatched his hand back; the bullet striking the railing less than an inch from his thumb.

He was smart enough to back up as he searched, wide-eyed, for his attacker. Silas didn't attempt to hide. He braced the TS13 against his thigh and waved to be sure Orion spotted him. When they made eye contact, he pointed at Orion and then the ground. He only gestured one time.

Chapter 5

"You're done." Christian waved the guards away. When they disappeared around the corner, he let himself into the room, walking past the bed. He scanned the area out of her fourth-floor window before making himself comfortable in the room's only chair. He'd wait. She hadn't so much as fluttered an eyelash, but she was awake. If she wanted to lay there like a zombie, so be it. He'd wait.

Five minutes of total silence.

Now, he was bored. He reached for the remote and helped himself to her television. The weather channel. A shopping channel. A Spanish channel. The Food Network. *Hmm. Tough choice. The weather channel it is.*

The local forecast called for rain.

"About time, you stopped staring at me."

He turned toward the sound. Her eyes were opened and her voice clear; not a trace of the raspiness or confusion associated with sleep. Their eyes met and he wanted to smile. "I knew you weren't asleep."

She did smile. "I was asleep."

"You knew I was here."

"I heard you come in, but that's no reason for me to wake up."

"How are you feeling?" His eyes raked over her.

"Crappy. This isn't a spa."

"What happened?" He indicated her right wrist. Above the I.V. tape, a strap held her to the bed. Beneath it, an inch of purplish blue twisted its way around her arm.

Lareina glanced at the bruise and hunched her shoulder. "The straps are too tight. Like you care."

Christian rolled his eyes at her insult. Coming to her bedside, he withdrew his key ring and showed her the attached pocket knife—the one she gave him for his birthday. He cut the binding and with no thought to seek her permission, he reached beneath the covers, pulling her left hand into his sight. A second later, both hands were free. "Ankles?"

"Please." Lareina massaged her sore wrist.

Once freed, Lareina sat up, making herself more comfortable. "Would you do something about this?" She wiggled the I.V. tube.

"Nope." Christian helped himself to her chart. "According to this, you might be due for some scopolamine soon."

"Among other things. You didn't authorize that did you?"

"Nope. That came straight from the top. Administrating a truth serum to you is a waste of time and taxpayer money."

Lareina fluffed her pillow and leaned back. "Always concerned with the little people."

"I'm concerned about you, Lareina. You're in deep shit. I may not be able to save your ass."

She laughed and proceeded to remove the I.V. herself. "You think much too highly of yourself, Eugene. You can't save my ass."

"Are you saying it's too late?"

"I'm saying you're not capable."

"I've had a long day. Don't piss me off."

She opened her arms, indicating the bareness of her hospital room. "You seriously aren't expecting sympathy from me, are you? I've had several long days, thanks to you."

"Don't blame this shit on me. All I did was catch your ass. You F'd up." He pointed a satisfied finger at her. "Now quit making it worse on yourself."

"Worse? Seeing as you're planning to kill me, really, what could be worse?"

"I cannot believe you just said that to me, Lareina."

"Meaning you won't stay around to watch."

"Meaning you better stop plucking my nerves, girl. I need some information. Tell me something so I can get you out of here."

"Forgive me if I'm not buying it."

Christian shook his head. It was an attempt to shake his frustration away. Lareina always had that effect on him. "Maybe you'll buy this...There is a real war going on. Right here on American soil. Real American citizens are dying every day. A handful of people possess the talent to stop it. No, to win it, so we won't have to go through this shit ever again. It's our job—yours and mine—to find those people and get them prepared. Except, now, you are undermining that effort."

"You left out the part about those talented people being children, who have no idea what they are being prepared for."

"I could have already had you terminated if that's what I wanted."

"But, you won't. At least not yet, because you don't know what I know and that drives you up a wall."

"You drive me up a wall. Are you listening to me?"

"No. I've already heard this argument...from you."

He moved in close. "You better listen to me. You're in deep shit. If I don't report something useful to my superiors in..." he looked at his watch, "twenty minutes. They are expecting me to summon an assassin, which, I will do. After that, it's going to become damned annoying keeping you alive. You *might* want to work with me a little bit." Their eyes met and locked. Raw heat shot between them. Desire, overwhelming in its intensity, too dangerous to be freed; it pulled at them, drew them in. They wanted it. Wanted to give in, give all, if only...

Christian took a deep breath. He broke the eye contact, he had to.

Lareina took a deep breath. She gave no indication she noticed the jolt they shared. "Twenty minutes, huh? Who did you call? Geico?"

"Like you care." He threw her words back without focus, his mind elsewhere.

"Actually, I do. An assassin who has an interest in me is someone I care about."

Christian snorted. As long as he was there, Lareina didn't have to worry about anything. She knew that. He knew she knew that. "I'm going to call your boy."

"My boy?"

"Silas McKade." He watched her eyes. If she were going to give away anything, it would be with her eyes. Whenever she was troubled or needed a moment to compose herself, she threw a quick glance to the left of her subject. Such a slight movement wouldn't register with most people, even experts. But, he wasn't most people. And one of these days that glance was going to be his downfall—he had to pay attention.

And there it was.

"McKade huh? Well, don't I feel honored."

"You should feel afraid. He is unequivocally the best in his field. Aren't you a little scared of what he might do to you?"

She pretended to ponder it. "Hmm. That depends. Did you call him for my punishment or his?"

Christian cocked his head to the side. "Why his?"

She rolled her eyes. "Riiiiiight, because *you* forgot I used to babysit him. It just slipped *your* mind he went to school with my brother. *You* didn't remember he went into the military on my recommendation."

"Quit being a smartass."

"Quit being a dumbass. Do you think he'll enjoy this assignment?"

"Do you think he'll do the assignment? I believe he has a thing for you."

"A thing?" She almost smiled.

"A soft spot."

"If you assume that will keep him from doing his job, then I believe you have a soft spot. It's where your brain used to be." She pulled her covers back. "Help me up."

He obeyed without comment. Steadying her while she worked her foot into her slipper. He was taller, but not by an uncomfortable degree. The strength in his arms was a surety. "Wait a minute." Lareina shifted her weight so she could get her other foot secure. "The last I heard, McKade's unit is supposed to be working on something on the East Coast. Did you set him up?" Her tone was heavy with accusation. "You brought him here to see if he has any kind of loyalty to me over the Army." The lack of change in his expression verified her conclusion. Jerking her arm out of his grasp, she walked to her bathroom. "The only reason you would do something like that is to punish the kid for~"

"Kid?" He laughed outright. "That kid is ranked in the top ten most deadly people in the country. He hasn't been with the East Coast unit for almost a year. You didn't know that?"

"Why would I know that? I stopped babysitting him a long time ago." When she got to the door, she paused to look at Christian over her shoulder. "You're hoping to punish him for being good at what he does. I think you might be jealous because I know someone who's more deadly than you are."

He tried to laugh, but there was no real humor in him. "You're reaching. I said he's ranked in the top ten. So am I and I'm farther up. Trust me."

"Not likely. The fact that you've already thought about this tells me

I'm right, you are jealous." She closed the door before he could respond.

She didn't see his eyes narrow or his expression drop. She didn't get to know she had touched a nerve.

He didn't see her eyes light up or her smile breakthrough. He didn't get to know he had given her hope.

****

Silas watched Orion's descent with a lazy, almost bored expression. When the boy landed on the ground, he locked the safety and slung his TS13 over his shoulder. No point in putting it away, now. "You don't listen well, do you?"

"You got an antidote for that pill?" Although far from winded, Orion took a few deep breaths.

"Where's Yukiyo?"

Orion resigned himself to being bossed around for the moment. "She's in the building waiting for me to text her."

"So text her." Silas walked ahead. "Tell her to stay where she is. If she moves, you'll be dead and she'll be next." Pulling out his Chronos, he punched in the security code to Lareina's condo.

Access Denied.

He did not hit a wrong key.

Access Denied.

"What?"

Access Denied.

This time, Silas paused, verifying the number/letter combination.

Access Denied.

He installed the system himself. If she changed the code, he would have received the update. He'll give it one more shot—out of politeness.

Access Denied. That's all the chances you get. Stay out of my business.

Silas read the message and laughed.

"What?" Beside him, Orion had been silent, watching the unreadable emotions play across Silas' face.

As opposed to being offended, the challenge delighted Silas. "It's a good thing you didn't make it to that balcony."

"I could have gotten up there."

"I know. Somebody would have been there waiting for your sorry ass too. He saw you coming."

They reached the front doors to the complex. Silas held it open for Orion to pass in front of him. His thumb worked overtime as he talked, walked, recalculated, and texted.

"Why would somebody who doesn't know me or anything about me, be expecting me to climb up the back of the building?"

They took the stairs.

"Because this somebody is smart."

"You think I'm not?"

Ignoring him, Silas finished his message just as they came upon Yukiyo sitting on the steps outside the fourth-floor corridor. He looked at her as if he were seeing fresh road kill and hit send.

Nice trick. You got some skills. But not enough to beat me.

The floor went dark.

****

Alec read the message sent to his phone. "We might have a problem."

"What problem?" Kaiden and Fisher spoke in unison.

"Don't know." This was the most serious Alec had been since they met him. He studied his phone, pressing a few keys. "Somebody was trying to hack the system."

"How do you know?" Fisher asked.

Kaiden tuned in on the important word. "Was?"

"Shit." Alec frowned. "They got in."

The power went off.

They stood quiet. Kaiden slid his pistol from his waistband and all three of them hit the flashlights on their phones.

Alec had a gun too. Under different circumstances, it would have been unnerving that neither Kaiden nor Fisher thought to search him. Now, they didn't have time to care. "This way." He motioned for them to follow him.

"Don't do it."

The foreign voice was clear, authoritative, and deadly cold.

No one moved.

As suddenly as they went out, the lights came back on. The illumination revealed Kaiden and Fisher facing the front door, their guns trained on Yukiyo and Orion. The latter two, unarmed and frightened. Alec had taken three steps in the other direction, toward the bedrooms. A soldier blocked his path; the sight of his TS13 locked on Kaiden.

Even though Alec was armed and currently no one had a weapon on him, he sensed the danger radiating from the soldier. He didn't actually know how to shoot; best not to press his luck. He relaxed his stance. "I hope to God you're Silas."

"Be careful what you pray for," Silas answered. "Sometimes you get it."

With a dissatisfied huff, Kaiden put his gun away. "Silas."

"Kaiden." Silas gave a happy greeting. The sound was at odds with his actions, or rather, his lack of action. The TS13 hadn't budged.

"Man." Fisher lowered his weapon. "You always have to be the prom king."

Silas waited a moment longer. "It's a party." He locked his safety with a toothy grin.

Beyond the hugs of hello between Kaiden, Fisher, and Silas, it was anything but a party. Four suspicious, weary individuals, eyeballing one another and their surroundings; none of them fully comprehending the why of it, the other two calm, composed and comfortable. One of them with knowledge; the other in command.

"Team Stupid," Silas directed his attention to Yukiyo and Orion. "Come on in and grab a seat. Are you hungry?" He plucked a dining room chair for himself and straddled it. Next, he looked to Kaiden. "You got any food here. My lunch sucked." Without waiting for an answer, he studied Alec. "Unless somebody is hiding in the john, you must be the genius, because it ain't Fisher."

Alec chuckled.

"Kiss my ass, Silas." Fisher went back to his spot on the sofa.

Orion followed Yukiyo to the vacant loveseat. He and Alec watched each other.

"Hey, Alec." Yukiyo ignored the tension. "What are you doing here?"

"Hey, Yukiyo. The real question is what are you doing here? Why'd you bring him?" He glared at Orion. Hell would freeze over before he'd speak to him on purpose.

"Where's Miss Elliot?" Orion returned Alec's intensity with an equal measure of his own.

"Eeeeeeennn," Silas made a buzzer sound. "I ask the questions and I'll get to that when I get to it. This playground rivalry is going to have to take a nap. Yukiyo, I need your phone."

It suddenly occurred to Alec—his over active mind jumping back to Silas' request for food—Lareina would want him to be hospitable. He muttered, "I'll get you something," on his way to the kitchen.

"What do you need my phone for?"

"A telephone conversation. I'm waiting on a call."

"What are you doing here, Silas?" Kaiden tugged on his earring, half afraid he already knew the answer.

"Same thing as you, I expect."

It made Kaiden mad to have to ask, but he did. "Do you know where she is?"

It made Silas happy to make Kaiden mad. He didn't hide it. "Of course, I do."

"Where is she?"

"Where?"

"Where's she at?"

Fisher, Orion, and Yukiyo talked over one another.

Kaiden waited.

Silas waited.

Alec returned with a two-liter bottle of Sprite and a stack of plastic cups in one hand, a large bag of corn chips and a box of Ritz crackers in the other, a pack of Oreos rode in the crook of his arm. He released his offering onto the coffee table and focused on Silas. His eyes filmed over with emotion. "Is she hurt?"

The emotion touched Silas. "I don't know. We have a chance of getting her back, but we'll have to move fast and work together."

Alec nodded. He blinked and sighed, bringing himself under control. "Name's Alec. I know all about you." He offered Silas a cup.

"No, you don't." Silas took it and held it out so Alec could pour him a drink.

Alec didn't pour. Instead, he offered Silas the bottle to pour it himself. "I know enough. How's that?"

Kaiden came to the end of his patience. He grabbed the bottle and filled all the cups, more to give himself something to do than to be nice. "How about if you tell us where my sister is? Then we'll all know." He tossed the corn chips to Fisher and grabbed two of the drinks.

"She's at Alpena Regional. I don't know if it's a necessity or if they're just stashing her there. You have to get her out within the next hour or so."

Yukiyo helped herself to a sleeve of Ritz. She took her crackers and her drink with her as she examined the room. "That's a big building. Do we have a plan?"

"Partially," Silas said. "Which is why I need your phone."

"Who would call *you* on *my* phone?"

Kaiden narrowed his eyes on the red-headed chink. She needed to stop holding up the action with her inconsequential phone issues.

"The call I'm waiting for is the go-ahead for me to get over to Alpena Regional and kill Lareina." He turned to Kaiden. "You may want to get there ahead of me."

Chapter 6

"Seriously, we have about five minutes to get a plan and make it work." Silas paced back and forth as he talked.

"Let's go." Alec crossed his path. "We can plan in the car."

"Except, you ain't going." Kaiden leveled his stare at Alec.

Alec raised his eyebrows and cut a glance to Silas.

Silas didn't hesitate. "He would be right." He turned his attention to Orion and Yukiyo, ignoring Alec as he brushed past him. "You two aren't going either."

Orion pfff'd. "Who put you in charge?"

"Me. Remember. Sixty-nine hours to go. Don't forget I owe you for that spider-man stunt."

"I saw him coming. The balcony's rigged, anyway." The corners of Alec's mouth turned up slightly, fantasizing about what could have happened had Orion stepped on the balcony before returning his attention to the issue at hand. "You're wasting time telling me I ain't going because I am. Guarantee it."

Orion clenched his teeth but otherwise ignored Alec. "I'm going to get Miss Elliot. I'm the reason she got caught, I'm going to get her out."

If his admission shocked anyone, they were good about hiding it.

"Yeah, well, you can be all sorry later." Fisher clasped Orion's shoulder. "Y'all are too young. You're still in school which means you're useless and we don't have time to teach you shit."

"So you get to stay out of the way," Kaiden finished for him.

"This is what you can do, Clyde," Silas offered by way of a compromise. "You and Bonnie, over there," he pointed to Yukiyo, "can go ditch that stolen car you left outside. I'll tell you where to take it. If you're not there when I come for you, you'll be an easy mark when I hunt you down." He reached for his Chronos and paused.

Yukiyo erupted in a fit of giggles. "It was sweet." She leveled her gaze at Silas. "Watching you get took." She pointed to a spot over his shoulder. His phone lay on the ottoman two feet away—not where he put it—and Alec nowhere to be seen.

"I seriously don't have time for this shit." Silas grabbed the Chronos. The kid called himself. "Lovely," he mumbled.

****

"What are you doing?" In the short time Lareina had been excused, Christian had gathered her few possessions and various meds. They were in a small bag he procured from who-knows-where.

"Relocating you."

"Why?"

"I'm saving your life, my dear. Since you aren't capable of handling it yourself." Evidently, he felt good enough to enjoy his skill.

"Stealing my socks is now a life-saving technique?"

He huffed once, on his way to open the door. Lareina silently followed Christian. She didn't want to be in that room any more than he wanted her to be. They didn't encounter anyone and had a playful shoving match getting into the elevator.

"Planning to push me off the roof?" Lareina said when he used a key in conjunction with the up button.

"That is a dream of mine. But not tonight."

"If that's what you dream of, you lead a boring life."

They exited onto a floor few people visited. The lights were dim. No one utilized the lounge area. At the nurse's station, a middle-aged lady applied herself to the study of a *Southern Living* magazine. She forgot to look up. Two rooms down, he opened a door on the right.

Lareina arched her eyebrows. This room belonged in a high-end hotel; a soft grey down comforter with four matching overstuffed pillows covered a full sized bed, a round end-table with a lace skirt nestled between two recliners. A small kitchenette, mid-size bookshelf, and a large television completed the picture. The bathroom door stood open. There was a lot of room in there. "Wow, Eugene. You shouldn't have."

He strutted around, cutting on lights, adjusting the temperature to his comfort. "Even in this economy, you can't expect the wealthy to live like the rest of us."

"Of course not." She plucked a book off the shelf. "Ooh." He had gotten her the newest release from her favorite author. Taking it to the recliner, she folded her feet under her and wiggled into comfort.

Christian followed her. He stood before her, hands on hips, feet planted apart, towering over her. "Your dinner is in the fridge. You can have a glass of wine. Don't touch the Bourbon until I get back. It's my favorite."

She pursed her lips. "What am I, your mistress?"

"If only." He leaned down to brush a light kiss across her forehead. "Try to behave yourself until I get back."

"Hmmm." She started the prologue.

Christian left, seemingly unconcerned. He locked her in and jiggled the handle to be certain before he reached for his cell phone.

****

"That's it? That's your brilliant plan?" Yukiyo narrowed her gaze at Silas. "Those two wish-they-were-cowboys are going to stroll through the hospital, toting their guns, while you sit in a building across the street somewhere, magically opening doors for them. They are going to scoop up Miss Elliot and waltz her out so you can throw a fit because she's missing. Nobody is going to notice any of this and Orion and I might be stuck hitchhiking because you got your stupid self arrested."

Silas rocked his head, mentally checking off her points. "Pretty much, yeah. I don't advise hitchhiking. It's dangerous and you can't be seen."

"You are the definition of insanity."

"He's passed insane," Kaiden said as he put on his jacket. "Once we get in, we'll be in the cafeteria."

Fisher came right on his heels. "Later."

"There's a question," Kaiden said. "Why didn't you get in touch with me as soon as you found out something was wrong with my sister?"

Silas didn't look up. "Uhhhh let me think...Because I don't answer to you. Besides, I don't know if anything is wrong with your sister."

Kaiden turned. Fisher blocked him. "Let it go, man. Right now, we have to focus on Lareina."

Fisher was right. Kaiden knew it. He closed off his mind to everybody and everything but his sister.

"Oh. Give this to 'Reina when you see her." He reached into his pocket, chucked something minuscule to Fisher and returned his attention to his Chronos.

Yukiyo's phone blared. The loud obnoxious sound of drums being played offbeat and screeching that passed for a song. Silas winced but stretched out his hand. She didn't recognize the number, so she relinquished her lifeline.

"Yep." Silas held a finger to his lips to shush her.

Christian couldn't help appreciating Silas' efficiency. "I take it she's dead."

He watched Yukiyo's face as he talked. "She's sixteen. She'd have to be dead or maybe naked to be parted from her phone. If it were the latter, I wouldn't be on her phone—"

Yukiyo's mouth dropped.

"—except to take pictures."

She threw up a hand and walked out. Orion went with her.

"Spare me your fantasies. You still have work to do."

"I guess that means you found out what you needed to know."

"I guess you think questions are in your job description."

"I don't have to guess. She didn't tell you anything. Do you want me to interrogate her first?"

"I don't care what you do as long as you do it in the next hour."

"It's possible. Where is she?"

"Alpena Regional. CCU. Room 416. There's a useful rooftop across the lot. Call me back from this number when it's done."

"Because sporting a phone with a lavender skin is my thing. Are you going to cry?" He switched topics smoothly.

"Are you?" Came curtly through the phone.

"Cry for what? Lareina won't see me coming. She won't be thinking about me at all. You, on the other hand...She knows it was you. Her last thought will be 'I was right. Eugene is a dick.' Can you live with that?"

"You don't have permission to call me Eugene. She knows you're on the assignment. Her cooperation, or lack thereof, and her life, or lack thereof, is all about your conscience, or lack thereof."

"Okay. She knows what I lack and you're a dick. At least, she's informed. In this business, that's all that matters."

"Get to work, McKade." Christian hung up.

"ALEC!" Silas yelled when the phone went dead. He didn't get an answer. "Be that way." Silas collected his TS13, and a half opened sleeve of Ritz. He didn't make another sound as he exited Lareina's condo.

****

"May I help you, gentlemen?" The attendant at the registration desk turned her attention from the orderly she had been flirting with to address Kaiden and Fisher. She blatantly appraised the visitors and approved.

Fisher took the lead. "Which way is the cafeteria?"

"It's down there." The orderly pointed, dismissing them.

Fisher blew the attendant a kiss before they strolled in that general direction.

****

Silas parked the Genuine halfway between the hospital and the hospitality house on the opposite end of the visitor's parking lot. He went to work. From a metal case which resembled a lunchbox, he mixed chemicals. With steady hands and certain knowledge, he created his weapon. Confident in the potency of his mixture, he funneled it into four capsules—three more than necessary to his way of thinking. Next, he located and checked a carrier that might have held a laptop computer. Only, it didn't. Touching each one, he counted the various pieces he would shortly assemble into an LRSR. His TS13 was his baby, but people sitting in waiting rooms tended to get bored. Bored people noticed things because they didn't have anything else to focus on. A handsome soldier with a long-range weapon would be remembered. Not something he needed today.

Silas entered the lobby of the cancer treatment center located directly across the hospital's main parking lot. He ignored the registration desk, choosing instead to plop down in a chair in the farthest corner.

Family members of cancer patients read newspapers or watched the news. Three boys and a girl played a board game. A second girl sat at an ancient computer.

44

In his semi-seclusion, Silas studied his Chronos, or more aptly, he studied Christian Deverell on his Chronos. The tracking device he planted on Christian remained hidden and active. With a few keystrokes, he could see everywhere his target had been and how long he stayed. *416. On the side of the hospital with the easiest sniper shot. Of course.* Mr. Deverell had been in room 416 for almost forty-five minutes. *We can be certain she was in room 416...It took you almost an hour to get her out of there...and you pro-ba-bly...took...her...* he watched the tiny dot stand still in the south elevator... *one floor up... hung out in room 521 for twelve minutes...also on this side of the building, because you are a cocky asshole, aren't you? I bet it ain't facing the street, 'cause you're cocky, not stupid.* Silas pressed another button, cross-referencing. *Twelve minutes. And then you called me and...* he went back to his map...*and went to the men's room. Because I scare the shit out of you, don't I? The window in room 521 looks out over the courtyard. I-know-where-you-put-her...* he sang in his mind as he scouted Christian's current whereabouts. *Chief of staff's office? What are you, some kind of bad-ass? Going to tell him how to run his hospital? Well, I'm going to show him how bad his alarm system sucks.* Standing up and stretching, he looked left and right. A woman in her thirties worked diligently, crocheting something awful. *She definitely needs to take a break.* He directed his question to her. "Excuse me. Is there a restroom on this floor?"

She sat her pile of knotted yarn on her lap and pointed. "It's down the hall on the left."

"Thank you." He grabbed his case and went in that direction.

Into the restroom, out of the restroom and up the stairs; inserting his earpiece and disarming the cameras as he went. On the top floor, he paused beside the emergency exit. It would take a minute for the power-surge to disrupt the alarm system so he could slip out of the emergency exit and make his way to the roof. He chuckled at a random thought '*That Orion kid would have scaled the building and be up there already. Damn monkey.*' On that bizarre note, he refocused on the business at hand.

Kaiden picked up on the first ring.

"You don't waste a second, do you?"

"Not one."

"Good, 'cause you ain't got but a few of them." The building went dark. Silas let himself out of the emergency exit. As the door closed, the lights came back on. He headed toward the roof. He didn't ask where

Kaiden and Fisher were. He knew where Kaiden and Fisher were. Silas knew most things. "Take the hallway to the left, toward radiology. When you get to the security doors, don't touch them. Just wait. There'll be two sets. If anybody gets curious, you're looking for..." He checked his Chronos. "Dr. Chavez's office. Your wife's there."

"Alright," Kaiden said, "then what?"

"When you get to the second set of security doors, I'll let you know. First, we have to make sure you don't botch this much up."

Kaiden hung up on him.

While Silas assembled his rifle, Fisher called him back. Kaiden didn't have anything he wanted to discuss yet.

"Incoming call. F-two." Silas spoke the command. His hands were occupied. His voice communication with his Chronos was always frequency one—plain and simple. Telephone lines began with F-2 and were numbered accordingly. The computer connected the line.

"We're here." Fisher didn't bother with a greeting.

"Anybody around?"

"No. Not that I can see."

"Stand clear. F-One." The voice-command switched frequencies. "Passcode. A-7-1-4-D-2-5-9. F-Two." He could hear Kaiden talking to Fisher.

"How the hell does he do all of this?"

"I'm a god, how else?" Silas didn't expect Fisher to relay his answer but liked saying it anyway.

"Should I keep you on the phone or call you back?"

"You will be at your next set in about a minute. Why waste the effor~" Chronos switched frequencies. "What the...F-Two. Fisher?"

"Yeah?"

"Did you hear that?"

"Did you say something for me to hear? We're coming up on the doors."

"Hold that thought. F-One. History."

The Chronos replayed Silas' prior commands.

Passcode. A-7-1-4-D-2-5-9

Passcode. A-7-1-4-D-2-5-9

Incoming call. 3-1-8-6-7-2-8-6-8-7

Outgoing call 3-1-8- 4-9-5-5-1-6-5

"WTF?" Why is that command repeated? First things first. "Passcode. A-7-1-4-D-2-5-9. F-Two. Fisher, are you through?"

"We are now. Kaiden said hurry up."

"If Kaiden doesn't like my pace, he can do this himself. Oh, wait. He can't. There's a lounge, it's a small one somewhere off to your left. It's near the elevator you have to take. You need a key. You don't have one. Which means I have to wait for it to be empty before I can override the system. When you get to the lounge, sit your ass down somewhere, but be ready when I call Kaiden. F-One."

During that time, Silas assembled his weapon. Now he sat it aside. He needed hands on his Chronos. A few fast clicks and he laughed, relieved. He shoved it back into his pocket. "F-Three. Dialing out. 2-4-8-6-1-6-8-2-8-8."

Unlike Kaiden, Alec waited three full rings, before he answered. "Can I help you?"

"Congratulations. I'm not sure I would have come up with an adequate worm reversal in the time frame you had."

Feeling the compliment, Alec's burden lifted a bit. "I started working on it when you got to the house. I couldn't help it, what you did was nice, man."

"I had one on you. It is my system." Silas switched topics. "What floor are you on?"

"Third. I've been taking the public route. Less hassle, more people. I'm moving faster now that I don't have to pretend I'm lost."

"Good man. You can bet your ass she's locked in. If I give you the room number, can you work on the combination?"

Alec chuckled. Feeling a tingle of happiness, he was minutes away from achieving his goal. "Please. I'm in your system...somewhat. Give me the number. I'll get in. Guarantee it."

"I'm getting you a way out. 521. Be ready when they get there."

"Alright."

"F-One."

Chapter 7

Alec frowned at his phone. "5.2.1. That's the combination? The room number. Wouldn't want anybody to use their brains would they?" A part of him was dissatisfied at the lack of effort it took to accomplish his goal. On the other hand, the stuff he snatched off of Silas' micro-brain was amazing.

When Silas' override opened the elevator on the private fifth-floor wing, he shifted the bag he carried, from his left shoulder to his right. It gave him the extra moment he needed to arrange his features. At the nurses' station, a nurse gave instruction to a candy-striper. The candy-striper appeared less than enthused.

"Hey," he spoke kindly, flashing them an innocent smile. "I always get it backwards. 521 is this way?" He pointed to his left.

"Right there." The candy-striper indicated the correct door.

"Are you here with someone, young man?" The nurse took in his details.

"Yes, ma'am. My uncle's parking the car. I didn't want to wait."

"Aww. You're sweet," the volunteer said.

Alec went to room 521. He tapped in the combination. As soon as the door clicked open, he dismissed the women.

There she was.

"Not who I expected." Lareina sat her book down. "Much, much better!"

It was impossible to tell whose smile was brighter. They met in the middle of the floor, hugging and clinging to one another as a flood of emotion erupted. Relief, joy, excitement, and more relief. The past few days had been hell. More so because of the fear and anxiety each had for the other. The whole world could fall apart now, and it would be okay—because the other was okay.

****

"We're in," Kaiden said as the elevator doors closed.

"Good." Silas' voice had taken on a cold impersonal tone. "As soon as you get off grab the first female you see. Make her open the door to room 522. She has to walk in first."

"Or what?"

"Or I'll have one less dumbass to annoy me. Hurry up."

****

"I brought you some clothes." Alec held out the bag as if all he wanted to do was please her. That was all he wanted to do.

Lareina mussed the top of his head then kissed the mess she made. "Thank you. You're three steps ahead of everybody."

"What'd they get you for?"

"I don't know. They haven't shared."

"I thought it might have been because of me."

"Never." She smoothed his hair back in place and kissed it again. "They would have to be smarter than both of us for that."

He laughed at the absurdity.

She walked toward her bathroom. "Remind me to smack Silas for bringing you here and putting you in danger."

"He didn't. He wouldn't even let me come."

The pout she heard in his tone melted her heart. "In that case, remind me to smack Silas for not bringing you. If he hadn't held you up, we'd be gone by now."

"I know, right."

While Lareina changed, Alec checked in.

"Uh-huh." Silas didn't have time for words, he adjusted his sights and made calculations.

"I got her!"

"Good. Hold tight for a sec. Be ready to move on my signal."

"'Kay. What's the signal?"

Silas laughed.

****

"Can I~Aaaaaagggghhh..." The candy-striper talked, screamed and lost her ability to speak, all in one breath. Kaiden's gun touched her temple.

"Get up. Now." He wasn't in the mood to repeat himself.

Visibly shaking, the student-volunteer followed orders.

"Room 522."

"It's...it's..." she swallowed and cried. "It's em-empty," she managed to whisper through her tears.

They didn't comment, which scared her more. The reality of the gun so consumed her, she could barely walk. They stopped in front of room 522.

"Open the damn door." Kaiden gave her a little shake.

Her fingers punched the numbers too fast. It didn't work. It made her cry harder. She did it again, slower; terrified when they saw the empty room, she would be punished.

The door swung open. Kaiden shoved the petrified young woman forward.

BAM!!!

She stopped, stiffened, and crumbled to the floor, lifeless. Particles of blood, paint and plaster flew into the air when the tiny projectile exited the back of her head and embedded itself into the door frame.

"What the...?" Fisher looked at Kaiden.

Kaiden looked first at Fisher, next at the dead woman and finally at the bullet hole in the window.

"If you're not wearing Kevlar, I think you should leave."

Silas' cold voice talking into Kaiden's Bluetooth jerked him into the present. "What the hell did you do that for?!"

"Oops."

****

"Excellent choice." Lareina stepped out of the bathroom. "What do you think?" She spun in a little circle. Dark jeans, black t-shirt with purple and gold splotches across the front, black hoodie and black and gold tennis shoes.

"You look pretty." Alec loved everything about her.

She loved everything about him. He chose her outfit based on his own. Dark jeans, purple shirt with a gold crown centered, black hoodie, and almost identical black and gold tennis shoes. "So do you." She hugged him to her. Releasing him, she got to the business at hand. "What's the plan?"

"Supposed to wait for a signal. That's all he told me."

"Figures." She grabbed her book, stuffing it into the bag. "Can't forget this."

"Is it new?"

"Brand spankin'."

BAM!!!

Alec jumped, surprised. The sound was close.

"That would be your signal."

"Sweet."

She placed a restraining hand on his shoulder. "What did I say about killing?"

"Not without a reason."

She nodded once and released him.

Alec opened the door. Directly across the hall stood Kaiden and Fisher with a girl on the floor between them. "Sweet. Can we go now?"

Death was nothing. America had been in conflict since before Alec was born. He had seen so much death and destruction, he was mostly immune to the horror and finality. Mostly. He understood loss well enough. Thanks to the war, his real family died when he was a baby. He lived in an orphanage for eleven years until he was accepted into the Excellence Program. Until Lareina found him. In the last two years, she had given him a lifetime of love; she made up for his lack. He was never going to lose her. If it meant someone had to die, he didn't care. Death was nothing. His mother was everything.

****

"In about a minute, you all are going to be inhaling some serious sleeping gas."

As if on cue, they heard an odd hissing sound coming from the hole in the wall.

"Go down two floors, turn left, take the stairwell all the way at the end. Don't let anybody stop you."

Kaiden rushed to Lareina. One short hug from him; a quick kiss on his cheek from her. The rest would have to wait.

"'Reina!" Fisher elbowed his way in. He wasn't going to be denied.

"You don't listen to anybody, do you?" Kaiden addressed and then ignored Alec.

"Leave him be. He got here quicker than you," Lareina said.

Alec grinned.

Kaiden led the way. The elevator stood open—waiting for them. During the short ride down, Fisher remembered. "'Reina, Silas told me to give you this." He held up a bottle of pills. "Do you want them?"

"Yes, I do." She took the bottle. "Thank you, sir." She shook four pills into her palm and offered them up. "Be warned, they taste terrible."

"What is it?" Alec wrinkled his nose.

"Insurance." Lareina waited until Kaiden and Fisher took theirs. She swallowed one and tried to hand the last one to Alec. "No matter what happens when we get off this elevator, Silas will be able to find us. Even if we have to separate, for three days, he'll be our guardian angel."

Alec watched Kaiden make a sick face. Fisher gagged. Lareina, however, did not flinch. She waved the pill at him.

"No thanks." He shook his head. "I'll stay with you. He can find us both."

Kaiden huffed.

Lareina put the pill in his pocket. She had bigger battles to win. "You better stay with me."

The elevator opened. Two guards were waiting to go up. They didn't get an opportunity to respond. Kaiden got the one on the right while Fisher handled the one on the left. Both were down within seconds.

"Sweet," Alec approved. He slid Lareina's pistol out of his pocket.

"Give me that!" Lareina took it from him.

"I want to help."

"Not a chance," Lareina said. That was a battle she fully intended to win.

The shots vibrated throughout the hall. People screamed, ducked, and fell down. They made the most of the opportunity with Kaiden leading the charge. Alec and Lareina matched their pace, running after him. Fisher covered their backs a half a step behind.

A wave of hysteria followed them, driving people to move with them, away from them.

****

Silas made his first important call.

"Lieutenant Colonel Briggs."

"Lieutenant Colonel Briggs, sir. This is Corporal McKade reporting."

"What do you have for me, McKade?"

"Decoy."

"What?"

"My mark was not in the designated location. In fact, I haven't seen her. I believe I've been called in to pick up somebody's blame."

"Is the decoy dead?"

"Affirmative."

"You did your job, Corporal. The DoP can deal with their own shit. I'll see to that."

"Thank you, sir." Silas hung up. Shit was going to splatter now. Deverell should be calling him soon.

****

Halfway down the stairs, Kaiden squeezed off three rounds. A DoP officer and a security guard went down. A second DoP officer dived over the railing. A moment later he opened fire on them. Two on one—the firefight did not last long, but the blood and gore were extensive and quite impressive to Alec. Lareina had to pull him forward. After that, there was surprisingly little resistance.

A bold, noble, and altogether stupid doctor burst through the second-floor landing yelling, "I'm a doctor! I'm a doctor! They need my help!" In his haste, he didn't concern himself with the fugitives.

Other than to watch his crazy ascent as he passed while they reloaded, they didn't concern themselves overmuch with him. Kaiden concerned himself with Silas' next instruction.

"Cafeteria. Kitchens. Make a mess. Take a window."

Kaiden grunted. It wasn't anything he couldn't accomplish. It was the fact that he wouldn't know to accomplish it without Silas' aid. Still, he led them out.

Apparently, communications were down. No doubt, thanks to Silas. The people in the eatery did not seem to realize the hospital was in turmoil.

Their ignorance was cured.

Both Kaiden and Fisher fired off shots. Lareina and Alec helped turn over tables and knock over chairs. Alec flung sodas and trays into the fleeing crowd. Two slugs shattered the shatterproof glass. Fisher cleared out the rest with a plastic chair.

Charging forward onto the concrete, Kaiden and Fisher shared the same thought: 'Damn, Silas is good.'

He brought them out within sight of Kaiden's white Oneida. The final push; a mad dash across the parking lot.

Silas hawked them through his scope. They were going to make it. The full force of the Presque Isle Department of Protection & Peace had not yet arrived. Of course, Alpena Regional was having a little trouble with their communication system, their electrical system, in fact, all of their systems. Silas loved his Chronos almost as much as he loved himself.

A police cruiser with siren blaring and lights flashing turned in, angling to cut off their escape.

Silas cursed. He could take a shot...and blow his cover. *Might as well turn myself in while I'm at it. Whoa...*He did a double take. *Absolute zero listening skills.* Slightly amused, he watched Orion slide the not yet ditched Acura in front of the cruiser. The cop skidded, missing Yukiyo's door by what looked to be inches.

Kaiden kept going.

To his credit, Orion drove off in the opposite direction.

It would be so much easier to just kill them all. Silas disassembled his weapon.

****

Christian looked around the room. His eyes saw passed the bullet-hole in the doorframe. He saw into the mind of the killer. Across the hall, the door stood open, mocking him. In the corridor behind him, investigators scurried back and forth, searching for clues— searching for anything. The hospital cameras were dead and the potential witnesses were asleep. *How did she manage to drug the entire floor?*

"You got an explanation, Deverell?" Commander Joffener was pencil thin and lanky; a forty-six-year-old teenager who had yet to grow into his body. His eyes were mean. On purpose. He frowned all the time. Again, on purpose. He wanted there to be no mistake concerning his sour disposition and lack of humor.

"I don't need an explanation." Joffener was his superior, one of few, but Christian had more pressing things on his mind than the whims of bureaucrats.

"Why don't you give me one anyway. I've got the army riding my ass. Apparently, their little sharp shooter threw a big fit."

Christian didn't want to think about their little sharp shooter. He thought, instead, about his alibi. "I noticed some suspicious activity downstairs—too much movement for a secure location. I brought her up here so I could investigate. She," he pointed to the dead girl on the floor, "helped her escape."

"Witnesses saw Elliot with three men."

"I said she helped. If she were the mastermind, she wouldn't be the dead one." *Three men. Kaiden, Fisher and who? Who else would she contact? More pertinent, how did she contact?*

"You think people on the inside were involved?"

"I brought her up here so I could investigate."

****

Christian returned to the office he commandeered for the day. That was one hell of an unnecessary mess. He could kill Lareina for this! He'd review the security tapes and figure out who else she'd pulled out of her damn hat, but first, he had a pest problem to handle. He reached for his cell phone, retrieving the number with agitation.

****

Silas lounged in his jeep munching on his Ritz when the call came. Instead of speaking, he chewed into the receiver.

"McKade, you're in deep shit."

"Doubt it." Silas put another cracker in his mouth, crunching loudly.

"Where is she?"

"I don't know. Where'd you put her? She wasn't in room 416. I checked."

"So you did get my message?" Christian told the lie smoothly, testing the atmosphere.

Silas was exceptionally good at this type of game. "Of course, I did. It's a shame that decoy you set up had to die."

Christian was also exceptionally good at this type of game. "Not me. The person you killed was aiding the escape."

"Too bad you didn't get to interrogate her."

Apparently, one body was enough to cover both their asses.

"Where is she, McKade?"

"You tell me."

"Do you realize how hot the fire you're playing with is?"

"I'm not giving a shit. Do you realize that?"

Chapter 8

"Who was that?" Lareina watched the Acura glide out of sight.

"Orion Quade," Alec said. The name tasted like one of Silas' pills. "Mio Dia Yukiyo is with him. They're not supposed to be here."

"Neither are you," Fisher said from shotgun.

"Yes, he is."

"Yes, I am."

Lareina and Alec were in complete harmony. Kaiden glanced heavenward before changing the subject. "What's the plan?"

"We won't have more than an hour," Lareina said. "We'll need to get to my condo and get out pronto."

"An hour?" Kaiden said, "They should already be on our asses."

"If it were me, I'd be there waiting," Fisher agreed.

"Naw." Lareina shook her head. "The condo isn't common knowledge. It's not leased in my name. They won't trace it, at least not until they upgrade my status as a fugitive. Right now, there are only a handful of people on their side who would possibly know about it. Only one of them matters. He won't send anybody after me. Not yet."

"Is he helping us?" Alec asked.

"No, no, no. Not at all," she chuckled. "He'll want the pleasure of wringing my neck without any interference. He'll have to ditch whoever they send him first. But honestly, it won't take him long. No, rest assured, he's not on our side and he'll be there in no more than an hour. When he does catch us, he'll expect to be compensated for his generosity."

"When?" Kaiden zeroed in on the keyword.

"Ummhmm." Lareina didn't want to dwell on that yet. Her eyes lingered on Alec. "Have you eaten?"

"Not really." Alec pointed to the two in the front. "They left a mess in the living room."

"They can clean it up while we're packing. Give me your phone. I'll order us a pizza."

Alec's grin was wide enough to be seen in Kaiden's rearview mirror and Fisher mumbled something about, "useless kids."

****

Orion closed the door and wiped the handle. It was the best they could do. With bags in hand—all that either of them owned—he and Yukiyo moved away from Mr. Murer's Acura. He was glad to leave it in good shape. There weren't a lot of nice things in the world anymore. "Do you think he'll come and get us?" he wondered aloud. They were in Montmorency County. It felt like he and Yukiyo were the only people left in the world.

"Oh, he'll be here," Yukiyo said. "We've seen too much."

"He could just kill us."

"We helped them get Miss Elliot out of there. They owe us. If they try anything, I will go off on all their asses." She thought of Silas' ass in particular. He had her phone. That was all kinds of wrong.

Other than hearing he had a small part in Miss Elliot's escape, Yukiyo's tirade didn't move Orion. "Let's go over there." He pointed out a plaza which had seen better days.

"Fine," Yukiyo said. "You're buying."

****

Although it shouldn't have been, it was a small surprise to see Silas pull up to the curb beside them. He stared at the wayward pair with a look of bored annoyance. Neither Yukiyo nor Orion spoke. They climbed into the jeep. Daring Yukiyo on the passenger side, resigned Orion in the back.

Yukiyo broke the silence. "Did they get away? Is Miss Elliot okay?"

Silas gave no indication he heard her.

"What?" Yukiyo poked him in the shoulder. "Are you mad or something? Like I care."

Silas let a smile show. "Mad? No. Most likely, it's not your fault a Chihuahua can follow directions better than you two. No harm. You helped."

"Why aren't you talking to us?"

"You don't listen. I'm not going to waste my time talking."

"I asked you a question. You could answer it." Everything about Silas drove her up a wall.

"If I gave a damn about your questions I would, but I don't. Call your mothers. Tell them you're someplace safe. Let them know you're alright, but you don't know when you'll get to talk to them again. Tell them not to tell anyone they spoke to you. Then hang up and shut up."

"Give me my phone."

"Use Orion's."

They did what he said, each staying on the phone for a few moments. Afterwards, there was no conversation at all.

****

Inside of fifteen minutes, Silas pulled into a vacant parking lot outside a Pizza Palace. A white Oneida sat with its driver side doors opened. Beside it, a Marada Ex6 had its suicide doors opened. Between the two, Kaiden, Fisher, Alec, and Lareina scarfed pizza.

Silas stopped in front of the vehicles, blocking them both in.

"Took you long enough," Lareina greeted them.

"You're welcome. It took me less time to get you out of trouble than it took for you to get in it." Silas cut the engine and reached behind him, feeling for a large plastic bag. "And that included me making an extra stop."

Orion was the first one out—the first one over, almost knocking her down with his bear hug. "Miss Elliot!"

"Orion." She hugged him back.

"I'm so, so sorry...I didn't know...I didn't mean~"

"I'm glad you're safe. I was worried sick about you."

"I'm sorry, Miss Elliot. I didn't mean for this to happen to you."

"Shhh. You're good, but you're not that good. You didn't do this, honey. Mr. Deverell was born to be a pain in my butt. If you want to blame somebody, blame him."

Orion did.

"I can't wait to hear how many mountains you climbed to get out of that place."

Orion swelled at the sound of her approval. "It wasn't that hard."

"Of course not," Alec sneered. "If it was hard, you'd still be there."

"Al-lec."

Alec hated when she used that tone. It meant, 'be nice or I'll tear you a new butthole.' But seriously, it was Orion. What did she expect? He didn't want to be nice. He bit into his pizza, choosing instead to be silent...for the moment.

Orion went on, "I had to get out, Miss Elliot. I couldn't let you get into trouble for helping me."

"Oh, we're in trouble." Lareina kissed his forehead. "You may as well get used to calling me Lareina. School's out."

Behind Orion's back, Alec stuck his finger in his mouth, pretending to gag. Lareina pretended not to notice.

"Are you hungry? Get some pizza." She released Orion and looked to Yukiyo. The younger girl had not come forward. Lareina went to her. "Yukiyo. You have no idea how glad I am you're with us."

Not too many things surprised Yukiyo. That statement did. "I wasn't staying behind with all the mess. I want to know what's going on. G.I. Joke wouldn't tell us anything." She smoothed down the front of her skirt.

"You know more than most of them." Lareina jerked her head toward the males.

Yukiyo nodded in agreement. "That's some crew you got there."

"Precisely why I need you."

That was enough for Yukiyo. "Can I ride with you?"

"Do you think I'd leave you with those vultures? You might have to fight with Alec over the front seat."

"He can have the front seat. I want the radio. SOMEBODY took my phone."

Silas took his cue. He stepped in front of Yukiyo, gave Lareina a hug, offered her the plastic bag and said, "I set up the basics. Alec can finish it if he wants."

"'Course I do," Alec talked with a mouth full of pizza. "What is it?"

"Phones." Silas pointed to the pizza. Alec handed him the box in the middle. It hadn't been touched. Lareina had ordered that one specifically for Silas.

"Speaking of phones," Yukiyo placed a hand on her hip. "You got your call. Where IS my phone?"

Silas opened the box to peek. "Nice." He gave Lareina a peck on the cheek and said to Alec, "Hit me up, if you have any trouble." After inclining his head in departure, he hopped in his jeep, not bothering to notice anyone else and drove off.

Yukiyo seethed. "I hate him."

"You ain't the only one," Kaiden said.

"Amen to that," Fisher added.

Before Lareina could comment, the loud obnoxious sound of offbeat drums and screeching that passed for singing blared from the plastic bag. It took a moment of shuffling through the boxes within before Lareina found the phone and hit the button. She read the message and smiled. "I think it's for you." She offered the brand new, upgraded, violet encased device to Yukiyo.

Yukiyo read it and smiled too.

It's in your hand.

****

The hospital surveillance had been put out of commission inside, however, the outside cameras and the police dashcams worked fine. Christian sat at his desk, scowling at the photos in front of him. Every one of them was linked to Lareina for some reason or another that made sense to her alone. Even if it killed him, he would figure it out. If it did kill him, he was taking her with him. He thumbed through Bio's looking for clues, getting to know his enemies.

Name: Kaiden Elliot Age: 22 Gender: Male Height: 6'1" Weight: approx. 185lbs Hair color: Black Eye color: Brown Race/Nationality: African American Last Address: Red River, Louisiana Occupation: Mechanic owner/operator Notes: Armed and Dangerous. Family: Lareina Elliot (Presque Isle Academy counselor), Moses Elliot (war criminal)

Her baby brother. Enough said.

Name: Fisher Jessup Age: 22 Gender: Male Height: 6'0" Weight: approx. 200lbs Hair color: Black Eye color: Brown Race/Nationality: African American Last Address: Red River, Louisiana Occupation: Mechanic/supervisor Notes: Armed and Dangerous. Family: Lainey Jessup (war criminal)

You've been following Kaiden too long.

Name: Alec Rajar Tandon Age: 14 Gender: Male Height: 5'4" Weight: approx. 100lbs Hair color: Black Eye color: Black Race/Nationality: Native American Last Address: Presque Isle Academy Occupation: Student Notes: Unknown threat. No known family. Test acceptable for EP consideration.

Was she in the middle of a babysitting gig?

This is her escape team? A couple of criminals and a brat. "Pathetic, Lareina. I was planning to take you on a cruise, but you chose the welfare crowd instead. What a waste." He pushed those three aside.

Name: Orion Lucas Quade Age: 15 Gender: Male Height: 5'6" Weight: approx. 110lbs Hair color: blond Eye color: Green Race/Nationality: Caucasian Last Address: Hillcrest SoE Occupation: Student Notes: Unknown threat. Family: Amanda Quade (three siblings) Loyalist. EP accepted.

You were in the program for less than a week. You went through a lot of trouble for nothing. Which makes you a slippery little thief with a high IQ and a blown opportunity.

Christian didn't bother to read Yukiyo's bio – he already knew it: Seventeen. Japanese or some Asian descent. Red hair. Who gives a shit about her eyes? Lived with her mother & aunt; Father M.I.A.; Academy less than a year; began testing for the Excellence Program three months ago.

Am I supposed to believe you're dead? You suck at hide-and-seek. Dead people don't ride around in stolen cars. The real question is why aren't you dead? Silas or Lareina's call? Honestly, who would want you alive?

Name: Jack Magok Age: 33 Gender: Male Height: 5'9 1/2" Weight: approx. 245lbs Hair color: Brown Eye color: Green Race/Nationality: Caucasian Last Address: Montmorency County, Michigan Occupation: Unemployed Notes: Alcoholic. Family: 2 dependents (Loyalty unknown)

You're the stupid one, right? That's why they let you drive a stolen Acura to a hole-in-the-wall bar; where it was sure to be noticed. Because you found it. He looked at his bio again. *Yes, that's what I'd do with you too.*

Name: Gillian Foster Age: 27 Gender: Female Height: 5'7" Weight: approx. 160lbs Hair color: Brown Eye color: Brown Race/Nationality: Caucasian Last Address: Presque Isle Academy Occupation: Counselor Notes: Probation -DUI. Family: Joseph Foster, Carol Foster (Loyalist)

What do you have to do with anything? Yes, she worked at the Academy. She lived a few miles from Lareina's secret apartment. And, yes, she's been missing since Lareina got caught. Still, it didn't feel right to Christian. *Whatever's going on with you, this ain't it.* He moved her picture aside. He slid the next photo aside as well. The murdered candy-striper was innocent. He implicated her himself.

The next picture didn't come from the collection of possible suspects; he pulled it himself. The biochemist had covered his ass well; no one knew his involvement. No one but Christian. Christian had every intention of keeping it secret. When he crushed Silas, it would be without interference.

Lareina Elliot. The last photograph. He didn't concern himself with her profile. Five- five, brown hair, brown eyes, full lips, twenty-five-inch waist, C-cup; he knew more about her than any man on the planet, including her brothers. *"What are you doing?"* He spoke aloud because he wanted her to hear him. He wanted her to answer, to explain. He wanted her...

****

It had been one long, eight-hour haul, but Lareina didn't take unnecessary chances. They skirted Lake Erie and didn't stop until they hit the tip of the Ohio/Pennsylvania border.

She, Yukiyo and Alec checked into the Days Inn first. Fisher came next, by himself. And finally Kaiden and Orion. Alec threw a nice little fit when he learned he wasn't bunking with her. Other than that, all was quiet. From their respective beds, she and Yukiyo chatted.

"Fisher, Kaiden, Silas, me and a few others. We were a rag-a-muffin gang. We used to go where there had been fighting and loot. We'd steal stuff, rob corpses, anything that earned us a dollar or a meal."

"I can't see you doing anything dishonest or undignified." Yukiyo frowned, trying to picture Lareina as a criminal.

"Most things I do are not honest or dignified. Look at us now. I've kidnapped three minors."

"You welcomed three stowaways. How long did you live on the streets?"

"A few years. When my Uncle Moe got out of prison, he taught us how to be real felons. He was part of the movement that became the Revolutionaries. That's where I first met Christian. His father was the leader of another gang. They teamed up, ran arms and fought the administration hard. I learned a lot."

"You and Mr. Deverell were a couple, weren't you? How did that work?"

Lareina shook her head. "It didn't. Among other things, the white/black thing was bad for business. Fueled the mistrust. As an appeasement, his father sent him to military school. Christian retaliated by switching loyalties. See this." She pulled a necklace free from her nightgown. It held a charm; a ruby-eyed Bengal tiger, fangs exposed.

Yukiyo leaned forward. "Wow." It was more exquisite than any piece of jewelry she had ever been in contact with.

"It's my alter ego. Christian has one too. His is a snake."

Yukiyo laughed. "Is that why you have all those figurines in your apartment?"

Lareina hunched her shoulders. "I like snakes."

"Poor you."

"I know." She tucked the necklace away. "Christian and I met again in the Excellence Program where he broke my heart. Crushed it." Yukiyo's downturned mouth made her add, "Don't worry, I got over it."

"Good."

"Unfortunately, I'm the only one. Those three," she pointed to the rooms beyond, "have never forgiven him. They didn't like him for catching my eye in the first place. Then he did something that put them in his debt. They hate being grateful. When he broke my heart, it was the last straw. They love to hate him. It's been a motivating factor for Silas to become better than Christian at just about everything."

Yukiyo snuggled down in her blankets. "Sounds like testosterone overload."

"You've no idea."

"And you've added two more aggressive brain-dead males to your collection. What were you thinking?"

"Nothing good. That's for certain." Lareina cut out the light.

"Do you still love him?"

"That would be stupid. He's a snake. Snake cuddling will get you killed."

There was a slight pause before Yukiyo asked her final question. "Do you think he still loves you?"

There was a longer pause before Lareina answered. "I wouldn't be here if he didn't."

****

Hours later, Lareina couldn't sleep. She paced the balcony, trying to talk herself out of her inclination. She failed. With the action came the memory:

"*Are you kidding me?*"

"*No, Eugene, I'm serious.*"

"*Opt-In accounts? Are you aware the government took over the internet?*"

"*I know better than you, what they took over. I'm also aware the Revolutionaries took it over from them. And they took it back and so on and so forth etc, etc, etc.*"

"*And you want us to communicate through Opt-In?*"

"*Yes, it's ingenious.*"

"*How so? Because so far, that idea sucks. Filled with holes. You can do better.*"

"*Think about it. With all the alternatives it's practically obsolete. If we set up dummy accounts, bogus names, fictitious info, whatever—we'll always have a way to communicate. It will be neutral and safe because neither one of us would ever post anything incriminating. And we wouldn't have alerts or updates coming to our phones*"

"*Okay. One: Neither one of us would ever say or do anything that could be considered incriminating, that's a pointless argument. Two: We're on the same side. No need for neutral zones. And three: I have your number and you have mine. We can talk anytime.*"

"*That may not always be the case. Humor me.*"

He did. He did everything for her...except listen when she tried to tell him the truth.

"Lareina, it is what it is. Creating spy-plots won't bring her back."

"Spy-plots? What about saving you? Can a...spy-plot do that?"

****

Oh, that man. She didn't want to talk to him, she wanted to beat him with something. She posted her status anyway: All by myself tonight.

His response was immediate. You wouldn't be if you stayed your ass home where you belong.

I wasn't home.

You were with me. That's home.

We don't live in the same place anymore and I'm not fighting with you.

Too bad. If you didn't want to fight, you should've stayed home...Why?

Why...?

Why are you doing this?

Because it's the right thing to do.

There's nothing right about getting yourself hurt.

If you don't hurt me, I won't get hurt.

Are you willing to take the responsibility for the people around you?

Did you not read my first post? All by myself tonight.

I seriously doubt that. If I know your crew, which I do, probably better than you, there's no space in your hotel room. Don't make me jealous. That's all I'll say about that.

Lareina paused. She re-read the post three times. *Hotel? Hmmm, suppose that's not too hard to guess. We'll let that go.* Jealous? Please. Because you generally spend your nights all by your onesies, I'm sure.

Whose choice was that?

Whose fault was that?

It felt strangely comforting to be sparring with Eugene as if living was easy. Even now, their relationship transcended all boundaries.

She changed topics. Why are you up so late?

I have to pick up a hard-headed female who needs to be turned over my knee. She's not one for doing things the easy way.

Lareina paused again. He was too matter-of-fact about it all. No frustration, no twenty questions. No questions meant he already knew the answer. That could only mean one thing. "Yukiyo. Wake up honey. Throw on some clothes. I've got to get the boys in here." While she talked, she typed: Maybe you should get some sleep. If this person is as much trouble as you imply, you might want to recover your strength.

After I hand out a well-deserved lesson, I'll get all the sleep I want.

Sounds grim. No need to go to your eternal rest. Especially over a girl you can't get.

You misunderstand. First, somebody is going to their eternal rest for this shit. But trust me, it's not me. And second, not only am I going to get the girl, I already got the girl. Don't ever forget that.

You're a cocky bastard. I'm going to bed.

Thought so. I'll see you in the morning.

Not bloody likely, because I won't be here. You do that.

Lareina signed off and sent a message to wake up her boys. It was time to go.

Chapter 9

Alec pushed Fisher out of his way and climbed into Lareina's bed. He pulled the covers over his head for good measure. Right behind him, Kaiden stretched out across the bottom. After dressing, Yukiyo returned to the center of her own bed, resting against the headboard. Orion joined her there, eyes glazed, using her shoulder for a pillow. Only Fisher and Lareina were fully alert.

"You alright, 'Reina?" he asked.

"Yes and no." She pulled out her suitcase. "We've got a problem and I think it's me."

Alec's head popped into view, his eyes wide open.

Kaiden didn't move. "What do you mean?"

"Christian is following us. He'll be here in a few hours. We have to go."

"How does he know where we are?" Upon hearing Deverell's name, Alec dismissed the threat.

"Let him come." Kaiden covered his eyes with his forearm. "I'll merk his ass for getting me out of bed."

Lareina pursed her lips. "Yeah, no." In answering Alec's question, she said, "That's the real problem. I don't know how he knows, but we can't let him catch up."

"Silas?" The name came from Orion in the form of a question.

"No, you dumbass," Alec answered.

Kaiden punched Alec's leg. "Knock it off. It's a good question. Sneaky little~"

Alec kicked back. "Silas came to help Mr. Deverell. If he wanted to do his job, we wouldn't be here."

"He isn't here," Yukiyo added. "He's the only one involved who isn't. And..." She looked at Orion. "He gave us some pills. Some kind of tracking device."

"We all took those." Those weren't the trackers that concerned Lareina. "It's not him. We're talking about Silas, Kaid. Think about it. Would he use Christian?" She needed Kaiden's head in the right place. Alec was always on her side. Fisher and Yukiyo weren't pressed either way. And Orion...he wasn't feeling threatened enough to be a danger to anyone.

"Somebody got to him? Got into his stuff?" Fisher asked Lareina. Kaiden looked like he'd gone back to sleep.

"No," Lareina and Alec spoke in unison with absolute conviction.

"Anybody got another explanation?" Fisher asked.

"It's not Silas," Lareina said.

Before she could say more, Alec piped in. "Silas said, it's possible somebody named Eugene put something in with the Mepho...bar...bital. Whatever that is—"

"It's a truth serum, for lack of a better word. It just makes you want to talk."

"Oh. He said you'll have to run for another day or two until it's out of your system. He also said to tell Kaiden to kiss his ass."

Less oblivious than they assumed, Kaiden sat up. "Are you talking to him?"

Alec shrugged and pulled his cell from under the covers he'd burrowed into. He showed them a text message.

"If we're debating traitorous activity, why would you contact the would-be traitor in question? Kind of stupid. May as well shoot ourselves," Orion managed to talk and snore.

Alec flung a pillow. It hit Orion and Yukiyo. "How many times do you need to hear it's not him, are you stupid and deaf? Sorry, Yuke."

****

It was mid-morning before they chanced another hotel. This time, they went to the Renaissance, one of the few remaining decent hotels in Pittsburgh. The popular city on the mountain had not fared well in the war. More battles had been fought on that mountain side than anywhere else in the country. Streets were closed, buildings had been blown apart, and tunnels were caved in. There hadn't been a football game played there in almost twelve years. Not since Heinz Field had been obliterated.

Still, people overcrowded the streets and overtaxed the resources; the perfect place to hide.

Having determined Christian had either stopped to rest, or he was exhausted and in no condition for a confrontation, Lareina had them watch, eat, and rest in shifts.

****

Lareina noted with no small amount of amusement, when awake, everyone seemed to congregate in the room she shared with Yukiyo. It faced Sixth Street, one of the few unimpeded roads through town. Lareina sipped sweet tea and read her novel—courtesy of Christian—while Kaiden, Fisher and Orion played a round of poker. Yukiyo commandeered the television with no intention of relinquishing the remote and Alec was engaged in the apps he's snatched off of the Chronos.

Suddenly, as if the Doritos commercial reminded her, Yukiyo glanced up from the set. "Lareina, What are we doing?"

"A whole lot of nothing." Kaiden threw in two cards.

"If you have to ask," Alec said, "You shouldn't be doing it."

Yukiyo rolled her eyes. "I was talking to Lareina."

Lareina understood what she meant. "We're waiting. That's all we can do for now."

"When will I be able to call my mother?" Orion studied his cards. "I don't want them to worry," he added before Alec could make some smartass comment about him and his mommy.

"Probably, ne-ver," Fisher delivered the taunt as he laid down his hand, confident his full house/jacks high would take the pot.

"I wouldn't go that far, Fish." Lareina sat her book aside. It was time for some information. "You all have a choice to make."

Kaiden folded. Whatever Lareina had to say was more important than the game. He didn't have squat, anyway.

Yukiyo turned the volume down.

Fisher reached for the pile of coins they had been playing for.

Orion laid his cards across the money. Straight flush/king high.

"Damn it." Fisher pushed the cards and the money away from him.

Certain she had everyone's attention (Alec hadn't looked up, but he always paid attention; at least to her.) Lareina said, "The Excellence

Program is a brilliant, well-developed cover. It does what it's supposed to do, find gifted young minds and help them develop to their fullest potential." She waved her hand around the room. "But, it does so much more. Unbeknownst to the people who excel in the program, you all are fighting the war."

"What do you mean?" Orion leaned forward. The Excellence Program had been his life's goal, his family's way out of poverty. The only way he could get them out.

"Of course, they~we are fighting the war. Everybody's fighting the war." War was a touchy subject with Yukiyo. Her father was missing because of the war.

Lareina delivered the blow. "I said you were fighting the war. I didn't say you were fighting to win, or even stop the war. You're fighting to lose." Her voice dripped with liberal amounts of sarcasm and derision. "The brightest, sharpest minds in the country are being used, tricked into figuring out what will actually destroy them and their country."

Everyone stayed silent.

"I can't stop it," Lareina spoke again. "But I have been doing my best to frustrate their plans. I can get you home, but they'll come after you again. And again. You have abilities they need. You can stay and help me if you want." She closed her book. "It's a tough choice. You have to be the one to decide."

"While you're making decisions, don't forget," Alec added, looking up from his phone once, "you're already in deep trouble."

"What's going to happen to our families?" Orion took the conversation back to his most pressing issue.

"Do you know why the DoP is a hazard?" She didn't wait for an answer. "They get hired from prison." Three sets of brows furrowed, but the kids remained silent. "If your choice is loyalty or jail, you do whatever you're told without guilt or questions. Many of them are dishonest to begin with. By now, Christian has people watching all of your families. No contact is the best way to protect them. Once we've set up shop—if we set up shop—families are among our first priority."

"All of our families?" Yukiyo asked.

"All we can reach."

"What's wrong with the school?" Orion asked. It was hard letting go of his dreams.

"The original idea behind the school system dates back to segregation. The first wave was to stop the small battles and skirmishes by shipping government kids into Revolutionary territory and vice versa. No one would want to shoot at their own children." She took a drink of her beverage. "Creating legal hostages turned out to be a stroke of genius. It was the brainchild of Dr. Stephen Raysan, child prodigy. He did a lot in psychological advancement. He taught me when I went through the program. Thanks to Dr. Raysan, they got selective both of the integration process and the students who were elected. Anyway," she said. "The program started with a lottery. Kids were picked at random. But that changed. For a while, children of the rich or powerful made better hostages. Now, only children with certain aptitudes and predispositions are accepted. All successful candidates are sorted into one of four categories. You're not grouped by age or location, but by test scores and ability so the system management team can best expose and exploit your talents. Once you've gone through the ranks, a chosen few advance to the—" she air quoted, "—Excellence Program. Where they challenge you with various—" she air quoted again, "—peacekeeping tasks. These tasks are potential problems within the regime. Every time a task gets accomplished, the regime plugs the hole, and continues the fight everyone thinks is over."

"I'm not following," Fisher frowned.

"Like this," Alec said. "If I ask you to figure out how to make twenty dollars in twenty days and you come up with a way to do that, then I know what *not* to let people do if I don't want them to make that much money in that period of time."

"Exactly." Lareina pointed at him. "You think you are contributing to the effort to end the conflict, but they're using you, the smartest, brightest, best that America has to offer, to keep things the way they are."

"What happens if we don't cooperate?" Yukiyo asked. "I mean, we are talking about a bunch of would-be geniuses."

"One, you're being lied to. Until five minutes ago you believed the EP was good and you were helping. And two, if you did happen to get suspicious, if you prove to be non-cooperative or uncontrollable, you disappear. End of story." Lareina didn't give them much time to digest that tidbit before she continued, "A while ago, a student was tasked with figuring out a way to assure cooperation from reluctant...at the time, they were called soldiers. She suggested manipulating their family circumstances to reliability on the program at hand. The bare-bones of it is something akin to welfare. If you need help and there's only one place to get it, and you get it, you'll be grateful. Essentially, they're manipulating emotions." She shrugged. "They loved the idea. Put her to work in the organization. A few years later, she noticed a pattern. Students testing high in certain 'at risk' categories, all seemed to have a family circumstance which put them in need of the program's benefits. Some of the most dangerous minds in the country believe Presque Isle Academy is their only hope."

All eyes gravitated to Orion and for a moment, he felt like he had just lost his only hope.

Lareina wasn't having it. "Don't feel sorry for yourself. Turn it outwards. Now you know there's a reason your mom can't get hired." She turned to Yukiyo, "There's a reason your dad is missing." She aimed her thumb at Alec. "There's a reason his history has been deleted. There's a reason you all have full scholarships." She pointed to herself. "I know what I am talking about because that was my task, my plan. They twisted it and are using it to get you guys locked in and loyal. With the right resources, the right motivation, any one of you sitting here," she waved her hand, including Kaiden and Fisher, "could end this war."

One final pause to take in every thoughtful expression, and then Lareina smiled. "They didn't count on me telling you."

****

Kaiden moved to pick up the cards. Might as well play another round. If he won his money back from Orion, he wouldn't have to whip his ass and take it. It seemed like a plan. "What?" He looked up in time to catch Yukiyo staring at him.

She touched her chest, the place where a pendant would lay. "Your thing. You have one too. What's that about?"

Kaiden pulled his necklace free. As far as possessions went, this was his prize. "A present from Lareina." He flashed a chain with a large grey wolf, clearly on the hunt. Its ruby eyes sparkled, reflecting danger of the mortal kind. "It's what I am. It's what I do."

Everyone looked at it, but Yukiyo had already dismissed him. "What about you?" She asked Fisher. "Did Lareina give you yours?"

Fisher glanced down his shirt. His wasn't visible. "She did." He eyed Yukiyo strangely as he pulled his out for inspection. It was similar to Kaiden's. A different wolf, his more brown with amethyst for eyes, but part of the same pack. Just as he and Kaiden were from the same pack.

"Those are cool." Orion stared at the pieces.

"I want one," Alec cut in. "A cheetah."

"What made you pick wolves?" Yukiyo put the question out there for any of them to answer.

"Personalities." Lareina flipped the page in her book. "Wolves are extremely dangerous and fiercely loyal...usually at the same time." She waved a thumb at Kaiden and Fisher. "They run in packs. That makes your chances of winning against them about slim to none."

"Damn straight," Fisher added his agreement.

"They only have one serious predator."

Kaiden snorted his skepticism.

"And that," she pulled out her own chain with a flourish, "is the tiger."

"I want one," Alec repeated. "Get me a cheetah."

"What kind of animal is Silas?" Yukiyo had seen his necklace but had not asked him about it.

"Silas has one?" Orion's interest was focused. "Is he in the pack too?"

"No"

"Hell no."

Kaiden and Fisher spoke together.

"What are you, stupid?"

"I thought 'Reina said you were smart."

"Ignore them, Orion," Lareina said. "They're just a couple of dumb dogs. Silas is a peregrine falcon. Fastest moving creature on earth. World's greatest hunter. He hangs out up high, sees everything below and covers our butts." She hunched her shoulders. "What else would he be?"

"Fried, baked or barbecued." Kaiden dealt the cards.

"Those are nice, Lareina." Orion cast his wistful eyes downward. "After I take Kaiden's money, maybe I'll buy one."

"I'm getting a cheetah."

Everyone went back to what they were doing. They were secluded but comfortable. No one had gotten on anyone's nerves too bad.

Alec's phone bleeped. The sound was ominous. They all had new phones and no one outside that room except Silas had access to any number. Least of all Alec's, whose only family was Lareina. Alec checked the message.

Deverell will be in Pittsburgh in about forty minutes. My tracker is almost done so get your ass gone.

Apparently, one of Silas' apps allowed some sort of high priority bypass. Alec would have thought it cool had he not been annoyed Silas killed his game. But resetting would have to wait till later. He'd been re-routed and was now looking at a map of Pittsburgh. Silas highlighted the best possible escape route.

"Deverell's coming." Alec didn't bother telling them how he came by this information. They ought to know.

Lareina slapped the arm of her chair. "Ohhhhh. That man drives me crazy!"

Everybody got up, the urgency was tangible.

"Isn't Silas your friend?" Yukiyo asked Lareina. "Why does he always contact him?"

"Because I'm the smart one," Alec replied.

"It's safer," Lareina answered, distracted.

"It's safer because I'm the smart one."

"How does Silas know all this shit?" Fisher went to the window. He checked the street below.

"How does Christian keep finding us?" Kaiden tugged on his ear. He opened the door a crack, surveying the hallway. "Ain't nobody that lucky."

Lareina yanked her bag from under her bed. She flipped it open so she could collect her things. "This is what Silas does. He's an expert." She paid sparse attention to the conversation. By now, Yukiyo was half packed. Kaiden and Orion were on their way to the room they shared. Fisher was just leaving. "Honey," she said over her shoulder to Alec, "you better get moving." She threw her novel in the suitcase on her way to the bathroom to gather her toiletries. When she returned, only Alec and Yukiyo remained. Alec hadn't moved. "Alec, did you hear me?" She stopped talking to notice what he was staring at.

Alec raised her novel. "Is this the one you got from the hospital?"

Confusion gave way to thoughtfulness. Her demeanor changed from harassed to enraged. Lareina snatched the book from Alec's hand. "Sorry."

Alec remained quiet. He understood.

Yukiyo and Alec watched as Lareina thumbed through the pages once and then once again, slower. Until she stopped. "Uggghhhhh!" Lareina flung the book across the room. Just as quickly, she followed it. "You asshole! I wasn't done yet." She tossed the offending article on the bed, ran both hands through her hair and took a calming breath. "Yes Alec, you are the smart one. Can you do me a favor and find out where the nearest post office is, please. And what time is their next pick up? I've got something I need to mail."

****

The plan was simple; easy to execute. While Fisher made time getting the rest of them to Harrisburg, Kaiden and his new sidekick, Orion, drove the Oneida to nearby McKeesport.

They arrived at the post office ten minutes before the last pick-up.

****

Christian was annoyed. Pittsburgh, McKeesport, back to Pittsburgh. He wasn't going to chase her back and forth all night. He pulled into the first hotel parking lot he spotted. Whatever the hell she was up to, he'd kick her ass in the morning.

****

"Yes, sir. How may we help you?" The car salesman rushed over to Kaiden. They stood side by side facing the lot.

"Let's see," Kaiden said. "You close in..." he looked at his watch, "What? Twenty minutes. Let's make this short and sweet."

"Times being what they are, I'll make time if it will help you. What do we need to accomplish?"

"How fast can you sell me that?" Kaiden pointed to the vehicle of

Orion's choosing; an Oneida almost identical to the one they drove, except it was a year newer and black.

"We close in twenty. I can make you a deal in fifteen."

"If you accept the trade," he indicated his white Oneida, "I've got cash and I'm not in the mood to negotiate."

"For cash sir," the salesman said, "I'll make you a deal in ten."

"Do that."

****

While Kaiden signed the paperwork, Orion switched out their belongings. He shook his head in wonder. The Oneida had everything: cases of weapons, ammo, money, emergency provisions and more weapons. Come what may, they would be ready.

"How did you know to pack it like that?" he asked as they made their way back to the others.

"All of our vehicles are equipped this way. In this line of work, you have to be ready to move."

"What line of work? I thought you were a mechanic."

"Owning a garage isn't my line of work."

"What's your real job?"

"Smuggle things and people, usually at 'Reina's behest. Also, I protect my sister."

"That's a full-time job."

"Twenty-four, seven."

Chapter 10

He knew it. Being right pissed him off. What could he do about it now? What's three unnecessary days on the road? His week went to hell the moment she escaped. No, his week went to hell the moment she got caught. *Shit!* He was going to ring her neck. *And everyone one of those punks with her is going down. No doubt about it.* Christian hit 230 mph going through the dessert. It wasn't the Bugatti Veyron Phoenix's top speed, but it was fast enough to match his frustration. The 'Welcome to Las Vegas' sign blurred past. He didn't need to read it, he was home.

That's what confirmed the suspicion which had been growing in him since yesterday. Lareina wouldn't go to Vegas unless she were going to his house. No way in hell was Lareina going to his house. He knew that. He told himself that. He drove on because he couldn't afford to blow it off. *If she did show up at his house, she wasn't going to have to wait for him to get there.*

That pissed him off the most. He wasn't fooled. He wasn't following his trace because he thought she would be at the other end of it. No, he was going home, in case she needed him. He was going home because he didn't have a choice. *Damn it.*

Christian tried to take comfort in the knowledge that he couldn't do anything, anyway. She found the trace; he had to come back to get a lock on her. If she dumped the damned thing and kept going, that would have been fine. But she sent the book to Vegas, knowing he would follow, on the off chance it was legit. "Low, Lareina." He slammed the brakes, cruelly enjoying the screech and dust.

He wasn't waiting until tonight. He wasn't waiting until he got home. Hell, he wasn't waiting to find a place to park. There on the shoulder of the highway, Christian pulled up his Opt-In account—his one direct link to her.

Are you making dinner?

A total of two minutes and twelve seconds passed before he posted again.

You need to call me.

A minute and forty seconds.

NOW.

He smacked his steering wheel and drove off, checking his phone for updates every three or four miles.

****

Lareina looked around the darkened hotel room. It was the last one they'd be in, at least for a while. She had the keys to a rental in New York, the city she'd chosen long ago to get lost in. They could move in the morning. In the other queen bed, Yukiyo slept peacefully.

That didn't happen every night. Lareina worried at the younger girl's burden.

She reached for her phone and the hidden comfort within. It didn't take long to find what she sought. Lareina slapped her hand over her mouth to keep from giggling too loudly.

Impatient little something aren't you? She typed. I'm not making dinner. Take out. Sushi. Yum. Call you what?

Knowing Christian as she did, she wasn't expecting him to answer right away. He blew a gasket, found a distraction and was in the process of calming down. *He must have gotten his book back.*

Read any good books lately? I read one, a first edition, hasn't hit the street yet, but I didn't get to finish it because it wasn't mine and the original owner was looking everywhere for it.

He deserved the taunt. She hated not finishing a book.

****

"Oh, crap." Misty Wilson had worked for Christian Deverell for close to a year. Long enough to know the scowl he wore didn't bode well for anyone who crossed him. She bent her head over her computer, mumbled good morning and hoped to God he didn't notice her.

He noticed her. "Get Shivelly and Carter." He plopped an envelope of photographs on her desk. "I need background info on all of them. Don't leave out anything." He watched her grab the receiver and dial an extension. "Get Basser on it too. I want it in twenty minutes." Having given instruction, Christian walked off, done with conversation.

Misty jumped when he slammed his office door.

****

The house was perfect. Both of them. Lareina, currently using the alias 'Danica Stone' had rented the left side of a duplex. No one lived on the right side. The boys commandeered it; making short work of connecting the power, heat, and water. Silas arrived and cut a hole in the wall. No need to go outside if they didn't have to.

They got food, furniture, equipment, and weapons; the latter courtesy of Kaiden. Having acquired and shipped weapons all over the country, it wasn't hard for him to procure what they were looking for.

****

"We have two things we need to focus on," Lareina told them. "One, we need to discover who sold me out and why."

"Sold you out?" Alec wanted to know too...retribution.

"They didn't haul me in because I left a paper on my desk." She shook her head at Orion. "They were planning to grab someone when they got there. Again, we need to find out why."

This seemed to make sense to everybody.

"The other thing we have to do right now, is get you three," she pointed to Alec, Yukiyo, and Orion, "trained. That's what I want you three," this time, she pointed to Kaiden, Fisher, and Silas, "to focus on as much as you can. We have to get them up to speed. If I know Christian~"

"You do," was spoken in triplicate.

She ignored them. "He's going to flush us out. We need to stay a step ahead of him because once he gets a lead on us, which he will, we'll need to be able to use all of our available assets."

"You give him too much credit," Silas sneered.

"You don't give him enough credit. That's a mistake," she answered.

"Yeah, well~What the hell do you think you're doing?!" Silas snatched his TS13 out of Alec's grasp. "Touch it again and I will break your hand."

"Silas!" He was too serious for Lareina's liking.

"Don't ever touch it again."

"Didn't you hear her tell you to train us," Alec matched the sneer Silas used a moment ago.

"Don't ever touch it again."

Kaiden laughed. "Congratulations, little bro. You found a sore spot."

"Something you'll never be able to accomplish." Silas dismissed Kaiden, focusing instead on Lareina. "I'll take care of it."

"You better take care of it."

****

They converted the basement on the right side of the house into a training area. So far, the training room had a few weights, a lopsided punching bag hanging from the ceiling alongside some dry-rotted rope, a few seat cushions, five wooden baseball bats, an old mattress propped against one wall, and a dusty carpet.

Silas gave the explanation. "Fish is going to teach you how to fight. Kaid is going to teach you how to fight dirty. And then I'll teach you how to beat them both—"

Fisher and Kaiden simultaneously interrupted.

"Please."

"Right."

"—at the same time."

"He can show you how to get merked," Kaden said.

"We'll start one on one," Silas continued. "Yukiyo, go with Fisher. Don't let her get away with any 'I'm a girl' shit."

"You're a girl?" Fisher crinkled his forehead. "Who knew?"

Yukiyo ignored Silas, rolled her eyes at Fisher and shoved Alec for laughing.

Kaden said, "I'll take Alec. You might forget yourself and break his hand anyway."

"I might. Doesn't matter. I got a score to settle with Orion too." Silas cracked his knuckles. "It's overdue."

"What'd I do?" Orion took a step back.

"You need a lesson in listening."

"No, I don't."

"You're getting one, regardless."

From the center of the room, Yukiyo asked, "Where are the mats?"

"What mats?" Fisher looked left and right for something that wasn't there.

"Do you ever get tired of being an idiot?" Alec grabbed one of the ropes and swung. "How are you supposed to train us without mats? What are you going to do, knock us through the cement?"

Orion grabbed a second rope. He climbed to the top using the strength of his arms. "I hate to agree, but that rug is not a cushion."

Kaiden watched them ambivalently. "Any of you ever see a real street fight?"

"Yeah."

"Yep."

"Of course." Yukiyo stepped away from the swinging monkeys.

"Did you see anybody spreading mats around for them to fall on?"

Kaiden's question hung in the air. Instead of answering, Orion and Alec let go of the ropes. Yukiyo stood between them. Now, they were back to back to back. While they had been messing around, Silas, Kaiden, and Fisher strategically surrounded them.

"Quit posing," Alec said. "You're not going to hurt us. Mom would kill you."

"Mommm," Silas mimicked, "isn't down here for a reason."

"She told us to train you quick." Fisher spread his arms. "Think of the cement as incentive."

As a unit, the older guys pounced.

****

You've got one day.

Lareina frowned at the message. "What's that supposed to mean?" What's that supposed to mean?

Christian left the initial message a half hour earlier. It surprised her that his response came back so quickly. It means you have one day. Twenty-four hours. Clear?

As dirt. Twenty-four hours for what?

To get on a plane and get your ass home where I can protect you from yourself.

Hmmm. That's not going to happen.

You're going to be sorry and pissed off if you don't.

You're going to be sorry and pissed off WHEN I don't.

Turn on the news.

Lareina heaved a sigh. She was already sorry. She reached for the remote. What am I watching for?

Christian put her on hold.

****

"This is Basser."

"Basser, this is Deverell."

"Yes sir, Mr. Deverell."

"Is everything ready?"

"We've got the perimeter secured; awaiting your orders sir."

****

I'm back.

Lareina smacked the air, pretending it was the back of Christian's head. You forgot to mention you were leaving. I'm sitting here waiting for you while you're off getting a snack.

I can type and eat at the same time. I needed to make a phone call.

I can type and talk at the same time. Why am I watching the news?

Wait for it.

She slapped the air again. Not long after, there was a breaking news story. Lareina sat forward and turned up the volume when she read the headline: Live from Louisiana—Red River Bombing.

83

NO HE DIDN'T. Yes, he did. Kaiden's garage was gone. Lareina listened with dawning horror.

"In a plan that has been described as both primitive and violent, a mixture of oil and homemade acetone explosives were ignited in a small auto mechanic's garage. DoP authorities believe this is evidence of a fresh wave of violence by the anti-government group who call themselves Revolutionaries. The owner of the garage, Mr. Kaiden Elliot, is thought to have been targeted because of a close relative who may hold a position within the Educational and Advancement division. For safety reasons, the name of this faithful supporter is being withheld."

"Wow, Brenda, there hasn't been a bombing in months." A male newscaster, who had been silent through the report chimed in.

"No, it's been quiet and there had been talks of representatives of both sides meeting and hopefully bringing to a close, what has been a tumultuous time, filled with loss." She paused in an effort to appear heartfelt and sad. "Thankfully, there was no one in the building at the time. However, the property damage is catastrophic and none of the housed vehicles are able to be salvaged."

The unnamed male appeared on the TV again. "It has to make you wonder Brenda, what they were hoping to gain. How~"

Lareina violently hit the button to shut off the television. She knew what the revolutionaries gained, absolutely nothing because they didn't do it. Damn Christian and his damn connections. Even knowing he would do something like this didn't make it easier to stomach.

After forty minutes of silence, Christian commented. You've got twenty-four hours.

One sentence. But, she understood the message. The warning. He knew her crew and he would punish her through them. All of them.

She answered him because she had to, a parting shot. Oooohhh... He is going to be so mad at you. Mad was an understatement. Kaiden will be furious.

Didn't you listen? The Revolutionaries did it.

I'm sorry, I didn't catch that. I was tuning out the bullshit.

Chapter II

The early morning quiet filtered through the house. Lareina tip-toed past Alec and Yukiyo's bedrooms. Silas slept in the left side basement. Kaiden, Fisher, and Orion had taken the bedrooms on the other side.

Although Lareina had expected to be the first one up this morning, she wasn't at all surprised to see Kaiden and Fisher dressed and eating when she came into the kitchen. The large room had chipped counters and cracked cabinets lining two walls. A pantry, storage closet, and antiquated refrigerator filled the third. Three layers of worn linoleum peeled away from the baseboard near the stove. A farmhouse table with a bench and five mismatched chairs sat at the room's center.

She went for the coffee. "I'm sorry about your garage."

"I'm not. I not sorry I'm going to cap the son-of-a-bitch who did it, either." Kaiden shoved a spoonful of Reese's Puffs into his mouth. His matter-of-fact tone made Lareina wonder if he hadn't got up early because he planned to drive to Red River and kill someone this evening.

"How did you find out about it?" Fisher ate with his spoon in one hand and his 9mm in the other.

"News. I caught it last night."

"Revolutionaries didn't do that."

"No, Kaid. No, they didn't." Lareina saw no point in withholding the truth. Before she could expand, Silas strode into the room.

"Deverell," he said. "No doubt about it."

"Motherfucker." Fisher refilled his bowl and passed the box to Silas.

"He won't stop there," Lareina said. "When the others get up, we've got to make some plans and get to work, quick. He only gave me twenty-four hours."

"Twenty-four hours for what?" Kaiden asked, then turned to Fisher. "Do you want to get Orion up? We could be here until two waiting for his lazy ass. I swear Lareina, that boy don't wake up for shit."

Lareina said, "If I had my way, neither would I."

They sat in companionable silence as they waited for the others.

Yukiyo followed Fisher as he shoved Orion ahead of him. Orion stumbled around the room without opening his eyes. He banged into a chair, plopped down in it, reached for the cereal box and tried to use it for a pillow.

Kaiden snatched it out of his hand. He slid a bowl across the table. It hit Orion on the side of his face. Orion grunted something that sounded like 'thanks.'

"'Reina." Yukiyo had taken to using the informal moniker. Her spiky, red hair matched the flames emitting from the fierce dragon stalking across her graphic tee. "You may want to get that monster kid of yours before somebody kills him. He looked like he was sneaking off somewhere."

Lareina didn't bother with details. "ALEC!"

The entire kitchen except for Orion waited for the culprit to appear. Orion's head was still on the table and he snored lightly.

"ALEC!"

"I'm coming." They could hear him running up the steps from the training room/basement.

"What did you~What in the world do you think you're doing!"

"Practicing." Alec's brow creased. "What should I be doing?"

Lareina pointed to the TS13 clutched in his hands.

"It's not loaded yet."

Kaiden shook his head, momentarily distracted from his own troubles.

"Boy, she is going to fry your ass now," Fisher said. Seeing the fire in Lareina's eyes, he slid his 9mm into his waistband, out of the way.

Silas finished his cereal and chose that moment to rummage through the refrigerator. He wanted eggs.

"Why do you have Silas' rifle?" Lareina watched Silas, anticipating his reaction.

She went on high alert when he didn't turn around. She held out her hand for the weapon.

"This one's mine."

"What?" Her eyes snapped back to him.

Orion's head popped up. "Why does he get one, and not anyone else?"

Lareina ground her teeth. "I am not having this discussion because giving high-powered weapons to children isn't something anyone in this room would do...Silas."

"It's already mine." Alec took a step back and set his jaw. He wasn't relinquishing his new toy without a fight.

"I want one," Orion demanded.

"Silas." Lareina returned her attention to the other person who wanted to die.

"It's his."

"Silas!"

Silas gathered the egg carton, salt, pepper, butter, an onion and a pan. These he carried to the stove. "I told you I'd take care of it."

"Excuse me?"

"You didn't want me to kill the little bastard for touching my shit, so I told you, I would take care of it...I did." He rolled up his sleeves and started mixing.

The conversation sounded familiar, however, she had no recollection of telling either of them Alec could have a rifle; a sniper rifle at that! "No. Giving him a firearm is not how you take care of it."

"Yes, it is," he said over his shoulder.

"He can't have it."

"MOM!"

"I want one!" Orion repeated.

"I'll get you something good." Kaiden didn't want the other kid to be left out. He was cool; annoying and useless, but cool.

"No, you won't. Weren't you listening?" Lareina scowled at her soon-to-be-dead brother. She wanted to kill them all.

"We had them at that age," Fisher said. Lareina's look squelched whatever else he might have added.

"You said you wanted us trained," Alec cajoled, earning a glare of retribution.

"Not like that!"

"It's what I want to be trained in. I like it. C'mon, you're being...what's it called when someone thinks too much bad stuff is going to happen?" He walked over and not-so-subtly put her hand in his hair.

"Paranoid," she supplied, not at all happy, but she rubbed his hair anyway. He needed to feel loved; even when he irritated her. Especially when he irritated her.

"Yep, paranoid. You're being paranoid. Besides, he already gave it to me." It made perfect sense to Alec.

"I already gave it to him." It made perfect sense to Silas too.

"I don't care." She stopped rubbing. "Why do you want a sniper rifle?"

Alec moved his head; jumpstarting her hand. "So I can take care of business without always being in the mix."

Damn it. Alec not in the mix. That's all Lareina wanted. The silence stretched while Silas scrambled his eggs. "Fine," she gave up. "But this is ridiculous. You better train him to be better than you, Silas. And if he gets hurt, I'm coming after you."

"Don't we have some real issues to discuss?" Silas said. "Anybody want some eggs?"

"I do." Alec slung *his* TS13 over his shoulder. His smile lit up the kitchen and melted Lareina's heart.

"How about you, Trouble?" Silas glanced at Yukiyo.

"Yes. Trouble?"

"Who came in here and started all this unnecessary trouble?" he shot back.

"Kiss my ass." She took a seat.

"Leave her alone." Lareina wasn't over her attitude yet. "You're the ones in trouble." She turned toward Kaiden. "You too. You will make Orion an expert or else."

Silas ignored her.

Alec smiled. He wasn't in trouble.

Kaiden didn't answer.

Fisher wasn't trying to get involved.

Having procured Kaiden's promise to supply him, Orion nodded out again.

Lareina and Yukiyo passed a wearied look between them.

****

"We've got a lot to accomplish in a short time-frame." Lareina passed out a couple of folders. With the conclusion of breakfast, they moved to the dining room table which served as the conference room.

"Deverell blew up Kaiden's garage as a warning." She talked over the various reactions. "Short version, he knows who you are and considers you the enemy." She included them all in the circular motion of her finger. "Where you're concerned, he's out for blood and he's not going to be very nice when he goes after whatever weakness he can find."

"Our families," Orion stated.

"That'd be my first guess, yes."

"Do we do something for them or do we go after him?" Fisher asked.

"We go after him." Kaiden tugged on his earring. "No more Deverell, no more problems."

"Yeah, good luck with that." Silas demonstrated to Alec how to disassemble the TS13. "The only chance anybody who isn't me has of offing Deverell is if he doesn't know you're coming. He blew up your garage, Kaiden. He knows you're coming."

Lareina nodded. "Besides, that's what he wants. He's waiting on your retaliation, Kaid. I'd bet my life, he's expecting us to try to protect our families too. He can't find us, so he's trying to force us to surface."

"We will protect them, though, right?" Yukiyo asked.

"As best we can," Lareina said. "But not by exposing ourselves."

"What are you thinking?" Silas turned his focus to Yukiyo. "The seven of us are going to fly around the country, scooping up everybody's mommy and sissy and hide them in that closet over there," he pointed to the pantry, "and the Dopes won't notice and Deverell won't care."

Yukiyo remained undaunted. "I thought you had skills. When you were out getting us new identities, maybe you should have mass produced."

Lareina put a hand on Silas' shoulder, silencing any further comebacks. "Kaiden has people who can work their way in and move your immediate families underground. If they want to go. In the meantime, we'll tie his hands."

Everyone waited for further explanation.

"I need you three on the computers today." She tossed a red jump drive to Yukiyo and a blue one to Orion. Alec appeared to be engrossed in the dissembled weapon. "Put that thing away." She slid a green jump in front of him. "They stay in my car. Don't touch any color but your own. Now, to this," She tapped one of the folders. "On the first page, there's a set of names you'll be operating as. I wrote them down because I want them kept secret. If you're on the computer dealing with the DoP, you're the first person. If you happen to be interacting with the Revolutionaries, you're the second person. The third person is a name you can put out there on either side if you need to; a friend, a co-worker, whatever. It's just someone you know. Memorize them. Destroy the papers. And for all of our protection...Don't. Share."

"Who are these people?" Yukiyo glanced at her list.

Orion studied his names, already in process of committing them to memory.

Alec reassembled his rifle.

"Me," Lareina said. "It was a personal experiment that turned out to be a stroke of genius."

"Because you are a genius." Alec snapped the last piece in place with relish.

"Good time, you little suck-up." Silas checked his work.

"Pay attention." Lareina's order had no sting. "I created a person just to see how long it would take before they found out it was bogus. She's been getting a paycheck for over six years now."

"Are you kidding me?" Kaiden found the thought funny.

"No. That's how I finance things I don't want connected to Lareina Elliot. We've got a handful of good, hardworking, bogus people who have access to various parts of the federal government. It worked so well there, I thought it prudent to get a few on the Revolutionary payroll too."

"Don't they have to report somewhere, show up for work?" Orion asked. "I've got boy names."

"I could have sworn you said *don't* share," Alec said.

"That's fine," Lareina said. "But no more. Most of my jobs are in the field or in some virtual warehouse/office. As an added touch, a lot of my interactions are with myself."

"No kidding?" Kaiden loved it.

"Right down to the gossip and one office affair. Once I gave myself a letter of recommendation. It turned into a promotion."

"You're a little bit twisted." Silas had dissembled Alec's rifle. "Do it again."

Lareina chuckled. "Don't hate just because you only have three people."

"Four," Silas said. "That you're aware of."

"The whole government is probably run by bogus people," Fisher commented.

"It would explain a lot," Kaiden answered him.

"What are we supposed to do as these people?" A spark of excitement lit up Yukiyo's dark eyes.

"For now, research. The next three pages are histories. It should have an initial on it. Keep those for reference 'til you really know who you are. Once you're working, you can access a file with every interaction each person had." She came to the more serious part of the work. "We have three objectives. They came to the school looking for something. That tells me somebody was on to me or what I was doing. We have to find out who that somebody is and what they know. Then we have to shut them up. That's one. Clearly, there is a link between the administration and the Revolutionaries. We have to find out who it is. The good news is I've narrowed it down to three, possibly four people. The bad news is that's as far as I got. I suspect at least two of them are decoys. Most likely plants, for just such a scenario. If we snag the wrong guy, we blow the whole operation. That's two. Next, we have to find a guy named Marcus Mitchell. Marcus is a secret the DoP know nothing about. Christian will want to keep it that way. That's three."

The young ones were thunderstruck at the enormity of her instruction. Even Alec stared open-mouthed, speechless.

The older three had a different reaction altogether.

"Anything else?" Silas cut her a glance of immense boredom.

"You don't ask for much do you?" Fisher rocked back on his chair.

Kaiden had the nerve to yawn, "You want this done by tonight?"

****

Conversation became limited over the next six hours. Everyone stayed busy on an electronic device of one form or another. Less efficient at playing computer sleuth, Kaiden and Fisher were nonetheless helpful, doing grunt work. Whenever Orion, who was fast, or Alec, who was extremely fast would come across a large file or folder, they would shoot it to one or the other with instructions as to what they were searching for. The system worked well.

Yukiyo and Silas had somehow paired off. She at her computer;

headset on. He, only God and Lareina knew where. They traded ideas, or rather, she offered ideas and he shot them down. Whatever information she collected, he cross-referenced with his Chronos.

What Lareina did was anyone's guess as she hadn't spoken since they'd started.

The first breakthrough came from Alec. "Mom."

"Ummhmm."

"Can you help me for a second?"

"Yep." All it took was a second for Lareina to get to his side. "What do you have?"

"I've been going through your communications~"

"You've been doing what?"

"If I'm going to find whoever is in your business, I have to start with your business."

She couldn't fault his thinking. "That's why you're the genius." She rubbed his head.

"I've got all of your reports for the last three years." He clicked on a file. A list of documents popped up. "These," he highlighted a large section, "pertain to kids you've recommended to the excellence program."

"Okay."

"I've got a list of the ones you didn't recommend, but I'll get to that in a minute. Eighteen people get your reports on a regular basis. Deverell and this person, I think it's his secretary, 'cause she gets everything."

Lareina looked at the email address. "You'd be right. Deverell is my Liaison. We work together with most of these children. He and Misty get everything first. And this one," she pointed to another address. "She's his old secretary. Umm. I can't remember her name, but she got everything until last year." Lareina read through the list. "These six, are the review board. They're who the reports are for. And this one, this one, this one and...this one, were on the board at various times in my career. They shouldn't still be getting anything." She went over the list again. "Oh wait, this one is Amanda. She's my assistant. She would have access to most of these reports. I don't know who these last four are." She studied them, trying to make a connection.

"Me either," Alec changed screens and punched in some codes. "But see here, I'm cross tracking. Except for these guys you said aren't on the board anymore, most everybody sends stuff back and forth."

"Okay?"

"But not this one." He highlighted an address. "Somebody WP Somebody. This dude doesn't send anybody anything. But he's gets everything you send. And he gets everything Deverell sends."

"We'll have to find out who he is and why he doesn't share. Good job. Hold that thought." Lareina answered her phone on the first ring. "Yep?"

"I'm here," Silas said. "And guess what? So is Deverell."

"Your gamble paid off."

"I don't need to gamble. I'm always right."

"Whatever works. Got anything yet?"

"Would I be calling you if I didn't? I'll be done in a few hours."

"At the rate you're moving, Kaiden won't have time to miss you."

Kaiden looked up. "If that's Silas, tell him to stay wherever the hell he's at."

"Tell Kaiden to kiss my ass. I want some spaghetti when I get home. With Garlic bread, yeah."

She cracked a smile, listening to him rub his hands together in apparent anticipation. Opting to ignore the first request she asked, "When will you be back?"

"To-night."

"Don't get testy. I didn't know if you were coming straight home."

"Oh. Make me some spaghetti."

"Whatever you like." She hung up, shaking her head. Her assassin was preoccupied with noodles.

"Where is he?" Kaiden asked.

Lareina didn't see the harm in sharing. "Vegas. At least, that's where he's supposed to be."

"What?"

"He got a flight straight out. I imagine all that security clearance."

"I thought we had some sort of deadline," Fisher said. "Couldn't he work from here? The more the merrier and what not?"

"Not with Silas," Lareina smiled.

"Let him go," Kaiden added.

Lareina continued, "He needed to get where Christian is to do his magic. We took a chance Christian would be working from his home office. He won't hit the road until he starts flushing us out. Which won't be for another," she looked at the clock, "Nine or ten hours, at least."

"What's he trying to do?" Orion looked up from his screen.

"Attach another tracker to Christian and hopefully, hijack his phone records. The only way we're going to find Mr. Marcus Mitchell is through Mr. Christian Deverell. We need to know where he is before I talk to Christian again."

"Do you think he'll get it done?" Kaiden exchanged an our-baby-brother-is-annoying look with Fisher.

"Fifteen, twenty minutes tops." Alec never looked away from his work. "He's a sick man with a sick system."

****

Silas strolled through the medicine aisle. Breaking into Christian's house wasn't a problem; convincing Christian the break-in was random, that was going to be hard. Mentally shrugging, he went back to his current task; he'd worry about Deverell later. *Allergy meds...nausea meds...menst~fuck no! Bingo, pain relievers. Hmmm, Tylenol, Advil...no, Excedrin. I'm thinking Eugene is an Excedrin man. No second rate drugs for him.* "Prick." Judging from the amount of shelf-space allotted, he concluded it was the area's biggest seller. "High-priced and a follower, ouch Eugene." He chuckled, grabbing the 24 count capsules. Three aisles over, he picked up a six-pack of Bud, formulating a plan right there in the aisle. If Eugene was gone, he'd break in. If he was home, he'd offer him a beer.

****

Although every surface glowed spotlessly and the furniture was impeccably coordinated, the house had a neglected, unused feel. Christian didn't come home very often.

Bypassing the commercial security system wouldn't have caused Silas to raise an eyebrow, but he left it alone. It would have been a giveaway the break-in came from a professional. Not what he wanted. However, that only gave him four minutes to do what he had to do. Fortunately for all involved, he only needed two.

Ski mask...gloves...pills...chemical pack...syringe...Springfield T.45; everything he needed. By the time the alarm sounded he was already in.

Twenty seconds to disrupt the living room, then he went upstairs. First door on the left, as the Chronos blueprint indicated, was the bathroom. *Just like I thought, Excedrin. Damn, I'm good.* Luck didn't enter anywhere into Silas' consciousness. He switched the regular medicine with his tracker-laced pills—pills that would give him a headache and make him take more pills for a while. Another twenty seconds to knock over a few items in Christian's guest room and slide tiny envelopes with his own special white powder under the doors to Christian's office and bedroom, because there was no way in hell he would actually enter either of those places. Silas would bet his life both rooms were set up with more security than a bank vault. No thanks.

He made one final pause in the kitchen and opened the fridge. *Jackpot! Thanks for the snack.* He helped himself to a thigh from the bucket of chicken. No one wanted those anyway. He bit into it and held it with his teeth as he scanned the shelves, grunting when he spotted two Corona's. *Uhhhhh, no. Gotta be Bud, man.* He freed the syringe and stabbed the top of the closest bottle. Feeling no remorse in contaminating the foreign crap. The needle went through the cap, leaving a hole so small it was undetectable by the human eye. He did the same with the other bottle. *Here's to your first headache. Bottoms up, old man.*

Silas was already a block away when the sound waves from the security alarm detonated his hurricane dust. It wasn't much more than flash powder and sawdust infused with sodium silicate. Not powerful enough to destroy anything, but enough kick to rearrange the décor. *Hope you invested in a quality vacuum cleaner, old man. 'Cause you got a mess.*

****

"Bullshit."

"Pardon me, sir?"

"Bullshit," Christian repeated when the dispatcher gave him the news. "Did I hear you correctly, someone broke into my house?"

"Yes sir, I'm sorry. The perpetrator was obviously looking for something. The place has been trashed. They need you back there to identify what was taken."

"I'm on my way." Christian hung up. "Lareina." He shook his head. It was a small, tight, movement. That name summed up everything.

Chapter 12

"Lareina." Orion found her in the kitchen, stirring the contents of a large blue-grey stockpot. Beside it, a heavy saucepan filled with chunks of meat, tomatoes, mushrooms and peppers swimming in Italian herbs, softly bubbled. He inhaled deeply. The garlic bread was almost done. "Mmmm, smells good. You're a great cook."

"Not really." She dipped a spoon into the sauce and offered him a taste.

"MmmMmmm. Yes, really. Now, I can't wait for dinner."

"You'll have to wait. It's not ready yet."

He watched her fish out a spaghetti noodle, cut it in half with a fork and toss it against the nearest wall.

His eyebrows arched high. "Never seen that before. Why are you wasting the noodles? Is the wall going to tell you when it's ready?"

"It will." She peeled it off and wiped the spot with a wet paper towel. "And it did. The noodle sticks when it's done."

"Who came up with that?"

"No idea. I got it from my mom."

"If I did that, you'd probably yell at me for starting a food fight or something."

"If you're making spaghetti, you're fine. If it's already done, then yes, I'd yell at you." She turned off the burner.

"I have a question for you."

She took a peek at her bread. "That's what I've been waiting for."

"There's a man named W. Jericho Parks and a lady named Gillian Foster. Can you tell me anything about them?"

"Jeri," her grin was huge. "His name is William Jericho Parks. We went through the Excellence Program together. Jeri, Christian and I. We always hung out. Not so much in recent years. I haven't talked to him in a while."

Following the smell of tomato sauce and warm garlic bread, Alec sauntered in. "WP. Initials match," he said, referencing his earlier search. Wedging his way between her and Orion, he relieved Lareina of her stirring spoon and sampled the sauce. "Is it done?"

"Just about. The bread has another minute or two. Would you tell everyone dinner's ready?"

"Sure." He went to the doorway. "DINNER'S READY!"

"Thanks, Mr. Lazy." Lareina drained the water from the noodles.

"I'm not being lazy. I'm being efficient."

"Because she couldn't do that herself," Orion muttered.

"She can't," Alec said. "She's a lady. Ladies don't yell."

Orion made a face of reluctant agreement. He had a point, Lareina is a lady and Alec was efficient. Everybody heard him. Returning to his questions, he talked over the movement of people. "What about the woman, Gillian Foster?"

"She worked at the school. You might know her~"

"Guidance counselor for Sector B," Yukiyo joined in. "Always wore that yellow scarf, no matter what she had on." Unlike the boys, Yukiyo made herself useful. She grabbed a stack of plates and a handful of flatware. "She tried to be Lareina, but she sucked at it. Too nosey for her own good."

"She was just trying to fit in." Lareina went to work slicing the bread.

"She was bossy and a pain in the butt. No one respected her. They all laughed at her behind her back." Yukiyo collected an armful of glasses.

"Grab the salad out of the refrigerator for me, please," Lareina instructed Orion. She handed the basket of hot garlicky slices to Alec. "Put these on the table, please."

Alec put a piece in his mouth and the rest on the table.

Kaiden and Fisher were the last to enter and the first to sit down. Neither man had any qualms about not helping.

There was a sense of home to it. The meal. The interaction. The day. Before, they were just people, caught in something bigger than any one of them. Now, they had information. They were discovering. They were working together—becoming a team.

It wasn't until the end of dinner did the conversation get back to its original subject.

Lareina turned to Orion. "You never said. Why were you asking about

Jeri and Gillian?"

"I might be on to something suspicious."

"What's that?" Kaiden helped himself to thirds.

"For starters," Orion said, "What's up with you and your even numbers?" He looked at Lareina.

"I'm drawn to even numbers. I prefer to use them when I'm able."

"You use them all the time."

"Do you have a point?"

"Your friend, Mr. Parks. Do you know what his task was?"

"Nobody ever knew for sure what anybody's task was. They all had some generic glossed-over name. It tied into your major, like a dissertation, except they selected the topic for you. Nobody cared what anybody did. We had enough to do researching our own."

"I was investigating your classmates, trying to see who's still around."

"A good place to start." She thought he and Alec were similar in their objective, yet completely different in their approach.

"I came across this dude."

"Alright, you found an old boyfriend." Fisher took the liberty of getting the ice cream. He could help out that much. "What of it?" He picked up one bowl and one spoon. He didn't want to take over all the work. That wouldn't be fair.

Orion said, "Mr. Parks is very successful."

"I'm not surprised. Jeri had always been very ambitious."

"His task had something to do with patterns. How to use them, how to anticipate, how to hide them or possibly break them. I'm not sure exactly what."

Alec was already tracking with him. "Would he be somebody who would notice a pattern, like if somebody always used even numbers?"

"He noticed it alright."

"What do you mean?" Lareina was not a fan of surprises.

"He's got something going on with or about you."

"Because she's retarded with numbers?" Kaiden got a bowl for ice cream too. "Who cares?"

"How do you know he's got something going on with Lareina?" After watching Kaiden throw four full scoops into his bowl, reach into the gallon tub of Neapolitan for a fifth, Yukiyo got bowls for everyone else. If somebody didn't act fast, there wouldn't be any ice cream left.

"Because he's got a lot of megabytes invested in a folder her name is tagged in. I haven't been able to unlock it yet, but it's a subfolder in his patterns file." Orion went on, "I was messing with your number-thing, overlaying it with people in my testing class." He paused.

"Go ahead, Ori," Lareina encouraged. "If I messed up, we need to know so we can fix it."

"You didn't mess up." Alec pursed his lips.

"No. Not you," Orion said. "I think this jerk got lucky or something."

Lareina appreciated the support, but it wasn't necessary. "What happened when you played with the patterns?"

"Seven different times. Seven different ways." He couldn't help smirking a little. "I was the only one in the group you tested who didn't land on an odd spot on any list. No matter how random the names appeared. I tested higher than everyone but my name never came first, on anything. I was the one not attending Hillcrest. A betting person could have made some money on it."

"Most likely," Alec was still defending, "they weren't after you, specifically. They were waiting to see how Orion didn't get selected."

"Damn." Fisher's bowl was empty. He reached for the ice cream scoop to remedy that. "Y'all are some creepy kids. You should be playing video games, not computer mind games."

Yukiyo snatched the ice cream scoop from Fisher. She plopped one scoop into his bowl and moved it out of his reach.

"What are you? The ice cream Nazi?" Fisher grabbed it back. He added three more scoops on principle. He licked the scooper once, for good measure.

"Gross!" Yukiyo turned away. "Hey, Orion, what about Miss Foster?"

"Oh. Yeah. Seems to me they have some sort of thing going on. Lot of emails. Lot of talking. Mostly about you, Lareina, and how you spend your days."

"Hmm...interesting," Lareina mused. "I wonder if his wife knows."

****

Christian surveyed the damage around his house. A random robbery they said. The hell it was. He kicked some books aside. Nothing of value was missing, he'd bet on it. He waited until the police completed their report and the investigating officers were gone before he checked the hidden cameras. They weren't everywhere because he didn't want all his activities recorded. The last thing he needed was footage of him scratching his ass, but that didn't mean he didn't have strategic places. His front door, his bedroom, and his office were wired to the roof when he wasn't home. It's where he kept the things that needed watching.

He grabbed a beer and the leftover chicken, pausing over the bucket. One, two, three, four, five...one of those greedy ass cops ate his chicken. If he ever found out who, he'd kill the bastard on principle, just on principle.

Christian righted one of the chairs in the kitchen, unpacked his tablet from his bag, and took a long swallow of his beverage before logging on. Time to find out who was stupid enough to come to his house. He watched, transfixed, his frown deepening with each passing second. Nobody, not a damn soul anywhere on the video feeds. One minute the rooms were clean, the next, they were a mess, like an invisible tornado hit them. Why would someone avoid those rooms? The most likely place to look for anything?

"Because it wasn't a damn random robbery, that's why." He took a bite and washed it down with another swallow of beer. "Who are you and what were you after?" He thought it over for a few drawn out minutes. Scare tactics? Planting bugs? There were a million possibilities. "Let's see how dirty you're playing," he mused aloud. He tore off another piece of meat and dialed his assistant.

"Yes sir, Mr. Deverell?"

"Upload the photos from my last five containments. Special emphasis on the Elliot Case. I want them circulated at every airport, train station and bus terminal that comes into Vegas. Somebody somewhere has to have a security camera that saw something. Call me as soon as you get a hit."

"Right away sir."

He finished his beer and re-surveyed the mess. She was cleaning this shit up.

****

"How long do you think it will take to crack his files?" Lareina looked at Orion, but her thoughts were already on other things.

"I don't know." He wasn't discouraged. "Patterns lead to codes and all kinds of annoying things, but sooner or later..."

"We don't got 'sooner or later.'" Alec felt the need to point that out.

"To hell with his codes. Let's go get his ass," Kaiden said. "He can open the file for us with my nine in his ear."

Lareina studied her baby brother. Sometimes he was as merciless as the wolf he wore, but in this instance, he had a point. "Alright, Kaid. I think you're right. Let's go get him."

"Really? Fine, let's do it." Kaiden didn't expect her to agree with him, but he wasn't going to argue about it.

Neither did Fisher. "Did I hear you right? Let's go get him?"

"You heard me, Fish." She hid her amusement. "It would save us some time, provided we can find him."

"He's scheduled to be at the Library of Congress in a little less than three weeks." As soon as Alec pulled out his phone, Yukiyo went and stood behind his chair. She pointed over his shoulder to something showing on Chronos II, the name he had given to his newest appendage.

Orion rolled his eyes. "I was working on Parks."

Alec didn't notice. He smugly burst Yukiyo's bubble. "You need to be faster than that." He hit the previous page and pointed. "He'll be at some United People Conference at the Harvard School of Excellence in six days."

"How do you know this shit?" Fisher was intrigued.

"Chronos II knows all."

Kaiden didn't care. "Let's go pack." He got up from the table.

"Whoa, not so fast." Lareina tugged on his shirt. "We need some details. We need a plan. I need to make a couple of phone calls and you," she tugged again and let it go, "you and Fisher need to clean up this mess."

"Say what?"

"Clean up." She stood up. "I mean it. And don't take all night getting it done."

****

The thunder is getting loud.

Rather than text back, Silas dialed her. "What now?"

Lareina wasn't offended. "Almost to my deadline. Got anything?"

"Possibly. I've got his phone list uploaded. One likely candidate, but no pinpoint on the exact location."

"How long do you think before you'll have it?"

"I'll have it by the time you actually need it."

"How about I bluff my way through it?"

"Good idea. I'm sure Eugene won't call your ass on that." He laid a thick layer of sarcasm.

"Not if I don't get caught," Lareina said. "Where are you?"

"On a plane. Should be landing soon. Did you make me some spaghetti?"

"Of course, I did. Saved you garlic bread too. We're looking at a job. I'll fill you in when you get here."

"What kind of job?"

"Going to visit an old friend. He seems to have a preoccupation with my habits."

"I could make him a dead friend."

"Precisely why I'm inviting you."

"Texas."

"Pardon me?"

"My likely candidate just got confirmed. He's hiding in Texas. Out in the middle of the desert where nobody will bother looking for him."

"Except you." She was full of admiration for him.

"Except me." He was full of admiration for himself.

****

She wondered if Eugene was waiting. Am I early?

Of course, he was waiting. It's never too early. Why did you do it?

What am I being accused of this time?

I want my house cleaned by the end of the week. I want to know what you took.

It's great that you've set goals. Get some help accomplishing them. I'd assist you, but I won't be there. I've got things. As for your second demand: nothing. I wasn't there.

Are you denying you have something that's not yours?

If I have it, it's mine. If you didn't mess with other people's toys, you wouldn't have a need to be so paranoid.

The silence stretched for close to a half hour.

Are you coming home?

Not today.

You might want to think about that. I've been to your apartment. You've got some family and friends who may feel different about your decision. In a little while, I'm going to visit Wisconsin. I might stop off in Indiana and I'm definitely going to see what was delivered to Joy Road.

Now, she didn't respond for a little while.

You're almost out of time.

She knew that. She just wasn't talking to him at the moment. Even after what he'd done to Kaiden—her own brother—it was still hard to accept. Her Eugene. Her caring, sweet, sensible Eugene, a lowlife. No, he wasn't a lowlife. He was a high caliber, efficient, killer. It's not as if she didn't know. She knew him better than anyone. Wisconsin...Orion's sisters. Indiana...Yukiyo's mom. And...no...no...not Alec...no. How could he? What was he planning? Joy Road. The Christ Child Orphanage was on Joy Road in Detroit. *He better stay away from my baby.*

Now, you're really almost out of time.

I'm thinking about families and stuff. About living in Texas. My friend with the soft spot went there recently. He said it was almost empty. That could get lonely, don't you think? You might need someone to talk to. She counted to sixty. Let him wait. If I were you, I would change my itinerary. I'd think about paying a visit to Florida. If you can get past the soldiers, there are two, possibly three places you might like to see.

Christian couldn't say what he wanted. There was a lot he wanted to say. On one hand, she was blackmailing him. On the other offering him a lead. Why? Breadcrumbs to go with the vinegar. Why?

You seem hungry.

He couldn't talk to her anymore. Lareina gave him a headache. This time, literally. A painful throb signaled the beginning of a migraine.

He made his way up to his bathroom. It was a relief to see the bottle of Excedrin – he wasn't sure if he had anything –but paused over the bottle. Capsules? *Shit.* He hated capsules. He meant to buy caplets. *Whatever.* He swallowed two without liquid. Normally a silent sufferer, Christian didn't have time for a migraine tonight. He looked at his reflection. Lareina would say he was tired. She always knew when he was tired; usually before he did. On reflective instinct, or maybe some subconscious preparation, he shoved the pill bottle into his pocket; wanting them on hand.

The vibration of his cell phone recalled him to the present.

"I'm sorry to bother you, Mr. Deverell." Misty Wilson, his assistant, was nervous. "We got a call from McCarran International. They ID'd one of your suspects."

"Which?"

"Corporal Silas McKade."

No surprise there. He rubbed his temple, helping the Excedrin along. "Where did he come from and what time did he get here?"

Misty scanned her notes. "Flew out of JFK. Arrived two-forty p.m. today."

It was around five when my house was hit. The little bastard is fast. I'll give him that. "Was he alone?"

"It appears so, sir."

"Good work, Misty. I'm on my way there. Get back in touch with McCarran and also put in a call to Nellis Air Force Base. If he's still here, I want him detained. If not, I want to know when he left and where he's going. And I want to be on the first flight following him."

"Yes, sir. I'll take care of it."

****

"What'd you say?"

"Am I supposed to understand what this discussion is about, Silas?" Lareina adjusted the receiver so she could continue brushing her hair.

"Must have been some talk you had with Eugene. He just left his house and is doing upwards of ninety. Going somewhere in a hurry."

"I take it you are somehow able to track Christian's movements on a more permanent basis."

"Not permanent. But, now that he's had his beer, I'll be able to keep up with him longer than three days."

"That statement makes sense to you and you alone." It was one of those things Lareina knew better than to ask about. "I think we touched a nerve. He put it out there, he was going after Orion and Yukiyo so I mentioned Texas. He hasn't said anything to me since. That means he's pausing to regroup and change his strategy."

The fact that she didn't bring up Alec was not lost to Silas, but he didn't broach it. "You're welcome."

"I made you spaghetti."

Chapter 13

"Hey. What's up?"

"Hey. Did I wake you?"

"No, honey." She closed her book. "Come on in."

Orion hopped onto the foot of her bed, not the least bit sleepy.

"What's going on in that monstrous big brain of yours?"

"I don't know. Just thinking. Can I ask you a question?"

"Ask away."

"How'd you get like you?"

"Me? I am a product of my environment. Without a doubt."

"I want to live in your environment."

"Whose environment do you think you're living in now? You could do better."

"Doubt it. What was it like when you were my age?"

"Bullets, death, the usual."

"Com'on, 'Reina. Tell me something good. I want to hear 'bout when Kaiden wet the bed and Fisher sucked his thumb and... and Silas being a crybaby."

"True facts. All of it." She sat up, tucking her feet under her. "Alright. I'll try to think of something interesting." She tossed him a pillow. "Let me see. Hmmm. I didn't grow up in movie America. That was my mother's generation. According to her, America was all about convenience, comfort, and blame. Political hate, racial hate, religious hate, social hate, educational hate, you name it—somebody complained about it. She said they were too busy posting selfies to notice they were dying from cancer. Things got out of control and went to hell when they took the fight off the internet and put it on the streets. Apparently, they didn't realize civil war wasn't a video game."

Orion rolled his eyes in humored disbelief. "I never understood why anybody would want their picture all over the internet where everybody can find you."

"They thought it was fun."

"They were stupid."

"No argument. The government tried to establish its idea of order by taking away everybody's freedom."

"Everybody agreed, right?"

"They're still debating. Those bombs in Fresno last month meant, 'I'm not sure about this.' A funny little tidbit for you: Do you know how the Rev's were founded?"

"No. They don't teach that in school."

"No, they don't. Poor black people lived in inner-city ghettos~"

"Everywhere is a ghetto now."

"Pretty-much. They called the white-trash country version the sticks. Those two divisions had more in common than anybody gave them credit for. They didn't have a lot to begin with. When the fighting started, neither group had much to lose. Not only that, they knew how to survive, and how to get things. Guess which two groups the government couldn't control?"

"Did they get along with each other?"

"Not at first, but better than anyone imagined. Certainly better than either of them got along with the government. Anyway, that's where Kaiden's pissy pants come in. My family came from the ghetto side. Finding ways to live was a full-time job. The war wasn't officially 'war,'" she air quoted. "But there was fighting all the time. My dad died when I was four. My mother had to work. I had to watch the baby. For nine hours a day Kaiden and I were locked in a room with nothing but our beds, a potty, our toys and some food. Instead of a lunch break, she would come home for ten minutes every three hours to check on us. By the time I turned six, I was an expert nanny. Kaiden was three—bad as hell—and we had another kid locked in with us. Fisher's mom paid me five dollars a week to watch him."

"Babysitting at six? That's nuts."

"Babysitting at four. An expert at six. Thank you very much. There wasn't any choice."

"There were no other adults anywhere?"

"All over the place. That's why we were locked in. The country wasn't divided like a chess board. You didn't know who was on what side. You couldn't trust anyone with your business. Or not to sell or hurt your kids. That happened a lot because hungry people will do anything for money. My mother took a big risk helping Ms. Jessup. That five bucks she gave me was an act of faith. I don't know how many meals she skipped to keep Fisher safe. We put three dollars in the pot towards Christmas and Birthday presents, one dollar went toward a weekly treat and the last dollar was all mine. To make myself rich."

"The safest place for a toddler is with a six-year-old and another toddler." He whistled through his teeth. "That's scary."

"You've no idea. But I was a smart kid. Before my dad died, I knew the alphabet, I could count, and I had no trouble getting online. My mother read to me a lot. I had certain books memorized. I taught myself to read by word association. I potty trained Kaiden and Fisher and taught them how to walk, talk, and eventually to read and write."

"I wouldn't take too much credit if I were you. They're both idiots."

"Agreed. I contend they acquired some brain damage later on."

"I'll accept that. How'd Silas get in there?"

"All kinds of divine providence. I was about eight. We were still locked in, but I was old enough to have the key. Thank God. One night, our moms didn't come home. They didn't come back the next day either. The non-war fighting had been pretty heavy in our area. We had no idea what happened, but I had to get food and take care of two scared five-year-olds."

He talked through a yawn, "Weren't you scared too?"

"Very. But I was in charge. Something made me feel like we needed to get out of the house. I got us dressed and took all the money my mother had hidden, and Kaiden, Fisher and I went for a walk. My neighborhood looked like an earthquake hit it. It was a good thing we left. About twenty minutes later, it got blasted."

"Ouch."

"Ouch is right. Everyone went nuts, running everywhere, but not us. We were taking a walk."

"Where'd you go?"

"CVS. You only had to cross one street to get there."

"Brilliant." Orion scooched down into his pillow. Lareina's voice soothed him.

"Unbeknownst to me, we had been spotted and followed by a little tornado in dirty clothes."

He raised his head up at the perceived threat but let it plop back down.

"I marched them into the CVS like I knew what I was doing. We were the only ones in the store. The employees were gone. Hiding, watching, fighting, I don't know. We were shopping. I remember Kaiden and Fisher sitting on the floor playing with a box of animal crackers. I was climbing a shelf trying to reach the breakfast bars when we heard this clanging. Up the aisle comes this little kid pushing a shopping cart, knocking into everything. He gets it there, helps himself to a box of animal crackers, climbs into the front of the cart and tells me to push."

"What'd you do?"

"I pushed. Kaiden didn't like Silas taking a whole box of cookies without asking. Fisher didn't like that Silas wouldn't get out and let him have a turn. They've been bickering ever since."

"Supply. Take. Gloat. Sounds like Silas to me."

"He was born to be a pain. It's his life goal."

"Mission accomplished." Orion yawned again.

"We shopped for things I knew how to make: dry cereal, fruit cocktail, tuna fish, pudding cups and such. I left a whopping seven dollars at the register. We pushed the cart down the street looking for a new house to live in. We found one that didn't seem to be in bad shape. It had pretty yellow curtains. We went in and set up housekeeping in the living room."

"What happened next?" His eyes were starting to droop.

"Two days later, we found out a little old lady lived there. We called her Grandnan. Turns out, workers all over the city were locked up and held for various war-related annoying reasons. The DoP didn't know or didn't care about people stashing their kids. Might have been because of it, as retribution. Regardless, children were left on their own for days all over the place." Lareina shifted her position. "Because of her age, Grandnan was one of the first to be released. She let us stay and collected all the urchins she could find. Being an adult, she knew where to go and who to talk to. As they were released, our families found us. We all stayed with Grandnan after that. The adults worked. Grandnan watched us and I continued to raise Kaiden, Fisher and Silas."

Orion was asleep.

"We're a nice little gang of safe-house hunters." She flipped her comforter down to cover him. Last night it was Alec. Two nights prior, she and Fisher fell asleep on the sofa. For a single woman, she hardly ever slept alone.

"You forgot to mention we wouldn't have it any other way." Silas came around the corner carrying a half-eaten plate of spaghetti.

"How long have you been home? I didn't hear you come in."

"You weren't supposed to." He bit into his bread and gave her his plate. "Hold that." He kicked off his shoes, tugged off his shirt and removed his Kevlar. As a sniper, he understood the importance of protecting vital organs. Instead of the cumbersome vest which would limit his movement, he habitually wrapped his torso in the bullet resistant fabric. Once he made himself comfortable on the other side of her bed. He took his food back and dug in.

"How did we end up like we are?" She ruffled his hair, much like she did Alec's.

Silas closed his eyes. Like Alec, he loved her hands in his hair. "Because Kaid and Fish are dangerous, you're smart and I'm me."

"That clears it all up. Thanks."

"My pleasure. Rub my hair."

She had no one to blame but herself so she rubbed. "Everything go okay?"

"Of course. Except, I noticed the empty ice cream carton in the trash. Nobody thought to save me any?"

"Yukiyo tried. She was too obvious. Kaiden and Fisher took complete advantage."

"I'll take care of it. They're both overdue for a case of the shits." He handed her his empty plate and made himself comfortable on her pillows. "Goodnight."

She put his plate on her nightstand and clicked off the light. "I am plagued with intrusive males." She pulled the sheet up and curled into a ball so she wouldn't kick Orion.

"You like it."

"Do I?"

"Push."

****

The week started off worrisome. Christian made an appearance in New York a few hours after Silas returned home. He arrived by way of the same airport, Newark Liberty International. Everyone prepared to flee while Silas tracked his movements.

Two days later, Christian left the area and went to the Pentagon. It disturbed Lareina to have him so close when there had been no contact between them. She didn't dare give anything away by communicating with him.

The high note came with a special delivery for 'Danica Stone.' Lareina called for Alec, Orion, and Yukiyo to join her. The others came, just because. "I have something for you." She gave each one of them a smile of fondness. "That is, if you want it."

"Is it what I think it is?" Alec's entire face lit up with expectation.

"More than likely." She handed him the first of three small gift wrapped boxes.

"Cheetah," he grinned.

"Open it and see."

He did and was thrilled to see a man's necklace with an incredibly lifelike citrine cheetah with obsidian eyes. It came with a matching earring. He put the chain around his neck and threw his arms around his mom, squeezing her with the fullness of his love.

She hugged him back, placing a kiss on the top of his head and rubbing his hair for good measure.

Orion and Yukiyo each stared at theirs. Neither had ever received anything so expensive. Likewise, neither knew what to make of the animal she had chosen to represent them.

Orion held his up, awed. The gentle giant of a silverback gorilla twirled from the chain held tightly within his grasp. The deep emerald eyes portrayed calm assessing intelligence and keen understanding. By contrast, the bulking body with its prominent muscles, long arms, and opposable thumbs spoke of strength, agility, and swift retribution. He felt like he was looking at the real him—the him nobody knew. Lareina knew.

"You're a monkey," Silas said. "Good choice, 'Reina."

"Lord of the jungle," Lareina corrected. "Besides being the original parkour experts, gorillas have been known to test higher than some humans on a standard IQ test."

"Higher than Fisher," Alec interjected.

Fisher tried to shove him. He dodged out of the way. Lareina went on as if she had not been interrupted. "In one program, they trained a gorilla to sign over a thousand words. Gorillas are the only animal that can walk both sides of the line. They can do human, more human than some people we know. They're also at the top of the food chain. They don't have any natural predators except the leopard, going after the babies."

"Leopards," Alec singsonged, "cousin to the cheetah."

"Good thing I'm not a baby." Orion put on his necklace and playfully beat his chest. He was a gorilla.

Yukiyo remained quiet. She studied her pendant with a sly half-smile. She didn't know why it was chosen for her, but she loved it. She quirked her eyebrow at Lareina.

Lareina happily explained, "To put it bluntly, a shark is your worst-case scenario." When Yukiyo's smile broadened, Lareina continued, "You don't want to play hide and seek with that ladyfin. She can detect a glow ten times dimmer than anything we can see. If that's not impressive enough, a shark will notice a muscle twitch." Lareina smirked, "she can see what you're thinking a mile away. Only stupid people mess with her."

Yukiyo smirked too. It was nice to be understood.

Now, every member of their team had a personal symbol thanks to Lareina's analytical tendencies. She made no pretense about loving the very characteristics the Excellence Program would have wanted to control or crush.

No one could have voiced it, but the feeling was freedom; the freedom to be who they were born to be.

"FYI," Lareina said, "There are some practical purposes for your animals...besides your personalities."

"What's that?" Yukiyo rubbed her finger across her shark's fin, petting it.

"Silas will put a tiny but powerful microphone inside. The earring will hold your earpiece. From now on, these and your sunglasses will be standard equipment."

"Don't forget the best part," Alec reminded her.

"Which best part would that be?" Lareina asked.

"Espionage jewelry *has* to come with codenames. I'm the Cheetah aka Fast-track."

****

Lareina waited in the Oneida with Fisher. She needed to be close, but could not risk being seen. They parked on the far side of the Harvard Conference Center's parking lot. Fisher's job was to ensure a clean getaway. Kaiden parked closer to the entrance. The dark blue van had been stolen for the purpose of transporting Mr. W. Jericho Parks from the convention to an undisclosed location of Lareina's choosing.

Easily disguised as freshmen students, Yukiyo, Alec, and Orion were inside. Yukiyo was their lookout. As a watcher she was unequaled. If she couldn't see it, it wasn't there. It was her duty to direct the activities, let them know what to expect and to alert them of any possible complications. Alec was the diversion. He would be the source of Jericho's problems. And calm, easy talking Orion would play the savior. He'd lead their target straight to Kaiden.

Silas would be hawking them. Keeping them safe. All six of them.

****

"Nice building," Orion spoke into his microphone as he slid into a seat three rows back.

"Because somebody cares about shiny wood and pictures of old people." That came from Alec. It wasn't necessary for him to attend the seminar; he wasn't wasting his time.

"It's culture and history and prestige... in other words, stupid rich people." Silas felt compelled to point out.

"Things you'll never have," Yukiyo said. Having pinpointed the restrooms and the offices on that floor, she bypassed two milkshake sucking DoP guards and went in the direction of food. She took her time pacing the dining hall. Six television screens, six different programs; all government controlled news and educational stations. In her school, it was a cafeteria—no TV's—but here, even though Harvard had been taken over by the administration and was an Excellence School; it still had a Harvard feel, therefore food was served in the dining hall. There were several people spread around the spacious room. Apparently, not everyone cares about the United People Conference. She certainly didn't. She eyeballed the menu. *Ooh. YY's.* Her family's name for French Fries. It came from her two-year-old attempt at pronunciation. Her dad had gotten such a kick out of it, he started using the name. It became a fun family tradition.

Yukiyo did a double take. For a second, she thought one of the pictures flashing across the screen resembled her father. The television was halfway across the room. It was most likely because she was thinking of him. Still... they were talking about soldiers... plane crash... POW's...

"...This is Brenda Blair reporting to you live. We've just received photos of the wreckage. Earlier today, a single engine military aircraft piloted by remote ground control was being used to survey what has now been confirmed as a Revolutionary POW camp, hidden in Yellowstone National Park. The onboard navigating system malfunctioned, shutting off the preprogrammed autopilot and sending the aircraft plummeting into the heart of the camp. The camp reportedly housed twenty-two POW's. Ten of whom were killed by the impact or the explosion afterward. Four other American POW's were wounded. All four are listed in critical condition with little hope of recovery. Three rebel guards were also injured; one is listed in serious condition.

The families have been notified and we have here for you the names of those brave souls, who had already lost their freedom for our great country, but now have lost their lives just days before a planned rescue..."

Names and faces flashed across the screen: Pvt. Travis Anderson; Pvt. William B. Cutler; Sgt. Ed. Edwards; P2 Montgomery Ellis; Cpl. José A.J. Guerra; Pvt. David S. Higgit; Sgt. Jeffery D. Kellerman; Sgt. Mio Jun Kaori...

Yukiyo didn't hear any more. She saw her father's picture; nothing else mattered. Why would it be remote ground controlled and preprogrammed autopiloted? Her father. *Chichi.* Yukiyo scanned the room. All the happy little people eating their YY's...

"Yukiyo." Silas' voice was calm. Deadly. Whether he saw it in her eyes, the rigidly of her stance, or something else, the warning came to him. "There's a problem, Lareina. Alec, Orion, stand by."

Yukiyo had an HK T42. The tactical compact pistol was lightweight and easy for her to carry. After coaching from Silas, Kaiden, and Fisher, she was on her way to becoming dead-on accurate. Two DoP fighters slumped over bleeding, without heartbeats, before the shots registered. A third soldier crumbled to the floor, just as the panic hit.

Screaming people ran in every direction; some diving to the floor, under tables and behind counters and trash cans. Yukiyo shot two more uniforms as they charged her before she was blindsided by a heavy woman. The off-duty officer slammed Yukiyo's hand hard against the floor. She slammed it again, trying to break the girl's grip and possibly her knuckles.

Suddenly, the woman flew back. She lay on her side with a clean hole where her left eye used to be.

Someone did grab Yukiyo's gun. Alec. He had his hoodie over his head and the sunglasses Lareina made him carry in place. Beside him, Orion, dressed in a polo and blazer for his part, hastily pulled his undershirt up over his head. He also had a pair of Lareina standard issue sunglasses.

They stood one on each side of her and yanked her to her feet. Alec pulled her out of the building while Orion covered them. To her credit, Yukiyo didn't resist. She didn't see anyone in a DoP uniform; she didn't have anyone else she felt obligated to kill.

The dark blue van waited with the engine revved. Orion shut the door as Kaiden pulled off.

Fisher and Lareina were already gone when two more shots rang out. From his crow's nest, Silas took out the tires of the first two cop cars, putting a halt to anyone following them.

****

Meetings were the worst part of Christian's job. If he wanted to be an advisor, he would have applied for employment as an advisor. Lareina liked dealing with the bureaucratic bullshit, not him. He had field work to do. Sitting in information-less gatherings at the pentagon with inept military officials was not the way to get it done.

The dismissal didn't come soon enough. The timing created a cross mesh of people arriving and leaving the conference room.

"You must be Commander Joffener." A man blocked their path. "I'm Dr. Terrance Chezwick, Director of Operations." Terrance was slightly above average height but soft. A man used to getting his way; he would be most comfortable having lunch and having drinks.

"I am," Joffener replied. "This is Field Agent Deverell."

"Commander." Chezwick shook Joffener's hand and denied Christian's existence. "Pleasure to meet you, sir. Correct me if I'm wrong. Your office does such marvelous work with children."

"We run the Excellence Program. Educating and training gifted and talented youngsters. They are America's future."

"Indeed. Indeed. I'm in education and training as well. Our jobs are similar in that regard."

"You work with children?"

"Heh heh heh. I'm not so fortunate. I have chosen the incredibly difficult task of reconditioning misplaced adults. However, I do admire your work. Children are smart and easy to control. Adults tend to be one or the other, rarely both. Getting to them early is a benefit for all involved."

"You don't have kids of your own, do you?"

"The people I train are like children. I consider myself privileged to have so many under my wing. But no, I'm not a parent."

"Which makes your mistake understandable."

"My mistake?"

"About kids. The smart ones may be easy to control, but the smarter ones are near impossible. And we work with the smartest of all. You don't control them, you simply guide them."

Christian remained silent and blank, but he pulled pieces like a puzzle. *Joffener quoting Lareina? Coincidence? This bozo is more talkative than politeness dictates. Reason? Director of what operation exactly?*

****

Back at his hotel, he'd showered and packed. He'd get to eating at some point. Right now he had a killer headache. That and he was anxious to get back to New York. It may be a big city, but thanks to soldier-boy, he was certain he'd find Lareina in it.

He turned on the news...and smiled. "Well hello, Mio Dia Yukiyo," he said to the replay of the shooting. "You're looking well and precarious for someone who should be dead."

He cut the sound up.

An hour and a half later, Christian stretched across his hotel bed, relaxed and in much less of a hurry. He ordered room service, intending to watch a movie when it arrived. He still had a slight headache, a minor nuisance, nothing more. His research had been profitable. The news of

Mio Jun Kaori, Yukiyo's daddy, no doubt caused the Japanese ghost to have her little meltdown. *Right there on public television. Got her fifteen minutes of fame. I hope her mommy saw it.*

The two stooges with her and the big mysterious sniper proved it had been a family outing. The last question was why. And the answer was sweet.

The guest list for the United People Conference had a familiar name on it. A name that meant something to Lareina. A name that meant something to him. Lareina was after Jeri. She had to be. Christian hoped to God she found him.

He had eyes on Jeri ever since he discovered their old ambitious friend had been copying his files. If that wasn't nice enough, Jeri was giving a lecture in a few weeks, right here at the Library of Congress. It would be simple enough to plant a tracker on him. Headache or not, Christian was going to sleep good tonight. In the morning, he'd move into a company house. He'd be staying in the DC area longer than he originally planned; he might as well get comfortable.

****

They drove. Other than to ditch the van, collect their things and for Silas to give Yukiyo a sedative, the group did not stop. They were going to set up shop in DC.

Chapter 14

From Massachusetts to Maryland, Kaiden, Fisher and Silas made the eight hour trip in six. The safe house was blocks from the Capitol, the Smithsonian, and luckily, the Library of Congress. A four-story Harlem-style brownstone with four rooms and a bath on each of the three upper floors. Kaiden, Fisher and Orion slept on the second floor. Alec chose a room down the hall from Lareina's spacious third-floor bedroom. Yukiyo, still unconscious, had been placed across the hall. Silas commandeered the entire top level. Even so, there remained plenty of space for the rebels to live and train. Training never ceased.

****

"I'm sorry." Yukiyo's voice was small. Her disheveled hair was growing uneven. She looked frail and worn despite the fact Silas had kept her drugged and asleep for close to twenty hours.

Everyone gathered in the spacious kitchen where Fisher made a mountain of pancakes. She stood in the doorway of the unfamiliar room, hating herself and all of them. She knew she screwed up, but one apology was all she was capable of. Because of her, they didn't pick up Jericho Parks, but she wasn't sorry for shooting DoP minions. She'd do that again in a heartbeat. In fact, she didn't have to wonder. From now on, she was on the lookout for the DoP. They all had to die. If anybody staring at her had an issue with it, they could go to hell. She'd send them there herself.

She held herself stiffly.

"Come on in, honey." Lareina indicated the chair across from her. "We saw the news. We're the ones who are sorry."

There was something soothing in her mentor's quiet tone, but Yukiyo wasn't sure she wanted to be soothed. She took a seat close to the door.

Fisher put a stack of hotcakes in front of her.

Alec reached over with the bottle of syrup. He poured and didn't stop pouring until it dripped over the side of the plate. "Few weeks ago I would have done the same thing. No idea where mom was. If I saw her on the news, they would all be gone. Anyone that moved."

Yukiyo wasn't prepared for the understanding; the lack of condemnation. They didn't seem to care that she messed up the mission and killed two, three...she didn't know how many people she killed. Hopefully all of them. "It was that, but it was more."

"I figured out the 'more' too." Silas reached over to her plate, but it wasn't to offer anything. He used his fork to stab the top two pancakes and place them on his empty one.

"It's amazing you figured it out so fast," Lareina said, "especially given the circumstances."

Yukiyo didn't feel better. She couldn't feel better; her father was dead. But, she did feel...something.

"Figured out what?" Fisher put a platter down with enough pancakes for everyone.

Silas helped himself to three more.

"It wasn't an accident," Lareina stated.

Orion barely contributed to any breakfast conversation. His eyes were glossed over and his main focus was sleep and how to get more of it. "Was it Deverell?" he mumbled, making an effort for Yukiyo's sake.

"I don't know. I don't think so. My gut instinct tells me it wasn't him, but it's still something I'm going to check out."

Lareina's statement stilled something within Yukiyo. Her dad mattered to someone other than her. Now, she could be grateful. Sad, but grateful. She noticed everyone eating and picked up her fork.

"Thanks," she said to Alec and Orion (the latter blinked up at her before letting his head fall forward). She cut her eyes briefly toward Silas, innately knowing, somehow he saved her.

****

Lareina figured she might as well get straight to the point. What did you do?

Most recently: Took a piss. Anything further back requires specifics. Care to elaborate?

Am I picking up a note of joviality?

What if you are?

It would be a clear indication you've participated in ruining someone's life.

You break my heart with your unfounded accusations.

You don't have a heart.

No, I don't. I gave it away.

Pity you.

She waited for him to comment.

He waited for her to elaborate.

Her ability to wait was longer than his.

Do you want to know who I gave it to?

No.

I may tell you anyway.

I won't listen. Your good mood has me concerned.

Why don't you tell me what you think I did?

To tell or not to tell? We could go on all night with this. Did you give the order for Wyoming?

Why would I want to kill a dead girl's father? Would that somehow affect you?

Hmm. How to answer? Affect me? No. Are you trying to affect me?

Not my style. Aren't you supposed to be blackmailing me or something?

She knew it. He didn't do it. Or something.

How's that going to work when I get around to calling your bluff?

Who says I'm bluffing?

I do.

You have been known to be wrong upon occasion.

No, I haven't. What are your plans after you betray me? I'll still have a lot of family members to retaliate with.

Damn you Eugene. Don't you dare call my bluff. You wouldn't. Besides, you won't be able to retaliate from prison.

After a moment of no activity, the next message popped up. Prisons don't hold people like me. Besides, it's not as lonely as you think in Texas.

I am aware. For the moment, I'm the only one who is. Don't force my hand. I don't want you to.

I have no intention of forcing your hand. It would be an inconvenience.

She smacked the air where the back of his head should be. For her to expose the people in Texas, one being his younger brother; the man who fed the Revolutionaries intel; intel he acquired from Eugene. The man who was supposed to have died in a government sting; a sting Eugene himself led and later identified the remains of his dead brother... an inconvenience. Well good. No worries then.

What did you take from my house?

Ah ha. I almost forgot about that. You keep thinking I have something of yours and we'll all sleep easier. Me? Nothing. I haven't been to your house recently.

You'll be there soon enough.

So you say.

So I know.

Hmmm.

I'll see you soon.

You do that. Damn it. "What do you know that I'm not going to be happy about?" she mused aloud. Without saying, he gave her a reprieve. And, he hadn't executed Yukiyo's father. It was more than she'd expected.

****

Yukiyo couldn't be recognized in her dark, shoulder-length wig as she weaved through the crowd. Street vendors hawking t-shirts and souvenirs called out their bargains while ticket scalpers offered deals on the upcoming MIC Center events.

Inside the Library of Congress, a more dignified crowd milled about, discussing the conflict and the tremendous effort on the part of the United People Organization to end such uncalled for violence.

"Are you freaking kidding me?" Yukiyo spoke into her mouthpiece.

"People are actually interested in this crap?"

From his perch, Silas answered. "United People are a serious force. Everybody wants the war to end. They speak the loudest."

"It's bothersome that Jeri is a spokesman," Lareina said from her vantage point, this time, alone. "It's a conflict of interest. Working for the government and speaking out against the war."

"I'd think the government would appreciate it," Kaiden chimed in. "Makes them look all good doesn't it? Gives the impression they wouldn't off people for the hell of it."

"With somebody like Jeri, it could be risky," Lareina answered.

"That's what we're counting on," Silas reminded her.

Neither Alec nor Orion contributed to the conversation. Each concentrated on his own part of the plan. They didn't have the benefit of the school setting to camouflage their youth or intent. Execution had to be accurate.

Yukiyo was focused too. In the days since her father's death, no one trained harder, practiced more or studied longer. She researched far into the night and was consistently the first one in the practice rooms.

****

The conference concluded at six. The small but elite crowd thinned out as happy people made their way to their vehicles, thrilled to have something important to discuss. The security guards were scarce. Not much need for policing this group.

Yukiyo watched everyone parade by. The dignitaries. The cult followers. The DoP patrolmen, or as she thought of them, the walking dead men. She wanted to kill them all. But they could wait, she'd get them eventually. This mission would succeed—she'd see to it. Still, she kept a running count in case the opportunity presented itself.

"Here he comes, Ori." She looked down as W. Jericho Parks, briefcase in hand, exited the men's room.

Jericho appeared to be a thin man. Long face, sunken cheeks, his eyes were jaundice-tinged; he wasn't someone who cared for daylight. He wasn't fond of exercise or healthy eating, preferring to divide his time between his computer screen and his superiors. His overindulgence in artery-cloggers and preservatives had not overtly manifested itself as of yet. As long as he wore loose fitting clothing, he appeared to be a thin man.

"Pardon me, Mr. Parks, sir." Clean-cut, wholesome looking Orion held out his right hand.

W. Jericho Parks shook it. Fan attention pleased him.

"You gave an amazing speech."

"Thank you, young man. I~"

Alec crashed into Jericho. "Hey, watch it!" He pushed his way between them. Before anyone could react, he turned back, getting right up in Jericho's face. "You got something to say? I didn't think so. Watch where you're going, old man." When he made eye contact with Orion, there was no recognition reflected there. Alec took three steps and broke into a run.

He was fast; to the entrance and out of the door in a flash of black and gold.

"Hey!" Orion pointed. "He took your wallet! I saw him."

Jericho patted his blazer pocket in escalating panic. "Hell! I've been robbed!"

The few lingering tourists divided their attention between the pair of victims and the path the thief took. No one moved or offered help.

"I saw him!" Orion matched his excitement and pitch. "There's a cop." He pointed. Falling in step with Jericho, they ran to the uniformed officer, just outside.

"Officer! Officer!" Jericho waved to the cop standing beside a grey van with its door sitting open. He had Alec by the arm.

Alec struggled, but couldn't get away.

"That's him!" Jericho rushed over with Orion on his heels. "He stole my wallet! That punk took my wallet!"

"Really," the officer said.

"Yes, sir. I have a witness. He's the one!"

Officer Fisher let go of Alec's arm. Together they grabbed Jericho and yanked him into the van. Orion heaved from behind.

"I took your phone too." Alec just wanted to point that out.

The door slammed shut and Kaiden pulled off.

****

What are your plans for tomorrow?

Lareina loved the randomness of Christian's conversations. It didn't matter that they hadn't spoken in days. Visiting a few friends. Running some errands. Shopping. Why, are you coming over?

No. I'll wait for you to get home.

It could be a while.

Or not.

Chapter 15

A quarter-cup of water startled Jericho Parks awake. It wasn't cold, but it wasn't particularly warm either. He sputtered, blinking and squinting in a futile attempt to understand. He looked around, seeing cement walls and nothing else. He was tied to a chair; the ropes were uncomfortable but not cutting. He tugged, testing his restraints.

The scraping of a second chair caused him to jump.

"Morning, Jeri." A soldier straddled a chair directly in front of him. The chipperness in his voice made a cruel contradiction to the severity of the situation. Even without the BDU pants or the rifle slung over his back, Jeri would have known he was a soldier...of the dangerous sort. Those grey eyes were made of steel and dealt in death.

Jericho looked to the place the soldier's name should have been. It was missing. He had already been afraid, but a ripple of pure fear ran down his spine. "Who are you?" His voice cracked from lack of use. "Where am I? Why are you holding me here?"

"Morning, Jeri," Silas repeated.

Jeri stared at him, incredulous that this...this...soldier person, hostage-holder, expected him to be polite. "Good morning. How do I know it is morning?"

"Because I said good morning. Don't bother asking me any more questions, okay. That's not why you're here."

"Why am I here?"

"You don't listen well, do you? That will get you dead." There was an unnerving truth in Silas' tone. "I don't have a lot of time, so you don't get to waste it. What do you know about Lareina Elliot?" He let the name sink in. "Don't forget a fucking detail."

"I don't know...anybody by that name." Silas didn't change his expression. Jericho wasn't sure if he had bothered to blink. What was evident was the soldier's disbelief. "I swear. You've got the wrong person.

I don't know any Lar...Laurie Elliot."

Silas used his thumb to scratch the side of his face. He needed a shave. "Make that your last lie."

"I'm telling you, I don't know this person."

"Let me tell you what I know," Silas said. "I'm a patient man. I'll put up with your bullshit and make you pay for it later. But, the guy behind you...on a scale of one to ten, his patience is a negative six. He's about to stick a cannon in your ear. If you tell him you don't know one more time, he'll pull the trigger and you'll be telling the truth, 'cause after that, you won't know shit."

Jericho hadn't been aware anyone else was in the room until the tip of Kaiden's 9m bumped his ear. He jumped, the ropes preventing him from actually moving. Sweat broke across his brow. Nothing prevented his whimper. "Alright! Alright. What do you want to know? We went to school together, but I haven't seen her in years."

"What do you know about her?" Silas asked. "Don't make this take all day."

"It ain't going to take all day," Kaiden said. He tapped the gun against Jericho's earlobe.

"She used to work for the administration. Doing something with the Excellence Program. You know, helping children. She got caught passing information to the Revolutionaries. She was arrested a few weeks ago."

"Now, tell me something I don't know," Silas said.

Sweat ran into Jericho's eyes. "No one's seen or heard from her. By now she's imprisoned or dead."

"You better hope not." Kaiden cocked the pistol halfway.

"If-if you t-tell me what you want, I-I-I can get it f-for you. What do you need with her? If she knew something, I-I could find out."

"Now, you're talking." Silas nodded.

Believing he found an opening for negotiations, Jericho blurted out, "I have access. I can find out anything you want to know. Y-you tell me what you want and I'll get it."

There was a short minute of silence, then the light footsteps of someone graceful moving forward; someone else Jericho did not realize was in the room. "Tsk, tsk, tsk.... Je-ri. It didn't take you three minutes to sell me out." Lareina stepped into his line of vision. "That hurts."

"Lareina!" Jericho's relief mixed with agitation. "What the hell is this about?"

Silas' hand remained at his side. He raised a finger, requesting silence.

She honored it and tension filled the space.

"Lareina? I'm serious. What is this? I'm tied up."

The silence continued.

"Lareina?"

It stretched into minutes.

Finally, Jericho got it. "I guess I'm not supposed to ask questions, even though I'm the one being kidnapped."

Silas said, "You got it just in a nick of time too. Mr. Impatient, behind you, was starting to fidget."

"I think I might pull the trigger so I can rest my hand." Kaiden pressed the weapon against Jericho's head.

Lareina leaned forward, "If you cooperate, Jeri, it will be over before you know it. We know you've been watching me. We know you've hacked my files. And we know why." She stood back, watching his eyes grow larger with each statement. "What you get to do is defend your actions. Because you're a friend you get one chance, Jeri. But only one."

Jeri swallowed and thought about his choices. Nervous energy prompted a surge of daring. "Enough Lareina. First kidnapping. Now, threats. You must be a desperate little girl. I know about your...games. I've known for a while, and yet I've never interfered or harmed you in any way. Hell, in six months, maybe less, I would have opened doors for you, seen your work come to real fruition. But this..." he managed to sneer, "is you throwing away a pot of gold with both hands. Now," the condescension was thick, "for the sake of...past friendship and your obviously needy circumstance, you can release me. We can get something to eat. You can tell me what you've done and I will do what I can to help you."

Lareina couldn't help it. She laughed. It was rich, real amusement. The sound sent warmth through the cold, stark storage unit they were using for a prison. Humor lingered around her eyes as she leaned down once again to be face to face with Jericho. Even so, there was no mistaking that she was deadly serious. "Not going to happen. I haven't begun to repay you for the harm you and Gillian have caused me—" His gasp was confirmation enough, "—The DoP isn't bothering to search for you Jeri because you're an untrustworthy piece of crap everyone is better off without. I've decided I'm not wasting another minute on you because I don't have to. This," she pointed to him in his chair, "was a courtesy. If you want something—food, bathroom, sunlight, freedom, anything of the sort—you'll have to make it worth my while to give it to you." She straightened up, turned her back on him and spoke to her crew. "Are you guys hungry? I'm starved."

The impatient assassin pocketed his gun. Jericho exhaled relief and was surprised with a gag. The soldier raised the garage-style door. Light flooded the storage unit. Spotlighting the complete contents of the space: a port-a-potty, an end table with a styrofoam container presumably containing food, beside it, a large plastic cup with condensation around the bottom, and across the room, against the back wall...an extra folding chair and W. Jericho Parks.

The three exited the unit, pulling the door down and locking it behind them.

Jericho felt as if he ceased to exist.

They were traveling in the black Oneida. "How long before he cracks?" Kaiden hit the locks and opened the driver side door.

Lareina and Silas answered in the same moment, "Two days."

"That's about what I thought."

"Hold up," Silas said when Kaiden started the engine. He studied Chronos. "He's a block and a half over."

They didn't have to ask who 'he' was. They were playing a perilous game of cat and mouse, working in DC while Christian was still in the area. Thus far, he hadn't changed his pattern or given any indication he knew they were there. However, with Christian Eugene Deverell, nothing could be taken for granted.

****

Storage unit sixty-eight was almost in the middle of the row. The facility had over a hundred separate spaces of varying size. The front office lay to the left, behind a wide parking lot. The whole thing was surrounded by a high fence. Since the war, most places were surrounded by fences.

Alec loved his job. He was king of the world. All was as it should be. The streets were quiet. He had a cheesesteak sub, a double order of fries, a whole two-liter of sprite, and best of all, a snickers candy bar. His mom stuck it in his pocket right before he left. How she managed to get a hold of such rare treats was amazing.

All channels were active on Chronos II. His rifle was locked, loaded and in position. He was the sniper for the day. For the first time, he would handle his TS13 without Silas standing over his shoulder. A half hour before anyone went near storage unit sixty-eight, he climbed the fire escape of the warehouse which stood two buildings over (the exact reason Silas picked unit sixty-eight) and set up the 'eagle's nest' so he could protect his crew.

Not that there was anything to protect them from—Alec was a realist—an old man tied to a chair, going to the bathroom on himself didn't pose a real threat. Still, he had the important post. He had a TS13. He had a snickers. He was king of the world.

When Fisher and O-Whiny went to check on Parks yesterday morning, he yelled obscenities and made mad crazy demands. Later in the afternoon, Mom took Kaiden with her. The punk had wet himself and cried for her to release him. He didn't tell her anything hugely important, but he earned a trip to the port-a-pot and a half a sandwich by telling them the DoP wasn't originally after Lareina or anything having to do with her kids. That only came up because they were investigating a leak. His own words, 'a leak', because anybody with half a brain couldn't figure out Parks was the leak. He fed Lareina to the dogs to get them off of his scent. *I won't be forgetting that.* Alec checked the sights on his TS13.

Silas and Yukiyo should be there in a minute or two. The bastard probably needed to take a crap. *That ought to be worth something.*

Alec looked out behind him. On the other side, he could make out the neighborhood where their safe house was hidden. It was a decent neighborhood. Not great, but decent; just a handful of lowlifes visible on any given day. A person with his ingenuity could set up shop and cash in. *Can't imagine getting Mom's approval for that.*

He faced front. The familiar Genuine pulled into the parking lot in front of unit sixty-eight. Alec unlocked his weapon and bit into his snickers.

****

Christian drove with his window down and his radio up. He changed his routine every three days. This was day one: If anybody was watching him, he could be counted on to do just about anything. He planned it that way.

At the light, he sent a quick text to his team leaders. Where are you?

In record time, he received two return texts: Ready and In position. *Good.* Those were the answers he expected.

****

Silas didn't know what Yukiyo had on, but he liked it. She had a way of making typically non-traditional things fit together in a way that worked for her. She wore a sleeveless dress over her jeans. He guessed the dress was supposed to be a top today. It might be a top. He'd seen her in it before. She didn't have any pants on with it, so he assumed it was a dress. Either way, it was nice. Not that he'd tell her. He wasn't telling her a damned thing.

Yukiyo was all about business. She leapt from the jeep and strolled forward purposefully. In her mind, this man, W. Jericho Parks was a direct link to her father's death. All of her feelings were going into the interrogation.

Silas was cool with it.

When he opened the unit's door, Jericho immediately turned toward the light. "I've had enough. Let me go. Please, help me."

"Help you do what?" Yukiyo said, "I ain't touching your pissy ass."

"I need help. Please. I can't take it anymore! Please."

Having secured the door, Silas came over. "It's up to you, Jeri. You know what you've got to do."

"What do I have to do? What else do you want to know?" Jericho cried. He had already been crying; no point in stopping now.

Silas opened up the spare folding chair. He straddled it, leaning forward. "Start talking and don't stop until I'm satisfied."

The scraping of the chair. The dampness of the storage unit. The intense Japanese girl. All of it, none of it. Everything. Jericho snapped. "You want me to talk. I'll talk. I'll tell you things you never knew about. Because it won't matter. Your ass is dead. All of you. Lareina too. I belong to The United People. They won't allow this. They won't tolerate this.

This is why they're taking over. The DoP can't control malcontents like you. Do you know what they do? I'll tell you what they do. The United People shuts down problems like you. Like Lareina. Do you think they'll let her get away with this? No, they won't. They've been crushing little peons for over a decade. Bit by bit, they're ending this war. And you warmongers won't stand a chance. They're using your own weapons against you. No. They're using Lareina's weapons against everybody. The Department of Protection & Peace doesn't have a chance. They think they do but they don't~"

Silas knew an opportunity. "What about the Revolutionaries. They can stop~"

"Please." Jeri made a disgusted face. "This time next year, the Revolutionaries won't exist. We've been wiping them out so fast; they don't know what's happening. They blame the DoP. The DoP blame them. Everybody takes credit, but it's the United People getting the work done. Go ahead, ask me questions. I'll tell you anything you want to know. None of it will make a difference. The United People won't stand for this."

"Can we move this along?" Yukiyo checked the time. "I have things."

"Yes. Yes, move this along," Jericho ranted. "You can take my life and hold me here for as long as you like, but now that I'm willing to cooperate, you want to rush me. Go ahead. It won't save you. Nothing will save you."

"You either," Silas mumbled to himself. "Why'd you pick Lareina? What made you think she was someone worth looking into?"

"Lareina Elliot. Apparently, you don't know who you're working with." Jericho sniffed. "Do you have any food with you?"

"Of course, I do." With an easy grace, Silas went to the back of Jericho's chair and deftly released the knots. It was far from the truth, but the soldier seemed unconcerned with Jericho making a grab at him or anything that may be used for a weapon. He had four reasons for his projected complacency.

First: Jericho had already tried it once, taking a swing at Orion. Ori had been expecting it. He ducked and came up with his pistol in hand; the barrel wedged in the crook of Jericho's neck. A half beat later, Fisher lodged his 9mm into the hollow of his cheek. They adequately dissuaded him from that course of action.

Second: Yukiyo was faster than Orion and Fisher. She'd nail him for twitching in the wrong direction. Silas didn't have a doubt about her.

Third: Jericho didn't own a bone. He may have thought he could overpower a kid, but in reality, Jeri was not brave.

And finally, he was Silas McKade. Enough said.

Yukiyo tossed a small bag to Jericho. A turkey sandwich, chips, a bottled drink and an apple. Jericho tore into his meal as if he'd been starved; which was somewhat true. The food was enough to entice Jericho into full cooperation. He talked as he ate. "You'd have to be an idiot not to keep tabs on Lareina. They don't have charts for her level of intelligence. MmmMmm. This is good. Did you make this?" he asked Yukiyo.

"With my own two hands." She faked smiled and genuinely frowned.

He shoved a handful of chips into his mouth, uncaring of her attitude. "The DoP is in fact, made up entirely of idiots. But, I've always had an eye on Lareina. Trained her. Chris too. Deverell. You don't know him. Believe me, you don't want to. I created a monster with that one. It's suicidal to make him your enemy." He took a swig of juice. "A note-to-self, for you." Two more bites of his sandwich. "If they wanted, they could probably take over and end this damned conflict. That's how good I made them...and how much information they could access between them." He had a few bites left. He slowed down, wanting to make them last. "If I told them everything...boy...I'm telling you, there wouldn't be anything left."

"What do you know that they don't?"

Jericho gulped half the bottle. "Lareina is the good one, Chris is dangerous, and I'm...I am the smart one—"

One out of three. Shows what you know. Notta.

"—I knew there had to be something better and they would get me there. Voilà, they did." The sandwich was gone. The apple was next. "I'm the one with the real contacts. The real power. Those people don't know who has the real power, but I do."

"You do?"

"Yes. I do." Jericho tried to look down his nose and smushed it against his apple.

Chapter 16

"Oh shit! Y'all better move."

That was Alec's way of giving a warning.

"What's out there?" Silas talked into the undetectable microphone concealed in his bird-of-prey necklace.

"Four squad cars and I think, one unmarked. Coming up on the gates."

Yukiyo and Silas locked eyes. Her gaze shifted from Silas to Jericho and back, her brow arched in a way that plainly asked, 'should we take him?'

Silas got up, slammed Jericho into his chair and looped the rope over his hands, tightening the knot.

Yukiyo assumed that meant no. Eager to help, she gagged their hostage, pulling the cloth tight enough to cut his mouth across the corners. With Jericho wiggling and grunting in the background, they flattened themselves against the wall beside the garage opener.

"Oh shit!" Following the sounds of sirens, Alec cast a glance behind him. He saw a train of flashing lights headed toward the house. There was no explanation for how he knew, but he wasn't wrong. He didn't have time to be wrong.

He was on channel with everybody, but he only cared about one person. "MOM! Get the hell out of there!"

"I'm already out. Kaiden, do you copy?" The serenity in her voice, the complete calm in her tone stilled Alec's rising panic.

"Dammit," Kaiden said.

If Kaiden was on the move, Lareina didn't have to worry about Fisher. Silas would see to Yukiyo. She needed to hear from her other child. "Orion?"

"Packed!"

"We got him."

The two spoke at once. Kaiden's impatient attitude nearly blanketed Orion's excited pitch.

"Good." Putting her attention where she needed it, she said, "Do what you have to do, baby. I'm on my way."

Alec never doubted it. His job was protecting Silas and Yukiyo. He had work to do. "Like I said, y'all better move. Front gate is bottled up; back gate is going to be a pain in the ass. If you don't hit it right now, you'll have to make your own exit through the fence."

****

Silas didn't need to be told again. Sliding the door up, he glanced left and right, moving with animal-like stealth as he led the way to the Genuine. The top was down. That could be problematic, but he had confidence in Alec. Less than ten paces put him in. Yukiyo's door slammed shut and he turned the key.

Rapid fire echoed to his left. He drove toward the sound. His confidence in Alec was well placed. The kid was clearing a path for him.

****

Christian lowered his binoculars and smiled. He found what he'd been searching for.

****

Two patrol cars at the back gate. Two officers down, a third wounded. Alec was a natural. "Good job, kid." Silas skidded around one of the cars and out the gate. He swerved first right and then left. Almost casually, he threw his arm around Yukiyo and slammed her head down across his lap.

Yukiyo didn't ask why. She didn't yell or complain. She could hear for herself, the shower of bullets spraying the air where her head had been.

****

"'ELLLLLLP!!!!!! MMMMMM!!!! ELLLLLP MMMM!!!!!" Jericho tried to yell. He bounced in his seat, hoping to gain attention. Three DoP officers converged on the unit. Jericho wet himself again, from sheer relief.

"Mr. Deverell, sir." The ranking officer used his two-way.

"What do you have?" Christian spoke low, not willing to give away his location.

"We've found the hostage, sir."

"Alive?"

"Affirmative, sir."

"Green warehouse. Second building. Fire escape. Bring him here." By the time they arrived with Parks, McKade would be done breathing. He would see to that. *Hell.* Christian's good mood suddenly evaporated. He had been slightly concerned when he couldn't locate the vehicle McKade would use to escape. Now, he knew why. He didn't recognize the RX8, but there was no mistaking the driver. *Hell.* This was the last damned place he wanted Lareina. He gave unit two special instruction regarding her. Somebody's ass was fried.

Christian watched Alec skipping down the fire escape; rifle over his shoulder, two-liter drink under his arm. *Cocky little punk.* He didn't know Alec personally, but he was certain his description was accurate. It grated him that it wasn't the cocky little punk he was waiting for. It didn't matter. This one was obviously extra special to Lareina. *Reason enough to kill him.* He slid his gun free. "Stop right there you little bastard."

Alec did.

Christian could see the intelligence in those dark eyes. *The little shit is debating it.* "You move. You die." Gut instinct prompted him to add, "And Lareina gets to watch."

Now, Alec obeyed.

"Climb down off that last step and put your hands up. You blink in the wrong direction and I will personally hand her the pieces."

Alec didn't answer. He was thinking.

"Leave him alone, Eugene."

Together Christian and Alec watched her approach. This was no place for a lady.

Only Lareina would stroll down a blind, back alley, toward a loaded weapon, wearing stilettos. Christian couldn't remember a day when she didn't look good. He'd never admit it, but he'd been agonizing over her since the hospital. He had been worried. Hell, he missed her. And there she was: green top—too low in the front, dark jeans—as tight as can be, dangly earrings, glossy lips, an arm full of bangles, and those damned sexy-ass stilettos.

Armed with an air of supreme poise, Lareina came forth. "Get in the car, honey." She ruffled Alec's hair but didn't stop until she stood directly in front of Christian. His gun was less than three inches from her heart.

Alec hadn't moved. She hadn't expected him to, but it was worth a try. No matter. Now, that she was there, he was safe enough.

"What are you doing here, Lareina?" Christian lowered his weapon.

"Getting my child. What's it look like?" She had the nerve to grin. "How did you find us?"

He arched an eyebrow at her and cast a speculative glance at Alec, exaggerating the act long enough to make sure she noted it before he let the topic go. "What did you want with Jeri?"

"Jeri's a bastard."

"No shit, Sherlock. Tell me something I don't know."

"It was news to me. That M-F'er has been stealing my files. He sold me out. It seemed prudent to find out some particulars."

"It wasn't to the government because you're a criminal?"

She pursed her lips at him.

Not the government. Then who? Something started to click, but Christian couldn't finger it. "You know I'm taking you in, right?"

"You can't. Not today anyway."

"Why not today?" He could hear them coming.

So could she. "Because my son can't drive."

"Yes, I can." If they wanted to pretend this was normal, Alec was cool with it.

Lareina glanced at him, affectionately. "Not legally."

He gave an indignant huff. "Because that matters."

"Lareina." Christian didn't have time for this shit.

"Christian. I'm getting my child out of here." There was no mistaking the resolution in her tone. "If you want to shoot me, you'll have to do it in the back."

He leveled her a mean look.

"Mr. Deverell, sir." An officer came into view. Two others followed him escorting Jericho Parks.

"That's her!" Jericho pointed. "That's her! She did it. She's responsible. I want to press full charges! She was behind it all!"

His outburst made up Christian's mind. He raised his weapon and unloaded three caps. Like dominoes, the DoP's went down one after the other. Jericho screamed. He fell to his knees and covered his head. Christian studied Lareina. "Three days."

He watched her eyes dart to the left in that telltale manner.

"I need at least a week." Urgency caused her voice to rise.

"You're only getting three days." He was in no mood to bend. Three soldiers lay dead. He had compromised enough.

"Fine. I've got to go."

One hand extended, gun still pointed toward Jericho, in the event he attempted to run, with his other, Christian grabbed Lareina's arm, pulling her to him. He put every ounce of his frustration into his kiss. It was either that or break her neck. And he was strongly contemplating the latter.

Lareina allowed it. She wanted, craved his touch as much as he craved hers. Theirs was a dance with the devil; irresistible and impossible. The tangles had become knots and he only gave her three days. It wasn't enough. She could hardly wait.

The kiss ended, but the intensity remained. He sighed, letting the heat recede.

She whispered, "I have a pretty long to-do list, Christian. Unfortunately, you're not on it."

He licked the corner of her mouth, matching her tone. "I am the list."

She pressed her cheek against his lips. "Well, you're not getting done tonight."

"Don't fool yourself, Lareina," he said. "I am going to have you."

The absolute authority rippling through the huskiness in his voice made her nerves tingle with anticipation. It was a future fact. The next time, they wouldn't be in the middle of a shootout. There would be no high emotions or weak moments to blame it on. It would be intentional. It would be permanent.

Summoning strength he didn't like to utilize, Christian pulled back an inch, tugging on her bottom lip a moment longer. "Don't stop." His eyes were serious.

"Be careful." Her eyes were worried.

With nothing more to say, she turned, moving away as fast as her stilettos would allow. Alec fell into step beside her. They were to the car, backing out and pulling into traffic when they heard a noise. It sounded like a gunshot.

Chapter 17

Christian watched her walk away. Even Jericho's simpering did not distract him. He thought Lareina needed Jeri's help. She wanted him to work for her cause—whatever the hell that was. But that wasn't it. It would have been easier if that had been the case. It would have at least made sense, but, no, she'd been wronged by Jeri. Jeri was a piece of shit. But, what was Lareina to him? "Get up Jeri." Christian raked his eyes over his former friend. It wasn't a pretty sight but he'd seen worse.

Jericho's knees were wobbly. Relief and anxiety jumbled his speech. "Th-thank me~you. Thank you Ch-Chris. I thought...I thought she was going to kill you~me. I thought *you* were going to kill me...I-I-I don't know w-what's going on. What's happening?"

"Chris?" He frowned at the moniker. "I am going to kill you."

Jericho gasped then turned it into a deep calming breath. He believed, in spite of the circumstances, Christian was showing humor.

"What's this about?"

"Lareina is dangerous. She's no good to me~to anyone." Another deep breath and Jericho managed to step forward. "I'm glad you got her. I told Commander Joffener she was the leak. Did you know you had a leak in your department? She was passing information to the Revolutionaries. If she could get out from that—which she can't—I'll see to that. Kidnapping me...well, there's no mercy. We can tie everything up and be... done..." He stopped. The scene registered. Lareina wasn't there. His DoP escort lay dead behind him. It wasn't right. "Chris?"

"My name isn't Chris."

Jericho swallowed bile. "You call me Jeri." He studied Christian's gun; the way he held it, leisurely, loose, almost as if he'd forgotten it was in his hand.

"That's because you think we're friends."

"We are friends. We've been friends for years. Since school."

"You, me and Lareina. Lareina was supposed to be your friend."

"I thought so too...until she did this to me." He searched Christian's face for sympathy, understanding. He found none.

"No, you didn't. You set her up. Why did you pick Lareina to fuck with Jeri? You knew how that would go over with me."

Jericho weighed his options and realized he did not have any.

"How long you breathe will be determined by how fast you talk." Christian crossed his arms. He had things to do and standing in a dank alley was starting to get boring.

Jericho had one chance. Intrigue. It drew them together. It was the basis of their friendship. He leapt on it. "I work for some people."

"Don't we all?"

"Some big people. People who can do what the government cannot."

Christian arched an eyebrow. "Revolutionaries?"

"Those idiots? Their big dream is to send us back a half century. No, Chris. Not the Revolutionaries. The Revs are pawns. There's no war without pawns."

"You're working for someone the government doesn't know about?"

"Call it a better government."

"Siphoning our files is your way of contributing?"

Jericho gave a short pause. Christian's knowledge impressed him. He had been nearly undetectable. However, this could work for his benefit. "One of my many ways of contributing. This is a big thing, Chris. You're loyal to the losing side. We can change that."

"My loyalties or my side?"

"Same difference." Jeri nodded, agreeing with himself. Intrigue. With Chris, it was a sure bet.

"Was Lareina on to you? Is that why you gave her up?"

"It wasn't quite like that. I wasn't given a choice. Lareina was doing something dicey. She was undermining everything. The administration, my people, probably the Revolutionaries. She was siphoning talent, the best talent. I was watching, trying to find them but...but I made a mistake. When they started investigating...I...I thought it prudent and useful to put an end to her meddling." Before Christian could respond, he added, "I wasn't worried. I knew between the two of us, we'd protect her. She wouldn't get into any real trouble. I had it under control. If I couldn't, you would have saved her. She should have known that. She should have known."

Christian smiled. "She knows."

Sensing a victory, Jericho said, "Yes, she does. There was no call for this nonsense. She may have jeopardized an important mission."

"She's human, Jeri," Christian said. "We all make mistakes. Take you for example. You should have known I would kill you for fucking with Lareina. You should have known."

Jericho tensed, waiting for the shot that would end his life.

Contrary to his words, Christian did not shoot. He walked forward, bending over the nearest cadaver. Officer Bregget. *Pity. I liked him.* Christian helped himself to Bregget's handcuffs and slapped them on Jericho.

Surprised to still be alive, Jericho let himself be cuffed without a struggle. "Where are we going?" he asked when Christian nudged him and they started walking.

"I'm not done with you, Jeri, but I have a mess to clean up. So we're going to put you someplace safe until we can finish this discussion."

"Oh. Safe. Good." Jericho was alright with that. Jericho was alright with anything that kept him breathing. "Can I get cleaned up? Maybe something to eat?"

"Of course, you can." They stopped at Christian's car.

Jeri waited for him to open the door. "You can take these cuffs off, Chris. I'm not going anywhere. I'm on your side."

Christian opened his trunk. "You're damned right you aren't going anywhere." He shoved him in. "I don't have a gag. If I have to silence you, I'll do it with this." He waved his gun once. Once was enough. Jericho Parks was smart enough to know Christian was telling the absolute truth.

The trunk closed and Jericho was left thinking he was better off as Lareina's hostage than Christian's.

****

"Okay. What was that?"

Lareina cut Alec a sly glance. She wondered when he would start. "What was what?"

"Mom."

"That was me saving your butt. Christian was pissed. I'd rather not give him someone I care about as a stress reliever. Okay."

"Probably thought Silas was the sniper."

"Probably."

"But that's not my question. What are you doing in three days? 'Cause you can't go to him."

It was impossible not to laugh. He somehow made impertinence a desirable quality. "Whose father are you?"

"Yours while you need one. You still haven't explained what all that was about anyway," Alec replied.

"I've got to tell him what we're up to."

"Says who?"

"Honey, I do."

"Why?"

"Oh, he had us. Wrapped up tighter than you know. He knew where we were staying. Where Jeri was hidden. He had us. Think about it, he could have gotten us at three in the morning. He could have snatched Jeri anytime he pleased. But he didn't. He wanted us scattered, so I would have a better chance of getting away. He did that for me. I bet you're right about him stalking Silas. I don't know what he would have done with you, but he let us go. Possibly jeopardizing himself. That comes with a high price tag, baby. If I don't pay it, the next time, and believe me, with Christian, there will definitely be a next time, he won't be so nice."

"Pfffph." Alec rolled his eyes. "What's he going to do?"

"I shudder to think." Lareina became quiet as the possibilities crept through her brain. She knew how he would react. Her lack of cooperation at this point would be nothing short of betrayal. Even if she could contemplate betraying him and leaving him to his fate, it wouldn't end well. It would lead to their own personal war, with a lot of people being caught in the middle. By her own actions, she told him precisely which person would be his best weapon against her. She wouldn't allow that to happen. She would do whatever he wanted. And, they both knew it.

"You give him too much credit. How do you know he'll find us again?"

She smiled at him and rubbed his hair, enjoying his ego-laced innocence. "We can't hide forever, we wouldn't get anything done. Even if we could, he would find us because he always finds us."

"That's not an answer."

"Sure it is. He's found us so far hasn't he? A week...a month...he'll find us. He'll never quit, baby."

"That's partly because you keep in contact with him." There was a note of accusation in his tone.

Lareina ignored it. "Yes, yes I do. If we get caught, we have to fall into his hands. He's the only chance we have."

"Why not get him on our side? He must like you since he keeps saving you and all." He didn't mention the kissing.

"I tried." She turned left and applied a little more gas.

"And?"

"Christian lets his feelings blind him to the facts. He thinks the Rev's took something from him, and he's not willing to admit they may be a better option than the government. He won't turn me in himself, but he doesn't understand. I'm guessing his ideal solution would be to lock me in a tower somewhere," she chuckled.

Alec thought about this for a long minute, his brow drawn in concentration. "On the one side, he's getting in the way, but on the other, you're keeping him close in case you need him. You know, those two plans aren't compatible."

"Now, you understand why he's a pain in my butt."

"What are you going to tell him when we meet him in three days?"

"We? What's this 'we'? *We* are not meeting him in three days. *I* am meeting him alone."

"Pfffph."

"We're not having this conversation. You are not going anywhere near that man."

"I won't if you don't."

****

If it was important, it was assumed to be in one of the cars, everything else was expendable. Kaiden, Fisher and Orion left the house, grabbing only what was within their reach at the time of the warning. They were in the Oneida and backing out of the drive when the police turned on their street.

People ran every which way, trying to see and not be seen. Kaiden gunned it. They cleared the next block before it could be closed off. Several cruisers pursued them while patrolmen searched the house.

From his position at shotgun, Fisher aimed at the lead car, stopping it from following them. On the other side, Orion did his part, taking out the tires of the next car to come within range.

They hit the fourth block and Kaiden spoke into his mouthpiece. "We got three riding our ass, but we're clear."

"I'd do something about that if I were you," came Silas' calm reply. He too was being chased, but only Yukiyo knew it. "'Reina where are you?"

"Alec and I are doing the speed limit, because we can," she taunted.

"Because she won't let me drive," Alec said.

"Not a chance," she told him. To the others, she said, "We're not being chased because we're that good."

"I don't need to know if you're good," Silas said. "I need to know if you're clear."

"Yesss, Silasss. We're clear."

"Thank you."

There were ten seconds of silence.

BOOM!

The explosion could be heard for miles in every direction.

They knew Silas had the house rigged, but it was unnerving to realize, evidently, they were living in an extremely large bomb.

"Damn, Silas." Fisher stopped firing, momentarily distracted by the flames and the dark billowing cloud of smoke in his direct line of vision.

"Don't blame me. Most of that came from Orion."

Orion shrugged. "It was a big house, hard to guess." In the same manner Alec had taken to Chronos and the possibilities of advanced computer magic, Orion had attached himself to Silas' chemistry set. The result being, all manner of chemical warfare and explosives came at the hands of the monkey-king. "Slurries are cool." He grinned at the smoke cloud.

****

The explosion served its purpose. The brownstone was gone, as were two houses on either side of it. Severe damage had been done to many others. Across the street, the fronts of several homes were missing. It did not end there. Cars were totaled. People lay bleeding or dead. Fires burned out of control, adding to the destruction.

"You are some kind of freak of nature." Yukiyo sat low in her seat, hanging on while Silas weaved through the city, leading the cops through his own personal maze.

"You know you like it."

Unsure of his meaning, she chose not to answer.

"Reach down under your seat and grab that brown box."

Her expression didn't change while she did as he asked. She opened the case and saw a half dozen hand grenades. "How many do you want?"

He cocked his head at her. "Do you want to do it?"

The idea brought a reluctant smile to her hesitant lips.

"Do you?"

She nodded once, a thrill brightening her eyes.

"Hold it this way." He demonstrated while taking them around a hairpin turn that shouldn't have been. "When you pull the pin, pull it back like this...you don't want the grenade coming toward you."

"Okay."

"When you throw it, the only rule is, do it in under four seconds."

That struck her as funny for some reason. "I'll do it in two. Where am I aiming?"

"Anywhere you want, sweetheart."

The grenade bounced off the hood of the lead car following them. Not knowing what it was, the driver kept moving and drove over it. It was directly under the muffler when it exploded. The car behind it wasn't spared.

"Whoooooooaaa!!!" Something broke free in Yukiyo. It wasn't murder. They were DoP—the bastards who killed her father—not real people. Silas hit another corner. She held on, giggling like she was on an amusement park ride. "I want to do another one!"

"You are some kind of freak of nature," Silas echoed her earlier comment.

A bubble of happy laughter escaped Yukiyo as she tossed a second hand grenade.

Chapter 18

"Like it or not. That's the plan." Lareina folded her arms tight. There would be no further debate.

Kaiden threw his hands in the air. "You should have told us to leave you at the hospital. Save everybody some trouble!"

Lareina cut him a hard glare. "I didn't have my phone on me." Kaiden wasn't into reasoning at the moment. Neither was she. The team reunited in Phoenix, North Carolina, some six hours after the raid. They arrived by different routes with no one chasing any of them that far. They weren't at a safe house, but a lavish vacation home belonging to Lareina and Kaiden's Uncle Moe. Moe had been a Mafia linchpin; the house was secure—no one would be able to sneak up on them. There was plenty of space— everybody needed a break. Moe had a collection of cars—Kaiden and Silas would need new ones. And most importantly, it was just a half hour from the cabin Christian built on Lareina's Lake Waccamaw property. It belonged to both of them. Alec had been told how to get there, but warned never to go unless Lareina was dead. The same information had been passed on to one other child. No one else knew of the cabin's existence. It was the only truly safe place in the world for either of them. He would be expecting her. She didn't need a tracker to know where he was heading. It was for such a time as this, the cabin had been built.

"We got each other's backs," Orion said. "Somebody *has* to go with you." The thing about Orion was that was exactly the way he saw it. Loyalty meant loyalty.

She loved her kids, every one of them, but she would not jeopardize Christian's life or Alec's future by disclosing the cabin's location. "But you can't." Lareina had already said this once or twice or ten times. "He can't, he can't, she can't, he can't, and definitely not him." She pointed to each person, ending with Silas. "You can't. It would be different if I were in danger~"

"You might be~"

"I'm not," she talked over Fisher. "But your company would put me at a grave disadvantage."

Yukiyo's arched eyebrows prompted her to repeat, "Christian would use you as a weapon against me. Silas is supposed to be in Canada on assignment. He can't be seen."

"You say that like I can be seen."

There was no environment Silas wasn't comfortably cocky in.

"If we put Silas and Christian in the same room," Lareina said, "one of them is going to end up dead."

"Him." Silas didn't deny it.

"I need you both, so stay the hell away from me while he and I are talking."

Silas shook his head at her lack of understanding. "I'm not your problem. I don't give a shit what you and Eugene do. I know he's not going to hurt you. If he did, I know how to find him. Hell, you ain't going nowhere I can't get to. If these babies can't do without their mommy for a damn day, send them to daycare."

Lareina wanted to laugh, but that would no doubt piss them all off. Instead, she used his speech to her advantage. "Well good. If you're not worried, I can't imagine why anybody else should be."

"He ain't your brother."

"He ain't your son."

Alec and Kaiden spoke in the same moment, using the same tone. Kaiden tugged on his earring.

"I'm both and more," Silas snapped. He clarified his point. "I'm not worried about Deverell. I'm worried about what you're going to tell him."

Lareina was honest. "I have to tell him...a lot."

They locked eyes—the mastermind and the assassin. Anything in the wrong hands could get them killed. She wanted to give up 'a lot.' They both knew Christian would protect her with his life; he already had. But, what would he do for the rest of them? Lareina trusted him. Silas did not.

She knew his thoughts. She'd had most of the drive to dwell on it. She'd been thorough with the cost/profit ratio. Silas was going to have to trust her, and she was going to have to trust Christian...and have a backup plan, just in case. "Silas." There was a quiet confidence in her voice. "Have you been keeping up with Marcus Mitchell? That guy in Texas."

Silas didn't understand the sudden change of topic, but she'd tell him soon enough. "Deverell doesn't talk to him often. Two or three times a month, max. I haven't listened to the conversations, but I can."

"You don't need to." She waved him off. "But secure that connection and don't ever lose it." That was all she would say. That was enough. Silas recognized it as insurance of some sort. A hidden ace if they needed it.

"Will it be enough?"

Lareina thought about what Christian would do if he knew she was using his biggest secret as bait. For Silas, no less. He'd put a bullet in her head. That's what he'd do. "If it's not enough, God help us because not even you will be able to save me."

Her level of sincerity was enough to convince Silas. "That's some scary shit." As far as he knew, there wasn't anything he couldn't save her from.

Alec knew when to interrupt. "Silas can't save you, but we're supposed to sit here and let you go off with him alone? What sense does that make?"

Rather than answer, Lareina hugged him to her. "Here's your assignment, Silas. Keep this one out of the mix. Christian already knows he's a sore spot."

"I got him. The little shit ain't going nowhere."

Alec huffed.

Silas huffed, imitating him.

"Fisher, I'm putting you on Orion."

"If you say so, boss." Fisher studied Orion, wondering how soon he should tie him down.

"I'm not doing anything!" Orion caught that look and moved to the other side of the room.

"Uh huh," Lareina said. "You're not doing anything at the moment, but according to you, somebody *has* to go with me. According to me, it won't be you."

His stern look told her that he strongly disagreed.

"Kaid."

"Ain't no *Kaid* nothing. No. I am going with you."

"I know," Lareina conceded.

"What?"

"Huh?"

"What?"

"Why?"

Kaiden and Silas remained silent. It wasn't that simple. Lareina wouldn't have wasted an hour arguing if it were going to be that simple.

"You can drive me to a neutral meeting place. Christian knows you, he knows what to expect. You can deliver me to him, spew all kinds of threats, throw a punch at him for blowing up your garage—he owes you that—then, once you are assured of my safety, you can get the hell out of dodge. That's my deal. Take it or I'll have Silas restrain you too."

His focus went precisely where she wanted it. Kaiden looked directly at Silas. "Try it and I will lay your punk-ass out."

Silas grinned. "I'm a soldier. I always follow orders."

Alec wasn't having it. "How come he can go but I can't?"

Neither was Orion. "Why can't I go?"

"Because, I can't trust either one of you to leave when you're supposed to. Also, I am not letting Christian get anywhere near you. We're not having another round of this. Yukiyo." She shut off further protests. "I have an assignment for you."

"What is it?" Unlike the boys, Yukiyo had no intention of going anywhere near Deverell.

"Get working on Gillian Foster. We're only going to be here a few days. While we're relocating, I'd like you and Kaiden to bring her by for a visit."

"Kaiden and Yukiyo? That's an odd combination." Silas' words were slow and measured.

"Yukiyo can identify her, but I'm not sending her off on her own. You'll be busy, and Kaiden's a better driver anyway," she teased.

"Ah-ha," Kaiden mocked, enjoying the one-up on Silas.

Silas ignored him but cocked a brow at Lareina. She had another reason, he was certain of it.

****

Latest intel reports enough finding to substantiate an investigation.

Possible Revolutionary HQ located in Seattle Washington.

A dozen more embedded micro-trackers are set to go live.

And why did he need to care?

Meetings were hell. Reports were hell. Life was hell. *Lareina had better make this shit worthwhile.* That singular thought looped through Christian's brain. Everything he thought, said or did, began and ended with his rendezvous with her.

It wasn't often, but there were a few times he was called to account for his actions. A bombing in DC happened to be one of them. Dozens injured, dead DoP soldiers, missing hostage; this was worse than the mess she made at the hospital. He was going to let her know—in great detail—how much trouble she caused.

And now, he was being watched. *Hell no.* He wasn't worried about being followed. Commander Joffener, his superior (one of few), knew better than to put a physical being on his tail. There wasn't a physical being in his department who would attempt it. It would be the same as volunteering to get murdered. Christian Deverell had a world-wide security clearance at a higher level than most world leaders. One part of his job—a part not on paper—was to determine who had outlived their usefulness. He had less than one percent accountability for these decisions. It was the part of his job he relished most.

Joffener wanted him to report his activities. He expected to be updated on Christian's progress with the Elliot-case. He wanted Christian to make it a team effort. *Hell no.* Because of his relationship with Lareina, Joffener had given him the freedom to bring her in on his own terms. But, with everything going from damn to shit to fuck, daily; Joffener was getting suspicious. Christian didn't have time for this shit.

He was agitated beyond redemption. He did the one thing that was guaranteed to make it worse...He got on Opt-In.

We need to talk.

Seeing the words—her words—soothed him. Without having to identify it, the anxiety which had been building all day, faded. She was safe. Regardless of what was to come, he had protected her. She had gotten out of there. She was safe.

Now, he could kill her. That is the plan.

There are a few things you might need to know beforehand.

There's a whole lot of shit I need to know.

No, no, no...there's a whole lot of shit you WANT to know. There's only a few you need to know. There is a difference.

Not hardly. The things I want are the things I need, the things I need are the things I get. That simple.

The sparring was nice. Right now, it was the only thing that made sense in either of their worlds.

You are simple. I'll give you that much.

Are you trying to give me a headache?

As if it requires effort. Take a pill.

Pills? It shouldn't have, but her suggestion made him suspicious. Was she giving him headaches in reality? McKade was going to die.

When are you coming home?

In three days...Or so I've been told.

You've got less time than that.

So do you. Which brings us back to my first comment. We need to talk. There are some things you need to know beforehand.

Explain.

My project, you interrupted. I need to know about the GF. I need my file code. And I need to know the contact.

You sound like a needy person. What's this have to do with me?

Seeing as you interrupted me. You have to finish the work.

Says who?

That would be me. Of course, you may not be able to finish the work. In that event, everything would then become a massive waste of time.

You are failing in your attempt to bait me. What am I getting out of this?

Am I? Let me make this as simple as possible, I know you have a hard time keeping up. That information is necessary for all involved. You included. Without it, we're shooting blind. The project has a three-day shelf-life, of which you have wasted one. You can try to obtain the info in the time remaining, or you can return the project to me so I can do my job. As for what you're getting out of this deal, other than the obvious benefit of my presence, you get to realize I was right all along. As a bonus, if you ask nicely, I'll let you come along for the rest of the project.

She made him laugh. That was her specialty. Is that all you need?

She didn't doubt him. She never doubted him. That would be the general gist, but I won't say no to extras.

Three days? I knew you were incompetent. I only need one.

You've got two. No worries then.

I'll see you at home.

You just might.

I will.

Cocky bum. NCC then.

Yes and yes. Christian smiled. His stress evaporated. He'd get her information, with time to waste. Of that he was certain. And, she was coming home. That was all he ever wanted.

****

Christian got up early. He made his coffee and went for a run. He grabbed a shower and treated himself to an amazing western omelet with hash browns. It was one of those simple pleasures that made for a good day. The Pentagon City house he resided in was nice. It was the type of house that in the old days would have had a homemaker making a home and a breadwinner winning some bread. Together, they would have produced three or four self-absorbed, ungrateful, mini-citizens who would have nothing useful to contribute to society. The American Dream. A waste of time. Some dreams weren't worth having.

Chloe has dreams. She dreams about magic fairies and presents from her daddy. Marie had dreams too. See where that got her. Christian frowned. He bit into a piece of toast, determined to change the direction his thoughts had taken. He didn't let Marie come to mind often. Because some dreams weren't worth having. Omelets were good. It was a nice house. He liked the colors; a lot of blues and greens. He especially liked the spacious garage. He had three cars parked there. It was time to look in one of them.

****

Christian popped the trunk. "Oh. That's where I put you. I couldn't remember. Damn. You look like shit." He reached in, grabbed Jericho by the arm and yanked. He ignored Jeri's moans and shoved him away from the car. "If I'm understanding correctly, you don't have a lot of time. So, this is how this is going to go down, Jeri. You're going to tell me everything I want to know and you're going to do that right now."

Jericho tried to stand. His legs were unstable and his joints were tight. His wrists were still cuffed and chafed. He'd lost track of how long he'd been in there. "Chris. Chris," his voice was hoarse and his throat dry. "What is this? I don't understand."

Christian walked up to him. "Chris?" He smashed his left fist into Jericho's face. Jericho stumbled backward, stunned. Christian stalked him, punching him again and again. He slammed Jeri's head into the car and threw him into a rack of power tools. "You call me Chris again; it will put me in a bad mood." He followed that comment with his right fist into Jericho's jaw.

****

When Jericho came to, he was seated at a desk. The monitor displayed his personal screensaver. For a moment, he thought he had fallen asleep at work. The confusion set in when he tried to rub his eyes. Once again, he found himself tied to a chair. A rush of panic clashed with a surge of pain. His eyes were swollen, one he could not open. His jaw hurt when he moved it. He thought it might be broken. His nose was broken. He lifted his head and from his partially good eye, he saw Christian sitting beside him. Panic became the dominant emotion. Fear made him numb.

"Welcome back, Jeri." Christian was jovial. "You've wasted a little bit of time here. You'll have to make up for it. Perhaps I wasn't clear. You don't have a choice and this is why...I'm the only possible chance you have of getting out of this at all, much less alive." Watching Jericho's battered face go bloodless, he said, "Don't panic yet. That's not the worst of it. Your family, your mom, your brothers, your wife; that stupid little bitch you've been cheating on her with. What's her name? Gillian. Yes, I know about Gillian. You're about to get them all killed. Ain't a damn soul can help you, but me. Everyone will know they died because you are a coward-ass traitor who could have saved them but chose not to. And if that's not bad enough, I have the antidote to the poison that's eating you alive. What I need is a reason to give it to you." He nodded toward the computer screen.

"Wha' do you wan' me to do?" W. Jericho Parks was broken. Days locked away without food; cold terrifying nights. He had no defiance left. The abuse he suffered from Deverell's hands had sapped his will. He didn't have any strength. He didn't have anything.

"Tell...and show...me everything." Christian leaned forward. He pulled his key ring out of his pocket and showed Jericho the knife Lareina had given him for his birthday. "I'm going to free your hands."

Jericho nodded in understanding. Then he howled in agony. Blood spilled down his leg where Christian stabbed him behind his knee. He twisted the knife and severed part of the muscle. "Don't let having your hands free give you any ideas about running away." Christian removed the cuffs. "We don't have that kind of time."

Minutes ticked by with no other sounds than an occasional whimper and the clicking of the keys. Jericho opened his files, one after the other in robotic fashion. He did not care what he showed Christian, who he exposed. He was dying; he knew it. In light of that, everything became irrelevant. His mind was engaged in blocking out the pain. He had so much pain.

Beside him, Christian scanned the screen. He had his prisoner make digital and hard copies. His scowl deepened as his understanding increased. His mood grew darker.

Jericho's fingers paused. His hand hovered. He had come to the last folder, his last secret. By shaky inches, he turned his head. His eyes, once vivid, now murky in their sunken sockets, locked with Christian's true-blue steel gaze. His thoughts were concise and for the first time that day his voice rang clear. "I know wha' this mus' seem like too you. Readin' this, I see it too. But, tha's not the way it was. I was doin' good things. I was winnin' the game. Smar'er than everyone. I was makin' money. I was bea'ing all the systems. I was winnin'. It wasn' people. It wasn' personal beyond me. It was winnin'. If I woul' have known wha' woul' happen, I wouldn' have done it."

He felt that he should explain, but he didn't expect compassion or sympathy from Deverell. In that respect, Christian was predictable. He received none. Not a flash of emotion. Not a glint of understanding. Not an iota of concern.

"You lost. Open the damn file."

****

The hot water cascaded down Jericho's battered body with soothing richness. He didn't mind the soap stinging as it seeped into his multitude of cuts and abrasions. He felt clean. A shower meant hope. When Christian directed him to the bathroom and told him to bathe, Jericho wept. He stood under the showerhead, sore and bleeding, weeping with gratitude. There would be no point in offering him a shower if Christian wanted to kill him.

Fifty minutes later, when the water ran cold and Jericho forced himself to move, Christian set his nose, gave him a bandage for his leg, two pieces of toast and a glass of water.

"If you can keep that down, we'll get you something more substantial," he said.

Jeri was going to keep it down. He wasn't going to lose a crumb. To be safe, he forced himself to eat slowly. Dry toast. It was the best tasting food in the world. He couldn't remember if he had ever given toast a thought before. He was a different man now. He would think about a lot of things. He would prove to Christian he was strong enough to eat more.

Afterwards, Christian let him sleep. In a bed. A real bed. He didn't know how long he got to rest, but it was the best nap he ever had. He would have laid there longer, but Christian stood over him, offering him clothes. It was the same outfit he had been wearing when he'd been abducted, now washed, ironed, stain-free and fresh.

Getting into the car scared him, but it was a different vehicle and Christian wasn't forcing him into the trunk. Jericho swallowed his fears and remained obedient. His heart raced when they stopped at the order menu at the KFC drive-thru and Christian asked him what he wanted.

He wanted a lot, but humbly inquired as to what he would be allowed.

"All you can eat," came the tolerant answer.

A ten piece bucket, four sides, six biscuits and two extra-large Cokes for Jeri. Christian ordered nothing for himself. Jericho hoped he wouldn't be required to share.

Christian let him eat in the car. Jericho began demurely. By the third piece of chicken, he forgot his manners and half way through, he shoved it in without bothering to breathe.

A good chunk of the night had been used when they turned off the road at a deserted rest stop near a body of water. Jericho hadn't noticed a sign; he had no idea where they were. Seven pieces of chicken, three and a half sides, all six biscuits and everything but the ice from the cokes were gone. Jeri nursed a pleasant belly ache. He assumed he was to follow when Christian got out of the car. He grabbed a leg (it was just a little one) and happily limped behind his savior. That's how he regarded Deverell now. The beating, the stabbing, was less important than the shower and the food.

Christian sat down at a lopsided picnic table out of the line of vision from the roadway. Jericho stretched and sat across from him. He shook his hands and wiggled his feet. They were little numb. He and Christian hadn't talked much, but he felt safe. "What are we doing here?"

"Waiting." Christian studied the water.

"Is somebody meeting us?"

Christian continued to study the water.

Accepting he wasn't going to get an answer, Jeri thought about the leftover macaroni. He wanted it. Maybe it would be better to share. "You didn't get anything to eat. Are you hungry? I have some left. I'll go get it~"

"Sit down. Jeri."

Jeri hadn't moved more than an inch or two. The authority in Christian's tone sat him back down. That small movement was costly. His body felt like dead weight.

Christian raked his eyes over him and let a long minute pass before he stood up. "I'll be back."

Jericho assumed he was going to get the food. He hoped so. The food was there and he wanted to eat it, but he didn't have the energy to move. He had been through a heavy ordeal. He needed more sleep.

Emma. His wife's face popped into his head. Funny, he hadn't considered Emma; what she must be going through. He thought about her in the beginning, when Lareina had him in that storage unit. In the later days, he hadn't thought about much of anything. Christian mentioned her. He mentioned Gillian too. He didn't give a shit about Gillian, except she had a nice ass. Not really, but it was nice enough. She offered it to him. What was he going to do? Say no? There was still chicken and mashed potatoes...Gillian always wanted something...Emma always wanted something...Shopping, buy me, give me, take me....she thought he worked for her. He wasn't working for her. He worked for the Vanguard. They paid out the ass...Gillian had an ass...His brothers...something about his brothers...they weren't shit. He was the smart one... He wasn't sharing his biscuits... Emma...was worried...Emma would be... happy... Chris...no Christian...Christian told him he shouldn't have...fucked with Lareina...Christian was right...

****

From behind the wheel, Christian watched his old friend take his last breaths and idly wondered what he was thinking. Did Jeri remember about the poison? Didn't matter. He should not have fucked with Lareina.

****

W. Jericho Parks slumped over. His lifeless eyes stared across the body of water he could not name. Christian started his engine and drove away. He had a meeting scheduled.

Chapter 19

Alec opened his eyes. His curtains were drawn, but he could tell it was light. It didn't make sense for him to be sleepy. He never slept in. It was daytime...

When his next coherent thought came, it was later. How much later, he didn't know. His mouth was dry and he wouldn't have any problem falling back to sleep if he just turned over...

Wait. Why was he in bed? He skimmed his nightstand, confused. He gave his head a violent shake, trying to rid himself of the cobwebs. His clock was unplugged. His watch was gone. *What the..?* He forced his mind to work. His mom wouldn't take his watch, she knew he loved it. She gave it to him. Probably Orion, jackass...but that didn't explain the clock. Why would Orion care if he knew the time? It clicked. Meeting. Deverell. He had to go.

He didn't know how long he tried to force his body to work, to force himself to move. Nothing. All he could do now was let whatever the hell was in his system work its way through...and plan. He was sure Orion hadn't done this one; at least not alone. He wasn't that smart, despite his test scores. No, this drug came from Silas. Silas. He expected something, but he'd been careful to pay attention whenever the bastard was around him. This was crossing the line. He felt tears threaten as he laid there helplessly, wondering about his mother. If he lost her, there wasn't a place on the whole freakin' planet Silas or Deverell could hide. He'd find them, he'd kill them, and he'd laugh. They deserved it.

He nurtured the anger, it kept the fear and uncertainty at bay. He knew he wouldn't kill Silas, mom would be upset. She needed him. But he'd make sure neither he nor Orion—if he helped—ever did this shit again. He didn't know what Silas drugged him with, but he was going to rearrange his chemistry set. Better yet... *Wait for it, you traitorous bastard...*

****

BAM!!!

The loud sudden noise repeated. BAM! Several blows resounded. Along with the racket came the agonized shrieks of an angry gorilla, venting his frustration at being betrayed. Quiet, Orion wasn't quiet today. He was heated.

He opened his eyes, feeling more rested than he'd been in a long time. He went to the bathroom and brushed his teeth, idly trying to recall what he did this morning. He woke up every morning around two. He had been doing it for as long as he could remember. Before, he would go from bedroom to bedroom, checking on his mom and sisters; pulling up covers, closing windows and picking up toys. After his selection into the Excellence Program, he would wander the halls, dodging the cameras and the night staff, snatching food from the kitchen. Lately, since he'd been with Lareina, he would read or talk to her. Somehow, she always managed to be up about that time. He didn't think it was a coincidence. He loved her for it. They would hang out and talk—him and her—about nothing important. Life. Wild animals, amusement parks, or whatever happened to cross his mind. Sometimes they watched parkour clips on youtube. She made time for him...on his own crazy schedule. He loved her for it.

He wanted to tell her about the chemical compound he figured out. He didn't recall talking to Lareina this morning. He didn't remember fiddling with his stuff either. He reached up, grabbing the clock off of the top shelf, to get a better look at the time. He thought about why he would have slept so long. Why didn't Fisher get him up for breakfast? Fisher never lets him sleep in. Breakfast. Hell. It was past lunch. Way past lunch. Lareina? Fisher. "Fucking asshole!"

Orion sailed the clock. It hit the shower door and smashed into a hundred fragments. Not that he noticed. He pulled the towel rack out of the wall. The screws came free, taking paint and drywall with it. Orion used the rack as a sledgehammer to break his way out of the bathroom. Rage ate through his veins, a fiery hunger that fed on everything. The brute strength contained in his lithe frame was scary when adrenaline set it free. The door splintered and hung off its hinges. Still, Orion was not satisfied. He went down the hall, smashing pictures, throwing things;

seeking a bigger target. Seeking Fisher.

On the steps, he substituted the towel rack for a banister rail. It came free easily. Its solid mass felt good in his hands. It would do damage, but the actual banister would do more. He used the rail to liberate a section of the wood. It made a perfect weapon.

A curio cabinet sat at the bottom of the stairwell. It fell in the wake of Orion's wrath. Over the cracking of glass and splattering of souvenirs, a voice penetrated the red haze covering his mind.

"Why don't you knock it off," Yukiyo spoke from the dining room where she set up a workstation to research Gillian Foster as Lareina requested. She paused in her typing long enough to take a sip from a tall glass.

Orion went for her.

In spite of being focused on her screen, she knew exactly when he crossed the threshold. "Don't come any further. They've got you tagged, boy."

It wasn't her words, but the casualness of her tone. Her nonchalance gave him pause. "What?"

"Tagged, man. You are going to be it. If you come any closer, you're probably going to get knocked out with a double dose of whatever they gave you last night. I bet when you wake up the next time, you'll be tied to a chair."

Orion's heartrate slowed but he remained apprehensive. Not of Yukiyo—he believed her. He wanted to know Fisher's location. More importantly, where was Silas? A cold chill ran down his spine. He glanced quickly over his shoulder. "How do you know?"

"Pfffph. You know it has to be something like that. Do you see Fisher or Silas around here anywhere? How much you want to bet, I'm the bait." She glanced out of the window, not expecting to see anything. "You've been awake for five minutes and you're breaking people's stuff with a banister." She pointed to the hunk of wood resting on his shoulder. "If you come anywhere near me swinging that, I guarantee you're going down. Now, what I suggest is you sit your happy ass down right there," she pointed, "where you can be seen. You can look at this for me." She slid a notepad in his direction. "I think it might be some type of code."

****

The drug was mostly out of his system, but Alec waited another hour—on principle—before venturing out of his room. Whatever they were expecting, he wasn't supplying. He used the time to analyze his suspicions.

Last night, Mom retired first. She announced she had a new novel and a full bottle of bubble bath. She was going to see which lasted longer—the book or the soap. She kissed him goodnight and that was the last he saw of her. When she kissed him goodbye in the morning (he never doubted she did), she probably thought he was in a deep sleep. If something went wrong, she would want him alert to be able to follow her emergency instructions. No way did she give Silas permission to drug him.

Didn't know about Yukiyo. She's not big on being bothered. That was a plus. However, she was starting to get pretty big on Silas. If Silas asked her to do something, she would. But Silas doesn't need any help. Jury's still out on Yukiyo. If he found out she was involved...Nope. This was Silas' fault. All Silas. If anybody helped him, it was Fisher and Orion. Mom had basically put Fisher and Silas on a team. And Orion was a stupid ass with a knack for chemical warfare. That's all there was to it.

Kaiden didn't count. Kaiden didn't care. He got to go with her. He wouldn't have time to mess with anybody. Anyway, Kaiden wouldn't help Silas do anything other than to protect Mom. Silas wouldn't ask him. This was Silas. All Silas.

Alright, now he was hungry. He wasn't going to starve just because Silas was a dick. Alec got out of bed, a little unsteady, but not feeling any ill effects from the drug. His mood improved a bit. Right outside of his door, he paused to survey the damage and rethink his position. The trail began at Orion's bathroom. Orion wasn't on anybody's side. Orion tried to tear the house down. Alec whistled low when he saw the damaged done on the stairs and the shattered glass below. His mood rose another notch. He didn't like Orion at all. However, that didn't stop him from appreciating Orion's handiwork. It made a statement.

****

Kaiden held the door open and followed Lareina into the post office. He watched her fumble through a handful of mailbox keys, seeking one that belonged to one of the one hundred and fifty P.O. boxes lining the wall in front of them. He noted that she had a lot of mailbox keys.

She found her box and retrieved the large brown envelope; a package she had obviously been expecting.

They made their way across the street to Millie's Café. They seated themselves at a window booth. Kaiden wanted to see. Lareina wanted to be seen. Millie's Café looked like it had been decorated sometime before the Civil War and so far nobody had gotten around to updating it. Kaiden hoped that meant the current owners gave all of their attention to the food. By the look of the menu, he doubted it.

Other than the name, Kaiden knew nothing of Kelly, North Carolina. It didn't seem to him there was much to know. "Do they have a hotel anywhere in this town?"

Lareina looked up from surveying the contents of her package. "I wouldn't know where. I've never been here overnight before."

The waitress interrupted Kaiden's retort to take their order of two coffees and an appetizer of onion rings. Lareina picked up the conversation, "I think they used to have a Walmart, but they were everywhere before the war."

"How long are we going to be here?"

"You're leaving in about ten or fifteen minutes. I don't know how long I'll be."

"Come on 'Reina. You know I'm not leaving you." He tugged on his earring.

"Come on Kaid. I'm not doing this with you." She had to wait while the waitress served their coffee and assured them the onion rings would be out momentarily. "You already know I'm going to be fine. I need you to get Yukiyo and find Gillian. She's our only shot of not doing this blind. That's more important than you hovering over me while I manipulate Christian."

"Suppose he manipulates you?"

"He can try." She smiled as she held up the first item out of the package—a disposable phone. It had one number programmed in. She dialed it.

"Don't eat a lot. We're going to have lunch."

Some greeting. She wondered how long he'd been watching her. Most likely since they arrived. "But I'm hungry now."

"I guess it sucks to be you. How long are you babysitting?"

Instead of answering, Lareina passed the phone to Kaiden.

"What do I want that for?"

It was phenomenal, the amount of testosterone she was forced to put up with. "Why are you here if you don't want to talk to him?"

Kaiden snatched the phone. "What are you up to?"

Lareina stifled a giggle. *Christian is going to lovvve that tone.* The waitress arrived. Lareina could tell by the stiff, quick landing of the onion rings that Kaiden's greeting had been overheard. She thanked the lady, not wanting her to think it was directed toward her or in any way personal.

Christian did not like Kaiden's tone at all. "Eat your lunch. Don't share. Get in your truck. Go back to where you came from. Now, put Lareina on the phone. I didn't call you."

Kaiden did not like Christian's tone either. "I ain't putting Lareina nowhere. You got something to say, tell it to me. Come at me straight, man to man."

Lareina munched on a fried onion and inspected a second item from the envelope. A car key. *Where's the car?*

"I can wait. Tell Lareina to quit eating." Click.

"The bastard hung up on me!" Kaiden threw the phone on the bench beside him. "I don't care how you feel about him, 'Reina. I'm going to merk his ass."

Lareina sipped her coffee. "You should know better. We're sitting in his little sandbox. You can't come here uninvited, shooting off orders, expecting him to play his game your way."

"Watch me."

"Alrighty then." She surprised herself by not sounding condescending. "Did he say anything?"

"He'll wait. Like I give a shit. And for you not to eat." He pushed the plate in front of her. "Eat."

"In another circumstance, this would be amusing. Christian has little patience." She plucked a few onion rings to appease him, before sliding the plate back across the table. "You, have none. Give me the phone." Kaiden would have denied, but she said, "Kaid. He doesn't care about me eating..." she paused, rethinking. "Yes, he does, but that's not his point. He can see us. He's got everything set up, his way. He will out wait you."

As if on cue, the reluctant waitress returned to their table. She refilled their coffee cups. "If you want something else, let me know. But, your bill's already been paid." She looked from the sister to the brother and back again. "The gentlemen said, you may want something else, sir, but the lady was done. I guess y'all know what that's all about."

Kaiden whipped his head around. "Where the hell is he?"

Lareina laughed. "Give me that phone."

She had barely closed her fingers around the contraption when it rang again. "Are we done?" she said as if she were indulging a child.

He used the same indulging manner. "Tell Kaiden, you have to leave now. When you get outside, go left."

"And then what?"

"And then nothing. You keep walking until I'm certain he's not following you."

She had on a skirt and he knew her shoe preference. Hiking was not in today's forecast. "Where's my car?"

"I'll tell you when he's gone."

She made a face, and clawed her hand, briefly entertaining the thought of strangling him. No, she needed him. Better to end this round. "You blew up his garage, Eugene."

"Didn't you hear? Revolutionaries did it."

"How would you expect him to act regarding me? He *is* my brother."

"How old are you?"

He pointedly did not listen, which Lareina knew had a point all its own. "What would you do in his place?"

"He's been compensated. It's time for him to go about his day and leave his betters to their work."

"Why don't *you* quit irritating *your* betters. I'll see you in a minute." She disconnected, not giving him a chance to respond. She slid out of the booth, slipping the phone into her bag as she moved. "Alright Kaid, I'll walk out with you."

Kaiden quirked an eyebrow but followed her out.

Outside, Kaiden took the lead and picked up the pace. Lareina briefly thought about giving him the slip, thus ending the unnecessary battle of wills, but decided not to. One, it would hurt Kaiden's feelings, and two, she wasn't sixteen. She wasn't sneaking out. End of story.

They reached the truck and Kaiden ripped the manila envelope off the hood before Lareina fully identified what she saw. "What is this?" he asked as he tore open the end. A visa-check card fell into his palm. A hand-written note came out with another shake.

Congratulations.
Your insurance came through. Buy a real garage.

"What does he think I need his money for?" Kaiden gave Lareina the note and put the visa card in his wallet. Need it or not, he'd take anybody's money if they offered it.

Lareina scanned the note. "Truce, peace offering, acknowledgment, whatever you were hoping for—this is it." She flipped it over to be certain there was nothing else. "Take it or leave it. Now, it's your turn."

Kaiden knew what that meant. Deverell started it. Kaiden just brought it to him. But the money was a table-turner. Any aggression from Kaiden today made it Kaiden's war.

Lareina helped his thoughts along. "You know he's got a plan B. And a C and a D if he needs it. I'd like to wrap up the real business a little sooner than that. Please. I brought you here so you wouldn't worry. Have a little faith in me. Please."

Kaiden threw his arm around her shoulder. Even in her heels, she was inches shorter than he. "I don't trust him."

"You trust him to be him. Has he ever hurt me before? Trust isn't your problem. You don't like him."

"No, I don't."

She burrowed into his shoulder. "Me either."

They both snickered.

"I wish."

Still smiling, she said, "I brought you here because you're you. Now, indulge me. I'll call you when I'm done."

"You'll call me tonight. Because you ain't staying over."

She smacked his chest and freed herself from his embrace. "I'll call you when I'm done. Go, check on my boys. I have no idea what Silas did, but I'm positive my Rajar won't be happy about it."

"Your Rajar?" He knew who she meant, but he had never heard her refer to him by that name.

"Alec Rajar," she supplied. "I tend to think of him as Rajar when he's in a dangerous place."

He quirked an eyebrow. "Dangerous? Of course, he's dangerous. If he wasn't, you wouldn't be attached to him. Do you hang around anybody who isn't dangerous in some way or another?"

She leaned in to peck his cheek. "Only you."

In response, he did the brotherly thing. He shoved her.

Chapter 20

As soon as Kaiden got in his truck, Lareina walked in the direction Christian indicated. She knew her baby brother would second guess himself. When he did, she didn't plan to be anywhere near. The phone rang before she reached the corner. "Uh-huh?"

"You certainly know how to waste my time don't you?"

"Where's my car?"

"If you didn't insist on wearing those damned shoes, you wouldn't be complaining."

"If you're going to be of no use, I'll get my brother to drive me to the house."

"Quit playing. Your car is around the corner. I assume you'll be able to get out of here without your shadow."

"I don't need to worry about it. That's why I keep you around." She spotted the Whitferde Subprei and grinned. Brand new. Blue and silver. It might not be her Marada Ex6, but it was hot. "I'm keeping this one."

He grunted. Not in the least surprised.

****

There was nothing like the open highway. Lareina hadn't felt this kind of liberty in months. She sailed down the road thinking what it would be like to forget everything and everybody. To drive and drive, doing ninety until she hit the ocean... Nope. Not without Alec.

She wasn't going anywhere without Alec.

A spot in the distance rolling in like thunder caught her attention. It was thunder—her personal storm. He had to be pushing a hundred and ten as fast as he was coming up on her. She could drive as far and as fast as she wanted, it wouldn't matter. Christian would always catch up. "Hmmm." She checked the roadway. No other car in sight. "To dust or not to dust? Whatever shall I do?" She wished he could see her grin as she mashed the gas.

Lareina answered the call on the first ring. "Do you want something?"

"Slow your ass down."

"No, thank you. I don't think I will just yet."

"Considering your activities of late, it would be idiotic to get picked up for speeding. Don't you think?"

"I have no intention of getting picked up for speeding, or anything else for that matter."

"I'm not concerned with your intentions."

A moment later, she realized his intentions. "You killjoy!" She watched the needle on her speedometer slide to the left. She was glad she couldn't see his grin. Of course, he would be able to control her car. Eighty-five. Eighty. "What are you going to do to make up for this travesty?" Seventy-five. Seventy. "Alright, that's enough." Sixty-five. "Come on now."

He caught up to her and flashed the charm she selected for him—the first one she selected. Crushed black diamonds made up the glittery scales of a black mamba, poised to strike. Many considered the snake the most treacherous of its species.

He showed her his grin when he rolled past. Content to remain on the wrong side of the road, he let her fall behind for a mile or so before bringing her speed up to ninety—equal to his.

She liked that.

So did he.

Side by side they coasted along the deserted highway to a destination they, two children and no other living soul knew existed.

****

Off the main highway, the road narrowed to one lane. Now, they drove slow, cautious, one after the other with him leading. He always took the lead. It mattered little that she was a fast thinker and could easily discern any telling nuance that could affect their situation. He deemed, with him in front of her, she could discern his reaction and get the hell out of the way. If something came at them, whatever it was, it wasn't going to touch Lareina without going through Christian.

Lareina argued, they'd be safer with her up front, representing less of a threat. Lareina never won that debate. In Christian's mind, Lareina wasn't a target. She wasn't bait. She wasn't taking the lead.

Several miles along, an unused dirt road lay to the right. Christian took the turn with an everyday easiness. Lareina drove in his tracks, giving the impression of one vehicle. Through a private gate and down a winding road that was little more than a large trail in the woods. Lareina could tell Christian had already been there. The path was clear and drivable. It took a while, but the secrecy was well worth it.

A cabin stood at the edge of the clearing. Their cabin. The house he built on her property. It was a cabin in that the outside was made of cedar. But that was it. Lareina didn't do rustic. Christian had built her a luxurious four-bedroom vacation home, with all the trimmings. Indoor pool, hot tub, gourmet kitchen, deck, balcony, game room, gym and a huge three-car garage with every tool imaginable; all the toys either of them wanted. The outside of the house just happened to be covered in cedar.

Lareina loved their house. It was the only place in their life that hadn't gone to hell. Here, they pretended they were normal; the way people used to be when a house and family and fun were all that mattered in the world. More importantly, here—and only here—they could be with each other the way they wanted to, the way they would have been, if they were normal people and a house and family and fun were all that mattered.

She followed him into the garage, pulling into her spot and cutting off the engine. He was already at the control panel when she disembarked. "Get that thing out of my car. Today."

He cut her an indolent glance and went back to securing the premises. "I can control more than your speed." No signals, no electronics, not even satellite would get through the scramblers he turned on. No one could track them here. It was as if they bleeped off the map. It didn't matter that they couldn't watch television or use the internet. They didn't come to the cabin to watch TV.

"All the more reason for you to take it out."

"No." He finished arming the security system and gave her a little nudge in the direction he wanted her to go.

She pursed her lips, not at all done with the topic, but decided to wait.

He'll want something and then I'll bargain. She led the way up the steps, into the house. Christian was content to follow her now. They both knew why.

Just as she thought, he had already been there. Everything had been uncovered, aired out and stocked up. Fresh and clean. It felt good to be home.

She started toward a second flight of stairs. Her bedroom, her bathroom, her balcony.

He grabbed her by the belt loop on the back of her denim skirt. "Hurry up. You wasted all of my time, now you have to help me cook."

"Pffffph." She tugged forward a step. "I didn't come here to cook."

"But you will anyway."

****

They made tacos, complete with salsa and corncake. They had a cookies and cream pie for dessert. Many of the ingredients were rare these days, but tacos were Christian's favorite. He always managed to get what he needed. Afterward, they lounged on the deck and shared some bourbon. He tapped the bottle. "Remember this?"

"No." She did, but that wasn't his business.

"Yes, you do."

"I don't care to."

"You left it at the hospital."

"Why would I want to remember it?"

They were silent. The bourbon was warm.

"When was the last time we were here?" He watched a hummingbird raid a vine of honeysuckles.

"Ummmm. Let me think." She stretched it out, just because. "Two summers ago." She remembered. It wasn't a time she was likely to forget. Christian had been shot. No one knew it. He removed the bullet himself and called her. She brought him here to heal in safety. Those days were crazy scary. She still hadn't fully forgiven him for getting hurt.

He remembered too. He could have died. She saved him. Afterwards, they could have chosen a different course. But they didn't. They were already on this reckless path to consumption and destruction. Nothing to do now, but see it through. "Do I have to admit you were right?" His thoughts were distant.

She sensed the edginess of his mood. "What did you find out?"

He guzzled his drink and refilled his glass. "Gillian Foster. I'll get to her in a minute. Your file code is miss-know-it-all. One word. No spaces. Very appropriate~"

"My ass is heart-shaped and sweet like a Hershey's. Why don't you kiss it?"

He snorted at the imagery. "Later."

"Only in your most vivid fantasies. What about the contact?"

"I'll deal with the contact."

She quirked an eyebrow at him. "I'll handle my own business, thank you."

"Your files are on the desk. I know how much you enjoy reading so I took the liberty of making you a hard copy."

Changing the subject, I wonder why. "Anything good?"

"Everything but when you come on your period."

"Can't imagine why he wouldn't find that interesting."

"Maybe because it's obvious." He smiled at that.

She smiled too. "Kiss my ass."

"I told you, later."

I can change the subject too. "How was Jeri?"

"Dead, the last time I saw him." He studied her, checking for regret. He found a little, but not enough to wonder over. "It was the best thing for him. He talked too much and didn't have the faintest idea he had positioned himself to be everybody's goat. There's a lot of shit happening and anybody could point to him and make it go away."

"I'm surprised he lasted this long."

"Keeping all that shit on file, could get a lot of people killed. Starting with Gillian." Christian said, "You have to find her."

"Why? Wait, back up. What did you find out? Summarize it and we'll go from there."

Christian didn't want to summarize. He didn't want Lareina involved. He wanted to go kill some people and get on with his life. "Fine." He refilled their glasses. "You were right. This war isn't the government and the Revolutionaries trying to decide who runs our lives."

No shit.

"Jeri signed on with a third organization." He knew he wasn't telling her anything she didn't already try to convince him of. "The Vanguard. It seems that they are in the business of keeping war alive on American soil. It's Joffener."

"Excuse me."

"You heard me. Joffener's the bastard working the carousel. He's the liaison for whoever the Vanguard put in there."

"The Excellence Program belongs to them," Lareina said. "Their main purpose, as far as I can ascertain, is to collect the biggest brains. They have various plans for children with the most potential. They use these kids to keep the war going."

"If it works, great," his voice was flat, his mind traveled. "If not... a battle breaks loose...a person disappears...blame it on the Revs...blame it on the government...blame it on the war...and keep fighting...the more fighting there is, the more money they make."

She watched him reconnect the pieces she already connected. There was nothing for it, but the truth. "Marie didn't have the necessary killer instincts. She told them no. That was no accident. That's where my research began."

Marie was the single weak link between them. They never spoke of her; never talked about what happened. Lareina had been shocked, devastated, to learn that he had gotten Jericho's cousin, Marie, pregnant. For a while, they couldn't get around it and it seemed as if their relationship was over. But Christian and Lareina's bond didn't die. Even when badly neglected, it wouldn't go away.

For Christian's sake, Lareina became the strength gentle Marie never had. Lareina became Marie's friend, her confidant. Lareina volunteered to babysit little Chloe and gave up her seat on the train so Marie could spend the weekend with Christian at his temporary duty station. Lareina hid his infant daughter, so everyone would believe she perished with her mother.

Christian allowed it, knew it was the safest thing for Chloe, even as he refused to believe her theories...

Lareina had just put the baby to bed when she heard something scraping against the lock. Taking the offense, she snatched the door open, startling the would-be intruder. "Can I help you?" The gun in her pocket was loaded and cocked, but he didn't need to know that.

"Oh. Uhhh. Pardon me." The man raised his hand, touching the brim of his hat. "Lareina? What are you doing here?" It was Sergeant Joffener. Other than his

name, Lareina didn't know much about him except that he was on the review board. "I thought you were off to Disneyland this weekend?" He closed his fist over something that did not look like a key.

She played along. "House sitting." She smiled indulgently, "I switched weekends with Marie. She needed to see Christian more than I needed to see Mickey Mouse."

He chuckled. "How kind of you. I hope they realize what a good friend you are."

"I doubt it. Do you want me to take a message for her?"

"No. Not at all. I'll see her on Monday." He left.

Lareina wondered why he tried to pick the lock. She wondered why someone would target a passenger train with no one notable and nothing of true value onboard. She wondered why the investigation closed in under four days with no conclusion, no motive, and no proof of any kind that rebels were involved.

She wondered what Marie had learned that made her desperate to see Christian right away—without the baby. What message couldn't Lareina pass on to him? What difference would one week have made?

Mostly, she wondered what if she had been on the train instead...

The memory of Marie went through Christian like a spear. He wanted it and the pain it invoked gone. He came to his feet and pulled Lareina to hers. His grip was viselike. Unyielding. He couldn't keep the emotions at bay. He had to react, respond, fight. She crossed the line; saying what never should be said. Spoke the name that should never be spoken. He pulled her closer and punished her with a kiss. He needed to wipe it away. The name, the memory, the horror, the guilt. All of it. He couldn't live with it, any of it. He couldn't live with the knowing. Knowing he had not saved Marie. Knowing he had been hoping to see Lareina and was grateful, thankful even, when he learned she had given up her seat. Knowing he could not separate the guilt from the gratitude.

That was the truth of what kept them apart. He'd lost Lareina. Just when he became certain he wanted her back, he lost Marie. She was out of reach, but always between them. He couldn't save the one and he couldn't have the other. Chloe suffers for it. His daughter had to be hidden from the world, without any mother's love. Not Marie's. Not Lareina's.

Christian Eugene Deverell. Invincible, except for one area. He couldn't protect the hearts of the women who loved him. He hated himself for his failure. He hated them for it too. But Chloe was innocent. Marie was gone. Lareina was here. She was the only one who could take it.

Lareina.

He tightened his embrace and deepened the kiss.

He hadn't had a full night's sleep since he got the call telling him she'd been caught. He was going to protect her. He was going to save her. He was going to get lost in her...

Lareina knew. She always knew. The whole of their relationship was a pyre doused in oil. They waited tensely for one of them to strike the match. Ignite the flame that would consume them. It would burn out of control and utterly destroy them. It would turn them into ash and dust and silence. But until then...the blaze...the blaze would be glorious. The blaze would linger in their memories and sustain them long after the fire grew cold...

His lips slid from her mouth—her mouth already belonged to him—to claim the soft skin along her jaw, down the column of her throat. Her skin was coffee; warm, brown, and stimulating. He breathed her in, her Jazzmonet fragrance drugged him. She rolled her shoulder back—an offering he greedily took. He buried his head in the hollow of her neck and nibbled. Her soft moan nearly undid him. He pressed into her, uncaring that his arousal was evident. She already knew what she did to him.

Lareina knew, she always knew. This would be the end of them. She luxuriated in the silky feel of his hair cascading through her fingers. She moved, impatient as he took his time feeling his way beneath her top. Her breasts were heavy in his palm. He sighed, content with the weight.

She and Christian were the mythical Thorn-Birds, searching for thorn trees from the day they hatch. When they find the perfect thorn, they impale themselves and sing a song of untainted beauty as they die.

With his thumb, he slid his pinky ring free. He brought it to eye level so she could see the pure gold band detailed with diamonds and rubies. The tiger and the snake. Blood and venom.

Her emotions were raw, her tears instant.

"Always."

She presented him with her hand. "Always."

They couldn't get married. Organized religion was illegal. Marriage licenses required a background check. No courthouse in the country would deem Christian and Lareina compatible; they would never be given permission to wed. Moreover, each was a liability for the other's activities. Not, that either of them could overcome their past. Chloe made it so she could not forget and he would not regret.

Marie wasn't there. The government wasn't there. The war wasn't there. Just him and her and the promise of their hearts. He slipped his ring onto her finger and his tongue into her mouth, nipping and sucking and dueling with hers. His body was hard and unyielding. He used it to direct hers. He backed her into the doorframe and even then, he did not stop. Fingers entwined, lips fused, he ground against her as if she were his life's substance. Indeed, she was. She was all that mattered—her and his need to dominate her in that moment.

Lareina slid her leg along his thigh, feeling his urgency, encouraging it. The intensity was already becoming too much. The ache was exquisite...

Chapter 21

They were spooning. Christian nuzzled her awake.

"What time is it?"

"Time for sex." He rubbed his half hard cock against her ass.

"Already." She moved her arm, giving his wandering hand better access. "How'd you get so horny?"

"Don't piss me off." Christian never repeated a mistake. His love life consisted of Lareina or nothing. It was the same for her. And not just because he would bury any man stupid enough to touch her. He tweaked her nipple and slid his fingers lower.

She didn't want to fight; she wanted him to stroke her. "Regardless, your stamina is impressive."

"I intend to be." He knew what she wanted...and complied.

Lareina and Christian had known one another since they were thirteen and fourteen respectively, but they had only been physically intimate in three seasons. The first when she was fifteen. One of her uncle's drug deals went south. She got snatched as a bargaining piece. Christian retrieved her before anyone knew where to look. He didn't take her home that night. He brought her here, when the place was little more than a two-room hunting shack. He didn't want to leave her and she didn't want to be left. He took her virginity and promised he would always protect her.

Her Uncle Moe, while grateful for Christian's rescue, was furious they'd been together. Old school Niggas and Rednecks got along fine; worked together great; remembered which lines not to cross. Christian's father had him out of the cartel and in military school before Lareina's next period.

A year and a half later, they rekindled their love affair. They were both enrolled in the Excellence Program. The time was magic, it had to happen. The night she said yes was the happiest in his life. Making love to his best friend. There was no feeling like it. There was no bond to match it.

He never expected to feel that way with Marie. He loved Marie, but she wasn't his best friend. He didn't know how her every thought clicked into place. She didn't touch every inch of his life. He could marry her. She could stay home while he cleaned up the world. They could be happy and have children and bring back the American post-card life. But if he wanted the feeling, the power, the release that came from making love to his best friend, he needed Lareina.

Lareina. He promised to protect her, but he watched her die the day he told her of Marie's pregnancy. He died with her. He knew who he loved, who he wanted. But he chose Marie. Lareina never let him touch her again...

Until the day he almost died. She was terrified for him, would not leave his side. Not even to sleep. The night his fever broke, they got married. Not legally, but the marriage which had always been. The one in their hearts. He put his ring on her finger and for days after, they made love as if there was no world beyond their door. For those few days, there wasn't.

But the ring couldn't stay. He was a government agent and she a revolutionary sympathizer. Eventually, his world and her world separated them. They were riding a wave. Sometimes breaking against the shore, sometimes swept out to sea. Swirling, foaming, moving, crashing. So close, yet, always out of reach.

Until today. Today, the sex was an explosive event. It started with him screwing her. Fully clothed and impatient, he took her against the doorframe. He had to. It had been more than two years since he held her. The hell she put him through these last months. The shit circumstance they were in. This week alone, he killed four people for that ass. No preliminaries. No coaxing. No sweet talk. Just his lust, his animalistic urge to slake it and her willingness to oblige.

She was willing to oblige. More than willing. She loved him best when he was at his very worst. Hard, controlling, dominating, man.

It was powerful and fast, not lasting more than a few minutes. Just what he needed to take the edge off his haze so he could think.

Lareina couldn't think. When he led her upstairs to his bedroom, she couldn't think. When he undressed her and made love to her, she couldn't think. Long slow strokes to the tempo of low whispered words of love and desire. Soft cries of pleasure, deep groans of satisfaction, and still they did not stop. They could not stop. Two years they waited. They may never have another opportunity. They had to love, for as long as they could. Right now.

That was two hours ago.

Two glorious hours of afterglow. They dozed, entwined, content and happily in love.

Now it was time for part three. Challenging, playfully combative, intensely hot, sex. For as long as they were able, they took turns dominating and gratifying one another for the sheer fun of reckless abandonment and wild release.

****

One of the quirks in Lareina and Christian's relationship was they were able to read each other's moods and shift gears accordingly. It wasn't a trait they always appreciated, but it was comforting just the same. They devoted the remainder of the evening to business. Christian's interrogation and Jericho's files gave them a lot of information to sort through.

Lareina resigned herself to the fact that Christian was a part of her team. Now, she just had to convince the others to accept him. The prospect held all the promise of convincing five bricks and a wall.

As far as Christian was concerned, he was the team. She could send her kids out for recess and resign herself to being sidelined until he was done.

"Him." Christian pointed to a name. "Terrance Chezwick. He's the link. I met him once. Not that he'd remember it."

"Oh. What of it?"

"Nothing. I didn't like him."

"Well, that settles it."

"He's your link."

"You're probably right, but I want to get Gillian before we act on it. Not something we can afford to be wrong about."

"Jeri dealt more with him than any of your other suspects."

She played devil's advocate. "It is possible they were doing legitimate work. You know the EP is a place of employment for many."

"Could be, but they weren't. Chezwick isn't in the EP. He was out of the office the day you got arrested. His email to Jeri the day before was 'I don't want any problems. Hand-deliver it.'" He shook his head. "It's not a coincidence he was out of the way. And I don't think he wanted Jeri to bring him doughnuts."

"I don't disagree with you, Christian. But that's not enough for me to tip my hand. I want to~"

"My hand. You're done."

She ignored him. "I have somebody tracking Gillian down. Hopefully, we'll locate her in the next day or so~"

"You didn't hear me. You're done."

"No. We're done. This is getting pointless." She got up from the sofa they were sharing. "It's getting late. I've got to get back." With obvious reluctance, she slid his ring off her finger. Only in their house, would she be his wife. "I've got things."

She would never see the wound she inflicted. Lareina trusted him with her life, but not her heart. She trusted him with her heart once and he broke it. And like him, Lareina never made the same mistake twice. No matter how much she loved him, he loved her, on the other side of these walls, she would not trust him with her heart.

Standing up beside her, he accepted the ring and kissed the tip of her nose. "Go take care of your children. But don't leave for forty-five minutes."

"Forty-five minutes?"

"You better be happy I'm letting you go. I can make it not start."

Like she wanted to be reminded of that.

"Park it at the restaurant. I'll have somebody take care of it. Leave the phone in the glove box."

"I want to keep it."

"Is it your birthday?"

"Does it matter?"

"You want it? Stay your ass home."

"Pfffph. I'm done talking to you." The wheels in his head were spinning and it hadn't occurred to him she had no intentions of fitting into his little dream-scenario. Best to leave him to his delusions so she could get on with the real work. "Why fort~" she stopped herself. She didn't need to care.

"Make sure you lock the back door. After I get this shit cleaned up, we'll come back. I may let you drive it then." He walked to the door leading to the basement. "Forty-five minutes."

"And what am I supposed to do in the meantime?" She didn't doubt he would stall her car if she didn't abide by his silly rules.

He called back from halfway down the steps. "Finish your book. I left it on your nightstand."

"Bastard," she mumbled, knowing she would get her book and do exactly what he said. "You better be happy I don't call Silas!"

"You're going to get McKade killed. You know that, right?" He shut his car door and revved the engine.

****

Fisher, Alec and Orion showed up at the diner thirty-five minutes after Lareina called for a ride. Fisher brought them along partly as a peace offering and mostly because they weren't letting him leave without them.

Yukiyo found Gillian Foster or someone using her credit card in Virginia. She and Kaiden had already been on the road for an hour and a half.

No one had seen Silas. At some point during the day, while he was instructing Yukiyo, his TS13 went missing. Rather than cut anybody's throat, he took off for an unknown destination promising to kick both of their asses when he returned. Alec confessed that Silas was a little scary, but he wasn't worried—he didn't do anything. Alec also informed her that Orion didn't have anything to be concerned about either. After the way he had trashed the house, Silas should be scared of him.

Lareina already missed the cabin.

****

The ring woke her out of a dead sleep. Silas' ringtone at 0-dark-thirty was not a good thing. "Hello?" Lareina answered without opening her eyes.

"They got Deverell."

She sat up, fully alert, fully alarmed. "What happened?"

"Don't know. But we've got a twelve-hour window. Maybe less. That is, *if*, you want me to save his ass. Because I don't have to. I'm just letting you know."

"Silas." Her heart raced. She threw the covers back, searching for clothes. This wasn't a time for games. Sadly, she knew Silas wasn't joking. "What do you know?"

"I was in New York replacing my TS13. I'm retaliating on both of those little fuckers, just so you know. Your boy can thank them I'm up here and visible."

"Why?" She located her shoes. Flats. Lareina had every intention of being extremely dangerous.

"Because I'm close and I'm available. I got the call from Lieutenant Colonel Briggs, my commander. He got it straight from Commander Joffener, Deverell's superior. I'm scheduled for a ten a.m. flight to Dulles. They want me to replace Eugene's brain with a bullet by three o'clock this afternoon."

Lareina gasped. The thought of it was terrible. Having it verbalized made it ten times worse. "Ten a.m.," she breathed. "Where are you now?"

"Already in D.C."

That and a hundred other reasons was why she loved Silas. "I'll be there in time for breakfast. Save him, Silas. Please."

****

Kaiden and Yukiyo were in Virginia, hopefully retrieving Gillian. Silas was in DC, hopefully locating Christian. She and the others would have to meet Silas, get Christian, meet Kaiden, and get some place safe—before three o'clock. Hopefully, someone would come up with a plan between now and then. Lareina's arrangements were usually thought through right down to the minute details. They didn't have time for any of that. "Damn you, Christian. You know I hate surprises." *What he better know is that I'm on my way.* She threw open her bedroom door. "Alec! Ori! Fish! We gotta go!"

****

Yukiyo sat in the front seat of Kaiden's Fiesta Sig. All the vehicles from his uncle's house were built for criminal activities. Kaiden had built secrets into this one himself. He kept Uncle Moe supplied with transportation during his drug cartel days. Of course, Uncle Moe always kept him supplied with cash. It was a win/win for all involved.

Kaiden stretched out in the back. They were casing the place Yukiyo targeted as Gillian's current residence. But it wasn't his shift. He didn't need to be awake.

Yukiyo went over the agreed-upon plan. She'd point Gillian out. Kaiden would grab her. Not a lot to remember. It was Kaiden's favorite way to operate. Everything was good.

The front door of the apartment building opened inward and a slim, blond-wig wearing figure bounced out, carrying an oversized hobo bag. "Kaid." Yukiyo spoke over her shoulder, "Wake up. It's her." She wrinkled her nose in distaste at Gillian's tacky disguise. She was too happy for this time of morning. That woman couldn't touch Lareina's class if Lareina gave her private lessons and an interactive DVD.

Kaiden woke up when he heard his name. He sat up when he heard the subject. He waited for Gillian to strut by and slid out directly behind her. Yukiyo got into the back seat. Kaiden slapped his hand over Gillian's mouth and shoved her into the car before it registered she was in trouble.

The first thing Gillian saw was Yukiyo's lightweight HK T42. Her scream lodged in her throat along with her air. She gagged.

Yukiyo arched a disinterested eyebrow. "Hi, Miss Foster. Why don't you take off that stupid wig." She helped out by yanking the offending hairpiece. Kaiden got behind the wheel. He started the engine and headed back the way he came.

The wig came off easily and a brown mop of curly hair spilled around Gillian's shoulders. "Mio Dia Yukiyo? What is this?"

"This is a gun." Yukiyo wiggled it for her benefit. "It's got bullets. Want to see?" She cocked it.

Gillian shrank back and covered her head with her hands. "I don't know anything. I don't know why you're doing this. Please. Let me go. Let me go."

"Shut her the hell up," Kaiden complained. "We haven't gone five miles and I already have a headache."

Gillian became hysterical. "NO! NO! I'll be quiet. I'll tell you what you want to know. Don't hurt me. Don't hurt me." She made herself small, pulling her feet up to her chest and curling over into a ball.

Yukiyo found her to be quite amusing. While Gillian cringed she reached into her pocket and retrieved the syringe-pak Silas gave her. Gillian did not realize she had been poked. The drug took about a minute to take effect. Gillian fell back, with an unconscious grin that gave the impression she would not be opposed to the effects of cocaine. Silas' drugs were awesome. It made her happy he hooked her up. For Orion and Alec's sake, Yukiyo hoped Silas found his rifle.

Chapter 22

Alec couldn't take Lareina's haunted expression and distant thoughts any longer. "Mom."

"Ummhmm."

"You know, the last time we were in D.C., Silas and Orion blew up a house. You don't suppose they've forgotten, do you?" He attempted humor for her benefit.

"One can hope."

"Never forget." Orion spoke from the front seat.

"If they give us any trouble, I suggest we give them Orion."

She laughed for him. That's what he wanted.

"Turn your head, 'Reina." Orion raised his middle finger high enough for Alec to see.

Happy with her reaction, Alec ignored Orion. "Are you going to be okay?"

She put her arm around him and hugged him to her. He brought her so much comfort. "I won't lie, I am worried. But, I'll be alright. We'll find him."

In the front seat, Orion prepared for a nap while Fisher drove, keeping a silent vigil.

Alec looked at her steadily, his obsidian eyes deep and serious. He had more to say.

"What is it?" she coaxed.

He waited a moment longer. He did not have a good feeling about this mission. He wasn't going to tell his mom that, but he did have something he needed to know. "Will you get okay if...if this doesn't turn out right?"

No, she wouldn't, but he didn't need to know that. She didn't need to think about that. It *was* going to turn out right. She gifted him with a loving smile, pulled his head down to her shoulder and massaged his scalp. "As long as I have you guys, I'll be alright."

"You have me."

"Then, I'll be alright."

That's what he wanted to hear.

He would make her alright.

****

The sun was blinking over the horizon when Lareina's phone rang. "Hello."

"We got her, 'Reina."

At least that was good news. "Thanks, Kaid. Are you and Yukiyo okay?"

"Yep. Took about two minutes."

"Excellent. Don't bother going to Uncle Moe's. We're done there."

Kaiden went on high alert. "Why? What happened?"

"They got Christian. We're going to get him."

"'Reina!" No. She wasn't going off on any wild-ass assignments without him. "Where the hell is Silas?" That jack-wad should know better.

"He's in D.C. That's where we're heading."

"The last time we were there, Silas let Orion blow up a house. And you couldn't wait for me?"

"They're going to kill him if we don't get there in time."

He didn't give a shit, but he wouldn't say that aloud. "I'll meet you there."

"No, you won't. You have to get Gillian underground. You might have to get her talking. Once we pick up Christian, our very small window of opportunity will be a whole lot smaller."

Kaiden was antsy, but he wasn't stupid. "Fine. Where to now?"

"Hmmm." She had a fair few safe-houses and places to lie low, but at the rate they were going, they'd be through them inside two years. It wasn't like she was still at work, organizing and stocking up. Once they got Christian, they were going to have to get way out of dodge. In fact, the East Coast may be off limits. "Head west, no southwest."

"New Orleans?" Being the person who smuggled in the weapons that stocked most of her safe houses, Kaiden knew their locations. "Or New Mexico?"

"Doesn't matter. You pick."

"Alright. Where are you now?"

"Coming up on D.C. We're going to meet Silas and go over the plan." By that, she meant when they met Silas, if he didn't have a plan, they would come up with one. But Kaiden didn't need details.

Kaiden knew enough to draw his own conclusions. Once they met up again, he was going to kick Silas' ass for letting Lareina out of his sight. He was going to kick Christian's ass for causing this trouble. Nope, he was going to kick Christian's ass on principle. Fisher better not let him down.

"You better keep me posted."

"Yes, sir." She loved the way he protected her whether she needed it or not.

A minute after Kaiden hung up, Fisher's phone rang. He had it in his hand waiting. "I got her."

"I know you do. Right now, you're the only one who does."

"That's why I'm here, man."

Kaiden took a breath. Fisher was his right arm. Having him with Lareina was the same thing as being there himself. Screw Christian. Screw Silas. He had Fisher. Fisher would watch out for Lareina. Always had. Always will. It wasn't a question. "Thanks."

"I like this car. It's smooth." Fisher's change of topic was exactly how they rolled. No questions. No debts.

Kaiden didn't know which one of his uncle's vehicles they were using, but he didn't have to. "Keep it."

"I think I will."

****

"We've just parked. Where are you?" Lareina didn't expect to see Silas, but she looked around anyway. She hadn't been to Pentagon Row in years, but it remained virtually unchanged. International cuisine, major shops and elite boutiques; before the war, Pentagon City had been dubbed fashion central. Even now, its inhabitants strived to maintain the façade. If nothing else, it still looked like an oasis for the wealthy and/or fun loving and/or shallow.

"I see you. I'll meet you at the Nopre Grill in a minute."

Lareina led the way past Ice Queen's and the JapAsian Bistro. It made her think of sushi and days when simple pleasures were easy to come by.

She didn't care how he made it happen, but Christian would be settling his debt with sushi. The thought made her happy.

****

"Where's Silas?" Orion slid into the booth first. He scooted across the seat to make room for Fisher.

Lareina sat directly across from him. As always, Alec was beside her. "He said he'd meet us here in a minute."

They had eaten on the road, so they ordered a round of drinks. Fisher kept his menu. He flipped the pages, not caring for the fancy stuff and settled on something he knew. "I'll have the steak and eggs with a double stack of pancakes and a side of hash browns. Don't forget the steak sauce, ketchup, and maple syrup." Once the young lady disappeared with his order, he returned to the subject. "If I know Silas—and I do—he's making sure we weren't being followed."

"We weren't." Alec had been checking the whole time.

"I know that," Fisher said, "but Silas doesn't."

Orion added, "To Silas, what he knows is all that matters."

Not long after, Silas strode in wearing full military attire—TS13 included. He sat down, crowding Alec, and by extension, Lareina. Disregarding salutations, he got to the point. "His office at the Pentagon is locked down. They have a whole brigade guarding his office here." He pointed out the window in the general direction of a swank high-rise administrative building.

"Which one is our target?" Orion asked.

"What chance do we have of snatching him from one of those places?" The dessert menu currently had most of Fisher's attention.

"His office isn't our target," Silas said. "Good thing too because our chance of success would be one hundred percent of zero in either situation."

"Where is he, Silas?" Lareina locked gazes with his.

He returned the stare, honesty for honesty. "They have him on house arrest. Minimum security."

"That should help, shouldn't it?" Orion was hopeful.

Lareina asked the real question. "Why?"

Alec had already caught on. "No, it won't help."

Silas remained silent. He nodded once, encouraging his protégé to continue.

Alec saw it. "Most likely, it's an ambush and they're using him for bait." He half turned in his seat. "I think they're expecting you, Mom."

Lareina had no intention of being swayed, thwarted or manipulated. "Well good. I hate to disappoint."

****

Christian noted the irony with detached humor. The last time he was here, he held Jericho hostage. Now, he found himself in the same position, tied to the same chair. Only, he wasn't Jericho. His keys were still in his pocket. And every last one of those stupid asses was going to die. He rethought the events that landed him in this circumstance. Not with regret; he hadn't done anything he needed to regret. He wanted everything fresh, to keep his adrenaline going.

He had Misty, his assistant, schedule an appointment with Dr. Terrance Chezwick. He had every intention of visiting the man and ending his life, plain and simple. Forty minutes later, Misty called him back. Commander Joffener wanted him a.s.a.p. Come to his office and nowhere else. The message should have been the tipoff. Joffener knew how to reach him directly. He was one of the few who did. He left the message with Misty because he didn't want to risk giving anything away. Christian hadn't forgotten, but he hadn't recalled either. Joffener trained him. Christian had been the Commander's field replacement. The man had been doing double cross and legal assassination before Christian knew it came with a job title.

Times change, of course. Christian earned his position. Joffener wasn't up on the rules of engagement. Telling Christian he put him on the Elliot case, not because he thought Christian would succeed, but because of his relationship with Lareina, was a bad idea. Letting Christian know he had been used, would be the last mistake Joffener got to make.

Commander Joffener didn't understand, Lareina wouldn't come for him. She'd want to, but she'd know better. Christian wouldn't allow it. He'd kick her ass for putting herself in danger when she knew his capabilities. With any luck, he'd dispatch Joffener and be on his way to Chezwick before she found out he'd been taken.

He didn't turn, or move, or give any acknowledgment he heard them, but he knew they were there, walking in slowly, behind him. Three. Three dead men, as far as he was concerned. He smelled it and took a deep breath before the chloroform drenched cloth covered his nose and mouth.

Seconds later, Christian's head slumped forward.

The man holding the cloth straightened up. He looked to Commander Joffener for further instruction.

"Open the curtain. I want to make sure he can be seen. I want to make sure the sniper has a clear shot. Missing won't be an option."

The second assistant did as bidden.

"Put that shit away, or we'll all be sleep."

The first man capped the bottle of chloroform. "Do you want us to untie him now? Lay him on the bed?"

"Oh, hell no." Joffener shook his head to be sure his point was made. "Deverell is lethal."

"He's knocked out, boss. He will be for the rest of his short life."

Joffener snorted. "I can't vouch that will stop him. I personally wouldn't put it past him to kill you while unconscious." Warming to his subject, he continued, "Gentlemen, you won't meet a more dangerous man than Christian Deverell. Unless it's the guy I'm hoping to replace him with."

"Who?"

"A young soldier by the name of Silas McKade. He's the sniper. He doesn't miss." Joffener checked the window, searching the nearby rooftops and trees for a glimpse of the legendary McKade. "If you put the two of them together, I have no doubt they could end this entire war in a matter of weeks. In fact, I've had my hands full keeping them both occupied and inattentive these last few months."

"Why aren't we doing that?" the second assistant asked. "Seems like a waste of talent to kill him if he's so effective and he'd be a part of an unstoppable team."

"I said they would be great together. Not that it would be possible. I'm convinced there is only one person on this planet who could get them to cooperate." The Commander looked from one of his henchmen to the other. "It's a woman~"

"Who else but?"

Joffener nodded. "Not just any woman. A dangerous woman in her own right, because of her knowledge-base and her ability to influence people we don't need influenced. She's the one we're getting ready to collect."

The first man snorted. The situation becoming clear. "I guess Deverell won't be pleased."

"Not one bit," Joffener said. "If my intelligence is correct, neither will Corporeal McKade."

"Ouch. What are we going to do about him?"

That depends on the Corporeal. If he kills Deverell, he's useful. If not, he belongs to her and we'll have to put him down too." Joffener tsk'd the thought of waste.

"Put him down? Won't he see us coming?"

"No." Joffener smirked at this part of his plan. He thought of it himself. "McKade isn't the only sniper I'm expecting." He left it there.

****

"What's the plan?" Alec had a bad feeling about this. He hoped Silas would grant him some peace.

"There is no plan."

Whatever Alec expected, that wasn't it. Orion and Fisher echoed his 'what?' Lareina kept quiet.

Silas directed his explanation to her. "We don't know what's going on inside that house, other than they're expecting company. I don't feel like shitting around. I'm going to put them all to sleep. Once they're down, two of your stooges can grab Eugene and the other one can hold your hand, 'til it's over."

"It's nervy as hell," Fisher said. "I like it."

"Me too," Lareina answered. "Except the part about holding my hand. I'm not sending anybody in. I'll do it myself."

"Oh, yeah," Silas sneered. "Unless your boy is a sleep walker, how do you plan to get him out?"

She hunched her shoulder daintily, "I have on flats. I'll manage."

Chapter 23

The late morning hour felt fresh. A cleansing breeze danced through leafy trees, spilling sunlight across manicured lawns and painted flowerbeds. It was a day for grass cutting and gardening and pretending all was right in the worn out world. A jogger bypassed a dog-walker. They both waved at a car-washer.

Alec had been let out at the top of the block. Silas dropped Orion off at the other end. The boys worked their way around garages and through back yards; an excellent pair of lookouts. Across the street and two houses down, the split-foyer didn't look as if anyone was home. Fisher parked in the driveway. Sunglass clad Lareina rang the bell. Satisfied they were alone, Fisher and Lareina jokingly reminisced about their younger years as they kept a sharp vigilance.

The oak Silas chose looked to be over sixty feet tall. Hfe only needed thirty feet for his purpose. Tossing a rope over a sturdy branch, he cleared the first ten feet in under a minute. The rest didn't take much longer. Situating himself on a branch strong enough to stretch out upon, Silas took in the scenery. He faced the front of the house as opposed to the back where he would be expected to take his kill-shot. More importantly, he could see everyone he needed to protect.

He inserted his earpiece and went to work. "F-one." Chronos went into voice command. "Dial out two, dial out four, dial out six, dial out seven." He called all the team players at once.

Lareina, Fisher, Alec, and Orion each checked in. It wouldn't be long now.

****

Christian listened for the door to close and the footsteps to fade before he moved. Inch by cautious inch, he turned his head into his shoulder, wiping off the poison as best he could. He hadn't inhaled it, but having it smeared across his nose and lips still had an effect. He was groggy. It was work making himself focus, but he kept shaking his head and recalling thoughts and words that would help him stay conscious. He judged it would take about twenty minutes for it to burn off. Twenty minutes. It felt like a long time to him, but in Joffener's case, it wasn't long at all. Twenty minutes was the rest of his life. That was a thought Christian could hold on to.

****

"Movement in the front," Alec whispered from somewhere too close to the house for Lareina's liking.

The front door opened. A man—Joffener—stepped outside to take a call. He left the door open. Silas put his eye to his scope and smiled.

Alec turned up the transmitter on Chronos II and Joffener's conversation became a lot less private. "ETA? Perfect. I want you in place at least an hour before he sets up. Are we clear?"

"I guess somebody else is coming," Fisher explained the obvious. "What type of party are we having here?"

"That is just rude," Silas replied, unperturbed. "I might take my toys and go home."

"Don't be a spoiled-sport, Silas," Lareina pretended to chide. "You need to play with everyone."

"Do you promise?"

"I'm not worried about Elliot—" The mention of Lareina silenced the eavesdroppers. "Deverell will be dead long before she arrives. We won't tell her until after she's been subdued. With any luck, she'll have her motley-crew with her and we can get this mopped up today."

"I can blow a hole in his head right now," Alec offered.

"So can I," Silas said. "But killing people outside the house won't do much to help us get inside. That's ultimately where we need to be. So sit tight and take your happy finger off that trigger."

"You take the don't-talk-about-my-mother attitude way too far, Alec," Orion said.

"How about I talk about your mother down on the block," Alec fired back.

"Kiss my ass."

"That's enough." Lareina ended the debate.

"I agree," Fisher announced. He filled the silence with an explanation. "Alec takes his attitude too far and Orion's mother should meet me on the block."

"I said that's enough," Lareina talked over Alec and Silas' laughter.

They watched Joffener stride the length of the walkway and back, listening intently, adding an occasional question or comment, but nothing to gain them further insight.

"Orion?" Lareina noted his silence. This wasn't a good time to have any of them off kilter or annoyed. She called him a second time before he answered.

"Can't talk." He spoke so softly, they would not have heard him had they not all been silently listening.

"Silas?"

"On it."

His response came the moment she called his name. Easily, he spotted Orion. The boy crouched low on the roof of the house next door. How he got up there was anybody's guess. It gave him a clear vantage point to see both the front and back of Christian's house. But there must be a problem. Orion was statue-still which told Silas he was in danger of being seen. Silas repositioned, scanning the area slowly, seeking out the threat.

A hundred yards out, less than half the distance to the back yard trees Silas was supposed to be hiding in, the glint of shine. Silas knew exactly what it was; sunlight reflecting off the barrow of a shotgun.

Clarity of reason came with the full discernment of the situation. Silas understood, and reacted in the only manner fitting. He switched clips and shifted his sights.

It was another sniper setting up. From his position, he would have a clear view of Orion; most likely assume he was the sniper sent to take out Deverell. Silas had total recall of Joffener's conversation. It was simple to interpret—the commander planned for someone to take him out. It spoke to the warrior in Silas. "Fucker."

The low-pitched monotone was a warning to Lareina. "What is it, Silas?"

It was an open challenge. That's what it was.

Corporal Silas McKade, Special Ops CT was a power you did not challenge.

"Fucker." Silas squeezed the trigger.

****

The echo of the gunshot. The short terrified scream. The snapping of limbs and the thump of a body hitting the ground was one sound. It was the sound of the trumpet calling the charge. Shuffling of feet and hustling of bodies had a handful of people pouring out the back, searching for the trouble and its cause.

The old plan changed. The new plan became 'Go!' There was no real awareness of who uttered the word, indeed, who thought they should move. But they heard it as one and all of them obeyed. Lareina and Fisher jumped from the car and flew at the front door.

Joffener was on the porch when he heard the first shot. The second shot didn't matter to him. It was Alec, making good on his offer. The commander lay lifeless—a hole in his brain. Alec had cleared the way because his mom was coming.

He went into the house first. Her shield. Fisher came right behind him. He stepped in front of Alec before Lareina got through the doorway. Gunfire exploded in the back. Orion and Silas held their attention and kept them busy. Cautiously, the trio went from room to room, weapons out, tracking in every direction.

****

When the sniper screamed, Orion moved. He went down the side of the house faster than he climbed up. By the time Joffener's men reached the back yard, he was properly concealed, close enough to pick them off.

Silas was already picking them off. Anybody who wasn't on his team was a threat—a threat that needed to be eliminated. Agents scattered, seeking cover, attempting to return fire.

Sirens roared. Rubber burned as federal agents zeroed in on the house. An overload of backup was on the way.

****

Fisher started up the steps but halted midway. There was movement. Lareina and Alec paused behind him. Nobody liked what they heard. An audible click. At the foot of the stairs, a lone man made an appearance behind a semi-automatic. "Stop, right there. Just stop," he said.

Another agent stepped into view at the top of the stairs. He fixed his gun on Lareina. "That was so dumb, it almost worked." He sneered. "Get on up here. You can drop those toys right here, at my feet."

As one, Fisher and Alec turned to Lareina. Caught in a crossfire with nowhere to run wasn't the ideal circumstance, but all it would take was a nod from her and they'd go at it, right there.

Lareina would do it. She had confidence in her boys. And getting caught was never an option. They both knew where to aim; she and Alec would target the semi-automatic, two on one, while Fisher dealt with the jerk at the top. She hesitated. She wouldn't if Alec weren't in danger. There was something else, too. She couldn't name it, but she wasn't out of hope. Not yet. She made the decision, breathing it in one clear word, "Up."

Fisher understood it. He did not like it, but there wasn't anything to like in any regard. He nodded and led the way up. Alec walked up backward, never taking his eyes off the man with the semi.

Their captor gloated. He beckoned them forward and pointed to his shoes. "Put it here." On the tail end of his words, he stiffened. His eyes bulged. He gasped once before a strong hand clasped over his mouth and he was pulled back into the shadows. The people on the steps gave no indication anything was amiss. The man below remained ignorant of the change.

Fisher came to the landing and released his almost empty clip from the magazine. It hit the floor with a clang. He stepped off to the side.

Lareina pursed her lips at the outstretched hand but willingly surrendered her weapon. The other hand snapped twice and she rolled her eyes but gave up the spare ammo to go with it. *Cocky Bastard.* She moved over beside Fisher.

Alec followed her. He neither stopped to note the current state of affairs nor to relinquish his weapon. He wasn't giving up his gun for anybody.

It didn't matter. The guy holding the semi-automatic followed them up the stairs. As soon as Alec was clear, Christian appeared around the corner. He unloaded four shots: two to the head, two to the chest. Having a semi didn't account for anything. The man, his finger already on the trigger, died before his finger moved. He fell backward down the steps, still holding his semi-automatic at the ready.

The front door burst back upon its hinge. The room flooded with agents.

From her waistband, Lareina produced a second weapon. She came here to free Christian. Arming him was part of that procedure.

Christian pulled back around the corner. Reaching to the dead man on the floor, he retrieved the knife protruding from his victim's punctured lung. The knife he used to free himself. The knife Lareina had given him for his birthday. He led them down the hall, toward the master suite and balcony. They were going to have to take their chances with whoever waited for them outside.

The agents reached the top of the stairs and all of hell happened.

Fisher shoved Lareina in front of him. Her grip on Alec brought him along. Christian and Fisher followed them in and took turns firing down the hallway, holding back the tide while Alec and Lareina hunted for a way out.

****

Officer Leeds searched left and right, positive he saw someone or something dive into the bushes. Whatever it was he was going to kill it. A sliding door caught his attention. He turned toward the sound and recognized two of the escaping suspects. The boy was closer. He took aim...

BAM!
BAM!

Orion did not hesitate, he cleared the tree he was hiding behind and shot Officer Leeds at point blank range. The splattering blood told him he had left himself open before the blinding pain snatched his thought.

Alec didn't hesitate either. He screamed his outrage as he took out

Orion's attacker. Not willing to stop there, he leapt from the second-floor balcony, shooting his way down. He landed at a run, dodging through a rain of fire. With the same adrenaline-laced superhuman strength Orion used to tear Uncle Moe's house apart, Alec hefted Orion across his shoulder. Alive or dead, he wasn't leaving him.

By now, Christian and Fisher had retreated to the balcony. Lareina jumped. She covered Alec as he sprinted to safety with Orion's blood dripping down his back. Every time she pulled the trigger, it was with the full force of a mother's anguish and rage.

Christian jumped with Fisher a half pace behind. Bullets came from below and behind as agents rushed the balcony and swamped the yard. Christian landed in a roll. He came up shooting and did not stop. Lareina was still within his sight. He followed her trail, took a hit in his leg and kept moving, looking back only once.

Fisher landed on one knee. The one-second pause was too long. He pushed his weight off the ground and his forward motion met with a wall of heat. The energy held him upright, arms flung wide, suspended for one glorious moment before he collapsed with five slugs buried in his chest and two in the back of his head. Fisher didn't know it. He didn't feel it. He didn't have to care anymore.

Chapter 24

Standard for any getaway plan, Fisher's keys were still in the ignition. Lareina snatched the back door open then sprinted around to the driver's side. Alec shoved Orion in and closed the door behind himself. Lareina whipped out of the driveway and angled the car toward Christian.

Christian cleared the yard and dove for the front passenger seat. "GO!" he shouted.

"Fisher!" she shouted back.

His look told her more than she wanted to know.

Silas' voice, silent until now, speaking in her earpiece confirmed her horror. Calm. Without debate. Final. "'Reina go."

She mashed the gas. She did not see how to get by the road block. She did not think to dodge the firepower coming their way. She did not know she undertook the impossible. Fisher was dead. There was no world beyond that.

****

So far, Silas hadn't missed. With the rest of them gone, the fight took on a new perspective. He cleared the yard. Unable to detect the sniper's location, officers and agents retreated to the safety of the house. That made Silas smile. He switched his magazine, firing two of the original capsules into the house—one upstairs, one down. While he waited for the sleeping gas to take effect, he made a necessary phone call.

"Lieutenant Colonel Briggs."

"Lieutenant Colonel Briggs, sir. This is Corporal McKade reporting."

"McKade."

"Permission to be blunt, sir?"

"Permission granted."

"Sir, I'm getting tired of being Deverell's bitch."

"What happened?"

"I walked into what I perceive to be an ambush, sir. From what I gather, a sniper had already been assigned. I suspect he's working for Deverell or someone higher up. Commander Joffener was apparently the true target. I arrived in the middle of a bloodbath. I have not gone in to assess the damage. I can do that if you'd like the information, sir. Or, I can leave now with services untendered. Your call."

"Are you in any danger, soldier?"

"No, sir. Not that I am aware of."

"Why don't you see what you can find out? See who survived. I'd be interested to know who was more dangerous, Deverell or Joffener."

"I'll get right on it, sir."

"Good man, McKade. I'm guessing you've got a promotion due."

"Thank you, sir." Silas disconnected. He knew who was more dangerous. Him.

****

Silas worked his way through the carnage. There were a lot of bodies, mostly the result of his skill. He used his boot to flip Officer Leeds on his back. The shiny glint of police issued handcuffs winked up at him with the key swinging next to it. *Bastard.* The tree blocked his shot, but damned if Alec didn't answer. On impulse, Silas helped himself to the cuffs. He suspected they would come in handy. He moved on. He had a job to do and he wasn't going to fail. Bending over the body of his fallen teammate, Silas removed Fisher's personal items: his wallet, his phone, his jewelry—two rings, an earring and a necklace. The necklace was especially important. It was Fisher's identity as surely as his fingerprint. Fisher was a wolf, ferocious and loyal.

He lifted Fisher's battered body and moved it closer to the house, talking to him as he walked. "Don't worry about it, man. I know my part. I won't let anybody mess with you." Gently, he laid him down on Christian's deck and watched him for a moment. Hating that there was nothing more he could do, he bid his final farewell, "Later, Fish."

Without a backwards glance, he walked away. Popping a pin on a grenade, he tossed it over his shoulder and sprinted. Four seconds and then the explosion. Christian's house and everyone in it gone for no other reason than to keep his promise. No one would mess with Fisher.

****

"Did you see Joffener?" Christian said. He held his hand over the wound in his calf, staunching the blood flow. If he were in pain, it did not register.

"Ummhmm," Lareina nodded tightly. "He was the first one." She wouldn't say dead. Only Fisher was dead.

"Second," Alec corrected. "Silas shot first." His attention went to Orion. He didn't know what he was looking at or for, but none of it looked good. "He's bad, Mom."

Lareina was not losing another family member. "Christian?"

"There's a doctor in Alexandria. He's not on anybody's side. He works for cash and doesn't keep records. Probably our best chance."

That was the chance she wanted. The best one.

****

Five hours. They reached the doctor's office, commanded and received immediate attention, waited for Silas, commandeered a vehicle and transferred twenty-five thousand, illegally hacked, dollars to the Doctor's personal account. They accomplished everything without obstruction, which was telling. The firefight and explosion would no-doubt be credited to the war, but the lack of a serious manhunt could only mean one thing. Some entity within the organization did not want them caught. Not yet, anyway.

Silas drove his jeep—this one a Phoenix—with Orion, still unconscious in the back. Alec drove the new car. Christian rode shotgun and Lareina lay unconscious on the back seat. She accepted the sedative not because of an external injury, but to earn some release from the wound that would not heal. She wore Fisher's necklace, the wolf charm with Amethyst for eyes, tightly clasped in her palm.

****

Kaiden wasn't what anyone would consider an early riser. He wasn't anti-morning like Orion, but he would never be able to hop up, fully charged like Alec. He didn't know why he woke up early this morning. Maybe it was the silence. Not the decibel level. New Orleans was never completely quiet, not even at this before dawn hour. He made a pot of coffee, watched it perk. He hadn't heard from his team since he texted Lareina his choice for their safe house. She Ok'd it and they went to communication silence. He and Yukiyo got the crying 'ho undercover while the rest of them went about securing Christian's sorry ass. He didn't know why Silas didn't put a cap in him and make all of their lives easier. Yes, he did. For the same reason, he, Kaiden, didn't do the same thing. The only reason for anything. Lareina. His pain-in-the-ass-sister who gave her everything for him, always. His whole life, she did all of whatever to see that he wanted for nothing. And not just him. Not more than a kid herself, she raised Fisher and Silas. Lost causes, both of them. Now, she was taking care of the next generation of rejects: Yuke, Ori and Alec. She would turn them into something important because that's what she did, saved the world, one screwed-up kid at a time. He watched the last drops of hot caffeine slip from the filter. Who was he to begrudge her favorite brand of entertainment—Deverell. The creep should be happy Lareina likes him. That's about all that kept him from getting merked.

On the front porch, coffee mug in hand, Kaiden searched the horizon, not looking for anything in particular; not even the dawn. It would arrive with or without his notice. His problem was the silence. Silence might be necessary sometimes, but it wasn't sitting well with him. He'd chill until he finished his coffee. Then he'd be done with the silence.

Yukiyo pushed the door open. Her hair flying in every direction. "Have you heard from anybody?" She removed a clump from her eye.

"No. I'm getting ready to wake somebody up now."

"Good." She came out on the porch carrying a bag he recognized but didn't remember from where. She helped herself to his mug and took two long sips. "Mmm. Good. Did you make a pot?"

"Yeah. Now, give me my cup back and go get your own." He reached for his mug and pointed at her bag. "Where are you going?"

She relinquished it after two swallows. "Nowhere you idiot." She pushed an overflowing flowerpot out of her way and sat down opposite him. "This belongs to Miss Foster. I spent half the night reading what's in it. And," she pulled out a small recorder, "listening to this."

"What's it called when you go through other people's mail?" He finished off his brew.

"Being smart. If you bring me a cup of coffee, I'll tell you what I learned."

"Bring you a cup? What do I look like, your slave?"

"I wouldn't have you," she sneered. "You're about to get some more anyway. Try being nice for one day."

Damn. Her sense of observance was phenomenal. He only glanced at the mug, had barely moved his leg. She recognized his intentions as soon as they appeared. He got up. "I know why 'Reina wanted you. You notice too much to be on the other side."

"Thanks," she muttered, unused to admiration. She pushed a stray lock out of her face. "I want more sugar."

****

Christian stared out the window. He neither saw nor cared to see the mileage markers. He hadn't chosen their destination, he had no reason to concern himself with the timeline or details of their arrival. He was waiting. His next course of action wouldn't come until he and Lareina could speak privately. Until he knew for certain whether or not she held him accountable for Fisher's death. He was responsible to some degree, they both were, but where the blame went meant everything. If she blamed herself, he would not leave her. He would help her work through her grief. If, however, she blamed him, he'd be gone before she could think to apologize. For now, he waited.

****

Yukiyo's findings were just short of a miracle. A stroke of luck had given them the exact information they needed.

"What are the chances we would grab her on the very day she decided to transport this?" Kaiden wasn't altogether certain of what he read, but he knew enough to recognize its significance. "Lareina is going to have a heart attack."

"I know." Yukiyo was quite pleased. "That's why Gillian was so willing to talk. I think she hoped if she cooperated, we wouldn't bother searching, 'cause she was dirty as hell."

"That and possibly trying to buy some time. Now, that we got all this, we don't need her."

The early hours of morning slipped by, unnoticed by the two engrossed in their findings. It was odd seeing Alec behind the wheel, pulling into the drive. Silas came right behind him.

Alec moved stiffly, making eye contact but not greeting Kaiden or Yukiyo. Instead, he opened the back door to help his mom.

Kaiden was glad he had forgotten to call. Obviously, they'd had a hard time. They didn't need any shit from him.

Christian got out and limped to Lareina's other side. The three didn't come any closer but waited on Silas as he assisted Orion.

Kaiden could see Orion had clearly gotten the worst. Thank God they were home.

Yukiyo gasped. Her hand covered her mouth and tears filled her eyes.

Ori's upper body was bandaged. His left arm was in a cast. His head bowed and his eyes were unfocused. He leaned heavily on Silas, letting him take all of his weight. Alec got behind them, supporting Orion's back to keep him balanced as they ascended the three steps to the porch.

The group was quiet. Too quiet, as if they couldn't speak.

Yukiyo's crying accelerated. She paced and wailed. She kicked the nearest flower pot, snatched her coffee mug and flung it.

Kaiden grabbed her arm. "Hey!" he yelled, stunning her into silence. "Breathe." He didn't know what made her pop off, her reactions were normally cold. Except when her Dad... His eyes darted over the group. Fish..."Where's Fisher?"

"Get him." Silas heaved a sigh and shifted so Alec could take his position. "Help Alec," he ordered Yukiyo. Better to get her out of the way. It was going to be hard enough without her losing her shit. Silas knew better than anybody what to expect. Lareina needed him to be ready for it.

"Aww hell NO!" Kaiden's world narrowed. His entire focus went to Christian. It was because of him. There was no way in hell Christian was going to breathe air that Fisher couldn't! He bellowed his outrage and dived at Christian, plowing into him, his momentum throwing them both to the ground.

Whether it was a surprise, or his injury, or some form of compassion; perhaps it was Lareina's scream. Whatever the reason, Christian did not put up any resistance. He seemed willing to let Kaiden put his anger wherever he needed it to go.

Kaiden had only steeled his fingers around Christian's throat when he was yanked backward. Before he could react, Silas rocked him. The punch landed in the center of Kaiden's lips, with enough force to snap his head back.

Lareina's second scream was quickly muffled, presumably by Christian. Her protests soon faded, presumably because she had been taken into the house. Neither Silas nor Kaiden looked to be sure.

For one long moment, Kaiden stared at Silas, too stunned to react. And then he gave Silas his full attention. His response time was a second shorter than Silas anticipated. The soldier had only braced himself for the retaliation when it came.

Kaiden connected with Silas' jaw. Silas stumbled back a step, blinked hard as he absorbed the pain. *Damn.* It had been a while. He had forgotten how hard Kaiden's punches were. Good thing too. Otherwise, he'd have let Christian take that first hit. *Oh, well.* He got what he wanted. *Back to business.*

He stepped in close enough for Kaiden to swing before neatly ducking and landing a fierce blow to Kaiden's gut. Kaiden doubled over with the wind knocked out of him.

"Too slow," Silas taunted as he danced out of the way, giving Kaiden a chance to catch his breath.

The taunt affected Kaiden more than the punch did. He charged Silas with the full force of his rage. But Silas was his match. He did not have Kaiden's brute strength, but what he had, was military skill and old fashion street know-how. Like everything in Silas' hands, it was a deadly combination. And Silas could think. It made him superior in this clash. In fact, it was the reason they were fighting.

In grief, Kaiden couldn't think. His first response to pain was anger. The bigger the injury, the madder Kaiden became. Fisher was Kaiden's right arm, his best friend. They'd been together since they were babies. He needed to pass off the pain he didn't want to feel. Christian was the blame, Christian was going to suffer. That simple.

Not, that Silas cared about Christian. *To hell with him.* He did, however, care a great deal about Lareina. And, although he pretended not to, he cared about Kaiden.

"Come on, son," Silas teased. "Whatcha got?" He tagged him and backed pedaled. "Nothing. You ain't got nothing."

"I'm getting ready to drop your ass." Kaiden connected with Silas' chest. "That's what I got."

"Not shit, son. You ain't got shit, but a bunch of anger and no focus." To prove his point, in rapid secession, Silas blocked a shot, elbowed him in the ribs and smashed the back of his fist into Kaiden's jaw.

"Why are you in my business anyway, huh?" Kaiden landed two rights which made Silas stumble and a left that had him seeing fireworks. "This ain't got nothing to do with you. Or does it?" His first coherent thoughts, an indication the red haze was leaving his mind.

"Everybody had something to do with it. Even Fisher." Silas had to duck fast. He came up behind Kaiden and tripped him. He held him down for a moment and released him just as Kaiden flipped. They jumped to their feet, breathing heavy, eying one another wearily. Kaiden still fumed, but the blind rage had begun to recede.

"Why him? Why not me?" Silas favored his left leg. Kaiden punched the thigh twice, intending to weaken it further.

Silas blocked a third swing and used the same leg to kick Kaiden, first in the stomach and then in the face. "Because that's how it played out. You weren't there. Fisher was." He put Kaiden in a headlock and threw him down. "About the only thing we know for certain is that it wouldn't have happened if you could have been there."

"No, the hell it wouldn't have! I'd have fucked him up for being in the line of fire."

Now, they were wrestling; burning off fumes of anger and restless energy.

"He would have listened to you too."

"Damn straight."

"He had her back, Kaid. Lareina was in some shit and he got her out of it. He got them all out." They were on the ground now. Wrestling and rolling, going for the pin instead of the injury.

"Hell yeah, he did. What did you think he would do? He probably saved all of their asses."

"I saw it. He did save their asses. All of them."

They struggled a few more minutes before Silas let Kaiden push his shoulders down. The fight was over. Kaiden needed the win. Kaiden held him there, feeling as if he had truly accomplished something, wanting to die because he didn't have Fisher there to share it with him. He released Silas, grateful for the sweat running down his face. It made him believe his tears were hidden.

He sat back, giving Silas room to sit up. They panted, trying to catch their breath. Silas reached into his pocket and retrieved Fisher's rings. Palm open, he showed them to Kaiden. "Nobody is going to mess with him. I made sure."

Kaiden tugged on his earring and nodded. "Thanks, man." He looked at the rings and didn't care if Silas saw him crying.

"I want to keep one." The request surprised him as much as it did Kaiden. Silas was not one to ask for things, he either took them or did without. But, Fisher was his brother too. He needed to own something of Fisher's.

Kaiden made his hand move. His fingers clamped around the first ring he touched. "Yeah, okay." He tried to shrug, to pretend the anguish wasn't eating him alive. He stared at the ring, the reminder of what he'd lost. Fisher had been with him through it all, since the beginning. Silas too. Silas deserved to have a memory. Fisher deserved to be remembered. "You should keep one." He meant it. He slid his memento onto his finger and held it there.

Silas' eyes filmed. It seemed alright, this one time, to let his grief show. Mimicking Kaiden's gesture, he put the remaining ring on his finger and likewise held it there. "Thanks."

When there seemed nothing more to say, nothing else to do, they struggled to their feet. Already the bruises were starting to show, they'd both be black and blue tomorrow. They made their way to the house, limping and grimacing. Outside the door, Silas made a confession. "I hope you won't mind, but I was thinking about your garage, so took the liberty of blowing up Deverell's house."

Somewhere through Kaiden's heartache, a snicker bubbled up. "I hope somebody took pictures."

Chapter 25

Inside, the house was a tomb. Yukiyo stayed with Orion. Lareina, Alec, and Christian were at opposite ends of the living room. Christian sat tensely on one of the twin recliners. As far away from Christian as possible, Alec propped on one end of the sofa, his eyes glued on his mother. He had a bad feeling about the mission from the beginning, but she told him she'd be alright. He'd wait. When she was ready, he'd do his part to make her alright.

Lareina stood near Alec, her hand massaging his hair. But, she wasn't alright. She wasn't anything. A large oil painting hung above the sofa. She stared at it intently, not caring to see the detailed images or the precision brush strokes. She didn't bother to notice the vivid colors. The hand-carved wooden frame escaped her appreciation. Her fingers gently combed through his rich ebony mane, her gaze fixed some place beyond the portrait.

Across the room, Christian stared intently at Lareina. The silence stretched between them, but only Christian felt the weight of it. Technically, Lareina wasn't there. She left him alone. It was paralyzing him. He hated feeling numb. He needed to know where things stood between them, but he couldn't do that with her gone. His length of patience was shorter than most people's. He accepted that. "Are you done?" His tone had an edge.

Other than a glare from Alec, his question went unanswered. He would not accept that. "LAREINA."

She turned, compelled by the absolute command in his voice.

"It's time for you to get your shit together, don't you think?" His words carried enough bite to force a reaction.

The reaction came.

"Who the fuck are you yelling at?" Kaiden walked in and went straight for Christian.

Silas went to claim a bedroom. He did his part. He didn't have to care anymore.

"You ain't hiding somewhere, talking shit on the phone, Christian." Kaiden brought to mind their last conversation. "What do you have to say now, huh?"

Christian stood up.

Alec stood up.

The activities of all four men combined brought Lareina to the present. Silas left her. She could sum up the others with one word each: shouldn't, couldn't and wouldn't—all negatives. She needed to be present.

"Kaiden, don't." She watched her fire-breathing brother. "He's trying to help me. Trying to get me to focus, that's all." Her voice shook, but it rang with clarity of thought and clear understanding.

Alec breathed a sigh of relief. She wasn't better, but she'd get there.

It didn't matter to Christian what she said. He noted the lack of accusation in her tone. That was all he needed to hear. Later, they would deal with the rest of it, together, without blame. He would have responded to Kaiden's threat, but Lareina continued to speak.

"Kaid." She filled with a fresh wash of tears. "I'm sorry. I'm so sorry."

"You didn't do it." Kaiden was there, gathering her close. "Shit happens." He cried with her. He couldn't help it; he didn't want to help it. "It just do."

"Fisher..." she collapsed against him, beating his chest, wailing. The floodgates of her agony burst.

"Noooo...not Fish...damn, Fisher...damn..." He cradled her and let his tears spill over to join with hers. They sagged under the weight of their pain, sliding to the floor in a heap of arms, legs, and memories.

Alec brought over a box of Kleenex, sitting it within easy reach, and then retreated to the sofa where he could keep watch in case his mom needed something. Christian went to explore the house. His immediate concern addressed, he and Lareina would talk after a while. Right now, she needed to cry it out with her brother.

****

Christian found Silas interrogating Gillian. He made himself useful. Neither one had any qualms about working with the other. They were both cocky enough to believe they alone controlled the situation and the other man was *not* a notable threat.

As much as possible, Yukiyo steered clear. She didn't like Christian. She stayed close to Orion and Lareina—they needed her. Kaiden and Alec were self-reliant. Silas and Christian could fend for themselves.

****

The house in New Orleans had the unlucky benefit of not having any memories of Fisher. For one reason or another, he had never been there during their stocking-up days. No room carried an echo of his memory. On some days, it was a blessing, nothing to stir a sudden recollection. Other days, it was a cause for heartache, as if he never existed.

****

"How are you feeling?" Yukiyo let herself into Orion's room. It was organized and clean. All of their rooms were—Lareina mandate. It made for easier getaways. His navy blue curtains hung open to give him a view of the back yard.

"Not like me." Orion put his cell phone down and squirmed against his pillows.

She adjusted them for him and fixed his covers too. "I hardly ever feel like me."

"Thanks. What's wrong with us?" He scooted over to make room for her to sit.

"You've been shot. It's going to take a minute to get over that. Me, I'm just crazy."

"We're all crazy."

"Not like me. Something happens and I... I don't know. I lose it." She looked at her fingers.

"What'd you do?"

"Nothing. Not really. I just saw you and Fish. I didn't see Fish. I couldn't function. I almost lost my mind."

"That's the best compliment I ever got. Fisher would appreciate it too."

She wasn't sure what the compliment was.

He put his hand on hers. "It's hard to make your give-a-shit list, Yuke, because if you have to give a shit, you will."

"You make it sound like instability is a good thing."

"Superhero trait."

"What about super villains?"

"Double dose. I'm a chemist. I should know."

"I guess you better heal fast in case I need to be drugged or something. I'll feel better knowing somebody is prepared."

"You're the one everybody watches. We all know you're crazy." He made her smile. That was something.

****

Orion had taken two hits—one in the shoulder and the other one making a neat hole in his chest, barely missing his lung. He was fortunate. Alec's speed was the main contributor to his continued existence. They saved each other's lives. Lareina was grateful to both of them, for both of them.

Three weeks was all the time Orion would allow for lying in bed, recuperating. He diagnosed himself as being ready for physical therapy. Against all advice, he practically lived in the training room.

He wasn't alone. More often than not, Orion could be found in Kaiden's company. There was solace in their quiet companionship—the boy who almost died and the man who was barely alive. The mission had cost them both. Wounds that never fully heal forge bonds that are not easily broken.

****

Silas went and came. Not only did he have duties, but it was vital for him to circulate and collect information. Other than his movement, the days were quiet. The occupants of the Willow Avenue house fell into a habit. Breakfast was scattered, where before it was a family event and the start of all strategy meetings. More often than not, Fisher had been the breakfast chef. Now, it was just easier to get it over with. Kaiden didn't want to be around Christian in the morning, anyway.

Practice was a one hundred percent focus activity. Nobody had time for excess conversation. All energy went into working off frustration. Kaiden didn't want to discuss things with Christian, anyway.

Afternoons and evenings were spent doing whatever anybody felt like doing. Structure disappeared, conversation was limited. There was nothing anybody needed to do. Kaiden didn't want anything to do with Christian, anyway.

Everyone seemed to be waiting on Lareina. She had become lethargic in her grief and had not moved them.

Silas came home and unleashed the cure.

"'Reina?"

"Ummhmm?" Lareina stared out the window. Rain fell heavy, splattering the glass, impairing her vision. She didn't notice.

"I'm going to have Alec kill Gillian Foster, alright?"

His matter-of-fact tone reached her in a way soft comfort never could. "Excuse me?"

"He could use the practice."

"Practice? Killing somebody? Have you lost your mind?"

Silas could see himself reflected in the brown of her irises. It was a good indication she was all there. "You want him good don't you?"

"Yeahhhh." Alec was nearby. He was always nearby. His enthusiasm did and did not help matters.

"Noooo." She cut him an are-you-insane, glare. "We're not having this conversation." To Silas, she said, "Isn't it enough that it tears me apart knowing he already had to kill people. That's not what boys do."

"Yes, it is." Alec cut her an are-you-insane, glare.

Silas was having this conversation. "Quit babying him. He needs to practice."

"Would you like me to practice killing someone on you?" she asked.

"Alright. Leave the wuss out of it."

Alec gave him the Finger.

Silas ignored it, goading Lareina was his project. "Orion?"

"NO."

"Fine. Braid their hair and put them in dresses. I'll do it myself."

"No, you won't."

"We got what we want. What do we need her for?"

"A few things, I think." She paused to decide if the statement were true.

"Such as?" Christian cut in. Although they hadn't talked much, he was never far from Lareina. "Identifying Miss Mio Dia Yukiyo? I can't imagine Gillian as the silent, non-fingerpointing type."

That made her eyebrows go up. *Christian in agreement with Silas?* Time to get back to reality. She addressed Silas. "We don't 'got what we need.' Not yet. Alec, honey," she turned to her son. "Would you get Yukiyo for me, please? Tell her to bring everything she has. I'm ready to be updated."

The direction of her thought, the surety of her words, and especially the gentle evenness of her tone washed over Alec. His smile washed over the room. Mom was back. "Yep," he slid Chronos II into his pocket, "I'll get her." He flashed Lareina a happy grin. "I won't even yell." Thrilled with her answering smile, he added, "Just so you know, Yuke might not want to talk. She don't like him." He pointed to Christian. "He gives her the creeps."

Before Lareina could respond, Christian caught hold of the uplifted mood and answered in kind. "That's alright, I don't like her either. She's not going to say anything I don't already know, anyway."

Not to be discouraged, Alec answered, "If that's the case, no point in you being here when I get back." Having gotten the last word he left to do his mother's bidding.

"What is with you and these kids?" Christian huffed.

Lareina's response was to look daggers at him.

"Ohh, a fight," Silas said without conviction. "Weren't you paying attention? I got twenty dollars that says she'll lay your ass out over that one." He nodded his head in the direction Alec had taken.

"I don't have to bet." Christian didn't bother to look at him. "When I want your money, I'll take it."

"And welcome back to reality," Lareina muttered to herself. "We do have real business to address if anyone is interested."

****

Christian was annoyed. If no one else knew it, Lareina did. Whatever Christian's issue was, it was going to have to wait. They were working now. Everyone huddled around the dining room table. For the most part, Christian ignored them. He confiscated a deck of cards and entertained himself. The task seemed to have his full concentration, but Lareina knew better. He hadn't missed anything. Likewise, Alec and Silas were side-by-side, researching and/or programming data into Chronos and Chronos II.

They were engrossed in their activity, but Lareina knew they missed about as much as Christian did. Which was nothing.

Kaiden stared at the ring he spun like a top on the hardwood table. Silent and sad, but half listening anyway. Only Orion showed focus. One elbow on the table, his cheek rested on his knuckles, he watched every word as it tumbled out of Yukiyo's mouth. He heard Lareina's questions and absorbed every possibility.

"Start from the beginning, honey," Lareina encouraged. "We all need to be brought up to speed."

Yukiyo got right to it. "After numerous conversations that could be defined as nothing short of odd, I stumbled on to what I thought might be some type of code, secret language, whatever." She shook a red-brown lock of hair out of her eye. It hadn't been dyed in months "I wouldn't have noticed if y'all hadn't been talking so much about patterns. I couldn't make much sense of it, but I tracked it anyway. Glad I did, because when we grabbed Miss Foster, we hit the lottery." This time, she used her hand to attack the offending piece of hair. "She had a bag full of transcripts. Phone calls. Face-to-face conversations. They were encoded messages and she had the translations." Yukiyo stopped talking. She left the table, left the room.

"What's she doing?" Orion turned a puzzled glance to the others.

"Who knows with that girl." Kaiden spun Fisher's ring twice more and then stopped. He slid it onto his finger.

"You can wait a minute." Yukiyo returned with a pair of scissors in one hand and the bothersome lock of hair in the other. Before their eyes, she snipped it to a less annoying length.

"That explains a lot," Christian said to no one in particular.

Yukiyo didn't seem to hear him. She continued speaking as if she never stopped. "She had three of the same conversations I tracked. And she had them decoded. It gave me the key to decode the rest of them."

"Why would she have all of this stuff?" Lareina asked the obvious question. "And why would she have something so important on her person?"

Silas picked up the conversation from there. "She was on her way to a meeting with a man named Terrance Chezwick~"

"How many days ago did I tell you it was him," Christian said to Lareina.

"It ain't what you say." Silas kept the attention. "It's what you do. What did you do? Get caught." Before Lareina could scold, he went on to say, "Putting the puzzle together, it looks like she was preparing to blackmail him. Something Jericho thought up, no doubt. We lucked out and caught her dirty."

"Does she know what she gave us?" Orion asked.

Yukiyo found the thought amusing. "That dumb bitch? I told you she was stupid. After I copied everything, I gave her bag back. Told her I checked it for bugs."

"Did you?" Alec glanced up from Chronos II.

"That's your job," she shot back.

"Then you know it got done." He went back to what he deemed important.

"So what did you find out?" Lareina began firing questions at Yukiyo.

"Well," Yukiyo replied. "There's a room at Fort Detrick, in Maryland. It contains a button. When it gets pressed, a missile-carrying drone is going to take off and there's going to be an explosion which will result in a pretty nasty mess."

"Who's supposed to press it?"

"The white house."

"Where do they want it to land?"

"They want it to land in Seattle. They have accurate intel where Revolutionary Headquarters is located. The idea is to take out the leaders and end this thing all la-dee-da."

"That's where they want it to land. Where is it going to land?"

Kaiden contributed the next piece of information. "That one is going to do exactly what they'd like."

"That one? That's not the only one?"

"That's the only one they know about," Yukiyo explained. "That little button in that room is nifty. It can send out two drones at once."

"Where's the other one going to land?"

"On the white house."

"They're going to blow themselves up?" Alec set Chronos II aside. This was getting too good to miss.

"Umm hmm. And the Rev's are going to get blamed for it. And that's not all."

"What else?"

"Unbeknownst to either side, that nasty second explosion will come from a... what'd you call it, Silas?"

"A Reaper."

"A Reaper?" The word echoed around the table.

"A Reaper," he repeated. "A drone that carries nuclear warheads."

Orion's mouth hung open. "That's nuts."

"That's what I said." Kaiden nodded.

"There's a better than good chance," Yukiyo said, "Maryland and Virginia won't be around when the dust settles."

"Do we know when this is supposed to happen?" Lareina asked.

"Not sure. Soon. Maybe a month."

"Six weeks." Silas was matter-of-fact. "I have to report to a base in Ohio to prepare for a mission west in six weeks. No excuses. I'm not the only one. I'm betting they're rounding us up to clean up Seattle." No one questioned his reasoning.

"Let me guess." Lareina didn't need to guess. "When the dust does settle, the Vanguard will be there to put everything back in order."

"With no one to oppose them," Christian added.

"Except me," Silas said. "Is it safe to say, we're done with Gillian now?"

"Si-las."

Chapter 26

"So, in a nutshell," Kaiden said, "we've discovered a situation. If we go to the Feds, we're all going to jail. Or worse."

"You're all going to jail or worse, anyway." Silas hunched his shoulders. "It doesn't matter if we tell them what we know."

"If you ain't going, I ain't going," Alec told him.

Orion kept the conversation on point. "I think telling them would only speed up the process."

"Not telling them won't slow anything down. Especially not a nuke."

"I'm glad you understand," Lareina interrupted the discussion her boys were having. "Going to the Feds isn't a viable option. Neither is going to the Revs. We don't work for them. They wouldn't hesitate to grab us."

"You work for them," Alec said.

"No. I sympathize. I was useful to Uncle Moe, but that's about it."

"Even if they listened and believed us," Yukiyo said, "they'd just abandon Seattle and say screw the East Coast."

Amid the chorus of agreement and added comments Christian stood up. Talking about the Revs left him bitter. "When you get done playing, Lareina, come find me. I'll let you know what we're doing." He left the room.

Ten minutes worth of complaints. Another ten minutes to calm her team and redirect their thought process. And a final ten to push his buttons. Now, Lareina was ready to confront Christian.

****

"Where are you going?"

Inwardly, Lareina cringed. She had been hoping to get under Alec's radar. "I need to speak with Christian." She ruffled his hair once. "Shouldn't take but a minute."

"Oh. Cool. When we're done, do you want to watch a movie?"

"What's with this we?"

"'Cause that's what we are." He picked up her hand. "Rub my hair."

"Monster." She complied. "I have to talk to Christian. You go start the movie. When I'm done, I'll catch up."

"We'll go tell him what he needs to do. Then, we'll start the movie together. You won't need to catch up."

She put her hands on her hips, preparing to set the little beast straight.

He wasn't having it. "Rub my hair. What do you need to talk to him about?"

"I need to make sure he's okay. I need to see what he's thinking and I need to see what we can do to help him. He's been through a lot."

"So have we."

"We have. That's why I need to check on him. Because we all need to be at our best if we're going to move. That includes Christian."

"Alright. Let's go hug the baby. Change his diaper. Tuck him in and get to the movie."

"Not we. Me."

"Mom~"

"No, mom nothing. When you're feeling junky, I make everybody lay off~"

"I'm your son. You're supposed to." His lip dropped—a telltale sign of his insecurity.

It broke her heart. "Without a doubt." She hugged him to her, still rubbing his hair. "Being nice to Christian doesn't change that. It helps him help us, so we can get this mess over with and you and I can go and have a real life."

Her assurance meant everything. "Go tuck the baby in. But hurry up."

She smiled at his bossiness. "If I miss more than half, I'll bring you a snickers."

"Bring me a snickers anyway."

She pretended to study him. "Come on. You can take one to everybody."

"Then I get two."

They took a short trip to the attic. Christian could wait a few more minutes. After all, she was intentionally pushing his buttons.

****

She found him in her room, lounging on her bed. The bastard was pushing buttons too.

"I don't believe I've given you permission to be in my private space."

"I didn't ask."

At least, his mood had improved. Lareina crossed the room and settled on the bed beside him. "What can I do for you, Christian?"

He had the nerve to smirk. "Do you want a list?"

"Are you going to get Silas to write it out for you? I know you have trouble with spelling."

That wiped his smirk off. He gave her the finger.

"Nice. Alec is starting to rub off on you. Good to see you fitting in."

"Not hardly." It was time to get serious. "What do you think you're doing? I get it. They're smart kids. It's a great idea to use that intelligence. You've pieced together an operation that neither the government nor the Revolutionaries can touch. You've even discovered a secret society nobody knew existed. But that's enough, Lareina. This, and you, has got to stop."

She folded her arms across her breasts, mentally preparing for a fight. "Stop what? Obtaining information?"

"Stop trying to save the world."

"I don't care about the world. Children being used as pawns because of my brain-child, that's something I care about. It has to stop. If the world gets saved in the process, don't blame me. It happens."

"You are done. Do you understand me?" He hadn't changed his position, but suddenly, he seemed intimidating. "You don't get to put yourself in any more danger. To hell with your ideals." His true-blue eyes burned hot like the center of a flame. His already tense muscles tightened. He was a black mamba coiled to strike.

And he was getting on her nerves. His mannerism. His words. Everything about him annoyed her sometimes. "Oh, alrighty then. We're playing the Christian-says game. I don't have time for it, Eugene." She made to move off the bed, but his hand locked around her arm. As easy as if she were a baby, he slid her back beside him, where he wanted her.

"Make time for it," he growled. "What were you doing at my house?"

Ahh. Now, we get to it. "Besides saving you? Not much. I don't fancy

D.C."

"Who told you to save me?"

She stared at him for a half a minute. The madder he got the better she felt. Once he vented, they could have a real conversation. "The same person who keeps telling you to be a pain in my ass. What kind of question is that? Who told you to change my location at the hospital? Who told you to let Alec and I walk away? Who told you to kill Jericho? Why would you think there would have been the slightest chance I wouldn't come?"

"I don't want you in jeopardy. Is that so hard for you to understand?"

"We're in a war. I'm a criminal. Is that so hard for you to understand? We're fresh out of those bubbles you like to put me in."

"You don't have to help them hurt you, Lareina. You don't."

"No. I can get to them first."

"That's what I'm for."

"I know."

There was nothing to say to that. They were silent.

Silas knocked once and let himself in. If he cared what they thought of his intrusion, it didn't show. "I'm here to interrupt your little powwow." He directed his conversation to Christian. "I know you're a big man, all scary and shit. But that don't mean a damned thing around here." He slapped two pills down on Lareina's nightstand. "Your antidote. You better take it within the hour." He ignored her raised eyebrows, keeping his focus on Christian. "You'll need one of those every night for at least a week. Here are your choices...You can be a part of the solution, or you can wake up and start chasing us again. But I have to say you really are shit at it. You ain't that hard to elude. So give it a good think." He turned to leave.

"Silas!" Lareina wanted to laugh. She sooo wanted to laugh. She put a restraining hand on Christian. "You drugged us?"

Silas glanced back, unrepentive. "My way is effective, decisive and keeps you out of the mix. You can't think straight with him around, anyway. Maybe you need to be asleep."

"Boy, I'm going to beat the snot out of you." Her uncontrolled grin nixed the threat.

"When I'm in the market for a mosquito bite, I'll let you know." He let himself out.

Silas was Silas. Lareina knew that when she collected him. She created him. *Damn, he was good.*

Christian was another matter altogether. He hadn't said a word. That was never a good thing. "Christian?"

It took a minute before he responded. When he did, it was devoid of emotion. He snapped his eyes at her, deeply sincere with his intent. "You might want to start getting unattached and resign yourself to knowing I'm going to kill him. I'm informing you now, so when it happens you will be able to recall I warned you."

Lareina felt a chill.

****

A video game. Leave it to Silas to flip the world over and then go play a video game. She plopped down beside him and picked up a second controller. "Reset it. I want to play."

He didn't hesitate to comply. He reset the game for two players and they took turns making their character selections.

Lareina waited until it was her turn before she got into her real reason for being there. "You shouldn't have done it. You know that, right?" She didn't waste time with preliminaries. Silas knew what she was talking about.

"You shouldn't have thought you could go off with him, making plans, expecting the rest of us to sit out."

"That's not what I was doing."

"That's what he was doing."

She couldn't disagree. "Aww man." She took a hit. "I'm going to kill that jerk." Her thumbs attacked with a vengeance. "We hadn't gotten to plans before you interrupted."

Silas' thumbs worked just as fast. "You wouldn't have. You both would have been asleep if I didn't come in when I did."

They cleared the board. Lareina turned to him while the next level loaded. "Silas, he's furious."

"And?"

She huffed. "Look, he's more than furious. This time, I'm concerned. I'm worried about you." She didn't mask her anxiety. Silas needed to see it.

He gave her a look which said he thought she should know better. "What are you worried about me for?" He went back to the game.

So did she. "I'm worried you've gone too far. Christian might do something drastic."

"Good."

"Good?"

"Good. It's been a long time coming. Time to get to it."

She hit the pause button. "Am I missing something?"

"Only because you're trying to be blind. Eugene and I can't share a world and we damned sure can't share you." He continued, uncaring if she understood him or not, "I tolerate him for your sake, but he and I have a silent agreement we don't want your opinion on, so stay out of it." He hit play.

"Stay out of it?" She hit pause again. "Really?! Are you kidding me? What agreement?"

"That one day he's going to snap and all hell is going to break on me. And then, I'll stop his breathing. I'm the one, 'Reina. He knows I'm the one. All this cat and mouse is him trying to get around the fact that he has to lose." He hit play again.

The game resumed but Lareina's mind was still on pause. Silas' cocksure attitude. The simple sincerity of his words. Lareina felt a chill. This wasn't going to end well.

****

They set their calendars by Silas' prediction; six weeks. They had to locate Terrance Chezwick and shut him down without anyone noticing. They also had to break into Fort Detrick and disarm two smart bombs without government help or military assistance. Killing Joffener did not help matters as it put them at the very top of The Department of Protection & Peace's most wanted list. Everyone was looking for them. Attempting either target would bring an end to their secrecy. The only chance of success would be to strike Chezwick and Ft. Detrick simultaneously. That would mean somehow getting Chezwick to Detrick and running a double sting.

Everything that could be learned about the base was investigated. Size, shape, security, personnel, no detail was too small to study. The same for Terrance Chezwick: his activities, his routines, his day to day living. Any scrap of information was valuable.

Instead of Silas, Alec was the hawk. It would be up to him to direct them out. Silas was going in. Not only was he their best chance of getting to the control room, he was their best chance of decoding and deactivating the drones. Kaiden would cover him, protect him while he worked.

Christian, Lareina and Orion would handle the most difficult part of the mission, taking out Chezwick. A head-on collision with one of the world's most treacherous men was sure to get messy.

Thanks to two well-learned lessons—one from Christian when he caught them with Jericho, and the other when they rescued Christian—they kept Yukiyo in reserve. Anyone who knew of them, knew there was a sniper in their midst. Her main purpose would be to guard Alec and provide a back door in the all too likely event things went more wrong than expected. She would also be in position to assist and/or rescue any team member who was in need. Her careful eye for detail made her the perfect insurance policy.

****

"Here you go." Silas passed out military IDs and dog tags. "Pay attention. Make sure you match up the right contacts."

Orion's short, neat, blond hair had grown to his shoulders. Now it was brown. Christian's was also brown. And where he always wore it in a ponytail, now it was cropped off. He and Kaiden had full beards. Kaiden's dreads were starting to lock.

Lareina and Yukiyo would be wearing wigs. Yukiyo donned a black one. Lareina chose the more standoutish red. It drew attention, but not enough to be memorable.

Alec agreed to the contacts and a hat. He wasn't cutting his hair, he wasn't coloring his hair. His mom liked his hair. He wasn't changing it for any reason.

Silas didn't change anything. He had more access being himself than anybody he could create.

****

Terrance sat at the bar inside the Irish Pub in downtown Frederick. He looked at his watch, expecting her to arrive any minute. Sasha Gammer. Her real name; not an internet pseudonym. It suited her; hot like her photo. He almost couldn't believe she was interested in spending time with him so soon after they met. A PFC, stationed at Ft. Detrick who knew nothing at all about him. He couldn't have planned it better. Although he had yet to make an appearance, he had business at Ft. Detrick. Business, that provided an excellent cover for his presence there and any potential liaisons.

It had a lot of potential. Sasha looked soft and willing. Dark hair, dark eyes, definitely of some Asian descent. Eighteen...ohh eighteen; old enough to be legal, young enough to make a tryst worthwhile. And here she comes. Long sexy legs in a short mini skirt. He hoped his fifty-two-year-old heart could take it.

Yukiyo looked around the bar. She spotted Terrance Chezwick, and took a deep breath. "Here we go," she muttered into the mouthpiece hidden on the underside of her great white and moved forward.

Terrance stood up, a true gentleman. "God, you're beautiful." He held the chair for her.

"Really?" Alec said to everyone listening, "That's his pick-up line?"

"I ordered you a drink." Terrance pointed to a wine glass then ran his finger up her arm. "Mmm. I knew you'd be soft."

It took effort for Yukiyo to suppress her revulsion.

"We can stay here and talk, or we could go somewhere, less active." If he didn't have to wait, all the better.

Her smile and thoughts were reptilian. "I don't think my sergeant would approve. I'm on detail in forty-five minutes." She let her gaze linger on his crotch. "I would have canceled, but I didn't want you to think I wasn't interested." *I am going to kill you, Orion, for suggesting this.* He traced Chezwick to four separate hook-up sites. Even so, nobody in their right mind would consider her bait. If it wasn't for Silas' goading, she wouldn't be here struggling to halt her gag-reflex.

Chezwick thought the gods were in attendance. He could smell it. She was ripe and ready. It didn't get any easier than this. "Here's one of my surprises for you, Sasha. I have some military authority."

Yukiyo feigned just the right amount of surprise.

"I researched you—"

Feigned suspicious surprise. *At least, this part is fun.*

"Lucky thing too—"

"Of course, it was," Silas said. "I put that profile there because you're a lucky kind of guy."

"You work in my department."

"Imagine that? Who'd have thought?" Lareina added her own comments.

"I can pull you for research," Terrance said, "or other work as needed. Heh heh heh."

The entire group of listeners chuckled in imitation.

He downed his drink and waited for Yukiyo's decision.

Oh goody. Back to feigned surprise, or whatever. How about if we go with a slight intake of breath, followed by dawning realization. "We could do whatever we want and it wouldn't be anybody's business." *I should be blond.* "Can you do that?" *Uggh. No, he did not get a boner. I'm done.*

He put his finger back on her arm. "Baby, I can do that and more...if you're willing."

In sync, the team imitated Terrance's chuckle again.

"How soon can you talk to them?" *Before I break your hand and put my heel through your eye socket, that is.*

"Baby, I have real clout. We can go right now."

Instead of answering, Yukiyo finished her wine, slid out of her chair and waited for him to join her. She swayed her hips provocatively as they made their exit.

Terrance Chezwick was sufficiently distracted, but he wasn't her motivation. She did not see him, but she knew Silas was somewhere near, watching her ass. She figured she might as well make it literal. He had some nerve naming her Sasha. As far as she was concerned, he could kiss her ass while he was at it.

Chapter 27

"Can I help you?" A soldier not much older than Orion addressed him from beside a four-drawer file.

Orion stepped into his role. "Is this the Education Center?"

The corporal glanced at Orion's rank—Private 1st class—and lost interest in being social. "Part of it."

"Good. I came to the right place. I'm looking for Staff Sergeant..." He snapped his fingers to help his memory. "I can't remember his name. Who's in this office?"

The corporal looked around dramatically. "You're looking at everybody who's here today. Can I help you?"

Orion grinned. "I bet you can." He revealed his pistol by placing the barrel against the corporal's forehead. "Sarcasm noted."

"Hey, man." The soldier raised his shaky hands above his head. "This ain't the answer. Don't be stupid."

"You appear to be an expert on stupid." Orion held the soldier's attention while Christian slipped into the room, Lareina a step behind.

A sudden prick, a widening of eyes and the young corporal fell forward, instantly knocked out by whatever was in the syringe Christian plunged into his neck.

Orion caught him. With Christian's help, they carried the unconscious soldier into an inner office and stored him in a closet.

"How long will that poison last?" Christian asked.

Orion said, "Mida z mix. Twenty-four hours, easy. I have something else if you want me to kill him."

"We got in and we got the office," Lareina mused. "I guess we're done with easy."

****

Silas and Kaiden waited until Yukiyo was out of the bar before they left their booth. Having parked closer, they reached Silas' Genuine and were on the road to Detrick ahead of Yukiyo and Chezwick. Silas stopped a few feet from the gate, not inclined to be processed yet.

A few minutes later, Chezwick pulled up to the gate and was waved through. Silas drove behind him.

The guard waited for him to roll down his window. "ID soldier?"

"Certainly." Silas handed him his military ID and passed Kaiden's fake one right behind it. "We're assigned to escort Dr. Chezwick." He waved a finger at the car in front of them.

That was enough information for the guard. He handed them back the ID's. Bigwigs and their entourages did nothing for him.

"You got a visual, kid?" It didn't matter that Silas didn't speak a name, everybody knew who he was talking to.

Alec had been on the base for most of the morning. He'd been in place for more than an hour. "I got her. Got you too in case I need a practice shot."

Silas turned left, driving away from Yukiyo and Chezwick. He parked the jeep close to the end of the PX parking lot. As they put on their gear, he noted Kaiden's grim smile. "What?"

"Having a loaded weapon hanging out in plain view. One less hassle. Makes things easy." He put on a pair of flesh-colored gloves.

Silas did the same. He slung his TS13 over his shoulder. "It's the little things that make our job worthwhile."

Together they jogged to the command center—the obvious place to launch a missile—and kept going to the out-of-the-way building behind it. It was Vanguard genius that the building itself was not within the restricted perimeters. It was a training facility that was secretly live. Assessable and close enough to lock on targets and override controls.

****

"Yukiyo, we're here. Education Center. Basement. Room 104."

"Ummhmm," Yukiyo said under her breath, quietly indicating she received Lareina's go-ahead.

"Hang a left at the next street." Alec fed her directions to repeat to Chezwick. "It's the third building on the left."

Orion joined them at the elevator. His thumbs moved swiftly as he texted. He seemed preoccupied and unaware of their presence.

Chezwick crowded Yukiyo. "This shouldn't take too long. Then we can get to business."

"I'm hoping it won't take long at all."

"Damn, man. Are you trying to look down her shirt?" Orion's bold address startled Chezwick. He took a guilty step back.

Yukiyo suppressed a grateful smile as she slipped a micro-tracker into his blazer pocket.

****

"Hold-up, Mom." The entire group could hear him, but his conversation was always for his mother. "I'm getting a weird readout."

"What's it say?"

"The best I can tell, Chezwick is hard-wired, maybe. Silas, what's up with that?"

"Shit." Christian understood it.

Silas was quiet, presumably working magic on his Chronos. After a long tense moment, he said. "You guessed it right. What colors are you reading?"

"Three bars. One blue. Two red."

"Shit!" Christian understood that too.

"Shit is right," Silas told them. "It means he's got an embedded tracker. If Chezwick dies, we're screwed. This base is going to go on automatic lock-down and every pecker with a gun will be told to hunt and shoot."

"Well, that's going to change some things," Lareina said.

"It does," Christian spoke into his mike even though Lareina stood beside him. "He gets to live fifteen minutes longer, until everybody is clear."

"Good job, baby," Lareina said to Alec. "You're awesome."

"Of course, I am."

****

"Man, this is pathetic." Kaiden said as he and Silas walked through the training center unchallenged. "This is the Military? Anybody can walk up in here."

"No, only military personnel with proper ID can get on this base. And nobody comes into these facilities unauthorized."

"Y'all hear that?" Kaiden said into his mouthpiece. "Ain't none of us here."

Silas rolled his eyes. "I'm authorized. Let's see you attempt it without me."

****

Lareina had taken the position vacated by the arrogant corporal. She looked up from the file drawer when Yukiyo and Terrance walked in. "May I help you?" she asked sweetly.

"I'm looking for..." Terrance flashed his badge and turned to Yukiyo.

"Staff Sergeant Riggs," she supplied the name.

"Staff Sergeant Riggs," he repeated.

"Do you have an appointment?"

Chezwick flashed his badge again, with flourish. "I think you will find I am exempt from appointments."

It took effort for Lareina not to imitate his chuckle. "Just a minute." She took his ID into the inner office. It wasn't long before she returned. "Staff Sergeant Riggs will see you now." She held the door open.

Chezwick walked in front of her.

Lareina followed him in, pulling the door shut behind her.

As soon as the door closed, Yukiyo backtracked out of the office.

Orion was stationed outside. He handed her a military-issued laundry bag containing a change of clothes and her HK T42. He gave her a mock salute. "See ya."

"You don't want to see me," Yukiyo said. "Next time you see me, I'll be kicking your ass for this one. That was your worst idea ever." She swept past him, on to her next assignment.

Orion chuckled. He knew what he was in trouble for. When she was out of sight, he let himself into the office and locked the door.

****

Silas and Kaiden walked the building a second time. The first was to jam the camera signal and loop the picture, so as to not alert anybody of their intended business. Also, for Chronos to collect data; specifically, heart rates and body heat. A headcount would work in their favor.

A single beep; unheard except by those who were listening for it. Silas stopped beside a windowed lab. Chronos had located the room with the control panel they required. From the window, they could see a series of computers and three people working within.

Kaiden looked to see if there were any more.

Chronos had Silas' attention. He stroked a few keys and waited. The combination lock clicked open. "Here we go," he announced to the group. He pushed the door open and Kaiden stepped through. Three shots whistled through his silencer. All three techs fell to the floor, unconscious; the last one cracking his head against the counter top.

"Ohh," Silas said, "he's going to have a nasty headache tomorrow." He used the tip of his boot to angle the soldier's head to view the gash. It was already turning purple.

"Better a nasty headache than not waking up at all." Darts weren't nearly as satisfying. Kaiden switched magazines. There would be no more innocent bystanders. He drew the curtains closed, leaving a slight gap between the window and the wall—wide enough to expose whoever went past, but not enough to show anything happening within.

"Alright," Silas talked as he fingered commands. "First thing, we stop whatever they were doing...computer glitch. Off-line for a bit." He spoke as if he were giving a tutorial. He punched some keys. "Then..." He punched some more. "We research the big-noise-machines that are active or semi-active on any base within a hundred miles of here." He got up from that station. "Keep an eye on it, will ya?" He moved to a second computer.

Kaiden eyed the screen, the door, and his curtain-peephole in turn.

Silas' fingers were all over the keyboard. By contrast, his voice remained steady and conversational. "We're looking for a six double-digit code. We already have two thanks to Gillian. I know I'll pull two by myself."

A woman wearing a white lab coat walked down the hall. The closed curtains didn't raise an alarm. She swept by without a pause.

"How long will this take?"

Chronos beeped. The computer shut down.

"That long." Silas moved to the next station. "'Reina's got the hard job. Chezwick has the numbers we need. She's got to get them and give me enough time to figure out where they go in the combo before Deverell kills him."

"What if that don't happen?"

"Then screw it. Instead of disarming them, we relocate and hit send."

"I heard 'Reina say something about discharging them over the ocean."

"Oh, no." Silas settled into the fourth and final station. This is where he'd do the rest of his work. "I don't waste taxpayer money. And I don't have a problem with the fish."

Kaiden almost didn't want to ask, but he did want to know. "If this shit goes south, which it probably will, where are you sending them?"

"According to Gillian, the Vanguard has a private island off the coast of North Korea. One's going there. The other one is going to Canada. Chezwick's mother's house."

"That would start two good wars."

"I'm a soldier. War is what I do."

"Lareina won't like that."

Silas paused long enough to quirk an eyebrow at Kaiden.

"Yeah, I know," Kaiden said, "she won't like the alternative."

"I was thinking, what can she do about it?"

"Ummumm." Lareina cleared her voice in a manner indicating she could hear them talking about her.

"Somebody need a cough drop?" Silas said into his mouthpiece.

****

Christian stood beside the large cherry desk belonging to someone he did not give a shit about. The ceiling-fan twirled lazily above him. "Dr. Chezwick, please." He gestured to a leather chair. "Have a seat."

"That won't be necessary, Staff Sergeant. I'm only here to make you aware of my need for one of your soldiers. I'm pulling PFC Gammer for an assignment. May take a few days."

Christian made a pained face. "Gee, I wish I could help you sir, but Gammer is being disciplined. She's restricted to the base. However..." He lit up with his bright idea. "I can offer you an alternative." He turned to Lareina. "Get PFC Odell in here." Back to Chezwick. "He's a good kid. Reliable."

"No, no, no." Chezwick waved Christian off. "I've already met with Gammer. She's been briefed and we're ready to go. You'll have to be a little lenient, Sergeant."

Christian sighed dramatically. "Let me explain why she's being disciplined." He sat on the edge of the desk.

"I'm not concerned with~"

"I think you will be. You see, we've recently learned PFC Gammer has been spending an excessive amount of time on the internet. Some sleazy dating site—"

Chezwick stiffened.

"—What was troubling, to me anyway, was that she caught the attention of a high-ranking military official—"

He held his breath.

"—We weren't positive if she knew her date was a top recruiter and preeminent spy for an elusive regiment secretly known as the Vanguard—"

Terrance dared not move, lest he give something away.

"The Vanguard, I'm sure you know, Dr. Chezwick, is an elite group of extreme thinkers. Their mission is to have America slowly kill itself. They make millions off of the war you see... That's not an idea I am fond of." Christian leaned forward and dropped all pretenses. "So sit your ass down before I show you what I am fond of."

Unnerved, Terrance Chezwick sank into the chair. He braved a glance behind him, noticing Yukiyo was not in the room. He thought the other woman remained, but she stood out of his line of vision. When he would have checked, Christian proved to be a thought ahead of him.

"Turn around." It was an order to be obeyed.

Chezwick was a man of espionage and war. He didn't make mistakes. "It appears I am being threatened. If this is the case, I suggest you get somebody with a higher rank than yours, *Sergeant*. You don't have the authority to wipe my ass, much less fantasize Mission Impossible."

Bolstered by his own speech, he returned to his former hauteur. "Is there a point to this colossal waste of my time? Or, is this a creative way for you to earn your demotions?"

The gold hoop earring dangling from Christian's left ear caught the light and sparkled. "I don't have any regard for authority." He gave Lareina a nod.

Silent steps brought her directly behind Chezwick. She nestled her gun behind his ear. The action made her smile. It was such a Kaiden-thing to do.

Christian rolled his eyes. *What could she possibly have to smile about?*

Seeing his reaction made her smile too.

Returning his mind to the work at hand, Christian patted Chezwick down, relieving him of his wallet, phone, handgun, and keys—the oversight which saved his life, was not something he would allow anyone else. He unloaded the gun and laid the items on the cherry desk, far out of Chezwick's reach. "My turn," he said pleasantly as he dislodged his own weapon. He held the pistol casually, but the relaxed stance fooled no one. "Don't have a reaction of any kind. Control your reflexes."

Before Chezwick could wonder, Lareina slapped her hand over his mouth. Two pills slid to the back of his throat. He swallowed the first pill before he could stop himself. He would have grabbed Lareina's hand, tried to throw her or use her as a shield, but Christian was poised, ready to strike. His stare hypnotic. The second pill went down quickly.

He made a gagging noise and Lareina freed his mouth. They weren't coming back.

"What did you give me!?"

"Wait for it."

Lareina plunged a syringe deep into the side of his neck. It was painful. She meant it to be.

"Ahhh!" Chezwick flinched. "What the hell are you doing to me!?"

"Ever hear of Mephobarbital?" Christian relaxed the moment Lareina stepped back. "No? Hmm, surprising for your line of work. No matter. It's rumored to be a truth serum. We didn't give you that because, if you heard of it, you'd know how it works. We gave you something that's about sixty percent stronger. And to keep you from talking too long about insignificant bullshit, we poisoned you."

"You want to kill me and you expect me to cooperate?"

"Who said anything about killing you? Although unfortunate accidents do happen, that's not part of the plan. Expand your vision. I'm foreseeing you as a semi-brain-dead vegetable. No vocal cords, no use of your extremities, in a Seattle nursing home under the care of the Revolutionaries, in dire need of someone with the authority to wipe your ass. Sound good?"

The references to Seattle and the Revolutionaries were not lost on Chezwick. Whoever these people were, two things were evident. One, they were on to him. And, two, this mystery group had their own set of rules. They were going to get what they wanted. He knew it. And they knew he knew it. "Who are you?"

"Don't trouble yourself. It won't change anything. Why don't you work on earning your antidote."

Chapter 28

"Hey, Yuke." Alec was disarmingly calm—a true sniper temperament. "I need you to relocate."

"You want your mother to beat the crap out of me. Why?" She referred to Lareina's explicit order that once Yukiyo was done with Chezwick, her objective was to back up Alec. That translated into 'protect my baby or else.' Who wanted to deal with Lareina's 'or else'?

"I'm the control tower. What do you think will happen if you don't follow my instructions?"

Lareina's lack of comment let Yukiyo know Alec had channeled her alone. He had Chronos II, he could do that. She got serious. "What do you need?"

"I believe somebody is setting up shop on the roof behind me. I need you to verify and if you can, get a fix on what he's looking at. Me or somebody else."

"Well, that ain't good." She was already on the move.

****

The serum was taking effect. Chezwick felt the rising panic. He didn't know what they were after. He didn't know what they knew. Anything he said could be potentially dangerous.

"I don't understand. What is it you want from me? What do you want to know?"

"You start talking," Christian said encouragingly, "and I'll tell you when to shut up. Try to say something that will prompt me to share my antidote."

****

Yukiyo was impressed with Alec. "What are you, telepathic? How did you figure that out?"

"Where's he at?"

"Directly behind you."

"Based on what went down last time, we didn't want to take a chance. That's why I've been here all day. I've got motion sensors set up on that roof and the two beside me. Chronos II picked up movement half an hour ago. What's he doing?"

"That, I can't tell you. He is a sniper. He knows you're there, but it doesn't look as if he's targeting you. At least not yet. He's not angled right."

****

"That's three," Silas said with his usual confidence. "We're halfway there."

Kaiden piled the last of the unconscious techs in an out of the way corner. "Are you kidding me? We haven't been here ten minutes yet."

"That's what makes the easy part easy. It's going to be hell from here on out."

"Define hell."

"Don't worry. I'm sure you'll get a feel for it."

****

Chezwick couldn't focus. Knowing he had been drugged did nothing whatsoever to diminish the effects of the drug. "I suspect," his pupils dilated. "That's why you told me isn't it? Because knowing makes it worse."

"Can't get anything past you can we?"

"No, you can't. Do you know why? I'll tell you that much. I've been in this business coming up on thirty years. That's forever by your count. You think I didn't make the connection to Detrick? You know what's here don't you? Too bad." He shrugged. "You're too early. We're not launching anything for another two weeks...at least."

"Who's launching them?"

Lareina thought to herself, *and it begins...*

****

"Can you find a spot where you can see him and me?"

"You don't ask for much do you?"

"I'm looking out for you." Throughout the conversation, Alec had not acted or moved in any way that would alert the sniper. "If you're not a good babysitter, my mom is going to kick your ass."

"You sent me here."

"Excuses."

In answer to his original question, Yukiyo said, "I can see you both."

"You in the building to my left?"

"Back window, three floors from the top. Some room they use for storage. A lot of furniture shoved in here."

"You lucked out. Good. Which way is he facing?"

"Profile's to you. Back's to me. Do you know who he's targeting?"

"That's a no-brainer. And no, we're not telling him unless it becomes necessary. The last time a sniper popped up, Silas went nuts. This ain't the day for it." Before she could comment, he clicked off of their private channel.

****

"Oh, excuse me." The same lab coat-wearing woman who passed by earlier entered the lab. "I didn't know anyone was in here." She shoved her hands into the deep pockets of her coat and gifted them with an inviting smile. "Are you going to be long?"

"Can we help you with something?" Kaiden moved away from Silas' workstation, putting the woman between them. As long as he kept her attention, her back would be to the unconscious trio.

"Yes, you can." She raised both of her hands. Each one held a pistol. One, she leveled with Silas' head. The other with Kaiden's chest. "You can drop that piece of shit you're hiding. Get back over there with your buddy. Don't test me. I'm PMSing."

"Do I need to stop what I'm doing?" Silas asked.

"On the contrary. You get to keep working. Speed it up if you can."

He returned his attention to the computer. "You don't need to kill her yet."

"Alright." Kaiden walked back over beside Silas.

Thrown off by their attitudes, the woman struggled for something to say. "I said, drop your weapon."

"Oh." Kaiden snapped his fingers. "You did say something about that didn't you." With almost absent-minded ease, he unclipped the military weapon attached to the uniform. He threw it aside as if it were a relief to not have to carry it. "Tell us your name and we'll start fighting over you." He winked at her.

"You know damned well I would win." Silas still hadn't missed a keystroke.

She tried to regain control. "You know, cocky dickheads bleed just like everybody else."

"No, they don't," The guys spoke in unison.

Orion whistled through his teeth. "That's some smooth shit, man. Feed me as much information as you can. We'll see if we can find out what she thought she was doing." He didn't have a Chronos, but between Silas and Alec, he didn't need one. His phone had enough perks to make it an easy task.

****

"...Do I know you? I think I'm supposed to know you." Chezwick crinkled his forehead. "I know lots of people. I could tell you some things. Believe me."

"What do you know about the Revolutionaries?"

"Puppets. Enough said. They won't ever get what they want. What they want is unattainable and thereby pointless. The good 'ol days. Bahhh." He waved a hand. "They were never that good."

"Who do you know within that group? Who do you work with?"

Chezwick shook a finger at Christian. "Uh, uh, uh. Trying to catch me. I know your tricks. If I talk about my contacts, you'll know everything. But what you won't know is my contacts with the Revolutionaries don't matter for this project." Chezwick kept talking, "What you really want to know is my government contacts. Willingly and otherwise," he chuckled and drooled, "they're helping us move this war where we need it to go. These missiles..." he paused. "I know you know about the missiles."

Christian nodded. "That's why we're here."

"I thought as much. Secretary of State, Baurer. He authorized it. See how high this goes? See why you don't want to be interfering?"

Christian kept his expression unreadable. "How high are you into this? Are you anybody of real importance?"

As expected, Chezwick was offended. "I'll have you know, I am the key official in this whole operation. I personally planned this coup. I am aware of what happens at every stage. The codes, the carriers, even the disposals."

"The disposals?"

"The carriers have to be disposed of. Layers. Everything gets done in layers, you see. Codes, pieces of codes, partial information. We make sure nobody ever gets to know everything..."

Lareina recorded the conversation. Her finger hovered over the pause button. That was a vital piece of information. She didn't know why she thought it, but she was certain. She didn't get to dwell on it. Chezwick grabbed his leg and cried out.

Christian checked the time. "You've drawn this out too long. From this point on, not only does it get painful, but the poison starts to become irreversible. The next words out of your mouth are going to be the launch codes and the chain of authority for those mass-Ds. Don't get forgetful. And, don't make a mistake."

The pain in Chezwick's leg was intense and traveling closer to his groin. *Oh, God. Please. No.* The serum. The poison. The pain. The thought of his manhood being threatened. It was too much. No one could be expected to have that much loyalty.

****

"You're not here to help us," Kaiden said to the woman holding the guns. "But you're not trying to stop us either. That's a pretty high fence you're trying to ride." He had been throwing random comments at her from the onset. Three-inch heels would put her at five-ten. Why did she dye her hair? The highlights looked good, but it must have been lighter. Probably the same shade of brown as her eyes. How long had she been in the military? She appeared to be a confident shot. She must have gotten a medal or something for accuracy. How old was she, twenty-two? Twenty-three? Was she stationed here? Why wasn't she in uniform? A lab coat wasn't much of a disguise. Did she eat lunch? Had she been on post all day?

While he talked, Orion sifted through outside camera shots of people coming into the training center. Silas jammed the signal for the ones inside. "Red top? Big heart-shaped necklace? About ten of them bracelet-things Lareina wears?"

"What I'm trying to do is none of your business. You're wearing me out with your description retrieving commentary. You should shut up now. You won't get a positive ID—"

"She don't know Chronos II," Alec piped in.

"—quit trying. You'll find out what I'm up to when you need to know."

"Exactly." Silas appeared to be agreeing with her.

Orion understood. "Got her. She's hot. I'm sending it to Alec. See if he can't get an information match."

"Waiting on it," Alec said. "Silas, I need a twenty-count when you're ready to get up, 'kay."

"Ummhmm," Silas confirmed. He'd find out why later.

"Touch-y." Kaiden grinned. "Oh, right. You did say you were PMSing." It was obvious, he did not think she would shoot him. It was equally obvious, she wanted to prove him wrong.

****

Christian repeated the code Chezwick gave him.

First, Silas keyed the numbers into Chronos. A green light and accompanying beep verified each set in the sequence. They had what they needed to disable the missiles. Next, he would reset the codes to a sequence that would make it impossible to rearm it without his assistance. They only needed a few more minutes.

****

Rather than lose his focus, Alec sent the information back to Orion. He could read it to them. "Abby Lancaster. She's a part of some black-ops team. Fifteen of them, I think. Recently recruited. There are six other names, not on that list exactly. They're on some kind of sub-list. They show up in red~"

"Means they're on something else we've referenced," Alec explained.

Orion kept going. "LTC Briggs, Gillian Foster, Terrance Chezwick, Misty Wilson, Carmen Newcomer and Captain Lawrence March. Mean anything?"

"I think it means there's another team here, targeting us, or our project. Since Abby is in the room with Kaiden and Silas and I've got a sniper behind me, my guess is we're the target."

No one said anything. Kaiden couldn't without giving the communication away. Christian, Silas, and Yukiyo had all received a shock. They recognized names, and the implications attached.

Lareina recognized names too. None of them meant anything good. She needed to do some fast thinking, figure out how to divert suspicions. The problem was she didn't know what to think herself. They had to get out of there. That much she knew. "First things first. Get this done and we'll deal with the rest of it later."

"Lareina. I didn't~"

"Calm down, honey," she told Yukiyo. "I didn't think you had. But first things first. Okay?"

"Okay. As long as you know." For the moment that was good enough for Yukiyo.

"Congratulations, O-dummy." Alec noted the position of his TS13. He marked the spot. "Apparently, you've discovered some new complication we'd be better off not knowing about until later."

"Or at all," Orion agreed.

With Silas, there were no first things first. All that mattered was what he understood. Hearing there was another sniper had the expected effect. He realized what Alec needed the twenty-count for. He was going to fuck up these drones. He was going to fuck up that team. And then he was going to fuck up Christian. He completed the code reset. "Twenty."

Chapter 29

Alec was the control tower. *Time to go to work.* While silently counting in his head, he turned around slowly, eyes focused, lining up his sights. "Heads up, Yuke." He squeezed the trigger and was already returning to his original position when his adversary fell over, not moving.

"You got him," Yukiyo said. "He ain't getting up."

"I know." Alec checked on his mom then refocused. "You're clear, Silas."

****

"Coming at you, Kaid."

Silas expected Kaiden to understand. And he did. Silas rolled to the right and Kaiden dived to the left, crossing paths with practiced ease. Abby's reaction—as expected—was to attempt tracking with the respective gun she had trained on them. The half-beat hesitation was more than enough time. Two shots were fired so close together it sounded like one. Twin spots of blood blossomed from her chest.

Faster than thought Silas collected his things and he and Kaiden left the lab. They moved steadily down the corridor, not wanting to draw attention to themselves. The attention came anyway. Two fully armed mercenaries came into sight, running hard, shooting first, dying quick.

"I'm guessing Abby's team had their own communication happening." Kaiden kicked the man he killed aside.

"Doubtless." Silas walked across his victim, never looking down. "No silencers. The idiots. We better move."

Kaiden didn't need to be told twice. As they made for the back stairs, they could hear voices and footfalls behind them. People were coming to investigate.

****

"Alec, you need to move," Yukiyo said. "I see armed-assholes dressed like your sniper friend. They're going into the building behind you. I'd bet you anything in about a minute somebody is going to pop out on that roof."

"I guess you better take care of it." Alec's eye was on his mother. He wasn't moving.

"No." Keeping her back to Chezwick and her voice down, Lareina stepped in front of the window. She wanted to be sure Alec could see her. Not wanting to risk Chezwick or anyone catching a name she addressed them in code. "Get the hell out of there, baby. Now. You too Ladyfin. Monkey King, get the car. Go meet them. Get out of the way, but don't leave the base yet." She wouldn't say, but she wanted to keep Alec close, in case they needed to make their own getaway.

"Mom~"

"Don't argue. You won't help me that way." To make her point, she purposely moved to the far end of the room, out of his line of vision. She heard him muttering under his breath.

"And she calls *me* hardheaded. Wonder where I get it from."

****

A flash of silver. Kaiden saw it, shoved Silas and followed him into a doorway. A moment later, rapid gunfire had them pinned. Somebody coming up the back steps had an Uzi. With no way to get down the steps, no option to return the way they came and no desire to remain, Kaiden and Silas threw their weight against the door. The wood splintered with a hard snap. They retreated into the room.

While, gunfire on a military base was not necessarily something to cause a stir, unidentified gunfire coming from the Command Center's training facility was something to be noted. MP's were alerted and came forth to investigate.

****

Chezwick struggled to breathe. He flopped back and forth in his chair like a dying fish. Christian watched him with an impassive eye. "We're not getting anything else. Probably best to leave." He reached out a hand to catch the dusting cloth Lareina threw him and wiped down the area.

Lareina did the same on her side of the room "Been waiting on you. Don't forget to clean his junk."

As if trying to communicate his fear of being left alone, Terrance threw himself out of his chair, falling hard onto the floor at Christian's feet.

"That's not going to be comfortable." He stepped around the still flailing man and joined Lareina at the door. He touched her elbow—his method of holding her in place—while he slid past her to take the lead.

They had just cleaned the outer office when they heard his strangled gasps turn to silence. They didn't have to look, but they did anyway. From the doorway, they could see Terrance lying on his back, his unseeing eyes staring at the ceiling fan twirling lazily above him.

"That shouldn't have killed him," Christian said, "not yet."

"Little good that knowledge will do Chezwick." Lareina turned away. "We have to get out of here."

"No, really?"

"Quit being a smartass."

"Quit being a dumbass."

In the hall, they could hear the commotion taking place outside. They didn't doubt it had to do with Kaiden and Silas. However, the more immediate problem for them was the tracker emitting from Chezwick's body. They only had minutes before the commotion came to them.

****

Alec was pinned. He lay flat on his belly, under a massive air handler, playing a deadly game of hide-and-seek. Four soldiers were investigating the rooftop behind him and the murder of their fallen comrade. Another two had been climbing the roof stairs just as he started his descent. He made a hasty retreat and barely missed being seen. He was out of Yukiyo's line of vision, but he fervently hoped his opponents weren't. He couldn't risk his position by communicating.

****

Orion wasn't certain what to do. It was impossible to get anywhere near the training center. The education center's parking lot was still in his rearview mirror when the MP's converged on it. Now, he was at the place Alec and Yukiyo should have been waiting. He didn't see either of them. However, he did see soldiers walking around on Alec's roof.

****

Kaiden looked around the room he and Silas were in; a lab similar to the one they had worked in. This one was smaller, darker, with an unused feel to it. There was an inner office door. However, nothing of use jumped out at him.

In the hall, the gunfire continued as the Black-ops team and the Military Police exchanged shots.

Chronos sounded. Silas moved off to retrieve the information.

Kaiden trained his guns on the splintered door. "We're trapped and you want to check your messages. Better be important." His humor and confidence were still intact.

"You're trapped. I have a way out." Silas waved his Chronos once. "This way." He nodded toward the inner office door. "Alec is still hawking us, but I think the little punk is in trouble. We have to get over there."

Kaiden thought of Fisher. "How are we getting out?"

"Next door is a restroom. Out this window and in that one. The vents in the restrooms are big. From there we can get to the other side of the building."

"I ain't crawling through no vents." Kaiden followed Silas to the window. "That's dirty, man."

One after the other they stepped onto the ledge and into the empty restroom, locking the window behind them. It took a moment for Silas to pry the vent cover open. He waited while Kaiden crawled through first—complaining the whole time. Behind him, from the inside, Silas jammed the cover back in place. It would be awhile before anyone figured out where they went.

****

MPs were everywhere. "This way." Christian and Lareina made a sharp turn down a foreign hallway.

"Might be better if we split up," Lareina said.

Christian rolled his eyes. "Keep moving."

****

The soldiers wouldn't find anything. Alec knew he was better than that. As per his training, he cleared away all evidence of his presence in real time. But his hiding spot only had one advantage. It was tiny, making it seem an unlikely place to hide. Already he was beginning to get a cramp. If they didn't move soon, he was going to shoot them and be done with it.

Next, he had his people to think about. He could hear what was happening, but he couldn't do much. It was risky sending Silas that message, but they needed his help. It was his job, damn it. He was the control tower. These assholes were interfering.

****

"On top!" Orion's voice sounded as he stepped onto the roof. "Second Line. Captain March." He bellowed the name as if it should have some meaning to the people within his hearing. It did. They lowered their weapons and relaxed their stance.

Alec was impressed with Orion's quick thinking. Good thing he sent him that list.

"Find anything?" Orion walked to where Alec should have been.

Alec slid forward. He needed to see.

"Nothing yet." Someone who appeared to be the leader said, "Who are you and why are you here?"

With ease, Orion gave his prepared line. "Why do you think I'm here? The second Lancaster went down, we got the call." He looked between the two soldiers, then over his shoulder at the four gathered on the roof behind him. "What? You thought you were the only ones? Funny." He sneered at the idea.

"Orion," Alec risked a whisper. "Under the air handler. About eight feet behind you."

Such was his relief, Orion leaned forward, one hand on his thigh for momentary support.

"Get them between us."

Orion straightened as the leader spoke. "There's another team?"

"Two. If my understanding is correct." Orion walked causally to the right. To his satisfaction, they followed his lead.

"Name, soldier?"

"PFC Odell." Orion pointed to the name stitched on his uniform.

"That your real name?" The second soldier, who had been mostly quiet, came closer. He leaned in to inspect the tag for authenticity.

BAM! BAM!
BAM! BAM!
BAM! BAM! BAM!

It took less than ten seconds to end all six lives. Alec shot both soldiers facing Orion. Orion reacted by aiming and shooting at the men on the other roof. He killed one, injured a second and was surprised to see all four go down without retaliation, until Yukiyo's ever calm, always sarcastic voice rang in their ears.

"Took you long enough." She never left her position. The moment Orion stepped onto the roof, she lined up her sights. "Can we go now?"

****

With nowhere to go but up, Lareina and Christian hopped in an empty elevator. On the second floor, they stayed unnoticed, coming to the last office in the hallway. It was locked. Lareina leaned against the door, blocking Christian's hands from view. While he picked the lock, she prayed there was no alarm. The door clicked open and there was blessed silence. They slipped inside.

"One of us has a plan, right?" Christian checked the room.

Lareina peeked out of the window. The building was surrounded. "Nope. But we will. Wait for it."

The quiet of the office was amplified by the chaos of the world beyond. Outside, barricades had been set up. Shootouts were erupting in several places. Over the years, the rigid military discipline, which had once been an American hallmark, had crumbled. People ran in frantic patterns, following whatever orders were uttered by anyone willing to be in control. Inside buildings, passageways echoed with footsteps, slamming doors, and intense yelling.

"Do you think they've already checked this office?" Lareina asked, reasoning as they waited. "Maybe that's why it was locked."

Christian nodded once, his thoughts on other matters. He tapped his necklace; turning his mic off. With a nod, he indicated for her to do the same.

Lareina easily complied. She wondered which Chronos would turn them back on.

He took a long minute to form his words. "You know you have a traitor on your little team, right?"

"If they haven't swept this office, they will. We don't have time for your unrealistic fantasies."

"We have to do this now. We don't have a choice. I'm not cooperating with your rescuers when I know at least one of them wants to kill you. Today."

"No, Christian. I do not have a traitor on my team."

Chapter 30

"Wow," Kaiden said. He and Silas came out in a vacant records room. "He's getting good, isn't he?"

"Better than anybody who isn't me." Silas checked their location on Chronos while Kaiden put the vent cover back in place. "Let's go." They could still hear gunshots but not at close range. Alec had managed to route them around their adversaries.

****

"Are you going to look at the facts, or are you going to let your feelings blind you into assuming they're not capable?"

"Capable?" She had to laugh. "Don't be stupid, my kids are more than capable."

He ignored the jibe. He'd get back to it later. "You think it's a matter of loyalty? That enough money, or power, or whatever hasn't changed a person's loyalty before."

"Christian, I'm not hosting a BFF club. I'm an Acquisitions Engineer~"

"You're a professional manipulator."

She pursed her lips. "And you're a maintenance man, slash, murderer, but it doesn't roll off the tongue quite like 'Crisis Containment and Suppression Architect.' Do you want to listen or not?" He gave her a droll stare which she assumed was permission to continue. "These aren't purchasable people, at least not right now. They took a lot of shit very personally. No, no, no. They're out for blood, lots of it and nothing less will do."

Not to be pacified, he said, "Yukiyo confessed to something."

"No, she didn't. Trust me, she was genuinely surprised."

"And you know this because...you can read minds now?"

"No, because believe it or not, I'm good at what I do."

They talked over their shoulders, with their backs to one another. Christian stood next to the door, listening for noises in the hallway. Likewise, Lareina stayed near the window. They wanted no surprises.

Deciding nothing would be lost by sharing, Lareina explained, "Carmen Newcomer *is* Yukiyo. It's one of the code names I assigned her. Educated guess, I'm thinking somebody caught on and decided to let her run with it. Somehow, they traced it back to her and by extension, us."

"Too easy. Silas would have picked up a trace."

"Silas wouldn't have known where to look. The code names are private."

Christian thought it over. It was a reasonable conclusion...for now. "Speaking of Silas, what excuse are you going to hand me to cover his ass? And don't tell me shit about coincidences. Briggs is his personal contact. He's been ass-deep in helping you rebel without so much as a speeding ticket. That kind of freedom has a price. I know it because believe it or not, I'm good at what I do."

****

"Hold it!"

As a unit, Kaiden and Silas turned. A young, nervous MP came up on them fast. His weapon drawn with shaky hands. They did as he commanded.

"Stand down, soldier," Silas said. He nodded in Kaiden's direction. "He's not a threat. He saw something. I'm taking him in for questioning. Kapeesh?"

Kaiden remained silent, but cut Silas an insulted stare.

The soldier gained interest and forgot his fear. He lowered his firearm. "What'd you see?"

Silas shook his head. The military used to be about discipline. "We've got a meeting in ten." He made to turn away and turned back. "You coming?"

The MP locked his weapon and put it away. He hurried to catch up.

Kaiden gave a low whistle through his teeth. *Unbelievable.*

****

Down on the street, the world had changed. So far, no one had yet to determine what manner of attack had come to Fort Detrick, Maryland. The only confirmed news was a top official had been killed. The base had been on high alert. The primary objective was to apprehend the murderer. Meanwhile, the Military Police were involved in various altercations with individuals unknown for reasons unclear. Orders came from opposing authorities. A true objective had yet to be established.

Alec and Orion emerged from an unguarded doorway. Yukiyo came down the sidewalk to join them.

"The car is over here." Orion led the way.

Yukiyo walked between the boys. "I don't know if we'll be able to get off the base."

"I'm not leaving," Alec muttered.

"Lareina doesn't want us to attempt getting out yet," Orion informed them. "We're supposed to regroup. It's going to be tough for her and Christian. I think we need to find Silas and Kaiden. The five of us should be able to pull them out."

"That's a plan," Yukiyo said.

Alec didn't respond. They turned to see if he had been paying attention. He wasn't. Alec was gone.

****

Ignorant as he was, the young soldier served Silas' purpose. The presence of an MP, Kaiden's stoic frown and Silas' natural swagger was enough to discourage questions. People were content to leave them to their business. They were out of the building and moving away from the barricade before the MP thought to ask "Where do we need to be?"

"Right there." Silas pointed. "There's his escort waiting."

This seemed to impress their companion. He eagerly led the way.

Yukiyo and Orion were driving toward the training facility and pulled over quickly upon spying Kaiden and Silas. They disembarked but did not move away from the car. They remained silent, waiting for a clue as to what game they were playing now.

"Good time, soldiers," Silas spoke with all the authority of a commanding officer. "Corporal Zane," he used the name assigned to Kaiden, "has a positive ID. You need to get him to Staff Sergeant Riggs," the name he assigned to Christian. "I believe he's in the education center."

"This must be serious," the MP interrupted enthusiastically. "The education center is on total lockdown."

Kaiden arched an eyebrow, refusing to comment now, just on principle.

Silas talked on, not bothering to acknowledge the MP. "Where's PFC RJae?"

"We believe he's already in route to the education center, sir," Orion answered as if he were giving a report.

"Where else?" Yukiyo muttered, uncaring of who listened.

"Good," Silas said. "They should be expecting you." He saluted, turned on his heel and strode away, leaving them all somewhat bemused. Whether he announced his own intentions, gave an order to Alec or something else altogether remained a mystery. It was clear they were to get to the Education Center, using Kaiden as their alibi and the MP as their shield.

****

Somebody, somewhere let loose a grenade. The building shuddered. Bits of debris shook free, raining dust, dirt and spiders. However, the tremor was not so big as to throw Christian or Lareina off balance.

Unaware of the exact activities outside, Lareina concentrated on the battle within. "Silas, a traitor? Come on, Eugene. Even with all of your prejudices, you can't make that believable."

"I don't have to make it anything. According to you, he's almost infallible. You don't get that way working for the little guy." He looked down his nose at her naïveté. "You don't. The son-of-a-bitch really is almost as good as me. That's saying a whole hell of a lot." Christian turned, giving Lareina his full attention. "Silas' number one priority is Silas and whatever he needs to do to be better at being Silas. Whether you admit it or not, I know, if it came down to it, your little teddy bear mascot would lay your ass out before he'd take the heat for anything. He's a key factor in everything you do. And yet, he's not wanted for shit. How is that even possible?" Christian crossed the room, closing half the distance between them. "I'll tell you how. It's possible because Silas McKade has been assigned to be your personal assassin. This has all been a big mousetrap for him. Now, that you're done doing whatever his superior... Briggs...wanted done, Silas summoned the mock bad guys. Although, I'm sure he'll want to do me himself." Christian hunched his shoulders. "That will work out. Makes it easy for me to find him, kill him and save your not-so-bright-ass from the monster you created."

Lareina had been quiet and still the whole time Christian talked. She remained quiet for a bit longer, letting his words settle over the room. "Some speech. Wordy but passionate. And very, very, wrong. Silas, a teddy bear? You get cuddly with him and you'll most likely lose an appendage." She frowned dramatically. "Mousetrap? No, no, no. He's a falcon. He doesn't play with his food. Half the time he's much too lofty and god-like to even bother with food~"

Christian cut her off. "Enough with the bullshit. You don't get to talk your way around this. The sooner you admit I'm right, the sooner we can get out of here. Because we can't move unless we're on the same page. He's going to come after us. Accept it, so I can kill him."

She sobered. "We don't have time for this. You're wrong. There won't be anything I can say to make you believe it, but you're still wrong~"

"Lareina, he's got a death warrant with your name on it. I signed it. He's walking around with permission to put a hole in your chest."

"And, he would if he needed to!" She was suddenly exasperated. She came forward, covering the space between them. "The bullet he would use would be filled with something he created to knock me out. It would stop the bleeding and make everyone think I'm dead. And you know what? I'd wake up in Peru for no other reason than it's near the equator and he knows I don't like hot places. That's what he'd do to me!"

In the corridor, just beyond the office where they were secluded, the ceiling tile moved.

Christian and Lareina stood almost touching toes. Under his contacts, his too-blue eyes locked with her fiery-copper stare; the heat that always lingering near the surface of their relationship swelled and threatened to explode. Hell was unfolding around them and he wanted to kiss her. He wanted to hold her, protect her until the insanity they were drowning in receded. He breathed her in, pleased that she wore the perfume he had given her. He wanted her, but he did not touch her...not yet.

Lareina spoke as if she were not affected although they both knew better. "You may not have noticed, but there's been no communication. Do you know what that means?"

"Everybody's fucked."

"They know we can't get out unseen. They're on their way. They don't want to talk to me because they don't want to hear me say no. Silas is racing Alec and Kaiden for the lead."

"Now, you're delusional. You cannot have that much burden of responsibility."

"It's not a burden. We call ourselves a team, but we're more than that. We're a family by choice. That's what makes us better than the government. Better than the Revolutionaries. Than the Vanguard. That's why we'll win, Christian. Silas doesn't need us. He's a one-man army on his worst day. He's with us because he's part of the family." As suddenly as her emotions flared up, they died down. She applied reasoning he couldn't deny. "You would champion every one of Chloe's causes. You don't even need to know what they are. Every resource at your disposal would be hers, because you love her. Just like we love each other."

He shifted, uncomfortable with his daughter's name being mentioned.

Lareina knew that. She leaned into him. "It might seem weird to you, but we're connected, codependent, fiercely loyal and we like it. So quit being a distraction and focus on the real issue here."

He enfolded her within his embrace, needing the comfort as much as she did. "Fine. But as soon as we get back, Silas is a dead man and I'm taking you home."

"You don't get to hurt someone I love."

"Love?" He leaned back to look into her eyes. "What do think this is? A Disney movie? This isn't a fairytale, Lareina. You're not Wendy. They aren't the Lost Boys and Silas damn sure isn't Peter Pan. He's a psychopath. The rest of them are sociopaths and narcissists. You've made them dangerous."

"I didn't make them dangerous. The world made them dangerous. I gave them a purpose and a choice."

"You should have given them a better choice."

"Maybe. It's a good thing we're family. Otherwise, they'd never forgive me."

"Why do you defend them? Defend him when you know what he is?"

"Why does she defend me?"

As far as they knew, Silas had materialized out of thin air.

Christian had his gun freed and cocked before recognition caught up.

Lareina's shuddered. "Give me a heart attack, why don't you?" She slid out of Christian's embrace.

"Pay attention." Silas didn't give her the courtesy of a glance. "Why does she defend me? It's her nature. She'll be defending you in a minute."

Silas' stance was aggressive. His TS13 was over his shoulder, but he had a pistol in his palm, fire-ready. His scowl prominent. Lareina took it all in, processing and rightly concluding he was not in the mood to listen. In fact, he was angry. This was her least favorite aspect of his personality. Silas could kill anybody. When he's angry, he kills everybody. "You lose a hand-grenade?"

"Everybody needs a distraction now and then. Ain't that right, Eugene?"

"I don't believe I've given you permission to be informal with me, Corporal. You don't have permission to call me Eugene."

Silas snorted. "I don't give a damn about you or your bullshit. Never have. You do know, I'm not letting you get away with it."

"Silas~"

"No, 'Reina. Not this time." Silas cut off her protest. "This is it."

There was something in Silas' expression that truly alarmed Lareina. He was in that place of no negotiation. However, it did not mean she wasn't going to try. "Spit it out, Si." Unlike the others, his name rarely got shortened. She used it when she was desperate to distract him; when Silas couldn't be reached. "You know better than we do how much time we don't have."

****

Kaiden tugged on his earring. If that wasn't a cue, he didn't know what was. He turned from the interrogation he, Yukiyo, and Orion were getting. He didn't have time for it. His teammates were in obvious agreement. They joined him—one on each side—all three ignoring the officer who questioned them and the MPs who followed; calling for them to stop.

****

Instead of answering Lareina, Silas studied Christian. "What are you, an idiot? Think I stopped monitoring your ass because you sleep upstairs. I can get you a good deal on those ice skates Chloe wants."

Christian's eyes narrowed.

"Think I don't know how many times you've been in contact with Misty Wilson. Can't call you a traitor because you were never a part of this team."

"Sloppy Silas. With one word, you've just lost this fight." Christian casually stepped away from Lareina. "Do you want to guess which one?"

Everything happened at once.

Silas raised his hand and pulled the trigger.

Christian mirrored the action.

Lareina slammed into Christian, intending to shove him out of the way and to misdirect his shot.

The bullets fired almost as one and mingled with a scream so pained, the third shot went unheard.

****

Kaiden ran with Orion on his heels. Yukiyo slowed down. The enormity of what she heard made her stop. She wasn't going there.

****

Two of the shots were true; one, unanticipated. A bullet drilled into the far wall, after tearing through clothes and flesh, paint and plaster. Another, aimed so well, it ripped the gun out of the startled bearer's hands. The third scorched a heated path and embedded itself into an irrelevant patch of Kevlar.

Lareina and Christian tumbled down together, a mass of arms, legs and splattered blood. She looked at him before her coppery-brown eyes closed in dark denial. His too-blue eyes stared beyond in silent sightless prayer.

Mere feet away, Silas sunk to his knees, then to the floor, unmoving. Incredulity frozen on his once expressionless features.

Alec, the last shooter, lowered his TS13. He had noiselessly come upon them and now he remained where he stood. Silent. Stunned. Disbelieving.

Chapter 31

The lack of sound drove the others to insanity and beyond. The trailing MPs gave Yukiyo a place to put her rage. She spun around to face behind her and opened fire on everything moving. Orion turned, whether it was to help her, save her or to get out of the way, in that panic-filled moment, he had no idea which.

Kaiden never stopped. Carried by the force of his love for Lareina, not even the barrage of bullets lighting up the hall around him could claim one iota of his focus. His sister needed him. He would never let her down, never let her go. He spotted Alec in the doorway. "MOVE!"

The raw pain, hard emotion, pushed through the younger man like a shot of adrenaline. Even so, he had just made it to Lareina, just touched her cool forehead when Kaiden joined him. "Mom?"

As if she were a bloody ragdoll, Kaiden snatched her up against him and fled the room. Not caring who saw, who came, who followed.

Kaiden's yell penetrated the fog. Christian sat up, dazed, soaked in blood with no visible wound. The horror replayed before his eyes. Lareina plowing into him. He anticipated she would, in fact, he counted on it. He shot around her and pulled her to him, dragging her to the ground. To safety. That was how it was supposed to work. But it didn't. Silas anticipated her movement as well, planned for it. But he was too focused. Too damned focused. He didn't calculate Christian's unyielding possessiveness. Silas expected him to keep Lareina safe by pushing her away, not pulling her in. He shot where Christian would have been; where Lareina was. Maybe it was him, Christian. He was too focused. He shouldn't have held her. He should have pushed her away.

That kid. Alec. Lareina's son shot the gun out of his hand. But not before he squeezed off a slug. It was still too late, Silas got his shot off first. Silas didn't miss. He was soaked in Lareina's blood because Silas doesn't miss.

The entire series of thoughts came in a matter of breaths. He was hauled up, yanked to his feet. That kid. Alec. Lareina's son grabbed his arm, shoved him. Alec called to Silas, shook him, yelled, but Silas didn't move. And now they were running behind Kaiden. Christian shook his head, one time to clear it. Kaiden carried Lareina. Alec moved to the lead. Christian closed the distance, guarding Kaiden's back. Anybody attempting to stop them was going straight to hell.

****

Intensity gave Orion strength. He needed every ounce of it to drag Yukiyo out of harm's way. They got to the office steps behind Kaiden but were too late, the others were gone. Everyone except Silas. And so, so much blood.

Yukiyo screamed, "The fuckers left him!" She ran to the downed soldier but not to awaken him, or mourn. "They sided with Deverell and left him!" She fumbled with his utility belt, locating what she sought. She slipped past, a grenade in each hand.

"Yukiyo!" Orion called after her. He did not know which way she ran, but he suspected it was what she considered treachery rather than the MPs that concerned her.

Orion hesitated. He had to get out. He had to collect Yukiyo. But he couldn't leave Silas. Not like this. He didn't know if he was dead or dying. Why would they leave him? There was nobody more vital to the team than Silas, except Lareina. He looked at the blood. Lareina. She was everything. She made them a family. He needed her but she wasn't talking. She wasn't telling them what to do.

He couldn't make it make sense. They had been doing a good thing. Righting wrongs. Saving kids. Saving the country. In their chaotic way, they were saving the world. Weren't they? "Lareina?"

****

The sight of three soldiers running, one carrying a bloody mass of a woman, momentarily halted the action on the grounds around the education center. This group must be on the saving side, not the killing side.

Uncaring of spectators, Alec led the charge toward a cluster of emergency vehicles. Nothing, not even their lives were more important than saving Lareina.

Whether by quick thinking or sheer instinct, Christian pointed and yelled, "Bomb!"

Everyone moved away from the building.

Behind them, another person emerged. She hurled a hand grenade in the direction of the sprinters. It landed on the sidewalk and exploded on impact, but missed the traitors she aimed for. In the midst of smoke and screams, before gunfire could resume, Yukiyo took off in the opposite direction, intent on two things: escape and retaliation.

Soldiers went after her, but to most of the people outside, it felt over. Yukiyo's departure marked an ending. Whatever this was, ended with her. They would search the building again, but the individuals responsible for the attack were gone or dead. Either way, it felt over.

In the confusion of movement, people helping the injured and/or searching for survivors and/or witnesses, no one paid attention to the lowly private doing his duty, moving a soldier who could not move himself.

****

Three silent soldiers crowded in the back of the ambulance as it drove to the surgical center in Frederick, six miles off base. Three silent soldiers crowded the hallway outside the operating room, making the staff inside feel as if their own lives were hanging upon the outcome of the lifesaving procedure they were attempting.

****

Christian came up with their alibi. He went undercover to infiltrate Lareina Elliot's gang. Kaiden and Alec worked for him and Lareina was his prisoner. They were caught in the crossfire of a riot which had broken out at Ft. Detrick. They weren't involved, but he needed his prisoner alive. His clearance check shut down further inquiry.

His resurfacing made him the senior ranking official in his department. As such, he became Joffener's replacement. He had been named to the position by Lieutenant Colonel Briggs, himself.

While Christian settled back into his old role and navigated the details of his new duties, Kaiden and Alec were left to wonder if parts of his alibi were true.

****

Thoughts and images collided in her head. Illogical words tumbled from her lips. Lareina opened her eyes, but the room did not come into focus. Kaiden. Blink. Christian. Blink. "No." That wasn't right. Blink. "Where's Fisher?" Alec was frowning. "I know. Rub your hair. Give Silas a snickers." Orion was running. "A red hair..."

Her second attempt at consciousness brought the room into focus. It was filled with pain. Hers. Everything went wrong. Christian and Silas. Someone was going to get hurt. The return of her last memory caused her to cry out in anguish.

They were there. All of them. Some of them. Called forth by her discomfort, Alec, Kaiden, and Christian, hovered around her bed. They touched her, kissed her, said things to soothe and reassure her and themselves. She was going to be alright. She was going to be alright. She wasn't going to be alright. "Silas..."

"He'll see you when he can," Kaiden said. "Relax, 'Reina. You'll be fine. I promise."

Neither Christian nor Alec contradicted him. They understood the necessity of keeping her calm at all costs. Even if it meant lying.

By the third day of her medically induced coma, they settled into shifts of making plans, sleeping and keeping vigil. Kaiden's time alone with her came in the late afternoon. He prayed for her. He read to her. He watched her breathe.

Quietly, her door eased open. Orion slipped in looking haggard and on edge. "Hey."

"Where the hell have you been?"

"Watching Silas and trying to find Yuke. Mostly watching Silas."

"He's..?" Kaiden couldn't say it. Had purposely not mentioned his name. Wouldn't think about Silas. He couldn't afford to think about Silas.

Orion went to Lareina's bedside. His eyes filmed. "Is she going to be okay?"

Kaiden nodded. "I think so. Might take a while."

Orion wilted. He had been too strong for too long. When he could speak he said, "I've been on suicide watch since it happened. Phone silence was his condition." He held Lareina's hand and let himself cry.

"Where is he?"

"Outside. Don't know what I would have done if I had to bring him bad news."

Kaiden strode past Orion, hugging him briefly on his way out.

Out of the building, across the parking lot, Kaiden had no particular destination in mind. Silas was the hawk, he was just making himself visible.

Five minutes into his stroll, the soldier let himself be seen. Kaiden caught sight of him and made a beeline in that direction.

Silas stood stoic; his face lined with anguish. Kaiden could do whatever he wanted. Silas wouldn't stop him.

Kaiden came right up on him and kept coming. It took a moment before Silas realized he was being embraced; longer to hear what Kaiden said.

"I thought you were dead. What the hell kind of shit is that, not letting me know you're alright? Don't you think I have enough to worry about without you going dark? You don't get to drop out. Do you understand me? You don't get to drop out..." The full range of his emotions went into his rant.

"I shot 'Raina man, I shot her." Silas didn't know anything beyond that. The image was seared into his mind and he could not function beyond it.

"Who gives a shit? She's okay and you're okay. What the fuck else matters?"

Silas cried harder and deeper than any other time in his life. He buckled under the weight of Kaiden's forgiveness. They sagged against one another. Afraid. Relieved. Together.

By the time Kaiden and Silas returned to Lareina's room, Alec was there with Orion. Kaiden motioned them out. "Give him a minute."

Orion did as bidden. Alec seemed not to have heard him. "You too." Kaiden came forward, intent on moving Alec.

"Leave him be." Silas studied Alec.

Alec studied Silas.

"We'll keep watch," Orion muttered and followed Kaiden out.

Alec stared at Silas.

Silas stared at Alec.

Each face expressionless. For a long moment, the only sound was Lareina's heart monitor keeping track of the beats.

"You shot my mother."

"Yes, I did."

If Alec expected further explanation, it wouldn't be coming from Silas. Instead, Silas went to Lareina. Leaning close, he stroked her hair, touched her face and kissed her. "You better get better," he whispered. He pulled in a deep breath and stood straight.

Alec watched him; his body language, his emotions, his personal pain. "Christian thinks you're dead."

"Keep him ignorant."

Having relived the moment a million times, Alec already had it worked out. "Did you think he would push her away?"

"If his love was right, he would have pushed her away."

"He should have. You would have. And so would I."

"We love her right."

They went back to expressionless staring, but the tension was passing. Alec moved away from the bed to look out of the window. "He was going for your head. I saved your ass."

"Of course, you did. You were the only one who could." Silas stroked Lareina's hair once more before facing Alec. "Somewhere down the line, you'll be the one to kill me. Because when I'm done training you, you'll be the only one who can."

"Deal. Is that the thing with you and him?"

"One of them."

"Next time, do it without warning. He'll still know who it was."

Silas cracked a smile. It was his first one in a long time. "Where's the fun in that? Besides, Lareina would never let me hear the end of it."

Alec smiled too. "She can be a pain. If you give me a heads-up, I'll take care of her."

"Deal." Silas wanted to make peace with Alec and he had. "I can't stay.

I have to find Yuke. Can you give 'Reina a message for me?"

"Yep."

"Tell her, it's been raining. Hard."

"She's supposed to know what that means?"

"She'll know." At the door Silas paused, needing to say one more thing. "Thanks."

Chapter 32

In the weeks following the fiasco, the news called it *The Detrick War*. An intense investigation turned up nothing solid, just speculation that somebody attempted to release warheads and somebody stopped them. Precisely who those somebodies were, had yet to be determined. The original settings of the warheads were discovered, although to date, no one could decode the resetting. They would have to be dismantled. This information was the beginning of 'talks' between the Pentagon and the Revolutionaries. It appeared they had common enemies and mutual friends.

Military discipline had been questioned. A training overhaul was being established. Intelligence and security were microscoped. America had a new focus.

****

"They got Yuke," Alec announced. He walked and studied Chronos II. It was a small wonder to see him out of the bedroom. Only necessity could get him out of the bedroom. In the living room, Kaiden cleaned their weapons; keeping everything at the ready. Likewise, Orion, with his chemistry case before him, measured liquids and cut powder. He wore gloves. Whatever he was preparing was potent and no doubt, dangerous. Christian read and reread reports. He was searching for something and would not be denied.

All three looked up. This news made it necessary for Alec to leave the bedroom.

"Who?" Christian asked.

"Not sure. All it says is, apprehended by authorities. Could be anybody, but we know the other team was EP graduates. They knew who we were. I'm betting they got her."

"We have to get her back," Orion said.

"Of course, we do."

They all turned toward the sound. And chastised in unison.

"Reina!"

"Mom!"

"Lareina!"

"Reina!"

Kaiden asked the question they were all thinking. "Why are you up?"

"I had to pee."

Nobody believed her.

Alec said, "I told you I'd be right back."

"I still had to pee and I wanted to know what was going on."

Rather than argue, as a group, they went to her. Alec taking the lead. Christian scooping her up with Kaiden right behind. Orion went to the kitchen.

"When we want you to know what's going on, we'll tell you," Kaiden said.

"Then I won't know anything."

"Too bad." Christian put her back in her bed. Lareina was far from healthy. Silas' bullet broke her ribs and collapsed her lung. The miracle of her life was due to her angle and the speed in which she received help. Like Orion, Lareina felt four weeks was too much time to be helpless. Unlike Orion, no one gave her a choice. "Move again and I will tie you down."

She looked from one male to the other, finding no sympathy; not even from Alec. Especially not from Alec. "Keep me in the loop."

"Fine." Alec made himself comfortable beside her. The others followed suit.

Orion joined them. He held a small glass in his hand. "I was saying, we have to get her back, but I don't know if she wants to be around us. She thinks Silas was betrayed." He gave the drink to Lareina.

"Silas was betrayed." Alec threw a glance at Christian.

Lareina accepted the liquid, had a sip, and talked over the retort. "She'll find out soon enough what's what. In the meantime, we've got something else to worry about." She settled back into her pillows. Being up for five minutes wore her out. "I want to dismantle the EP. I think we should shut it down." She took a large swallow.

"Can we wait until you're healed?" Kaiden couldn't help but smile. Her brain never took a break.

"I didn't say tomorrow," she yawned. "But it needs to be done. If I've overheard you correctly, the other team was EP. We can't let that happen. We've got to figure out how they got us. And we've got to stop them from sucking kids into this."

"Calm down," Christian said. "You're not going anywhere anytime soon. We've got plenty of time to work through it. If that's what you really want to do."

"It's what I really want to do."

"Okay." Christian had come too close to losing her. Never again. Every problem they've ever encountered came when he chose not to be on her side. He didn't have to care about the rest of them. He didn't have to think about the war. All he had to do was stay on her side.

Christian not fighting her. That was the biggest win Lareina could imagine. She savored it as her eyes drooped. "Ori. Did you drug me?" She didn't know if she asked the question or thought it.

"Every single time." He loosed the empty glass from her fingers. Lareina was asleep.

"That was fast," Alec said. "Keep that stuff away from me."

Orion grinned.

Quietly leaving the room, they continued the conversation.

"We still have to do something about Yuke," Kaiden said. "'Reina won't rest if she's in trouble."

"I'll get her." Christian took in their skeptical stares. It didn't bother him that they didn't trust him. They weren't his problem. "Anybody in this room more qualified? Have a better chance?" When no other suggestions came forth, he said, "Good." To Alec, he said, "Figure out where she is and find out what I need to know. As soon as you get it, I'll be gone."

"Incentive enough." Alec went somewhere to work.

****

The lighting in the interrogation room was dim. The room itself was predictably sparse. A table with three chairs. The interrogating officer sat beside the empty chair, sipping stale coffee. Across from him, Yukiyo faced the two-way mirror.

"Look," Captain March said. "I want to help you. Tell me how to do that?"

He was handsome, in Yukiyo's opinion. Mixed-race. Dark hair and skin permanently tanned. She couldn't be sure of his eyes; the room was too dark, but they were piercing and sincere. He had on a green t-shirt. His arms were ripped. Definitely handsome. It was nice to have a face to go with the name. She remembered his name. "You can't help me. But thank you, all the same."

"What are you thinking? Are your friends preparing to charge in here and rescue you?" He leaned back in his chair. "I'll admit they are better than average, but that's a tall order."

"I don't have any friends."

"Pretty girl like you?" He flashed her a row of almost even white teeth.

She didn't respond.

"Did you have a falling out? Don't think they'll care?"

"They care and they'll come."

"But they're not your friends?"

"I don't have any friends."

"Why are you expecting to be rescued?"

"I'm not expecting to be rescued. I wouldn't go with them if I was."

"Help me out here. Why would they attempt to rescue you?"

"Because they don't know I'm waiting to kill them." She looked past him, toward the mirror. "Is that enough information for you?"

****

On the other side, Lieutenant Colonel Briggs spoke to his companion. "Maybe we should keep her alive a while longer. Let her do the work. Save ourselves some trouble."

"Let her live if you want." The snake stared, transfixed on the girl in the other room. "But Miss Mio Dia Yukiyo is more trouble than we need."

"How's your other prisoner?" Briggs spoked casually, only mildly interested. With his round jovial face and laughing brown eyes, the Lieutenant Colonel had the ability to put people at ease. Make them comfortable and lax.

Christian wasn't most people. Briggs didn't waste words. Lareina's health didn't concern him.

"Healing. Should be feeling closer to herself by the time I return."

"You never said how you commandeered her team."

"I did not."

Briggs looked at him, checking for impertinence. "Say."

"They're smart kids. Lareina's life and their freedom are mine to control."

"Agreed. But at the moment, you're not there to control anything. What's stopping them from being smart enough to go underground?"

He was walking a thin line. He had to cooperate to keep the trust. Right now, he needed Briggs' trust. "Lareina's life and their freedom. Both would be greatly compromised without me. Besides, I have something they want."

"What's that?"

With a slight nod of his head, he indicated the prisoner on the other side of the glass. "Her."

****

For a cell, it was quite comfortable. Bedroom, private bath, living area, kitchenette; like a suite at a not luxurious, but well-kept hotel. Hues of rose and green dominated the décor, giving an element of style, maybe. Or, at least, a desire to match and blend. Yukiyo didn't care for any of it.

She didn't care about the three-station television—news, weather, and family movies from before she was born. She didn't care about the books or magazines piled on a small wooden bookshelf—stupid cozies and boring articles about pretend happy people. It was a farce. The idea that somewhere in the country, life remained carefree and easy.

She didn't care about the food in the fridge or the healthy snacks in the cabinet. She ate when she was hungry, ignored the rest and pretended not to notice when they restocked. Obviously, it wasn't poisoned. It tasted fine, but it wasn't truly good either. She would kill for one of Lareina's candy bars.

Yukiyo didn't care about anything in her cell, but she did care about her future and whatever crazy plans these people had for her. They wanted her to sell out her team, of course. That wasn't going to happen.

She suspected they already knew enough about them anyway. Lareina Elliot and the people closest to her—big secret, that. They also wanted her cooperation; her help to get to the others. Stop them, recruit them, whatever. Their plans had nothing to do with her plans so she didn't have to care. She cared about getting out.

They let her keep her personal items. It was weird to think a country that used to be so technologically advanced, couldn't find a transmitter in a neckless. Good. She couldn't reach anyone but she hoped Alec or Orion would be able to find a way to track her. Silas would have already been here by now.

She had cried some, but not much. They weren't anything. But they were supposed to be. She and Silas were realists. It would have happened eventually. They didn't need moonlight and sappy music to convince them to be together. They needed time. Time Deverell took from them.

****

Silas parked a block away from the gate. It was time to come up with a plan. He could go in through the front as himself, flash the death warrant and be on official business. Or, he could break in and steal her away. If his understanding was correct—which it was—either way would give her a heart attack, with him being dead and all. He smiled to himself. She wanted to kill everybody because she thought he was dead. A girl didn't get any sweeter than that.

Damn. He needed to see her. She was the last piece to getting their shit back together. They needed their shit together. And, he missed her. He worried about her. He thought about her; all pissed off and ready to kill for him. The best news he'd gotten after learning Lareina was going to make it was Alec's message giving him Yuke's location.

He'd break in, make it more fun. Hopefully, she was still wearing her necklace. He turned on the transmitters to track her, not talk; that would scare the shit out of her and possibly blow his cover.

Chronos beeped. He got a message.

Silas read the text and frowned. He hit the steering wheel. "Bastard!" He read it once again and banged his head against the headrest. He had to think about this.

Don't bother. Stay your ass still and I'll bring

her out. That's an order.

Christian. Couldn't be anybody but him. *How does that asshole know I'm alive? How does he know I'm here?* The damn transmitter. Deverell was still on frequency and *he* would notice when it went live. *What's Deverell doing here after hours?*

****

Christian knocked once and let himself in. It took Yukiyo a moment to hide her surprise.

"Good evening. I hope you've eaten."

She raised herself from the sofa. "Why are you here?"

Arms folded, stance ridged; Christian noted and ignored her attitude. "I'm here to take you home. Why else?"

Yukiyo sneered. "Tell the truth. You came here to kill me."

"If only. Sorry, my dear. If killing you were my plan, we wouldn't be having this conversation because you'd be dead. For some odd reason, Lareina wants you home. Get your shoes on."

"You work for them."

"No kidding."

"I'm not going anywhere with you."

"I'm not interested in traveling with you either. Shoes."

"You killed Silas~"

Christian walked up to her. "Miss Mio Dia Yukiyo, We're on a time schedule. You're leaving here tonight with or without your shoes. If you think there's an option other than cooperation, evidently, you don't know jack shit, or me. I won't ask you again."

She hated him but she didn't have a choice. All the more reason to kill him. Her uneven brown hair had grown to her shoulders. It whipped behind her as she made an abrupt about-face. She slipped her feet into her shoes and said, "I haven't eaten."

Christian ignored her. He led the way out.

****

Silas heard the conversation. Yuke was with him. What was Deverell up to?

He had just about decided he was done waiting when he received a second text.

Where?

Silas could play too. There's a grocery store on the main road, about two miles. Take her there. When Deverell arrived, he, Silas would be waiting for his ass.

****

Christian circled the parking lot. When he didn't see what he searched for, he spoke aloud. "I assume you're up some damn tree planning to screw up my evening. Don't. I'm hard-wired. Same program as Chezwick's. Anything happens to me and they'll be at Lareina's before you hit the bottom branch. Yukiyo has already wasted more time than I have. I'm doing this on my dinner break. I'm a grouchy bastard when I'm hungry, so get your ass here, now."

Yukiyo mostly ignored Christian. She fingered her shark, wondering to whom he connected. Alec? Possibly, but not alone. She hoped Orion wasn't there. Orion was the only one she didn't specifically plan to kill. She would if he got in her way, but she hoped he didn't.

****

Silas thought fast. Christian knew the transmitters were live, he had Yuke, and had the jump on him. Best not to force his hand. Yet.

****

Halfway through Christian's second pass, they were blinded by the headlights of an approaching vehicle. Christian stopped and waited while the other car did the same.

"Your ride."

Yukiyo stared at Christian. "You're going to let me leave?"

"If it wasn't my intention to let you leave, I'd be eating dinner."

"Whatever." She exited the one car and walked straight to the other. She got in, slammed the door and looked at the driver. Her breath caught and stayed caught.

Silas leaned over and kissed her. It wasn't long, but it was powerful. It tasted of surprise and relief and yearning. He pulled back and said, "Hold that thought." He drove forward, coming alongside Christian.

Christian didn't give him time to ask. "Your death was accepted a little too easily for it to have been legit. Five full minutes of research showed Briggs still had you active. I've been expecting you. By the way, you work for me now. I'll get you the details tonight. I'll be home in a few days. We'll start planning then."

Silas sneered. "I'm cooperating with you, why?"

"Do you have a choice?"

"You know I do."

"Choose wisely. Working together is good for Lareina and bad for everyone else."

"Can't fault your logic, Eugene. What makes you think I'm going to trust you?"

"It's good for Lareina and bad for everybody else. You have her." Christian nodded at Yukiyo. "When I see you again, you won't doubt my intentions. And, I'll give you an opportunity to earn *my* trust."

"Do I want it?"

"You do."

They could read each other. And they knew things other people did not. It was one of the many reasons they were both dangerous. They were reading one another right now. Christian wasn't a threat –at least, not for the moment. He did hand over Yukiyo, unharmed. He hadn't mentioned their last encounter. He didn't even bristle at being called Eugene. Silas was intrigued.

"You're driving out of here in front of me."

"I'm going into that store and getting some food. If you're still here when I get back, I'll forget the whole thing and arrest you both."

That made Silas laugh. "As if you could." He put the jeep in gear and drove off.

Chapter 33

Silas took Yukiyo to dinner, then he took her to a hotel.

Yukiyo surveyed the room. "Why would you get a room with one only bed?"

"Would you prefer to lose your virginity in the car?"

She failed at not smiling. "You're an asshole. I'm not sleeping with you. And, for your information, I'm not a virgin."

"The hell you ain't." He moved faster than she expected. Tackling her, he forced her to the bed and covered her body with his, using just enough of his weight to keep her pinned. "You're smart, you're sexy, you're dangerous, and you impress the hell out of me." He reached his hand between them to unbutton her pants.

"Get off." She resisted by squirming once. "That's not what you think."

"You're the liar in this relationship, not me." He undid her zipper and slid his hand inside. "You chose me. You defended me. Don't you think I owe you for that?" He slow stroked her, loving that even as her body went soft and she moved against his hand, she kept her eyes open, fixed on his. Watching her pupils dilate as he awakened her desire, took him from semi to fully erect. He rocked against her, teaching her body to follow his.

"Silas..." her lips quivered. Her heart-rate accelerated. She couldn't focus. Her body felt... He was making..."Oh, Silas..."

"Stay with me." He rubbed her faster, savoring her very first orgasm.

While her nerves were still jumping, and she trembled against his hand, he kissed her long and slow. He kissed her again then whispered in her ear, "I will love you forever and I'll remain unconditionally faithful as long as you don't break my heart."

Yukiyo could barely speak but she knew what she felt. "I won't hurt you, Silas. I'm as loyal as you are. I'm in love too."

"You are about to lose your virginity."

****

The family reunion brought joy unlike any other. Yukiyo wore a newly purchased yellow sundress. She was soft, full of giggles and genuine happiness.

If anyone was leery of an ulterior motive, it couldn't be felt in their welcoming embraces.

"I've been so, so worried about you." Lareina wouldn't stop hugging her.

Likewise, Yukiyo returned the affection. "Thank goodness, you're alive. Are you okay?" She did a visual check.

"Still a little weak, but getting there. Thanks to you."

Yukiyo arched an eyebrow. What did she do? Nothing besides lose her mind.

"Nothing mattered more than the diversion you created. We wouldn't be here without your sacrifice."

"It wasn't on purpose."

"Didn't need to be." Alec squeezed in for his hug. "As long as it worked."

Lareina released her. She wanted Silas.

Crying with happiness, she kissed him, hugged him, and kissed him again. She held his face and stared at him for a long minute. "How's the weather?"

Smiling through his own tears, he wiped the wetness from her cheek. "A little damp, but the storm's passing."

"It's sunshiny bright over here."

They embraced and laughed at themselves. For Lareina's people, other than making them stronger, mistakes didn't matter; couldn't matter. After all, she had created them to cause trouble. KAYOS was their destiny.

****

Later, over subs, they sorted through what they knew and their biggest problem: Christian.

"No, Kaid," Lareina said. "Killing Christian is not an option."

"It is to me." He took a huge bite out of his double meat cheesesteak.

Orion sliced his sub in half. "You can't work with somebody if you're not sure they're for or against you." He gave half of the spicy-Italian-combo to Alec. In return, Alec passed him half of his turkey-bacon-club.

"The guy who did my interrogation, Captain March, he was on the list. I think Deverell might know him." Yukiyo dunked a YY—her name for French Fries—into a puddle of barbeque sauce. "I didn't know he was there until he released me. He never bothered talking to me before then. He seemed to know his way around the place. People knew him...Granted, we only saw two, but they followed his orders without question. Considering my connection to you 'Reina, I can't imagine Deverell being in the dark about who's asking me questions."

"He wasn't in the dark." Silas helped himself to a few of her fries. He dipped them in her barbeque sauce. He had his own extra-large order of fries, but they were destined for ketchup. "If his files can be trusted, Briggs is our link. He's been onto us for a while. He put that team together to do what we do naturally. He wanted to see how we and they compared."

"What are we, his little toys?" Alec talked around his sandwich.

"*They* were his toys," Silas said. "His toys got bitch-slapped. Now, he wants us."

"Pardon me?" Lareina had to put her drink down, to be sure she understood.

"Instead of being on the run, he wants to legalize us and send us on assignments. One of the missions of the EP is to combine the talents of its A-crop. Create some unstoppable teams to get their work done for them." Silas reached for more of Yukiyo's fries. She slapped his hand. He slapped her hand, took some of her fries and a few of Lareina's for good measure. "Turns out, we put down one of his best combinations. We're better—by a wide margin—than any group out there. He's aching for us. Bad."

Orion asked, "Is that why everything's been quiet and kind of easy?"

"Yep. Deverell is his golden-boy because he thinks Eugene will deliver us to him. He gave him Lareina, he gave him Yuke. He gave him all of us, me included. We can do whatever we want as long as we do what Briggs' wants."

"What does he want us to do?" Kaiden also helped himself to Lareina's fries.

Silas sat back and grinned. "Lieutenant Colonel Briggs doesn't like the Dopes, the Rev's, and especially not the Vanguard. So, mostly, he wants us to do whatever the hell we think we should do."

Alec asked, "How do we know this isn't some BS cover-up of Deverell's?"

Silas pointed to him. "That's the problem, genius. We don't."

"Christian is not the enemy," Lareina said.

"Since when?"

"All of our problems somehow involve him."

"He's my enemy."

"Of course, you'd say that."

"I don't like him."

"He's not the enemy," she repeated.

****

By week's end, Silas and Yukiyo were comfortably back into the family routine, with the added dynamic of a developing relationship. All was peaceful until...

Orion trotted down the basement steps. "Christian's coming."

Lareina sat down the five-pound weight she'd been pulsing. Silas stood beside her, monitoring her movements. Across the room, Kaiden and Yukiyo were having target practice. It had been too long for Yukiyo, she didn't want to get rusty.

"Alec said to tell you, he's not alone."

Their current safe house was in Truth or Consequences, New Mexico. Closer to El Paso than Albuquerque, the location was chosen for no other reason than its name. They owned a little over ten acres in the just-about-ghost-town. There were three possible routes to their hidden ranch; one of which was known only to the occupants and all three were bogged with surveillance rigged by Alec and recently enhanced by Silas.

They crowded around Alec in the office he termed 'the command center.' Other than to point, indicating which one they should be watching, the wall of monitors before him didn't hold his attention. He had Chronos II in hand, fingers flying. "He's got two people with him. Can't get an ID on one and I can't even see the other."

Christian drove the Whitferde Subprei. The windows were tinted; they couldn't see anyone.

"How do you~" Kaiden started and stopped. If Alec said it, he knew.

"My car!" Lareina squealed and made for the front porch.

"Oooh. That's a pretty hot car." Yukiyo followed her out.

"Set-up?" Kaiden asked.

Silas said, "Definitely."

"What?" Orion didn't get it.

Kaiden pointed to the screen. "That little gift is his idea of bringing her flowers. She'll be too girly to fight him."

"He better have flowers for all of us." Alec got up. "'Cause I'm not too girly to fight him."

They left the room together, amid a chorus of agreement.

****

Lareina grinned when Christian pulled into the drive. She loved that car. "I hope you removed that offensive speedometer attachment."

"All in good time," Christian said.

Yukiyo joined her on the porch just as the other two passengers got out and Lareina's welcoming smile froze in place. A hundred guesses wouldn't have gotten it.

Marcus Mitchell, formally, Mark Deverell, rounded the car. "Hello, Lareina. Long time."

"Mark." It had been a long time. But he was not her primary focus. The blond-haired child resembled Christian so much, Lareina could pretend Marie wasn't her mother. But Lareina couldn't pretend.

"Is that her?" Chloe asked her dad.

"Yes, that's her," Christian answered without taking his eyes off Lareina.

Boldly, Chloe went to meet her. By habit, the Deverell brothers followed.

"Hi. I'm Chloe." Bright blue eyes stared up at Lareina.

Lareina swallowed her emotions. "Hi, Chloe. I met you a long time ago. When you were a baby."

"My daddy told me. He told me you love children and you'll be a good mommy."

"Did he now?" She shot Christian a look. *What the hell...*

Chloe took Lareina's hand as if it were the most natural thing in the world. Lareina *did* love children, it showed. She turned her attention to Yukiyo. "I know you too. You're my new big sister, Yukiyo."

"Big sister?"

"Daddy says you shouldn't do my hair, but I want you too. I want to look like you. You're pretty."

"Oh, I am so going to do your hair," Yukiyo said.

To his credit, Christian remained silent.

"Mark, this is Yukiyo." Keeping hold of Chloe's hand, Lareina led them inside. "Come on in. Meet the rest of the family."

Mark greeted Yukiyo and watched her from behind as they followed the girls into the house.

Christian caught the look and said, "Don't. Just don't."

****

The others were waiting, spread across the living room. No greetings, no courtesy, no expression whatsoever. Whatever Christian thought he was doing, he was not going to do it to them.

"Everyone, this is Mark, Christian's brother. And this is his daughter, Chloe."

"Daughter?" She looked old enough for Kaiden to have known about her.

"Chloe, this is my brother, Kaiden."

"He's my Uncle Kaiden."

"Anything's possible," Kaiden said. "Depends on why you're here."

"To live," Chloe answered. "Didn't they tell you?"

"Nope," Alec said. "Somebody forgot to send us a telegram so we could get everything all ready for you."

"Daddy?"

"It was meant to be a surprise."

"Oh." Chloe threw her hands in the air. "Surprise!"

It was hard not to smile. She was cute and it wasn't her fault.

"Orion... Alec..." Chloe took hold of Lareina's hand again. She looked between the remaining three unknown people. "I know I have two big brothers, but I don't know who you are."

"Him."

"Him."

Alec and Orion pointed to each other at the same time.

Chloe laughed. "Who's him?"

"That will be your first assignment," Lareina said. "You figure out which one's which without them telling you and show them they're not so smart."

"I will." Chloe beamed. "I don't want no help either." Turning to the last person, Chloe counted off names. "Uncle Kaiden, Alec, Yukiyo, Orion... SILAS!" Releasing Lareina's hand, she hurled herself into Silas' surprised arms. "I've been 'specially waiting to meet you!" She kissed his cheek.

"Why would you want to do that?"

What an odd picture it made, Silas holding a child instead of a rifle. Odd, but nice.

"Daddy said you were my uncle *and* my guardian angel. He said I was your special 'signment. You won't *ever* let anybody hurt me and if I get scared when he's not home, you'll fix it."

"Daddy says a whole lot of sh~things doesn't he? Anything else?"

"Umhmm. He said, you were getting me ice-skates. But you have to measure my feet." She stuck her foot out.

Forget smiling, Silas broke out into deep gut wrenching laughter. He remembered making the offer. Christian had indeed brought them all a present. Something they could not resist.

Lareina understood it better than anyone. Christian handed them his heart. Chloe was his dearest secret; the biggest weapon against him. "Alec, Ori. Would you please help Mark and Chloe with their things?"

"Yep."

"Sure."

As they moved past. Chloe grabbed Orion's shirt. "What's your name?"

He hunched his shoulders. "You won't catch me that easily. I'm used to being around little girls."

Lareina smiled. A moment with kids being kids. *Wow.*

"Speaking of that." Christian halted everybody's movement. "I've been in touch with Ms. Quade, Ms. Mio and Ms. Jessup. I think our safest option is to get everybody where we want them, turn this place into a compound."

This was a stunner. Bringing their families in. Including Fisher's mom. Christian was wiping away any possible resistance, if, he was legitimate. Giving his attention to Lareina, he said, "We need to talk."

"You think?" She quirked an eyebrow. "Yukiyo, honey, I hate to do this to you..."

"I don't mind." The possibility of seeing her family had an amazing effect on Yukiyo. That and Silas holding a child was humorous. "Come on, Chloe. We'll get the linens and make up the beds. When we're done, we can mess around in my make-up."

"Yes!" Chloe wiggled out of Silas' arms and latched on to Yukiyo. "I'm not lazy. I'll really help make up the beds and not just pretend."

"Good deal."

Orion, Alec and Mark went in one direction while Yukiyo and Chloe went in the other.

Kaiden and Silas hadn't budged. Neither Lareina nor Christian expected them to.

"What are you up to?" she asked.

"I thought it was obvious."

She folded her arms, preparing for the battle. "It is. The parts you want to be obvious."

Kaiden said to Silas, "Maybe she's not an idiot after all."

"Too early to tell," Silas replied.

Lareina and Christian ignored them.

"I'm combining our lives. You got a better idea?" Christian came forward but stopped short of touching her.

"That's never worked before."

"We never tried it before."

"Because it doesn't work," Silas said.

"Because it doesn't work," Lareina repeated.

"Different game. New rules. We're on the same side now."

"Says who?"

"Says me. We," he made a big circle with his finger, "are our own movement. You want to shut down the EP. We'll do it. Not the DoP. Not the Revs. Not the Vanguard. Us. We have enough power in this room, in this house to change things. Why not?" He glanced at Silas. "Killing each other didn't work out. We need to do something else."

"Try harder?" Silas suggested.

Her eyes darted to his left. "It's not that easy, Christian."

"Yes, it is." He slipped his pinky ring off. "Put on the damn ring and make it that easy."

Kaiden stood up. "Ring?"

Christian slid the gold band on her finger. "Don't take it off again."

"Again?" Silas joined Kaiden in surrounding Lareina. "What's this, 'again'?"

Lareina bit her lip to keep from smiling. "You are a snake."

"Of the worst sort. Don't take it off again."

"Lareina?"

Facing her brothers, Lareina took a deep breath. "Christian and I made an official commitment."

Kaiden tugged on his earring. "When?"

She hunched her shoulders and mumbled, "Couple years ago."

"And you're just getting around to telling us now?" Silas said, "Fuck, Lareina. Do you enjoy being the source of everybody's problems?"

"Clearly, it's complicated."

"You could have made things a little easier for us."

"How, Kaid? You already know I'm in love with him. Were you suddenly going to trust him because we got married?"

"Maybe a little," Silas said.

She wasn't expecting that. "Pardon me?"

"You're an idiot." To Kaiden, he said, "I told you to give it some time." Refocusing on Lareina, Silas continued, "'Reina, you're an idiot. Our biggest problem was that you were in love and Eugene hadn't made a commitment to you."

"I've been committed to her since she was thirteen. You knew that."

"I knew you broke her heart," Silas said. "I knew she wasn't wearing a ring."

"She is now."

"'Bout damn time," Kaiden said, "don't you think?"

"We'll see what Alec has to say about it." Silas smirked.

Lareina smirked with him. "You three are going to be in trouble."

Christian asked, "Why?"

"It's not like he'll blame me," she saifd. "He'll have Ori backing him up. Better keep an eye on your drinks." She admired her ring.

"Ain't neither one of them that stupid." Silas went to find Yukiyo.

"You ever find your rifle?" Kaiden followed him out.

Taking advantage of the moment alone, Christian pulled Lareina to him.

She came willingly. "Impressive. That was so much easier than I ever would have guessed."

"That was hard as hell." He kissed her.

~~~~~~~~~~~~~~~~~

Kaiden/Alec/Yukio/Orion/Silas
KAYOS

To learn more about Tracy and her
books please join her newsletter-
https://tracyaball.wordpress.com/the-book-i-write/

follow her on Twitter-https://twitter.com/Tra3ballA

or find her on Facebook-
https://www.facebook.com/Tra3Ball/

View other Black Rose Writing titles at and use promo code PRINT to receive a 20% discount when purchasing.

BLACK ROSE writing™